GHOST TO PARADISE

KRIS A.S.

GHOST TO PARADISE

KRIS A.S.

Dedicated to those searching for light in the dark.
This one's for you.

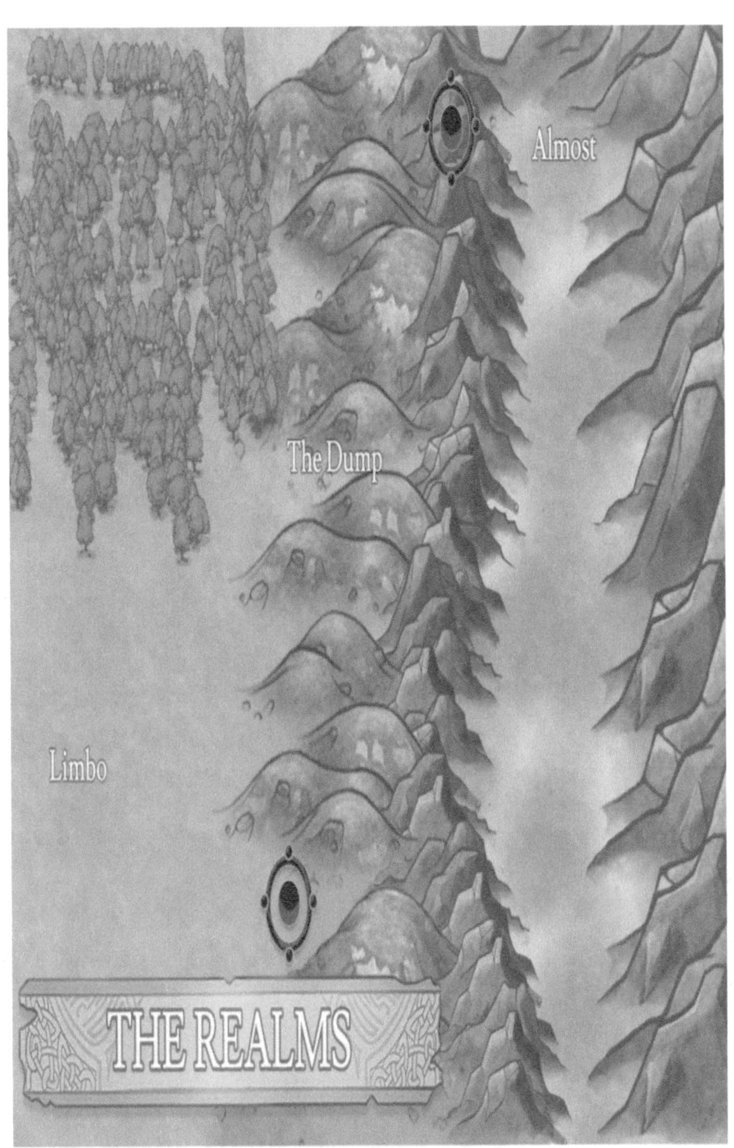

Almost
The Dump
Limbo
THE REALMS

CHAPTER 1
CA-CO-PHONY

In my usual corner, I sit with my arms wrapped around my knees. My human's snores go in one ear and out the other, and soon, I'm sitting in silence. Alone. I hold myself closer as a dreadful sensation crawls up my spine. I stare down at the short purple chain that haunts me like I haunt my human. The chain that only extends a few yards. The same chain that binds me to this wretched human world until the end of my human's life.

Dark thoughts begin to shoot through my mind. I close my eyes, but it only makes things worse. *I'm alone. For how long? Kill my human. Possess her body and do it! I'm fine. I'll just wait until she dies, and then, I'll die. And then...* My head spins, doubling over the uncertainty afterward, but in an instant, I jump to my feet, allowing my human's snoring to fade back in.

I take a deep breath—back to reality—forcing the bad thoughts to the back of my mind. My gaze then fixes on the dastardly chain before following it up to my human, and my face twists into a scowl. Her name's Kiara, but she's not that important. Plus, she reeks of alcohol, her wretched odor polluting the entire two-bedroom apartment. If an adult were ever present in this house on the weekends, she'd surely hear a mouthful.

Inching over to her with one hand covering my nose, annoyance plagues each of my heavy footsteps. When I pass by one of her many narcissistic mirrors, I keep from looking at myself—or rather, what I've become. I know what I look like, barefooted and dirty; I know I wear a dull tattered gown with holes in its flowery design. And underneath, spandex shorts cling to my golden brown yet ashen skin. I've looked like this since I got to this ghostly purgatory sixteen years ago.

Leaning over her bedside, I whisper, "Sweet nightmares."

Then, I reach out and touch her shoulder, and she shakes a vicious shiver. Her snores cut out. Her eyes tighten, scrunched up like her face, and the tension travels through her body and forces her hands clenched. Yet after a moment, her snores fade in again, and we do this same rodeo until she finally wakes up.

"Four-thirty in the afternoon already?" she yawns at her cellphone, scooting out of bed. She checks her messages and finds one from her mom, asking her to go grocery shopping because she's working another double shift. I mouth her catch-phrases as she says them. "Ugh, again? She's always working—how annoying. Fine."

Humans are so predictable.

By the time she showers, clothes herself, and finishes getting ready, I ease into her mother's cramped Volkswagen Beetle and pretend to strap on my seat belt. Then, I brace myself, latching onto the car door and my seat. Because beside me, once my human's seat belt clicks, she hammers on the gas.

I fly forward, and my grayish brown hair flies with me, my tight curls swaying to-and-fro on this rocky adventure. She floors it, brakes, and swerves all the way to the grocery store before zooming to an abrupt stop in the parking lot.

Snatching the key from the ignition, she creeps out of the

car like a celebrity in disguise. She wears tinted sunglasses to cover her hangover eyes and baggy clothes, which look like she's *obviously* trying to hide something. But I sigh, letting it go, and hurry after her into the grocery store.

Because *this* is what I've been waiting for all week—all fun, all games, and all pranks.

As soon as we enter, I wave at a bunch of fellow ghosts, who all simply glare at me. The ashen pallor of their skin reminds me of mine, serving as a permanent souvenir of this seemingly eternal hellhole. Nevertheless, it's always packed inside here no matter what time of day, and I love it. The more people, the better.

My human stops in the fruit and vegetable section, scrolling down her mother's long list, and practically swipes everything in sight. As we continue on to the first aisle, I look down in her cart and see a bunch of greens: spinach, kale, avocadoes, and celery. But I know the truth. Like every week, she and her mother buy all these fruits and vegetables in an attempt to be healthy, but her mother is always working—too busy to cook. And Kiara is too lazy to cook, so they'll just end up tossing them and resorting to takeout.

"Stupid humans," I mutter, as we stop in the first aisle.

Her phone rings, and she picks it up. "Hey, babe," she greets, her voice rising an octave. "I miss you too. Happy birthday!"

I suck my teeth at her. Because for one, that's Chesnutt High's infamous drug dealer—a.k.a. her *ex*-boyfriend. They hang out together at parties and have secret rendezvous but couldn't care less about each other—not even enough to cuddle after sex. Hence her wishing him a happy birthday but likely not going to see him today. Two, she doesn't miss him, especially since they just got drunk together last night. And three, birthdays aren't anything to celebrate. Humans are just one step closer to death, meanwhile ghosts can't even age.

"So, what are you doing for your birthday? Work, really?" Her voice reduces to a hushed whisper. "You shouldn't be doing *that stuff* on your special day.... Money isn't everything, Josh...."

Wandering down the aisle, I weave in between the many people and their ghosts, making awkward eye contact and cheap smiles with the latter while walking through numerous purple chains. My fingers whisk across the canned goods, and I knock one over.

The store's too noisy—no one reacts.

So, I keep moving and knock over three more. They plummet to the floor and make loud *pop* and *clink* noises, and I spin around, reacting like everyone else.

"Oh my!" an old lady with lively gray hair shouts in fright, the three cans rolling at her feet.

The aisle full of humans stare at her, and her eyes widen. She shakes her head, peering from the crowd to the cans on the floor. "Th-that wasn't me."

I duck my head, giggling.

"Seriously?" the old lady's ghost says to me. "I hate it here as much as you do. For once, can't you just make things easy on all of us?"

A slew of dead eyes turns to me, but just as I shrug them off, a high-pitched giggle sounds. I turn toward it to see a young girl, about my age, walking toward me. She wears a strawberry-colored bralette with harem jeans and sandals, showing off her pink toenails. Her tall, slender figure resembles that of a sculpted model, but her round baby face tells a tale of naïve innocence.

"That was pretty funny," she says across from me, her long, frizzy hair dangling over her shoulders.

A smirk tugs at my mouth as the other ghosts go back to their boring, nonexistent lives. "Thanks," I say before sticking out my tongue at the rest of them. "At least *somebody* has a sense of humor! *Agh*—"

My chain yanks me from the aisle like I'm some pet, and I stumble over. Grumbling, I stomp after my human who puts her phone away before weaving into another aisle. My vision instantly locks on my next victim, and I hurry to knock packets of instant ramen into their cart. However, a waving hand cuts me off.

"You're welcome!"

Mid-grab, I turn and come face-to-face with the same high-pitched girl. I raise a brow at her, releasing a packet of instant ramen into a random human's cart. "Huh?"

She nods with bubbly, light brown eyes, the same color as her hair and peanut skin. "I love a good prank, though I'm not so good at pulling them myself. I'd rather watch."

Confused, I stare at the rambling motormouth in awe.

"But then again, this is the first prank I've ever seen—or remember—so I guess I'm not too sure. I actually just got here about a month ago, and I'm kinda confused. Everything is..."

I roll my eyes, ignoring her. "Oh, a newbie."

Resuming my pranks, I wander down the aisle after my human and sneakily knock cans of soup into random humans' carts. Later, I'll laugh if I see them scrambling and confused at the cash register. A few ghosts catch me pulling this prank in the next aisle, but they don't say anything. Instead, they do what ghosts do best: play dead.

Meanwhile, the new girl follows me around like an annoying house fly. Her plump lips stay in constant motion while she gestures her hands with every other word. She paces beside me as if we're attached at the hip, working my nerves.

"When I got here, at first, I was scared, but then I was like, 'Wow, this is pretty cool!' I haven't been able to explore much, but I really want to. Can you show me around?"

I start to tip a bag of candy into a human's cart.

"Only if you're not busy!"

Her loud voice startles me, and I knock the candy over with a little too much force, sending it flying to the floor. It slams down with a low *clap*, not nearly loud enough to cause a scene. I ball my fists at the wasted prank.

"If you are, I'd completely understand. We can just hang out some other time, considering we're friends and all."

"Friends?" I shout, louder than intended. I whip around, step to her, and jab a finger at her chest. "I don't even know you! You just started following me and talking my ear off, ruining my fun! Leave. Me. Alone."

In an instant, her grin downturns to a frown, and her lips begin to quiver. She drops her head and puts an arm over her face, sniffling.

I furrow my brows at her in confusion before stalking off. That's when I see all ghostly eyes on me. Even though their blank expressions remain the same, they stare at me as if *I've* done something wrong. "*Tch.* What are you looking at?" I yap at one of them.

Finding my human at the end of the aisle, she browses an assortment of chips and popcorn with a hand to her chin, scoping the entire selection, and I know this is going to take a while. Still sniffling in the same spot, I look back at the new girl. She cups her rosy cheeks with both hands as her shoulders shudder.

I roll my eyes at her dramatics, but then a pang strikes the left side of my chest—where my heart's *supposed* to be. With a sigh, I trudge back over to her. She continues sobbing, so I reach out an awkward hand and pat her shoulder. "There, there. I didn't mean it."

She looks up with bright eyes. "Really?"

"Yeah," I grumble.

"Yay!" She pulls me into a sudden embrace, and my body goes stiff. "I'm so glad we met each other." She pulls back. "My name's Rina!"

"Slixx."

"Oh, cool name! I think we're gonna get along well."

Backing away, I nod with a cheap smile. "Yeah, yeah, see you around."

However, just as I turn around—

"Hiya, Slixx!" Eddy beams, jumping in my way. Tall and lanky, he wears his standard ankle bracelet, tattered jeans with loose frays dangling around his calves, elbow pads, and a plaid shirt. His skin isn't quite as dark as his thick eyebrows, but it comes close.

"Just great," I grumble, "another inconvenience." I flash him the usual *leave me alone* look, but he just smiles at me in awe. When I sidestep right, he sidesteps left. I go left. He goes right. Finally, I meet his dull hazel eyes with a glare.

"Now you gotta talk to me," he says.

"Over my dead body," I say snidely, pushing past him.

He giggles. "Technically, we're already...I see what you did there." He maneuvers around and stops in front of me, again.

"What do you want?" I snap.

"Hi there!" Rina greets, rushing over to Eddy. She hugs him with a big squeeze, exchanging names, while I try to sneak away. But then she throws an arm around me. "Any friend of Slixx is a friend of mine."

Out of the corner of my eye, I catch sight of my human leaving the aisle, knowing this to have been her last stop, and my palms grow clammy. Our short chain begins to extend, but I know it can only go so far. She's going to check out. Time's running out, and I haven't even pulled the grand finale prank yet.

Rubbing my hands together, I casually look both ways for

my last victim. First, I spot an old lady, but two of those in one day would be boring. A soccer mom? Her reaction probably wouldn't be satisfying. I gloss over a sea of kids. A young man in a suit? He's too far away. I scan the horde one more time, and an elderly man strikes me. His ivory skin and sharp nose draw me in.

I head for him with the slickest grin—

"Slixx!" Rina and Eddy call out, cutting me off mid-stride.

I glance over at my feeble old target who picks up eggs —he doesn't even have a ghost, *perfect*—but he, too, begins to leave. "What?" I grit through my teeth, fuming inside.

"Did you know Rina's new?" Eddy asks.

I shoo them away as I lock on a new target, creeping toward a young, blond girl. "Yeah, yeah, I think I remember her mentioning something like that."

"Mhmm, just got here about a month ago," Rina says, her and Eddy following me. "I've spent most of my time in the hospital with a baby—"

Approaching the blond girl, I crinkle my fingers back, readying for a good Scare, but then she runs off to her parents. A sigh escapes me. "Your human."

"My human?" Rina asks, a childlike finger to her lip.

Eddy nods. "Yep, every ghost here is 'born' with a baby, and that's your human who you'll be attached to for the rest of your time here."

"In this dead hell," I mumble.

"How cool," she beams. "How long is that?"

Looking past her, I study her chain, which is actually long and snakes out of the aisle. Then, I glance back at her starlit eyes filled with hope, and a thick slick of jealousy wells in my chest. That's how it always starts between ghost and human— happy and loving—until the resentment sets in and hatred grows with each passing pointless day. "Until your human dies."

"Slixx," Eddy scolds. "How morbid. It's until they *pass on*."

"Whatever."

My chain tugs before reeling me in like a caught fish, so I follow my human to checkout, Eddy and Rina at my heels. They chitchat back and forth about her new crappy life, while my human places items onto the conveyor belt. I fade into the background, desperately trying to pretend I'm elsewhere.

"Well, now that I'm here in this ghost world, what am I supposed to do?" Rina asks. "Are there, like, ghost police, or ghost jobs, or ghost hospitals?" She chuckles. "That'd be cool."

Unable to help it, I flick my gaze to her, deadpan. "No."

"So, what then?"

Before Eddy can answer, I smirk, knocking a pack of gum into my human's cart. "You can do whatever you want." We watch as she picks it up among other items, puzzled, before shrugging and tossing it on the conveyor belt with everything else. I chuckle. "See, Rina. No rules. Just fun."

However, her smile downturns to a frown.

"What's wrong?" Eddy asks.

I glance over at my human paying for her cartful of bagged groceries, relieved that it's almost time to leave.

Rina gulps. "What happens to us after our humans die?"

And just like that, a familiar wave of dread hits me. The same horror from this morning—that same horror that I've experienced nearly every day of being a dead shadow. I clench my jaw, dropping my head. It's as if a hand grabs my throat, choking me into despair. Dark clouds invade my mind as I shut my eyes. *What will happen to me after my human dies?*

"*Bliss!*" Eddy blurts out, snapping me back to reality.

"Huh?" Rina asks.

"*Bliss?*" I repeat, rolling my eyes. "Not this again. This is why everyone thinks you're the local town crazy." I palm my face as we all follow my human out of the store. "Look, Rina, don't listen to him. That place doesn't even exist."

Rina knits her brows, her attention shifting between me and Eddy.

"Just because you and everyone else refuse to believe the truth doesn't mean it's not *true*." Eddy tosses his hands behind his head, the sunlight highlighting his rich chocolate skin despite the ashen hue. "Do you even know what *Bliss* is?"

My human hurries through the parking lot as if paparazzi will pop out at any moment, while I desperately search for my last victim. My head whips in every direction, but no one's within reach except a brunette. Annoyance plagues my temples, knowing there wouldn't even be an audience to laugh at. "No. Uh, somewhat. Maybe—I don't know."

Eddy chuckles. "*Bliss* is like"—he taps his chin—"a garden of sweet peas flowering under a bright sun. With animals everywhere, especially dogs. And it's supposed to smell like pure goodness and sweet sugared almonds—so I've been told."

"Oh, that sounds lovely!" Rina says.

"If it were real," I snort.

Once we arrive back at the car, I throw up my hands in a huff. "Forget it," I grumble, sliding into the passenger seat while my human puts the groceries in the trunk. "Today was a bust—"

"Slixx!"

I jump in my seat with a gasp.

"Come with us," painfully familiar voices call out in unison.

Whipping around, I turn to see Eddy and Rina. Their faces and hands are pressed against the car window, and they smile with the biggest grins. "What the...? Are you two following me?"

Eddy raises a brow before gesturing at a middle-aged man

loading groceries into a luxury car beside us. The man wears a crimson bomber jacket with wrinkly jeans, but I don't get a good look at his pale face. A purple chain does link from him to Eddy's back, though. "Well, that's my human, Mr. Strife. *Soooo*, no."

"My human's across the street," Rina says, giggling between words. "It's his first time outside the hospital, so I thought I'd finally explore."

I cross my arms. "Whatever."

"Is that any way to talk to an old friend?" Eddy asks.

"Eddy, we're *not* friends."

"Really?" Rina asks. "I just met you guys, and you two seem pretty close to me."

Eddy dips his chin. "Exactly. And what do you call frequently running into a pal—for over a decade—and catching up?"

"A crazy person trying to start conversation with the same stranger over and over again, which is kind of creepy," I say.

Backing away, his smile slacks, and somewhere deep inside, a part of me aches for him. Even Rina pouts, rubbing Eddy's shoulder. I try to shake the feeling, but his now sad puppy-dog face moves me.

"Eddy, look, you're not *all the way* crazy—or *that* creepy."

In a snap, his mood chippers back up. "Really?"

I dip my chin.

"Then come with us."

"Mhmm, come!" Rina chimes in.

"Where?"

"To *Bliss*."

I roll my eyes with a sigh. Thankfully though, my human settles into the car, straps on her seat belt, and turns the key in the ignition. She then flicks on the radio to some mainstream song and blasts the volume.

Waving at me, Eddy and Rina try to get my attention. Their mouths move, but I let the loud music carry me away as we back out. "Sorry, can't hear you! See you around!"

We speed off without a second look back. However, as we come to a hard stop at the sign, my human's phone rings. She looks at the caller ID, rolls her eyes, and turns down the radio before answering. "What, babe?"

"Hey, hey, what's with the tone?" I overhear him laughing.

"Actually go celebrate your birthday instead of fake working."

"*Selling* is a real job."

"Not when it's done *illegally*."

Tuning them out, I palm my face as we turn onto the street. They bicker back and forth as per usual, and the onset of a headache strikes me. I massage my temples, but ever since they first met, it's been misery on my mental. (And yes, ghosts get exhausted, too.)

"Whatever, Josh," my human says. "Bye."

"No listen, I'm in kind of a pinch right now and need a favor—"

She hangs up on him, tossing her phone on the passenger's seat.

"Hey," I snap as it goes right through me. Then, instead of turning left back home, she makes a right into some popular fast food restaurant. "You have got to be kidding me. Stress-food?"

"I'm sure mother won't mind," she says to herself, taking out her mother's credit card. She then pulls up to the drive-through window, and the intercom greets her. I predict her regular plain dry sandwich order before tuning her out, again.

After they hand her the food, she veers off right to get back on the main street, but then her phone rings. She ignores it, though, waiting for the busy intersection to clear, and I ignore her, gazing out the window. I stare at the bright sky, annoyed by its beaming sunlight that I can never feel. A couple with a cute puppy crosses in front of us, and my face scrunches in revulsion since I'm not able to pet animals either. But then my eyes befall a big dumpster near a dark alley, and within that alley, I squint at a familiar human face surrounded by a bunch of thugs in black hoodies.

"Is that...?" I ask aloud as if she can hear me. The more I squint, the more I recognize that face from last night. My stomach tightens into knots, knowing whatever's over there must not be good. "Josh?"

Oblivious, my human simply turns up the radio, humming to the beat.

I keep my eyes peeled on the alley and the thugs closing in on Josh. Half of me yearns to mind my own business, while the other stupid half longs to help. "Do something!" I wave in front of my human's face, but obviously, she can't see me either. I pat her shoulder, but she just shivers before turning on the heat. "No, no, no..."

Suddenly, a silver flash twinkles from the alley as one of the thugs pulls out a weapon of some sort. They all charge at Josh, but he stands his ground. Meanwhile, I stare in awe. A rush of horror suddenly overcomes me, and my palms moisten like thick fog. If I had a heart, it'd surely either stop or beat out of my chest. I gulp, dread nearly paralyzing my limbs.

But just then, I jump into Kiara's body and melt into her limbs before swerving the car toward the shady alley.

CHAPTER 2
STRANGER DANGER

Ghosts possess an ability called *Possession*. This means that they can jump inside humans or animals but for only ten minutes, and if used for the entire time, Pepto-Bismol-like side effects may occur. It's also worth mentioning that the same human can only be possessed once a month, which takes the fun out of it. (Luckily, I've been saving mine up for a good prank.) Overall, Possession is pretty safe—as long as ghosts don't get into any trouble.

Unfortunately, my middle name (in my past life) must've been Trouble.

SKRRRT!

I pull up in front of the alley and hop out of the car, storming toward the scene. The thugs stop dead in their tracks, staring at me (Kiara) in confusion. I charge between them, counting five thugs total, and Josh.

"What's going on here?" I demand.

Now up-close, I see that all the thugs have knives pulled out, but that doesn't faze me. One of them has a ghost. While on the opposing side, one of Josh's feeble dealer friends stands beside him—hunched over in fear. I doubt he'd do much damage, but either way, they're still outnumbered.

Chuckling, the middle thug laughs first, clearly the leader, and the rest follow suit. A purple chain extends from his back up to the sky, so perhaps his ghost has strayed. "Who's this bitch?" he scoffs.

As if on command, I hawk and spit at his foul mouth, and the phlegm lands at his feet. His smirk drops. The rest of the thugs' laughter ceases. I stare each of them down until Josh calls my—I mean, Kiara's—name twice.

He pulls me toward him. "What are you doing here?" he asks in a low voice.

"Was just in the neighborhood. You looked like you needed some help." I side-eye his friend who quivers in fear. "Both of you."

Josh shakes his head. "Nah, this ain't no place for you. I'll be alright. Just go."

"Yeah, you heard the guy," the leader mocks from behind. "Get outta here before somebody gets hurt."

I open my mouth to reply, but Josh cuts me off.

"Hey, Ronny, relax. I told you I'm gonna get you the rest of your cut so lay off."

"That's what you said last time, Joshy. I thought we had an understandin'. If all the money's not here in Ronny's hand, then that's *your* ass. Ain't no such thing as comin' up short *twice*—unless you stealin' from Ronny." He snarls his nose like a bull-dog, twirling his knife about his finger. "There's two types of people I hate in this world: liars and thieves." He points his knife at Josh. "You were supposed to be my boy."

Josh holds up one hand. "Relax, Ronny. I said I got you."

Ronny heads toward us first, and then the rest of the thugs follow. "Nah, that ain't good enough no more."

Suddenly, all the thugs break out into sprints. They charge

at Josh and his scared friend, but the latter takes off down the alley. Two of the thugs chase after him, while the other three tackle Josh. Everything happens so fast, catapulting me into a whirlwind. They slam Josh against the wall, and he lets out the loudest grunt. I grab one of the boys with all my strength, but he knocks me down. I hit the ground on my back, and a sharp pain seizes my body. My vision toggles over Josh. He yelps as they beat the crap out of him, punching and kneeing him.

A rush of adrenaline surges me to my feet, and without thinking, I scan the alley for a weapon. The dumpster catches my eye first and then a rusty old crowbar. I act fast, retrieving it, and I whack one of the thugs over the head.

Crying out in pain, he hits the ground with a *thud*. I keep swinging, though, and hit another's side. This one stumbles back but doesn't fall, and it is then that fear overcomes me.

Ronny rises tall before storming at me. "You bitch!"

"Kiara, run!" Josh yells.

One second, I look over at Josh's bloody mouth, and then the next, a knife blinds my vision. I try to lurch back, but Ronny cuts across my neck and chest—or rather *Kiara's* neck and chest. A fiery pain devours me, tears unleashing by the bucket. I choke up blood before grabbing my neck. Blood squirts out and stains my hands as I fall to the ground.

Once Kiara's head hits the pavement, her body spits me out like a lost cause.

"Ronny, we gotta go!" one of the thugs cries out.

I pat my ghostly body even though I come out in one piece, but then I stare in horror at the sight of Kiara.

"Yo, she's bleedin' bad!"

"I ain't mean to—"

"Hey, what are you kids doing over there?" a raspy bass voice yells from down the alley. "The police are on the way!"

In an instant, the thugs take off down the alley, cursing at each other and stepping over Kiara's body as she bleeds out. My knees buckle beside her. Josh scrambles to her side, too. Cuts and bruises plague his bloody face while he holds his gashed arm.

"Slixx, are you okay?" Eddy shouts, sliding to my side.

When I look up at him, I catch a glimpse of his human, Mr. Strife, running after the thugs. They disappear into the darkness, but Eddy remains by my side, his long chain likely extending more than several yards. I start to wonder just how close he is with his human, but Kiara seizes my attention again.

Eddy throws his arms around me, but my limp limbs remain by my side. I stare at the puddle of blood beneath us before a remote holler erupts from down the alley. Immediately, Eddy snatches away and jumps to his feet with tiny horrified pupils.

"Your human?" I croak.

But he's already sprinting down the alley after him.

Returning to Kiara's bloodbath, guilt paralyzes me. Maybe I shouldn't have gotten involved. Maybe it wasn't my place. I blink long and hard, tears building up behind closed lids. "This...is all my fault," I whisper, my voice cracking. I tremble with blame, and the worst-case scenario shoots to the forefront of my mind.

Death.

If a ghost's human dies, they die.

If she dies, I die.

Kiara's eyes slowly close, her pale lips flat, and her chest rises one last time. Her heart was the one thing I envied about her. And now, it's no more. She's dying, and my skin begins to flicker in and out like a light. One second, I'm here, and the next, I'm gone. Questions swirl through my mind, pondering death and what will happen to me.

Approaching sirens sound in the distance as my chain starts

to flicker, too. It shimmers in and out of existence with me, and after a moment, I shut my eyes, bracing for the inevitable—*waiting to die.*

But I never do.

Our chain suddenly snaps. It clanks, and small metallic pieces fly everywhere. I shield myself as they rain down over me, pelting against my permanently re-solidified skin. And upon looking down, I stare in bewilderment at my dead human whose end of the chain dissolves.

Suddenly, a gust of wind whooshes from behind. I shield my face but hear unknown footsteps hit the pavement. The ambulance finally arrives, so I start to think it's them until an uncanny voice speaks.

"You," a man says as if in my ear.

I spin around to the deep voice and stop short of a strange tall ghost, who appears only a few years older than me. He wears a thick black chain around his neck that runs down his dark cloak, and his long platinum hair stops at his chest. His ebony eyes appear hollow, too—even more lifeless than the usual ghost.

When he squats down to level with me, I freeze at his deadpan expression. He still towers over me, sitting on his heels about an inch away, our bodies nearly touching. Up-close, he looks ill. Dark circles under his eyes sink into his skin, and his pasty lips beckon for moisture, too.

"What is your name?" he asks, his head tilted ever so slightly.

He appears like just another ghost, but something about him unnerves me. Anxiety cripples my throat. "S-Sli-Slixx…"

"Well, I have been searching centuries for you, Slixx."

I knit my brows. "Why?"

"Because you are my ticket to *Bliss.*"

It's as if time stops—just he and I in that moment. The

paramedics rush to Kiara, and the police spring into action after Eddy's human, but I find myself trapped in this strange ghost's magnetic pull. His eyes abruptly flush red, like coursing blood into water, until they're solid ruby.

I nearly become hypnotized in his deep crimson trance until his purple chain catches my eye. It rattles on the ground, trailing down the dark alley, before quickly rising in midair. I assume him to be the ghost of the thugs' leader. And the leader must be on the run as the chain's about to pull his ghost with him.

The strange ghost, however, grabs hold of the chain, wrangles it around his palm, and yanks it back with one hand. It must take a heap of strength, though, because he grits his teeth. "My name is Verquen, and I have spent most of my ghost life searching for a way to pass on, beyond my curse."

"Curse?" I furrow my brows in confusion before finding my voice, ire seeping into my bones. "You're the ghost of one of those thugs, right? Why didn't you stop them?"

"What humans do is none of my concern," he says without hesitation.

"If I...*we*...hadn't shown up, they would've hurt—or killed—that boy!"

"Pain is inevitable. Death is inevitable. My involvement would have probably turned out like yours, anyway."

Taken aback, my eyes widen in rage.

Above, the bright sun shines over the shady alley, but the warm weather contrasts with the spectacle below. Neither of us say a word as a cool breeze passes by. My dress blows in the wind, and Verquen's long hair picks up. Meanwhile, chaos and flashing lights ensue around us.

"I did those humans a favor and let their destructive behavior run rampant, so once the worst happened, they would be relinquished from this human world on their own terms, moving one step closer to peace—likewise with their ghosts. You, however, did not pass on with your human. And that is why you will lead me to *Bliss*."

"What the hell are you talking about?" I shout, rising to my numb feet. "Even if I knew what *Bliss* was, I'd never help you after what you've done. Or should I say, didn't d—"

In a snap, Verquen snatches my neck with his free hand. My eyes bulge as he cuts off my windpipe and lifts me off the ground. I try to claw at his hand, but his grip remains tight.

"You will lead me to *Bliss*. You just do not know it yet, Ticket."

His icy voice sends a shiver down my spine.

"Slixx!"

Although my hearing drones out to distant echoes, I recognize that voice. My mind scrambles on who, though, while my feet dangle in midair. The weight of the world pulls me down, and my vision blurs.

All I see is a devil with sinful eyes.

A distant voice cries out my name again, and this time, Verquen glances out of his peripheral. He then opens his mouth, and smoke fumes out. It encircles us, sweeping around our legs; his body begins to fade, blending with it.

Some yards away, Eddy and his human limp into view. His human holds the wall for support as the paramedics surround him, while Eddy breaks out into a sprint, darting my way. His quick, long legs barely touch the ground, and in the next breath, he lunges at Verquen.

CHAPTER 3

BLISS

/BLIS/

noun
1. perfect happiness; great joy.
a state of spiritual blessedness,
typically that reached after death.

This must be how I died.

There are few things ghosts can remember about their past lives, but how they died isn't one of them. Recalling a name or face is common, but even then, neither come with context. To be a ghost is to be dead—in limbo—without worries or regrets. Some call it "fake peace."

However, as I gasp for air, an angst wells deep inside my chest. This suffocating pressure around my neck feels *familiar* and so does staring into the eyes of a madman. My attempts at prying off Verquen's hand only drain my energy quicker. I try once more, but my arms fall flaccid like my stiff legs.

I croak for air, helplessness hanging me by the neck. Tires *skrrt* away in the distance. Flashing lights fade from my vision.

21

The world spins around me, while smoke continues to flood from Verquen's mouth. It wafts into mine like poisonous gas, and my heavy eyes begin to close for good.

A sudden image of Kiara's bloodbath flashes through my mind. And although I can no longer feel my face, I know tears finally singe my cheeks. Perhaps I deserve this—perhaps karma is righting my wronged interference. I wonder...I wonder...

"Slixx!"

Eddy, I think, catching a glimpse of hazel eyes. He sounds so far away—like at the bottom of some vast well. I follow his bouncy eyes as he leaps from right to left. A glimmer of his elbow pads shine. He yells in rage, throwing blow after blow, but Verquen's sinful gaze remains untouched.

When my eyes finally close, Verquen's voice startles me. His final words come out crisp and clear yet icier than a cold black heart. "In due time, you *will* lead me to *Bliss*, Ticket."

Then just like that, I hit the ground. I gasp for air, inhaling lungfuls, before coughing uncontrollably. My body naturally curls up into a fetal position as my vision slowly unblurs. I rub my sore throat to ease the pain, but then a hand touches my shoulder.

I jump.

"Relax, it's me."

Looking up, I exhale in relief. "Eddy? Don't scare me like that," I say, smacking his shoulder.

"Ouch!"

"Slixx! Eddy!" someone calls out from the street.

I look past Eddy as he looks over his shoulder, and we behold Rina.

She runs to us with flailing arms before hunching over, her hands on her knees. "I heard...ambulance," she pants, gesturing yonder. "I ran as fast as I could. You, and some guy, his hand... on your neck."

Remembering those ruby eyes, I whip around in search of Verquen. My neck cranes around in panic, but there's no sign of him. His smoke even dissipates. I keep my eyes peeled, though.

"Don't worry." Eddy extends a hand, lugging in heavy breaths himself. "He's gone."

I let out another relieving sigh.

Rina straightens up. "I saw him from afar, but when I got closer, it was like he disappeared."

"Yep, just vanished like magic," Eddy says. "Who the hell was that psycho anyway?"

Standing up, I start to grab his hand but use the wall for support instead. I take to my feet like a bird learning to fly. "One of those thugs' ghosts. He just appeared out of nowhere and started talking nonsense."

"Well, are you alright?" Rina asks.

A knot wells in my throat, and I look away.

"Sorry, I showed up late." Eddy stares down at the ground, pity in his lenses. "I tried to get him off you, but he used *Pellucid* and kept dodging all my attacks."

Rina knits her brows. "Pel-lu-cid?" she repeats, the word sounding odd out of her mouth. "What's that?"

"It's an ability where ghosts can make themselves transparent," Eddy explains. "So if I use it and you try to touch me, you'll fall right through." He motions for her to touch his shoulder, so she does, and her hand goes through his body. "But it only works when you're aware of the touch."

Rina slowly dips her chin in understanding, her hand retreating. "But if somebody catches you by surprise"—she punches his arm—"then you're caught."

"Ouch!" Eddy rubs his fresh bruise. "Exactly."

"I wish I'd used it when he grabbed me," I say. My voice cracks on the last word, and Eddy looks at me with that same pity, striking me to the core. Even Rina pouts her lips. I scowl at them. "Don't look at me like that."

"Like what?" Eddy asks in a low voice.

"As if this whole thing is my fault!" I yell.

Rina flinches. "Slixx, I don't know even know what—"

"I didn't—" Eddy shakes his head in confusion.

"Yeah, I possessed my human to come over here to save her drug-dealing ex-boyfriend. Yeah, I got you guys involved. Yeah, none of this would've happened if it wasn't for me. But I didn't mean to get her *killed*."

I look away as snot and riverbeds let loose. However, even with the crippling guilt on my chest, I keep a straight face and flick away the tears, forcing Kiara to the back of my mind. "I'm fine."

Staggering forward, Eddy reaches out for me.

I smack his hand down. "I said I'm fine."

Neither he nor Rina move for a moment, but then Eddy's gaze lands on my severed chain. He narrows his eyes as if putting the pieces together. "Your chain..."

Rina gasps, mouth agape. "It's broken! But I thought you guys said ghosts die with their humans?"

"They do," Eddy says with an edge in his voice. "They're *supposed* to."

"Then, how are you still alive, Slixx?" Rina asks.

I start to shrug, but then Eddy's face suddenly glitches. I furrow my brows, inspecting him from head to toe. His linked chain slithers behind him intact, but then his face glitches again like *his* human's dying. His body grows fainter by the second, too.

"What's wrong?" he asks, worry in his jittery eyes.

When Rina looks over at him, she winces. "Your skin—it's flickering!"

I simply point at Eddy's body, and as soon as he looks

down, his pupils shrink in panic. Speechless, I stare at him at a loss for words. He doesn't say anything either. Instead, he stumbles over to the crowbar, picks it up, and watches his reflection glitch.

Rina tugs my arm. "What's happening to Eddy?"

"Mr. Strife," I say in a low voice, sensing his dread from afar, but he stands frozen. "Something must've happened to his human."

"Like what?"

"His human chased after the thugs who stabbed my human, so he might've gotten hurt." I hesitate, pacing over to Eddy. "If you need me, I can come with you."

Still, no response.

Rina hurries to us. "Me, too!"

But he doesn't say a word.

"Eddy?" I ask.

Suddenly, he grabs my wrist and takes off running. I quickly grab ahold of Rina's hand, linking the three of us like a chain, and our rapid footsteps sync in cadence. We burst out onto the street in broad daylight as Eddy leads the way. Darting across the road, we run—fast and far—away from the dark alley, following Eddy's long chain.

CHAPTER 4

MAKE IT MAKE SENSE

Inside a Tucker Bay Hospital room, Rina, Eddy, and I listen as a doctor delivers news to Eddy's human. We sit near the window, while the doctor stands on the opposite side. He holds a clipboard, flipping over the pages, and glances up—only occasionally—with the firmest face.

Meanwhile, Mr. Strife clutches the bedsheets over his chest. He frowns, wrinkles around his mouth and across his forehead, and his cavernous eyes tell a painful tale.

"Fortunately, you only suffered a flesh wound," the doctor says. "But unfortunately, your heart is in critical condition. Are you aware of that, Mr. Strife?"

Mr. Strife nods with droopy brows, averting the doctor's gaze. He's paler than the dead and as red as a cherry. "Yes, suh."

"You already have heart disease, and amid the stabbing, it triggered an attack."

Out of my peripheral vision, I catch sight of Eddy's grave face. His clenched jaw hardens, and his big eyes widen even more. He hugs himself, looking onward as if *he's* just been delivered the news.

"Your heart was unable to receive enough oxygen—"

"Spare me the details, Doc," Mr. Strife says. "How long I got?"

The doctor clears his throat before clasping his wrist behind his back. He then looks his patient square in the eye and shakes his head. "Not long."

Tears well in Mr. Strife's eyes, but he swats them away.

"Do you have any family, Mr. Strife?"

He forces a laugh, massaging his temples. "One daughter that don't care to talk to me."

"Well, you might want to give her a call," the doctor says, leaving those as his departing words.

After he silently closes the door on his way out, Mr. Strife breaks down. Tears cascade down his plump cheeks, and he clutches the sheets even tighter. But not only his sobs fill the room—Eddy covers half of his face with an arm, and his shoulders shudder. Loose tears stain his jeans and checkerboard shirt.

Rina leans on him, rubbing his back. "I'm so sorry, Eddy," she whispers in his ear. "It's going to be alright. We're here for you."

We?

I reach for his hand but hesitate. Death and sorrow haunt the room, and grief builds up like the urge to cry in one's throat. I ball my hands into fists and set them on my lap, figuring the best I can do right now is just be here. Besides, Rina's consoling better than I ever could.

Scoping the room, my attention wanders down to my severed metal chain on the tiled floor.

"Slixx?" Eddy croaks.

"Yeah?" I say.

He rubs his face before finally putting his arm down.

"Take your time," Rina whispers, but he turns to me with the most intense gaze.

I meet his glossy hazel eyes. He fades in and out, his face still glitching—dying like his human. "When I saw your human's car parked near that shady alley, something seemed off. I guided Mr. Strife over, figuring he would know what to do. Of course he did. But I—"

"Eddy, it's not your fault. It was me—"

"When we got there, I saw your human bleeding out on the ground. She's really dead, isn't she?" He asks more so as a statement than a question.

"She can't be because that would mean..." Rina trails off.

But I dip my chin.

Her bubbly eyes widen. "How?"

Eddy slowly extends his hand in disbelief, and his eyes light up when he touches my shoulder. "You're not even fading.... How are you still alive?"

I shrug. "Technically, we're all dead."

Rina and I giggle, but Eddy glares at us, zipping Rina's lips. "You know what I mean."

I crack a smile. "Sometimes. I mean, you do have a reputation as the local town crazy."

Although I chuckle, he doesn't find any humor in my joke, retracting his hand. "Why was that psycho ghost choking you?"

"And how did he disappear?" Rina adds.

"Your guesses are as good as mine," I mumble, but Eddy shoots me a grim look. "I-I really don't know. All I remember is him talking crazy—like you—something about me being his ticket to *Bliss*."

In that moment, I didn't think it was possible, but Eddy's big eyes grow even larger. His pupils reduce to dots, gawking at me with the strangest expression. The top half of his face lights up, while the bottom half hangs flat. "What'd you just say?"

Rina grins, hopping up. "It is real!"

But I dare not speak, unsure if I *should.*

Suddenly, Eddy jumps up and begins to pace the room, muttering to himself. "Everyone said I was crazy. Said I had a screw loose. But I knew. I knew it. I knew!"

Dancing in place, Rina spins around like an elegant ballerina. She twirls her arms about to a nonexistent beat, and one of her legs bends with perfect form. "How exciting! I didn't doubt you for a second, Eddy."

Abruptly, he whirls to me, strides over in two steps, and sits back down. "Okay, what did that psycho ghost—"

"Verquen—" I correct.

"What did Verquen say *exactly*?"

Rina does one final spin before sitting back down. Although she still smiles, her eyebrows pinch with the slightest tension as she listens.

After I feed them the gist of Verquen's sick, twisted theology, their faces scrunch, now just as confused as me. Eddy twiddles his thumbs as he analyzes the lines on the floor, and the gears must turn inside his head. Whereas, Rina simply falls silent, staring off into space.

In the next moment, snoring erupts from Mr. Strife's bed. He tows in deep breaths, and his chest caves up and down. Dried tears stain his pale cheeks, snot running down to his big floppy ears. The muscles in his face relax, and temporary relief settles over the ill man. Hopefully, his dreams are better than reality.

"Don't waste your time trying to make it make sense." I sigh, facing them.

Rina slowly nods.

"He was obviously a psycho—"

"No," Eddy blurt outs, fixing on us with big bug eyes. "I get it! It's *bullshit*, but it makes sense."

I jerk my neck back in confusion. "What?"

"We have to get to Chesnutt Cemetery." He heads for the door, bouncing in excitement, and the tips of his dense hair blow behind him. He looks over his shoulder and motions an arm for us to c'mon.

"Chesnutt Cemetery?" Rina asks, standing up. "I'm in, but very confused."

I cross my arms. "I'm not going anywhere until you explain what's going on."

To my surprise, he paces back over and grabs one of my and Rina's hands. The corners of his mouth pinch into a thin smile. "*Bliss*, guys. I'm not crazy. Verquen was going to stand by and let those thugs kill each other, so they could pass on in peace." He raises a finger. "It's sadistic, but it works."

Rina falls back into a thoughtful daze; however, I slip my hand from Eddy's grasp and push a loose strand of hair behind my ear. I try to make sense of it all, knowing that humans who die with regret become ghosts and those who don't, find true peace.

"It's like a cycle," Eddy continues. "The sooner humans die, the sooner they can move on to the afterlife—whether that be as a ghost or to *Bliss*."

"But what about the ghosts that die?" Rina asks.

I peer into his starlit eyes. "If *I* had actually died?"

"Where do they go?"

Eddy winks. "That's what we're gonna find out."

For a second, a tide of hope wells inside me, but I push it down like vomit. "*Tch*. What a waste of time." I turn away. "Plus, I doubt Rina's chain would even make it that far?"

Rina's chin drops to her chest, studying her long chain which leads out of the room. "What do you mean 'make it that far'?"

Demonstrating, Eddy grabs his chain, walking closer to Mr.

Strife, and their link shrinks. "The length of a ghosts chain depends on the bond between them and their human." He walks back over to us, and his chain extends.

"Oh, I love my human!" Rina exclaims with a newfound smile. She twirls around with a sidestep, and her long, frizzy hair revolves around her. "He's so strong. He was born really early and really weak, but now he's fine—strong as an ox."

Eddy tugs my arm. "*Seeeee.* She'll be fine. She could probably travel across the country without her human."

"Just like you," I mock, but he simply smiles as if a proud father. I stick out my tongue in disgust, feigning a gag. "Stupid human lovers," I grumble.

"C'mon, Slixx," Eddy pleads. "Just come with us to the cemetery and let me show you something. Afterward, if you still don't believe, I'll leave you alone."

I raise an eyebrow. "That does sound promising, but I still don't think—"

"What's the worst that could happen?" Rina asks, twinkling.

They both stare at me with big pleading eyes—Rina like that of a baby and Eddy a puppy. Her rosy cheeks radiate like beams of light while his white smile brightens up the room.

I avert their gazes, disbelief swirling in my mind, but Verquen's ruby eyes flash in my head. I can't escape that cold scowl, that sinful gaze, or that *power.* Although I try to resist, somewhere deep in my gut beckons for me to go, and the many dark thoughts in my head from over the years merge and erupt into a new voice, screaming for me to take a chance *at life.*

"I still don't believe in this *Bliss* place," I scoff, ambling toward the door. I walk through it but leave half my body inside the room. "So, whatever's at Chesnutt Cemetery better be damn convincing."

Grinning, Rina and Eddy high-five like children.

But before we leave, Eddy walks over to his human and kisses him on the cheek. A small smile spreads across Mr. Strife's face like a newborn baby, surely relieving some of his pain. Because although ghosts are known for haunting, we can be healers, too.

CHAPTER 5
QUARTET

Contrary to what you might think, not even ghosts like cemeteries.

The moon looms overhead, and stars twinkle around the thin crescent. They shine down on the dark cemetery below, glowing bright even after death, but no amount of light could light up this wasteland. It smells of decay, mud, and dying soil, forcing me to cover my nose.

An old metal sign hangs over the entrance with thin gray letters inside that read **CHESNUTT CEMETERY**. The ends of the sign connect to two stones, and attached to that, a metal fence encloses the place. Even though the two front gates are open, the old rusty bars look less than inviting.

Rina and Eddy cling to my arms as we enter the cemetery, our chains rattling behind us. "This place gives me the c-creeps," Eddy mutters.

Rina sniffles. "Same."

I want to snark *did I give either of you permission to touch me?* but I hold my tongue. Instead, I say, "It was *you two's* idea to come here."

We bypass the many white chiseled tombstones, and a

spider crawls down my spine. Dark bouquets litter the grass, serving more as Halloween decorations rather than loving gifts in memory of the dead. I gulp, inching forward down the straight cobblestone path. "Where are we going anyway?"

"And how much farther?" Rina whines.

"T-t-to the fountain. N-not f-far." Eddy's teeth chatter like rattling skeleton bones. He whips his head both ways, eyes wide, and he tightens his hold on me. I nearly laugh at how big he is hunched over at my side. "It'll g-g-give you all the p-proof you need, Slixx."

"It better," I sigh.

Suddenly, a bushel of flowers ruffle. I freeze, Rina gasps, and Eddy yanks me close, nearly knocking me over. They point at a black blob that flies out of the bushel, and I stagger back. All our footsteps stammer against the ground, our chains jangling behind us. We watch the blob weave in between the tombstones as it nears us, but I've lost the ability to move.

Closer and closer it comes.

"*Ahhhh!*" Rina screams.

Closer.

Eddy tugs my dress, beckoning for us to flee as the big blob approaches us, and his chattering becomes even worse. "S-S-Slixx, w-w-we gotta g-go! S-Slixx! N-n-n-n-now!"

Although the night sky is bright, there is no other source of light in this cemetery—not a single lamp. Only the darkness surrounds us, and on top of our spooky noisy chains, the eerie sounds of nature stir the air, too. Crickets sing a horrific tune while flying insects scream in pain. Even the trees tousle, their branches clacking together in discord from the lowly wind. The black blob hides behind the last tombstone barrier before prowling out of the shadows. Rina's horrific screams and Eddy's chattering teeth fill my ears. I grip their wrists as a creature emerges.

"Woof!"

"A golden doggy!" Rina exclaims. Rushing toward it, she twirls in circles as her angelic laughter carries her away.

My jaw drops, but then after a moment, I let out the biggest exhale in history and pull away from Eddy. I clear my throat, pretending to dust off my permanently dirty dress. Meanwhile, hints of embarrassment and irritation press at my temples, but I just stride off, shaking my head.

However, Eddy quickly catches up and clasps my arm, again. A big smile spreads across his face as he chuckles and snuggles against my side. "You got scared, huh?"

"Did not!" I snap, trying to shake him off.

"Did too!"

Stopping dead in my tracks, I finally jerk him off, and he yelps. A familiar foreign sensation of pins and needles pricks at my skin, and a recurring load wells in my chest. I ball my fists and squeeze my eyes shut, hoping and waiting for this anxiety to go away.

"Did not," I grit through my teeth.

A moment of silence fleets by between us. The outdoor sounds seem to increase in volume, or maybe my hearing heightens because my eyes are closed—either-or. Nevertheless, Eddy doesn't speak for a long while, and by the time he does, I open my eyes, staring straight ahead at a large stone monument.

"Sorry..." he whispers.

Guilt overpowers my anxiety and crashes down on my limbs. "You don't have to—"

"I-I didn't mean to trigger your Truth."

I knit my brows, turning to him. "My *Truth*?"

His gaze shifts from the ground to me, and he narrows his eyes. He studies me like I'm some unknown specimen, as if analyzing the cracks and crevices of my mind. "You've never—"

"Guys!" Rina calls out. "I think something's wrong."

Eddy and I exchange worrisome glances before hurrying to her.

She now kneels at the foot of the dog, petting it, but her hand goes right through. She frowns, dropping her arm to her side. "Why can't I touch him?"

"Animals go through us like humans," Eddy answers. "Every living creature goes through us."

"Unless you scare them." I chuckle, reminiscing on a past prank.

"Or *heal* them," Eddy emphasizes.

I glower at him.

Rina tries to touch the dog one more time before giving up. She then grabs the left side of her chest and hunches over, hugging herself. "I don't know why, but I just got so sad. I think I used to have a dog...maybe in my past life."

"Nonsense," I groan, shooing her away with a wave.

But Eddy wraps his arms around her and pulls her to her feet. "Your Truth's been triggered."

"My Truth?" Rina parrots.

"What the hell does that even mean?" I snap.

"You just got here, so of course, you don't know," he says to Rina. "But you, Slixx..." His attention shifts to me, and those same squinty eyes pick me apart. "You've never been to a cemetery before?" he asks in his Eddy way of making a statement rather than asking a question.

I shake my head.

"Never?" he blurts out. "Your human never visited a loved one here? You never wandered off at night and went exploring?"

I cross my arms, dumbfounded. "First of all, my human was still a teenager and hadn't lost anyone yet. Second of all, our chain barely extended outside of her apartment."

"Probably because you hated her," he mumbles.

"I never said I *hated* her!" I yell much louder than intended, and he cowers away, Rina flinching beside him. My gaze then wanders down to their long, stupid chains. "Not everybody can be as freakishly close as you and your human."

"Sorry, bad joke. Too soon."

"Guys, don't fight," Rina says, her soft voice soothing.

Clearing my throat, I regain my composure. "Besides, why would I *wander* to a *cemetery*?" I raise my voice on the last word —an obvious *what the hell*—but Eddy doesn't seem to get it. "And I'm sure the latter isn't how you first came here either."

He averts his gaze, glancing back at his linked chain. Then he walks off, and Rina and I follow close behind. "Not at first. It's sad to say, but Mr. Strife's actually lost a ton of people during his lifetime. His mother, older sister, and wife. Damn sure isn't fair, but life isn't either."

He shrugs. "We'd come here every Sunday and lay flowers, and he'd pray even though he wasn't exactly a man of faith. And from there, I started coming here on my own at night. It's creepier than creepy. But something kept pulling me here."

"Something like what?" Rina asks.

Looking back at us over his shoulder, he smirks. "We're almost there."

"Woof!"

Gasping, all three of us whirl around, and that same golden dog peers up at us. His tongue hangs out of his mouth, and his floppy ears hang low. His small black eyes look like dots, but they glimmer with innocence like Rina's. He barks, again, before walking over to us.

Eddy stiffens, holding his breath, as the collarless dog sniffs him. Then he ambles over to me, sniffing at my feet.

I also tense up but do my best to keep pokerfaced, but when I look down, the angelic dog does the unthinkable—*licks* me. A ghost! His tongue connects with my thigh, and his saliva smears up my skin. I slowly tick my head to Rina and Eddy who both look just as surprised.

"He touched you!" Rina shouts, mesmerized by the dog.

When it leans in to lick me again, I jump back. "How's that possible?" I breathe. "Eddy?"

He shakes his head, wide-eyed. "I don't know."

Rina stoops down before the heavily panting dog, but her touch falls through again. "No fair. Slixx can touch him and I can't."

Eddy tiptoes forward next and bends down at the foot of the dog. He slowly reaches out with one hesitant hand, and a bead of sweat trickles off the tip of his sharp nose. The dog looks up at him with a smile. However, when the tips of Eddy's fingers pass through the dog's fur, his smile falters.

"Woof!" the dog barks, looking directly at Eddy, and Eddy perks back up.

"Can...can you see me, boy?"

"Woof!"

Rina and Eddy motion for me to come back, so I inch over to them.

Kneeling, I sit back on my heels as the dog licks me, again. His warm saliva swamps my cheek, but this time, I can't help but laugh. It's as if he's just told me the funniest joke. Butter melts inside my chest, and flowers bloom in my mind. My body feels light, too—so light that I reach out for the dog.

He caves at my touch, and sparks fly between us. His tail begins to wag just before he lies across my legs, nuzzling up against me. And the sweetest floral smell wafts up from his fur coat.

"Awwwwwwe," Eddy drones, poking fun.

"You guys are so cute together!" Rina says, and the dog barks in agreement. "Wanna come with us, boy?"

"Woof, woof!"

Eddy chuckles.

I giggle, petting him. "That must mean yes."

"Well then you're gonna need a name," Rina says to him in a baby voice.

"How about Yellow?" Eddy suggests.

The dog whines, and I say, "Nah."

Rina stares off into the distance, thinking. "Hmm... Cutiebooty?"

Eddy and I gawk at her.

She laughs. "Sorry, I'm bad at names."

"Butters?" I pose.

Eddy wags a finger. "No way. Sounds weird. What about Heads?"

Just then, a light bulb flickers in my head, and I chipper up. But I must move too quickly because the dog flinches, twisting around his alert head. His tail briefly stops wagging, but then it picks back up at top speed.

"What? What is it?" Rina asks, eagerly.

"Lay it on us," Eddy says.

The name flows out of my mouth, and the dog looks up at me with starlit eyes. He barks, licking my arm. I try to wipe off his spit, but he licks me again as if demanding I accept his affection. Laughter oozes out of me as I pet the newest addition to our team.

"I love it!" Rina shouts.

Chuckling beside me, Eddy extends a flat palm. "Pleased to meet ya, Tails."

Tails sits up and faces Eddy with the biggest grin. He reaches out to paw Eddy's hand, but his attempt falls through. He whines, trying again and again, and his ears twitch. But after a minute, it's as if a switch clicks in his head, and instead of trying to touch Eddy, he barks with a nod.

The three of us giggle.

Eddy wraps his arms around his knees before standing up. Then, he pats his lap and takes off running. "C'mon, boy! Let's show Slixx and Rina, *Bliss!*"

As if on command, Tails darts after him, his tongue flailing out the side of his mouth. He catches up to Eddy—Rina not too far behind them—and they all chitchat back and forth. Tails' innocent barks fill the cemetery, traveling up to the sky, and somehow, an invisible light ignites over the burial ground.

This cemetery doesn't seem so scary after all.

CHAPTER 6
RIDDLING ANSWERS

The cobblestone path breaks into two at the large monument, and Eddy leads us up the one on the left. We steadily climb the hill, passing by another litter of deceased and memoriam gifts. The tombstones read different names with various dates—some short-lived and some lengthy. Flags blow in the gentle wind, and leaves rustle from nearby scattered trees. Even balloons sway before one tombstone, the rubber chaffing against each other.

Outside of Tails, whose sweet smell lingers around our quartet, the cemetery's odor grows worse—like decomposing tissue and regretful sin.

"How much farther?" Rina moans.

I keep one hand on my hip and the other over my nose. "Yeah, it reeks."

Eddy points up the last stretch of the hill, and as we near the top, running water fades into the cacophony of nature sounds. "We're almost there," he says.

After several yards, the tip of a large gray fountain finally comes into view, and the rest of it arises with each step we take. It's divided into three tiers, a pointy crystal centered at the top.

Water gently falls from the crystal and trickles down to the first tier, and the overflow cascades to the next tier and then the next. The largest tier acts as a basin and holds the water, though, filtering it back up to the top to begin the cycle again.

We follow the rest of the path before finally reaching the fountain. Tails collapses in front of it like we're going to be here a while, and Eddy takes a seat on the fountain's ledge. He dips a hand in the water with closed eyes, inhaling a lungful of air.

"Uh…" Rina places a finger to her mouth, searching the dead zone. "Now what?"

Impatient, I tap my foot against the ground. "Where's the proof?"

Eddy's long lashes flutter as he turns to me. He scoots off the ledge and slides down to the ground beside Tails. "Right in front of you."

He motions his head for me and Rina to sit down, so we do. Then, he directs our attention to the very bottom of the fountain. The thick base tier starts off as just a small circle, but it widens in layers from the ground.

Eddy lies down on his stomach, ushering us to do the same, and that's when I see small squiggly words engraved on the stone, which round the entire fountain.

"Here's your proof," he says.

I squint at the tiny writing, while Rina reaches out to touch it. Her eyes light up in wonder as she runs the tips of her fingers along the base.

But just as I'm about to say it's too dark to read, Eddy lights a match. The words come alive on the stone and highlight neon purple, nearly dancing off into the air. I run my fingers over them, tracing each letter, and that same beckoning in my gut from before wells inside me.

"Read it, Slixx," Eddy says. "And if you still don't believe, I'll stay out of your sight."

I gulp, but Tails places a reassuring paw on my hand. He whines as if saying *it's okay*, and I believe him. "Everyone dies and how matters. Humans without regret go *Bliss*. Humans with sin and remorse go amiss."

Rina, Eddy, and I scoot over with each word, eventually rounding the entire fountain.

"Ghosts one – Limbo in murder and sickness, ghosts two – The Dump in natural quickness, ghosts three – Almost in self-witness. Never rising from infliction. Move forward not back. Stay still or attack. Hither toward sweet peas and pure canines (though beware of the Hellons). True peace you seek—to *Bliss* —despite hellish way, those might make it with a plum severed chain. Start at one, by human by way, death burns at daybreak."

After we round the fountain and wind up back where we started beside Tails, Eddy turns to me and Rina, who appears just as stupefied as me. He doesn't say anything for a long while, and all is quiet. The weak wind fades, calming the trees, while the gentle water soundtracks the twinkling stars above.

Serenity washes over my soul.

"We have to go," Rina whispers, a smile spreading across her face from ear to ear. She throws her arms around us, pulling us close, and our heads butt together. "Let's go!"

Eddy nods in excitement, but I stare at the inscriptions for another long minute before I finally open my mouth.

"*Bliss*…it's real?"

CHAPTER 7
LIMBO

"What does all that mean?" I ask, all of us now sitting on the fountain's ledge with Tails lying across my legs. I pet his soft fur as his back rises and falls.

Eddy stares at the trickling water. "To tell you the truth, I don't know. Some of it makes sense, but most of it…"

"Is like a puzzle with missing pieces," Rina finishes, leaning her head on my shoulder.

Taken aback, I glare down at her with twisted lips before letting it go. "Then can you start by explaining what makes sense because I'm totally lost."

He flashes us a smirk, and his infectious smile makes me laugh. "Forewarning, I'm only certain of three things, and the rest are just guesses."

I dip my chin. "Okay, spill."

He spins around and dips his feet into the fountain, and the water stops short of his tattered jeans. His ankle bracelet floats underneath the surface, the charmed ends pushing and pulling with the current. "Stating the obvious, every ghost already knows that humans who die with regret become ghosts and those who don't find peace—AKA *Bliss*. For us, it's like we're supposed to believe that this is as good as it gets. But I think *anyone* can go to *Bliss*. Just because we've already passed on as ghosts doesn't mean we can't make it."

Rina slowly nods in understanding. "We can just as much as humans can."

Tails barks as if to follow her declaration with an emphasized period.

"Okay, and what's the second thing?" I ask.

"All of us ghosts on this Earth—we're all in Limbo," he mutters, pity in his low voice. "Kind of like 'fake peace.' We have no recollection of our past lives. We just linger in this world without worries, cares, or regrets. No purpose."

He hunches over, placing his elbows on his knees, while Rina pouts her lips, grabbing her empty chest. I don't react, though—numb to this harsh reality for many years.

A brief moment of silence fleets by.

"And the third thing, our human selves died by homicide or sickness."

I cup my chin and take a moment to ponder the riddle engraved on the fountain. *Ghosts one – Limbo in murder and sickness.* "All that does make sense, fake peace and all. But how do we know which one of the two was our cause of death?"

Eddy turns to me. "We don't."

I swallow spit, and my palms grow moist. We stare into each other's eyes in silence for what feels like an eternity, awkward unease thawing inside me. Unsure how to respond, I shift my attention to the rippling water.

Thankfully, Rina breaks the ice. "So, Eddy, what about your guesses?"

Eddy's pitch rises, chippering up. He raises a finger so fast that Tails snaps his head to him, but he throws up his hands in peace just as fast. "My first guess is that there are three realms."

"Realms?" I tease.

He gives me a look. "Worlds, dimensions, whatever you wanna call it."

Catching on, Rina lists the three realms: "Limbo, The Dump, and Almost."

The gears slowly turn inside my mind. "And like you said, we're in Limbo right now. That guess makes sense. Go on."

To my surprise, he places a hand on my shoulder, and I freeze. He gazes into my eyes, deadpan. "Like Verquen said, *you're* our ticket to *Bliss*."

"Ticket?" Rina asks.

"Not this again," I groan.

"That psycho ghost from the alley said Slixx was the ticket to *Bliss*, and that she would lead him there." He raises a brow at me. "You still don't believe?"

"*Bliss* is probably real—"

"Probably?" Eddy exclaims, shocked.

"But me being this 'ticket' is a stretch."

"A stretch?" I shoot him a scowl, annoyed at the echo, and he recoils. "*Those might make it with a plum severed chain.* It's the most accurate guess I have."

"No, the 'realms' were a bit more believable."

Rina looks at me. "It does make sense, though, Slixx. And it might be more than just a coincidence that your broken chain led us here."

"Technically, Eddy led us here," I joke.

"Slixx." Eddy's tone drops, grave. "Your human died, and you *didn't*. Your chain literally *snapped*. Plus, Verquen came to *you*. You're the only one who can lead ghosts to *Bliss*."

Forcing back the thought of Kiara, Verquen's red eyes flash through my mind. *You will lead me to Bliss. You just do not know it yet, Ticket.* I shiver, rubbing the goosebumps on my arms, and my voice reduces to less than a murmur. "If that's true...and I do this, then maybe it'll make up for what I've done."

"You say something?" Eddy asks.

Rina, however, places a comforting hand on mine.

I shake my head, but Tails snuggles against me, giving me the courage to ask, "Why me?"

"That, I don't know." Eddy pulls his feet out of the fountain and spins around to the ground. "Just like *beware of the Hellons*—which I doubt means anything pleasant."

I crack a smile, cradling Tails in my arms. "I'm sure we'll find out sooner or later."

"Anymore guesses?" Rina asks.

"Yeah, just one." Eddy stands up and yawns before gazing up at the stars. He then speaks as if from stream of consciousness. "*Start at one, by human by way, death burns at daybreak.* I believe the first part of that means we're in realm one. The second part may have to do with Slixx's human."

I connect the dots, shifting my attention to Rina. She meets my gaze, and a mutual knowing transpires between us. We then look up at Eddy, and he looks down at me.

"We've got to find Kiara before sunrise," I say.

CHAPTER 8
THE CHASE

Initially, we thought finding a dead body would be easy, but as it turns out, we were wrong. We check the largest and closest hospital first—Tucker Bay Hospital—and of course, we get lost.

Rina and I eavesdrop on doctors and patients to figure out where the morgue is while Eddy checks in on Mr. Strife. He disappears through the door, leaving us alone to snoop around. Meanwhile, Tails waits for us outside, behind the building.

Taking the stairwell down a couple flights, I try to split up from Rina to cover more ground, but she stays glued to my hip. She clings to my arm and drags me halfway into random rooms before saying, "Not it," and checking an adjacent one. Her long, frizzy hair flips with every turn, and I have to spit it out of my mouth.

After the tenth door, she stops and waves at a distant ghost. "Maybe we should ask someone."

"Yeah right, they'll just look at us like I look at Eddy."

She giggles. "Like long lost lovers?"

I flinch, sticking out my tongue, but then a tall man dressed in blue and his ghost breeze past us. His clipboard catches my eye: **CORONER'S RELEASE FORM.**

"I'm not even going to dignify that with a response," I say, pivoting on my heels after the quick man, who also carries a cup of coffee.

"Where are we going?" Rina asks, hurrying after me.

The man rounds a corner so fast I have to jog to catch up, but when I do, I lose him in the busy hallway full of humans. "No, no, no," I mutter, hurrying down the hall.

"Wait, Slixx!" she calls out.

But I keep going, flying through humans until I reach the next corner, and then I spot a glimpse of the man in blue and his lackluster ghost. They turn another corner, the human's long legs propelling him yards ahead of me. It takes me a few seconds to catch up to them, but when I do, an empty elevator dings.

The doors open as Rina finally catches up, panting.

Before she can open her mouth, I grab her hand and slip inside the elevator with my targets, followed by a bunch of other humans and their ghosts. The man in blue slurps his coffee, most of it absorbing into his thick mustache, before pressing Floor B. Meanwhile, the other humans light up the elevator buttons like a Christmas tree, and we stop on just about every floor.

Wedged in between a plump man and a ghost lady in a thong, I hold my breath as my claustrophobia sets in, yet Rina beams with joy beside two elderly ghosts. She tries to make small talk, but they ignore her. Most ghosts aren't ones for small talk or engaging in conversation of any kind. Leading simple, boring, *dead* lives is the standard.

"Rina," I hiss, seizing her attention. She snaps to me, and I tip my chin at the man in blue's clipboard. "He's going to lead us to my human."

By the time Rina, our targets, and I reach the basement level, we're the only ones in the elevator. Rina and I follow the man in blue and his ghost out and down a dim hallway.

"Slixx, it's cold down here," Rina whispers, grabbing my arm.

I roll my eyes. "Human weather doesn't affect ghosts."

"Well, it sure *feels* like it."

Above, a couple lights flicker, and I fight the urge to hug myself. Dread seeps into my bones, filling my head with fright. But we continue down the hallway until our targets stop outside one of the many doors. The man chugs the rest of his coffee before disposing of it, and then he and his ghost enter the room. And we follow in after them.

Inside, only half the lights are on—creepier than creepy. On both sides, large drawers line along the metal walls, likely dead bodies stored inside. An empty stretcher rests in the middle of the room, and a sink lies against the back wall. The man glosses over his clipboard before putting it down and snapping on blue gloves. Meanwhile, his ghost plops down on the floor in a corner and tucks his head between his legs, becoming more invisible than ghostly possible.

"What's he doing?" Rina asks, watching the man closely.

When he walks over to one of the drawers, I suck in air and shield my eyes as he opens it. The metal drawer clamors out, bouncing off the walls, and a depressing sigh comes from way of the coroner.

Rina gasps, squeezing my arm. "You shouldn't look."

But I peek between my fingers and instantly regret it. Cold veins pop out of my human's pale tan skin, and a dingy white sheet barely covers her naked body. "Kiara," I whisper, an immense pressure toppling onto my chest.

Just then, the door swings open.

Rina and I jump.

Two more coroners dressed in blue enter the room—one middle-aged lady and one blond man—and they're both ghost-less. Straightaway, the middle-aged lady skims the clipboard, while the blond man helps the other lift my human's dead body onto the stretcher. Her limbs barely move, as stiff as cardboard.

Rina steps in front of me, shielding me from my sinful crime. She places her hands on my shoulders before pulling me into a warm hug, but I open my eyes, staring at my past.

"Kiara Thompson," the lady reads aloud. "Her family's ordered a rush delivery to Chesnutt's Funeral Home & Crematory. Hmm, rush delivery? We don't get those too often."

"Probably a religious thing," the first man says.

He's right. Not Kiara's mom, but her dad's side is a part of some cultish faith.

"Either way, this meaty one is definitely going to produce some ashes," the blond man jokes, and they all laugh.

I ball my fists. Their disgusting jokes contort my face as a fiery rage burns beneath my skin. I start to snatch away, but Rina hugs me even tighter. I try to hang onto her—onto the one pure thing in this room.

"Glad this unit isn't stacked with bodies like the rest. It actually doesn't smell that bad in here."

They all laugh, again.

Just as I snap, Rina whirls around. She stamps her foot, a dark shade over her eyes. "How can they be so mean?" She strides over to the blond man in two giant steps, and her fingers crinkle. Lurching forward, she touches the man's shoulders, and a powerful shiver tremors his body. He cries out, spooked.

"I'm impressed," I say with my hands on my hips. "Didn't think you had it in you to Scare, Human Lover."

Rina looks back at me and shrugs. "Well, humans are supposed to respect the d—"

"Sliiiixxxxx!" a super high-pitched voice yells from down

the hall. At first, I don't see the person, but then Eddy sprints past the door. His head whirls around, searching for me, and we lock eyes. "Rina!" He stammers to a stop and runs into the room. Sweat pools down his face as he snatches our wrists.

"*Agh!*" I yelp.

"*Ow!*" Rina shouts.

Eddy breaks off into a sprint again, dragging us with him, and we all run down the hallway.

"What's going on?" Rina asks.

I cover my nose, catching a whiff of vinegar. "And what's that smell?"

But before Eddy can speak, a monstrous cry as if from the pits of hell screeches behind us. I wheel around, and Rina and Eddy stop, too. My jaw drops at the sight of three large demons standing between the elevator and stairwell. Three horns protrude from their rough pinecone-shaped heads. Their sharp rows of teeth jut out their mouths in every direction like sharks, and their one long cylindrical eyes appear a swirling mix of black and violet.

Polluting the air around them, they breathe out toxic gas through their pea-sized emaciated noses, which cave into their rotten skin. They also hold pointy spears and shields in front of their scaly dragon-like bodies.

Rina gulps, her lips quivering as if on the verge of a scream.

"Eddy..." I say in a low voice. "What the hell are those things?"

He hesitates, his sweaty grasp slipping from my wrist. "I-I wanna say d-demons, but I think the accurate terminology from the fountain w-would be *Hellons*."

"Oh," I whisper. "Well, that's good to know."

"*HWAAAAAAH!*" all three Hellons screech, their piercing cries echoing down the empty hallway. The dim lights flicker. The glass windows shatter, shards flying everywhere. Rina,

Eddy and, I cover our ears as the vibrations hit us. Our hairs whip back, and my dress ripples behind me like a flag amid a windstorm. The three coroners and mindless ghost burst out of Kiara's room, scurrying down the hallway for the exit. "Hwa. Hwa! **HWA!**"

"We should probably run," I say.

Eddy inches back, letting go of our hands. "W-way ahead of you."

In a snap, the Hellons take off running, and so do Eddy and I. Rina, however, screams—motionless like a statue. I double back and snatch her hand. Then we sprint down the hallway with all our might, but the Hellons gain on us like Olympic sprinters. I lug in breaths before huffing them out, my feet only touching the ground for less than a second.

Eddy flies through a door ahead, and we follow him. The Hellons' screeches slam at us from behind, but we veer right. Flying through another door and then another, I pant. Eddy finally rams through a wall, but just as I pass through, I lock eyes with the biggest Hellon mere feet behind me. I gasp at the spear in its claws—aimed at Rina.

"No..." I gasp.

"*Hwaaaa!*" the big Hellon screams.

It cocks its claws back before letting the spear fly, and midstride, I freeze like I'm falling. I try to speak, but my throat feels like sandpaper. My limbs become leaden unlike my distant head, and all I can see is the horrifying Hellon before me. Green saliva drips from its wide-open mouth while its nostrils lug in ebony air.

I peer from the Hellon's swirling black eye to the spear just inches from Rina's back to Rina's terrified face. The other two Hellons trail the biggest one with hungry mouths, and I wonder if they're going to eat her, and then me. I think back on the sixteen years I've been a ghost—from haunting a baby to a grown human, all the times I pranked people, and the many ghosts that I've met. However, I come up short of anything—or anyone—that I'd miss. I can't even recall one time when I was *truly* happy. And in that moment, I ponder...*what if I actually made it to Bliss? What would that feel like?*

The Hellon's spear lurches forward, but acting fast, I fling Rina to the side. She flies left, while all my body weight sends me flying right—toward the spear. I wait for it to hit me, bracing myself for an impact that I'm strangely familiar with, but it never comes. Instead, a force yanks my arm, and a *ZOOM* sails past my ear.

Just as I stumble over, that same force grabs my wrist and heaves me back to my feet. My vision whiplashes before toggling on the back of Eddy's head. He guides me along before releasing my hand, so I kick my legs back into gear to pick up cadence with him. Beads of sweat pour from my face.

Despite all my might, a gap grows between me and Eddy as his long legs propel him forward—maybe he was a track star in his past life. Nevertheless, we burst through another wall and wind up outside. Our chains clank against the concrete, slithering behind us.

Above, the darkness in the sky has receded, and the subtlest layer of light now overcasts the moon. The litter of twinkling stars have also been replaced with thick clouds, drifting in peace.

"We don't have much time left," Eddy calls back over the Hellons' screeching behind us. We bypass a dumpster, and he cups his hands around his mouth. "Tails, let's go!"

Running through a slew of cars, I whip my head left then right, but there's no sign of Tails. Then a nerve strikes at the thought of Rina, panic arising in my chest. "Tails! Rina!"

Just as I ready my footing to change course, a bark sounds from ahead. I look over, facing forward, and Rina and Tails bolt from around a car. Tails bounds at my right side, his paws and my feet striding on one accord, while Rina falls into sync on the left.

I glance behind at the Hellons, who'll be catching up to us in no time. "What do we do?" I call out, but Eddy must not hear.

"I don't know!" Rina whimpers.

Tails barks before lowering to a snarling growl.

"If you're saying what I think you're saying," I pant, "then no! We can't fight those *things*!"

Tails barks in protest.

"For one, they're humongous, and you're tiny. And two, you probably can't even touch them!"

Headlights blind me as we cross the street, and a blaring car whirrs by. I peek down at Tails to make sure he's okay—he's unfazed, running by my side. However, a car swerves, and a loud bang alarms a car crash. Rina screams, ducking while running as if the car can actually hit her. I catch a glimpse of the damage out of the corner of my eye, glossing over an unconscious man pressed against an airbag.

Behind us, the Hellons continue screeching, cracking any glass in their path.

Eddy leads us into a dim forest, and I instinctively shield my face from the onslaught of branches. They pass through me (of course), but I keep my hands up, zooming by trees and crunching on twigs.

"Eddy, where are we going?" I call out over the chaos.

"*Ahh, ahh, ahh!*" Rina sounds off.

"Not sure!" he grunts back between her screams.

Tails then barks as if taking the words right out of my mouth, *what do you mean you're not sure?* He lugs in breaths and puffs them out in less than a second, and his paws barely touch the ground.

I shout Eddy's name in frustration, but when I look up at him, he's jumping down out of view.

"Cliff!" he says on his way down.

Tails runs ahead of me and Rina and soars off the cliff next, but anxiety builds in my chest. In that split second, I ponder the magnitude of the cliff—*how long is it, how far is the jump, is it sturdy, is it safe, will I lose my footing, will I even see it coming?* But all that goes out the window when the land ends and I actually leap off the cliff.

Despite Rina's manic shrieks, she leaps beside me like a majestic deer. Her wild hair flies up like my dress, and her arms fall with grace. She readies her feet for landing, while mine dangle in the air, waiting to hit the ground. A thrown spear and shield just miss me, whizzing between our heads, but then another set grazes my arm, green plasma (a.k.a. ghost blood) splattering out. I yelp.

"Slixx!" Rina cries out.

"Slixx!" Eddy's distant voice shouts in unison with Tails' bark.

My landing falters to a botched tuck and roll, and I go tumbling in the mud. *"Agh!"*

I slam into a tree, my back aching as I hunch over in pain. (Pellucid works in more ways than one. Ghosts may also be able to pass through things, but not if we don't see them coming.) Blood oozes from my wound, tainting the leaves, twigs, and small creatures beneath me.

My vision toggles on the brightening forest, the many trees blurring into a thousand more. The pain in my backside throbs, and it travels along my spinal cord. I try to reach for my back but can't...literally. My arms won't move. Perhaps the spear had poison on it. When I try to uncurl my body, my legs refuse to move either. I look up, and small rocks fall from underneath the cliff as the monstrous Hellons approach. I try one last time to move, but it's futile. It's as if I've lost connection with my body.

"*Hwaaaa!*"

I shut my eyes.

"Woof!"

My eyes shoot open to Tails who nudges against me. He scoops his nose under my side as his whimpers beckon me to either climb on his back or latch onto him. I try to move again, and this time, my fingers twitch. I then try to move with all my might, grunting and squeezing, but I barely manage to lift my head.

"C'mon," a soft voice says from above.

A shadowy figure bends over me, and frizzy hair brushes across my face. *Rina!*

"Give me your hands," she says to me, quickly finding them.

Tails barks as she mutters to him, and then she pulls me to my feet. I immediately topple over—unable to feel my legs—but she holds me up by my waist. Meanwhile, slews of rocks fall from the cliff as the Hellons draw near.

"Are you sure?" Rina asks in somewhat of a scream.

"Woof!"

"Okay, I'm trusting you!"

In an instant, she spins me around, and Tails bounds in front of me. She then tosses me onto his back like I'm riding a horse, a ghost's weight comparable to that of a feather. Her soft hands wrap mine around Tails' neck before they both take off running, Tails carrying me along with ease.

The darkness within the forest ebbs away as daybreak approaches, our precious time running out. Yellow shine glimmers through a cloudy barrier, and it faintly radiates across the horizon. The wind chills my face, a shiver seizing my half-paralyzed body.

We bypass shields on the ground and spears stuck high in

trees. Only one grand screech sounds behind us—the rest of the piercing chorus mute. When I peep over my shoulder, only the biggest Hellon charges for us. It smashes down trees in its path with its shield, its large scaly three-clawed feet chucking up mud.

Tails rounds a large oak tree, and my view of the Hellon cuts out. I face forward, batting my curls out of my eyes. A sweet flowery smell entices my nostrils, and I lean down to Tails' enchanting fur coat. Even during this crisis, the lovely smell clears my worries as if absolving them in sugary almonds. I inhale a lungful of air as we soar out of the forest and into oncoming traffic. It's backed up, so we weave in between cars.

Storming behind us, the single Hellon shakes up the cars in its path, and it lets out another earsplitting scream. Windshields and windows shatter on sight. Humans shield their faces, some covering their ears, and I can't tell whether or not they hear the Hellon. Shards of glass rain down on the concrete, clinking like crystals.

Tails takes us through a plaza before crossing a backstreet after Eddy.

Rina calls Eddy's name, but he doesn't seem to hear. I look back at the Hellon who runs after us with perfect form, its shield at its side. It screeches one last time, breaking the last store's windows.

"Eddy!" I yell, finding my voice as we enter Old Ches' Memorial Park. We pass under the large brick sign, and the lush green grass opens up to multiple trails. We follow along the main one, nearing a playground.

I glance over my shoulder and do a triple take before blinking in shock. "Stop!"

On command, Tails presses his paws to the pavement, and Rina skids to a stop, too. Eddy keeps on running, though, until I call his name. Then, he finally turns around and squints at me and the mind-boggling sight before us. He inches back over, panting heavily like Rina and Tails and scratching his head.

"Unbelievable..." he breathes.

Just outside Old Ches' Memorial Park's open gates, the biggest Hellon paces along the entrance. Its sharp toenails clink against the ground as it walks back and forth. It doesn't pass under the wide sign; it doesn't cross the painted entrance line; and it doesn't *enter* the park.

Rina, Eddy, and I look at each other. His wide eyes peer down at me in confusion, and I return the expression to Rina. Even Tails barks as if to join in on our clueless conversation. All four of us stare at each other before shifting to the Hellon stuck at the gate.

CHAPTER 9
ASHES

Rina, Eddy, Tails, and I decide to keep our distance since the Hellon has a spear—and thank goodness we do. Seconds after the Hellon stops pacing, it throws its shield like a frisbee. The wide disc slices through the air to get us, but luckily the paralysis has worn off my body.

We all dive out of the way.

And when the large Hellon's exhausted both its weapons, the craziest thing happens. It disappears, crumpling away to dust. It lets out one last demonic screech before disintegrating, and in the distance, glass shatters from the plaza across the street and cars nearby. Nevertheless, we all look at each other, knowing a bit more about Hellons than we did before.

"THEY DIE WITHOUT WEAPONS," Eddy says as we trek through the small park.

Rina shivers, still trembling in fear. "They're really ugly."

"And they can't throw to save their lives," I joke, and what sounds like a laugh emits from Tails. While walking, I still hold my arm even though Eddy tore off a piece of his plaid shirt and tied it around my gash. Dark blood stains the cloth, but it doesn't hurt anymore.

"They're after you, Slixx," Eddy says.

He hops onto the low wood surrounding the playground, following it along the perimeter, and Rina does the same. They teeter along like two children, while Tails and I crunch on the woodchips.

Before I can rebuttal, Eddy follows up with, "Back at the hospital, they were looking for you."

I raise a brow at him.

"I didn't know where you or Rina were. I had just come out of Mr. Strife's room and started looking for clues when the Hellons showed up. I think they chased me down to you."

Rina raises a hand. "But I was with Slixx. How do you know they weren't after me?"

"Exactly. And with the way they were after us, I'm pretty sure they were chasing *all* of us."

"I just have a gut feeling." Eddy gives me a look. "Why's all this so hard for you to believe?"

Because I don't want it to be true, I think. Kiara's humming rings in my ears from when she gaily vibed to the radio for the last time. *Any of it.*

I step off the woodchips, and we all amble across a field of grass. I glance down at my wound, remembering the pain and paralysis that traveled up my spine. Verquen's ruby eyes catch my mind off guard, and I suck in air, shaking him away. "First, it was *Bliss.* And now, I'm just supposed to believe *I'm* the ticket to get there?" I throw up my hands. "Why hasn't anyone else gone, hmm? I can't be the *only* 'ticket' to ever exist."

"Maybe there were others," Rina offers.

Eddy flashes me a smile. "Maybe they made it."

I stop, and he, Rina, and Tails turn around and look at me. "Maybe they didn't."

Rina drops her head.

Tails whines.

Even Eddy's smile wavers for a moment before spreading into a grin. He walks over to me and lifts my chain. "What you got to lose? You don't have a human anymore. Would you rather wander this realm without purpose or chase something that might be real—that *might* lead you to paradise?"

Suddenly, Eddy's skin flickers like a light. One second, he's here, and the next, he's gone. I gasp and point at him. "Eddy!"

His gaze wanders down to his hands, watching them in awe as he fades in and out. His body does that a few more times before permanently materializing, faint like before. He studies the specs on the ground. "I'm right there with you, Slixx—purposeless and a bit uncertain. Mr. Strife doesn't have much longer, and neither do I. I'd like to see *Bliss*—or at least chase it—before I go." He looks up at me with the warmest smirk. "It's not like we got anything to lose."

Twirling over, Rina throws an arm around Eddy's shoulder. She stares across at me with those big, bubbly, light brown eyes, and her innocent smile can only be compared to that of holy water. "In the short time I've known you guys, you've become my best—and only—friends." She giggles. "So, I don't care where we go as long as we go together. And regardless if *Bliss* is real, I say we chase it. What's the worst that could happen?"

For a long moment, I dare not say anything. My mind doubles over in contemplation, doubt, and hesitation. I explore the possibility of roaming this realm like a zombie—the only purpose us ghosts in Limbo have is our humans. Mine is dead, and I'm not. I try to find meaning in becoming a nomad and wonder how long I'd live or if I'd ever die without a human to die with.

Purpose drives not only the living but the dead, too. Call it what you want—goals, dreams, hopes, aspirations, faith—but purpose keeps humans going. They live for something, while the purposeless ones take their own lives. It works a similar way in this realm, too. Our sole purpose is to be attached to our humans, and when they give up or die, we die, too. (Well, I'm still here, so we're *supposed* to die, too.)

"Sooooo," Rina drawls, interrupting my train of thought.

"What do ya say, Slixx?" Eddy asks.

I shift my attention to the bright sky above. Almost fully risen, the sun ascends overhead and lightens up the land. Most of the park appears lit, while the other half remains a mere silhouette. Tails' fur looks even more beautiful under the sun— shiny, thick, and soft—while Eddy's hazel eyes twinkle with hope, staring into mine. His face appears gentle in natural light, and somehow, he seems to grow into his lanky body, his long limbs accentuating his height instead of acting as odd proportions. Meanwhile, Rina's smile warms me from the inside out, igniting a pure beam of light in my chest.

"Woof!"

I can't help but smile at Tails. His cute tail wags fast, and his long pink tongue hangs out of his mouth. He licks my thigh, runny snot smearing with his saliva.

"Gross!" I squawk with a laugh, and he does it again.

When I finally look back up at Rina and Eddy, they beam at me like they know what I'm going to say. "It's not like we have anything to lose. I'm in."

<hr>

BY THE TIME we reach the other end of the park, four Hellons await us at the exit. They stand outside the gate in a pack, and Rina, Eddy, Tails, and I freeze yards away, hoping they don't see us. Unfortunately for us, one does and alerts the rest. They begin screeching and readying their weapons for when we near them.

"Not good, not good," Rina says.

"Guys, what's the plan?" I ask.

Rina shakes her head. "Don't look at me."

We both turn to Eddy who's twiddling his thumbs in deep thought.

"Should we run through, split up, charge ahead—?"

He whirls to me. "Charge ahead? Only if you want us to get killed."

Rina wheezes in horror, but I crack a smile, holding back a laugh. "Then what's the plan, genius? We've got to get to Chesnutt's Funeral Home & Crematory and track down Kiara's body. Fast. It's already past daybreak—we might even be too late."

"Nonsense!" Eddy claps his hands, kneeling before Tails. He motions for us to stoop down, and reluctantly, I do. He then tosses his arms around me and Rina's shoulders with Tails in the middle of the circle. "Huddle up, team. Here's the plan. Since the Hellons are either blind or just have sucky vision like T-Rexes, we can use that to our advantage—that and the fact that they're only after me, Rina, and Tails because of Slixx. Therefore, me, Rina, and Tails are gonna create a distraction."

"What kind of distraction?" Rina asks.

"A distracting one."

Rina's eyebrows furrow with fear, but he flashes her a cheesy smile.

"As for you, Slixx, you're bait."

"Bait?" I snap.

"Woof!"

"Bait," Eddy confirms.

I jerk my neck back. "What do you mean bait?"

"You're gonna pop out after we create the distraction. Run out the middle of the park and when they chase you, run back in."

"Hopefully, a spear doesn't take me out," I mutter. "And then what—what's the rest of the plan?"

Eddy looks around, shifty eyed. "Uh, play it by ear?"

Rina's eyes swell as she falls into a petrified daze.

Fright wells in my bones, and I wag a shaky finger at Eddy's face. "Are you asking us or telling us?"

He shrugs, his white smile wider than ever, before rocking our huddle side to side. "Let's do this, team. One, two, three, break!" He throws up his hands and starts toward the exit, and Rina and Tails follow him.

"Wait," I hiss, but they're already gone.

Though after a few steps, Eddy turns around with scrunched brows, peering at me as if I'm missing something. "Hide," he mouths. "On my signal."

"Well you should've mentioned that," I grumble, creeping away. I tiptoe past a stone monument, over to a row of bushes, and hide behind there. Once I've nestled my way into one, I peek through the leaves like a spy.

The three of them mosey over to the exit, which looks exactly like the entrance. A brick sign hangs overhead and reads **Old Ches' Memorial Park**. The gates are open, welcoming and inviting, but the Hellons guard the deserted park. They wheel around to Rina, Eddy, and Tails, who approach them, and begin screaming like banshees.

"Hiya!" Eddy calls out as their voices die down, stopping just a few yards away from them. "How's it going? My name's Eddy. This is my new friend Rina, and my newest pal, Tails. We come in peace and are hoping to just pass through...right there—"

"HWAAAAAAH!" all four Hellons screech in unison.

The vibrations travel in rings, zooming through the air, and Rina, Eddy and Tails barely hold their footing. Rina's hair and Eddy's shirt blow back like Tails' fur. They dig their feet and paws into the ground just to brave through it.

After the Hellons settle down, Eddy prods a finger in his ear. "Okay, that didn't work."

"What now?" Rina asks in a loud, hushed whisper.

"They call this a distraction?" I mumble in disbelief. But then Eddy turns around with the biggest wink, scanning the area for me, and waves the most *unsubtle* thumbs-up. "He can't be serious."

Suddenly, the Hellons let out the loudest screeches, and glass breaks in the distance. They ready their spears as Rina, Eddy, and Tails fight to stay standing. Then one of them cocks its arm back to launch its spear, and neither Rina, Eddy, nor Tails sees it—Rina with her head buried down, Eddy with an arm over his face, and Tails with his head tucked down.

Just as the Hellon's arm flies to launch its spear, I bolt out of the bushes and dart straight for the border. I catch sight of the Hellons who take off like savages, and their screeches cut through the air.

When I fly through the gated bars, my eyes widen at the new Hellons out of my peripheral. Three more charge at me from the left, and they're silent until I gasp. Then they sound off like their brethren.

I curse under my breath. My thoughts scramble like eggs, and my mind scatters. All my weight plows full speed ahead, my body assuming control. I keep on running straight before veering off into zigzags. I then slip into a narrow alley, and all the Hellons race after me. Not too far behind, they sprint like a wild stampede, screaming and shattering the buildings' windows.

The alleys' walls are all painted with graffiti, and dumpsters, electrical boxes, and decrepit fire escapes line along them. The alley quickly turns into a maze with so many twists and turns and fine backstreets. My body tells me to turn at one of the many intersections, but my mind finally regains control. I continue running straight, knowing the Hellons would catch up if I changed course.

My average legs begin to burn as I spit out heavy breaths. Although apart from that and the deafening Hellons, all I hear is my noisy jangling chain acting as my personal manic soundtrack.

Bursting out onto a busy street, I cross it before slipping into another narrow alley. The Hellons hunt after me with clobbering steps, burrowing through the heavy morning traffic like ogres, and more car windows explode. A glass massacre breaks out, the pouring shards ringing against the ground like a sweet chaotic melody. However, a new sound erupts—faint yet present. Various voices hum in the distance, and they grow as I near the end of the long alley.

Another street comes into view up ahead, but this one is empty. I sprint with all my might, toward the voices, knowing all I can do is run—though I'm not sure for how much longer. I've never pushed myself to the limit before—or even know if ghosts *have* one—but judging by my burning legs and enflamed chest, I don't have much longer.

Rina, Eddy, and Tails suddenly dart past the alley—a few meters away. They don't see me. Eddy's thick hair breezes back as the wind wrinkles his clothes like a track star, and beside him, Rina's long hair and baggy jeans whip in the wind. Below, Tails runs at their side with his tongue out like the perfect companion. A smile remains plastered onto his face, and his agile paws drive into the ground.

I slurp in a breath to call out to them, but the words get

caught in my throat. I try again, but tumultuous voices roar in the distance. I try one last time as the nearing commotion grows louder, but it's futile. Instead, I focus on catching up to them, and my legs wobble like noodles as I race to the finish.

However, once I break out of the alleyway, I freeze at the sight before me—taken aback. An enormous assemblage of people and their ghosts crowd the area. They stand on both sides of a blocked street, while competitors take their marks underneath a starting line. I begin to scan the crowd until the Hellons' screams propel me forward.

I peek over my shoulder and see that they're just several feet away. That's enough to light a fire under my butt to get moving, so I huff in a breath and run through the humans and past their ghosts. The latter only react when they see the Hellons. Their gloomy faces turn starstruck, but that's it. They don't even move as the Hellons charge toward them, so the Hellons knock them out of the way.

A gun sounds nearby, and the human crowd cheers on racers. Meanwhile, I'm competing in a race of my own—the high stakes being my *life*.

My lungs burn with the intensity of a thousand flames, and the heat in my chest slows me down. I slurp in thick breaths, but they blow out as quickly as they're drawn in. I've lost all feeling in my legs, now running on adrenaline. I keep going, though, until someone grabs my arm.

Exhaling a long shaky breath, I freeze.

If I were alive, my heart would surely stop.

I wrack my panic-stricken mind for help, but it's futile as my body refuses to move. The grip on my arm tightens, and I gulp before slowly ticking my head to the side—toward my doom.

To my surprise, it's not a Hellon but rather a random human

woman. She looks like she's in her early twenties with hickory skin and long black hair. She wears a mini skort and a low V-neck, and her boobs appear one touch away from spilling out of her shirt. I crinkle my brows at the stranger, leaning forward to get a close-up of her eyes. "Eddy?"

"*Shh!*" a cocoa-skinned woman says from behind, her index finger to her lips. I turn and inspect the woman who wears a brown tracksuit, the color matching her pixie haircut. She smiles from ear to ear—that earnest smile a dead ringer for Rina.

"Woof!"

My gaze snaps down to Tails who stands at my feet. He heaves in exhaustion, and my breathing is just about as heavy as his. His golden coat shines, though, mimicking the risen sun that glimmers down on us.

Screeching like nails on a chalkboard, all four of us whirl around. The Hellons gain on us, too close for comfort, and the tracksuit woman—Rina—tugs my arm. "Hide," she says.

The other woman—Eddy—frantically nods. "This event is probably the only break we're gonna get with these things."

I desperately try to catch my breath. "Lucky us," I pant before spinning around. Then the first ghost-less human I lock onto, I jump inside. My body and chain melt into an older man's body as I gain control over him, and my eyes become his.

Another screech seizes my, Rina, Eddy, and Tails' attention, and our gazes shoot back to the alley. As we turn to look for the Hellons, the Hellons fly *through* us. Their heavy footsteps shake the ground, all of them stampeding through the crowd. The very last Hellon stops short of us, though, and whips its big ugly head in every direction. Its one eye swirls with darkness as it surveys the area, sniffing with its tiny nose.

When the Hellon takes a step forward, I suck in a breath, its spear at my chin. Tails' tail stops wagging. Rina clutches her heart. Eddy grabs his skort. The Hellon then crouches down and leans an inch away from me, turning the air poisonous black before inhaling. Its meaty nostrils nearly suck up my possessed human's short hair, but then the Hellon shifts to Rina, Eddy, and Tails.

None of us move—for what seems like hours. Sweat plagues my palms, while beads of it trickle down the sides of Eddy's angular face. Rina's lips pout with the deepest line across her chin, and below, Tails doesn't speak as if mute. We all hold our breaths until the Hellon searches the crowd one last time, swinging around its spear and shield, and finally decides to move on.

I exhale only after it's miles away.

"That was close," I mutter.

Rina gulps. "Too close."

"Very," Eddy says.

"Woof!"

The human crowd continues to cheer, so the four of us maneuver our way through the countless people, holding hands. I make sure Tails stays in my peripheral vision, while Eddy pulls my wrist and I pull Rina's. He leads us all like the natural born leader that he is. Certainly, he must've been a star or trailblazer in his past life. I can't take my eyes off him, losing myself in thought about the many possibilities of *human* Eddy and the way that he looked at his human—Mr. Strife—with such...*compassion*. I wonder—

"Watch it," a nagging brunette calls out at me. She lowers her tinted sunglasses before dusting off her shoulder. Her goth ghost stands beside her with her head down.

"Ignore her," Rina whispers in my ear.

But a low growl sounds from below, and I look down to see Tails snarling. His canines show, vicious like the livid wrinkles above his scrunched nose. Even his eyes boil tight. He jumps to my other side and acts as a barrier between me and the brunette. I scan him, analyzing every ounce of ire and savagery in his face and body, and a sense of protection washes over me.

"Tails…"

The brunette glances down at Tails and sucks her teeth. "You should really keep your dog on a leash, old man."

Out of nowhere, Eddy cuts in front of me, Tails, and Rina. He stands erect like a man with broad shoulders, but his womanly body appears odd in that stance, especially given his poked-out pelvis. Nevertheless, he jabs a finger at the brunette whose eyes widen. "And you should really mind your business," he mocks in a valley girl accent.

The brunette gasps.

Moving us along, Eddy pulls me forward, and I smirk in her face, pulling Rina who flashes the lady an amused smile. Even Tails growls until she's out of sight.

We soon get lost in the crowd, trying to find our way out. It takes another few minutes, but when we burst out of the sea of people, I stagger onto grass. The lush leaves crinkle beneath my thin sandals, pricking and tickling between my toes.

"Let's switch into fresh bodies and hitch a ride," Eddy says, feeling up his stomach. His wandering hands stop upon reaching his possessed human's boobs, and he squeezes them. Of course, they spill out of his hands, reminding me of Kiara's curvaceous figure.

Rina giggles yet also recoils in revulsion. "Ew, Eddy."

"That's disgusting," I say, scowling at him, but he's too busy fondling his nipples. "You act like you've never possessed a woman before."

He jerks his chin back, feigning shock. "Who do you take me for—a perverted heathen? I would never purposefully do so."

"Suuuuure." Rina gestures a finger around her ear. "You *are* the local town crazy."

His jaw drops. "Not you, too, Rina! Don't let Slixx influence you like that!"

I burst into laughter.

"Kidding, kidding," Rina jokes.

Backing away in glee, I motion for Tails to follow, and he trots after me. I sidestep to the nearest ghost-less human—a short college student wearing a mascot sweatshirt—and the slickest smirk arises on my face. I melt into her body like butter on a hot pan, sizzling as I settle in.

Tails barks while his tail wags in delight. He either likes my new look or is ready to get moving. He then barks at an approaching man and woman before running circles around them.

The man has on layered shirts, a thin jacket, and clean Timberland boots, and his thick full beard matches his edgy aesthetic. "Let's go," Eddy says, his voice oddly deeper than the bottom of an ocean.

Skipping beside him, Rina occupies the body of short woman with long hair and a baby face like hers. She wears a yellow sundress, accentuating her round hips, and her casual white shoes match her crystal earrings. "I've always wondered what it would be like to be short!" she exclaims, her new voice nasal.

I simply chuckle at her and pick up cadence with them.

Leading us down the block, Eddy pats his clothes as he walks, fishing for something. It only takes him a second as he pulls out a phone from one of his many pockets. Then, he closes his eyes to wrack his possessed human's brain before unlocking the phone. He swipes back and forth, picking at his beard like he's had it his whole life. And in that moment, I must admit, Eddy *feels* quite handsome.

Shaking away the putrid thought, I fold my arms. "What are you doing?"

"Dancing," Rina says, spinning on her tiptoes around Tails.

I roll my eyes. "Not you."

"Hitching us a ride," Eddy says. After he taps one final button on the phone, he stops at the corner, pats his lap, and Tails runs over to him. "I guess this is the only time I'm gonna get to touch you, boy."

Rina kneels beside them. She, too, reaches out and strokes Tails' fur for the first time. Her eyes light up in wonder at the touch, and she snuggles against him. "I can finally touch you—well not me, but you know! It's better than nothing. Aha, you like that, boy, huh?"

Tails whines, his tail wagging fast. He cranes his head around Rina's and Eddy's hands, and saliva drips from his tongue. A bit falls onto Eddy's fresh-out-the-box shoes as he licks him.

"I don't think this human's gonna like that," Eddy chuckles, sizing up the uncreased, spotless boots.

But Tails can't get enough, and eventually, Rina finds his soft spot. She massages the back of his ears, and he caves at the touch. He lets out a high-pitched moan, lying down on the ground.

Jealousy wells inside me. Their hands all over him. An overzealous yet familiar feeling of control seeps into my bones, and envy overflows my stomach. I narrow my brows at Rina and Eddy before bending down and swatting their hands away.

Tails perks up in confusion as I slide him closer to my side. He twists around to look at me, but I just smile and begin to pet him. Forgetting all worries, he instantly caves at the touch, wagging his tail in delight.

"What's wrong, Slixx?" Rina asks.

But I just turn my nose.

Eddy cocks his head to the side, studying me. "I can't tell if you're competitive or—"

"Or what?" I snap, glaring at him mere inches between us. His possessed human's eyes twinkle like his own, and his charming smirk...(charming?)...is *actually* charming. (Surely, the human's just handsome and *not* him.) My cheeks grow hot. I yank away my gaze. "Tails is *my* dog—you two know that, right?"

"Technically, we all found him," Rina says.

I flash her a dark scowl.

"But sure!"

Meanwhile, Eddy pauses for a moment, and I can feel his eyes searching me—piercing through my human flesh and bearing into my soul. "Or that," he finally finishes.

Puzzled, I scrunch my face. I open my mouth to rebuttal, but a *PING* sound cuts me off.

He looks down at his phone and smiles, waving for us to get moving. "Our ride's here." Once he sees me about to ask a question, he points up the street, and at the end of the block, a silver Nissan waits for us. But even after we jog to the car, it takes a ton of convincing for the ghost-less driver to let Tails in. The conversation goes a bit like this:

"Just let him in," I say. "We can't leave him!"

"Please," Rina pleads.

"Nah, ain't no way dat mutt's gettin' in my cah."

"Mutt?" I repeat, loud enough for the few people walking by on the sidewalk to turn around.

Rina pokes out her lips. "That wasn't a very nice thing to say, mister."

"Woof!"

"He's fully trained," Eddy chimes in, trying to diffuse the situation. "He won't pee or anything in your car." He flashes the driver his phone's lit screen. "It's only a four-minute drive."

After going back and forth—Eddy doing most of the persuading because I'm a 'say it once' type of ghost and Rina's clearly too nice for negotiations—the driver lets Tails hop in the car. He gives Tails the evil eyes, though, and Tails returns the look with a low growl. Startled, the driver jumps and hits his head against the ceiling. Eddy, however, reassures him one last time before we pull off.

We seem to hit every red light, making for an awkward car ride. Rina tries to talk to the driver, but he just blows her off with one-word responses. Eddy and I refuse to say anything while Tails lays over my lap, quiet as I pet his back. He keeps his eyes on the driver the *entire* time, though, ready to snap if need be.

Even after we step out the car, he frightens the driver with a ferocious growl, and the driver hits his head on the ceiling, again. "Yuh should really put a leash on dat ting—!"

I slam the car door.

"What an unpleasant man," Rina mutters.

Tails stifles a growl as the driver speeds off, and I bend down to pet him. His head bobs around my gentle hand. "Good boy, Tails," I say.

Suddenly, my possession over this human's body begins to fizzle away. I lose control of her legs first, then her arms, then her head, and then I get spit out altogether. I stumble backward on the pavement, grabbing my head, and my chain slithers behind me.

Eddy shoots out of his possessed human's body next, then Rina, and Tails just whips his head between us in awe. He wags his tail as if amused.

Eddy and I quickly regain our balance, but Rina stumbles back before landing on her butt. She yelps, rubbing her backside. Meanwhile, the three now unpossessed humans blink back into their bodies—in complete and utter confusion.

"I think I'm gonna throw up," Rina says, covering her mouth—what little color she has draining from her face.

"Nausea *is* a side effect of Possession," Eddy says. "It'll wear off within the hour, though."

Rina dry-heaves.

"How was your fit, Slixx? Mine was crammed." He lightly punches his legs as if to wake them up. Standing over his chain, it looks like a tail caught between his legs.

I shrug, massaging my temples. "Mine was a perfect fit." The humans then seize my attention, and I laugh at their stupefied faces. They stare at each other, patting down their bodies like in a movie, and I want to break out cackling. However, I suppress most of my boisterous laughter on account of my throbbing head.

Tails leans against me and places a comforting paw on my hand. He whines, probably a soothing sentiment, and his mere presence soothes me.

"Headache?" Eddy asks me as Rina gags aloud.

I nod.

Eddy's lips curl into a frown, and his thick eyebrows droop down. He shakes his head at me, motioning for me to give him a hug. "You poor child. Come here."

Chuckling, I wave him off as the sun makes a grand appearance. "Never."

Without a word, the three humans look each other up and down before parting ways. The short woman and college student scurry away, while the man ambles in the other direction, cursing about his shoes.

About halfway down the block, the hasty college girl nearly trips over a hole in the sidewalk, and it takes everything in me not to laugh out loud.

"You're really loving this, huh?" Eddy asks.

Unable to contain myself, I vigorously dip my chin in response.

"I'm glad one of us is having fun," Rina says. "Don't mind me—" Her cheeks puff up.

"Newbie," I joke, and Eddy and I laugh.

But after a minute, he straightens up, and his demeanor turns sour. The bright sunrays cast a silhouette on the left side of his body, which makes him look even graver, and the deep frown line under his chin strangely resembles that of a sad puppy.

Looking up at him, it's like I'm looking all the way up at the Eiffel Tower. He stands with poor posture, hunched over, but still appears tall, shading me, Rina, and Tails. His long arms hang by his knees, which are slightly bent, and his long neck tucks down to his chest.

He sighs, pointing ahead. "You gotta be kidding me."

"What now?" Rina somberly asks, finding her feet.

I follow Eddy's index finger yonder—across a quiet street—and lay eyes on a small plaza. It truly embodies every bit of the humanly idiotic phrase "ghost town," leaves and litter blowing across the huge empty parking lot. There are only about six stores clustered together in a strip, and chipped paint peels off the wide rusty building. One of the stores' signs flicker as if to spark a flame and bring this dead-end plaza back to life because the parking lot looks way too big to be empty. This was definitely a hotspot once upon a time.

Next to the flickering sign lies our destination in all black capital letters, reeking of death: **Chesnutt's Funeral Home & Crematory.**

"That ass hat dropped us off across the street," Eddy sulks. "Now we have to walk all the way over there."

"Ass hat?" Rina mutters, stifling a laugh.

I pet Tails one last time behind his ears before standing. "That's a terrible comeback, Eddy the Track Star."

"Huh?" he asks.

Striding off the sidewalk, I cross the thin street in a matter of seconds, and Tails trails after me. His nails click against the concrete like music to my ears. Glancing over my shoulder, I laugh at Eddy who still stands in place, bewilderingly staring at me.

"You were running all super-fast from the Hellons like this —" I mock his professional run with a giggle. "Remember?"

Beside Eddy, Rina finally catches on and runs across the street, doing her own imitation. "You were super fast but also super serious."

After a minute, Eddy finally begins walking, and he can't help but chuckle as he passes us. "You guys are something else."

"Hey! What does that mean?" I shout.

"Yeah, Eddy, what are you trying to say?" Rina parrots.

"Nothing. Nothing."

We cut through the grass, and our mindless banter carries us across the plaza's parking lot. We stop at the foot of the crematory, reading the sign posted on the door. It's a tattered blank sheet of paper, instructing visitors and guests to go through the entrance around back, so we do.

The back of the plaza looks just as shabby and dilapidated as the front, the chipped paint peeling in layers. We stride through the smaller parking lot and bypass a couple sparse parked cars, presumably employees, but several feet ahead, a cluster of cars park together in front of the crematory.

"Her parents," I whisper, recognizing their Toyotas. A lump gets caught in my throat, but I swallow it. The angst from before resurfaces in my chest as we near our destination.

"Are you okay?" Eddy asks, he and Rina glancing my way.

Tails even looks up at me for a response, so he must sense something's off.

I swallow another lump of grief and put on my best act. "*Tch*. Of course."

But Rina still takes my hand, and I let her.

Stopping a few feet from the glass backdoor, I stare in at Kiara's parents who sit on opposite sides of the spacious lobby. Dressed in blue uniform, her plump mother with cocoa skin bites her nails and vigorously shakes her legs, and Kiara's two older sisters sit on both sides of her. They all lean on each other for support as if about to crumble.

On the opposite side, Kiara's stone-cold father and his new family fill all the empty seats available. I recognize her many half-siblings but only from pictures, and some older gentlemen, I don't even recognize at all.

But what strikes me most is that all of them have ghosts. They stand behind or sit before their respective human, and of course, they all have that same sad pathetic expression— mummified. Some spot me, Rina, Eddy, and Tails, but when they do, they just return to staring off into space.

"You don't have to lie," Eddy says in a low voice, and Tails whines in agreement. "She was your human for..."

"Sixteen years," I finish.

"You watched her grow up," Rina says.

I crack a smile, shifting my gaze to the big picture of Kiara sloppily hung on the back wall. "She was a drunken mess." I chuckle. "But she was always kind—scared easily, for sure."

Eddy elbows me, and I look up at him. His starry eyes shimmer like a glittery ocean, highlighting his strong jaw and thick eyebrows. He peers down at me like we're the last two ghosts in the world. "Our emotions are every bit as real as humans. It's okay to feel them."

Speechless, I study him in awe. He reminds me of an unsolvable puzzle piece, and no matter what, I know I'll never figure him out. A moment of silence drifts by. Neither of us say a word, our eyes doing all the talking.

But then my conscious sets in, and I turn away. "She'd still be alive if it weren't for me."

"Slixx, it's not your—" Rina starts.

Eddy shakes his head. "You didn't mean t—"

"Guys, stop." I gulp, slipping my hand from Rina's. "Don't try to make me feel better."

"But..." Eddy's voice trails off to mute, allowing a long beat of silence to drift by.

"Why do you two love humans so much?" I finally ask in disgust. "We're just their ghosts, enslaved to them and their pathetic lives. Day in and day out, we watch them grow and mature—something we can never do again. Something we don't even *remember* doing in our past life. Humans are nothing more than scars on our backs that will never heal."

Rina hesitates, her mouth quivering. "Well, when my human had to stay in the hospital, I overheard so many conversations—some funny, a lot sad. But every time I'd listen, I'd hear something new. Then I'd start to daydream about my past life. My family, friends, pets, allergies—if I believed in ghosts." She chuckles. "It's fun to imagine and pretend, living vicariously through humans. I'd rather have them than be alone in some dark ghost realm."

I clench my jaw. "But what good is a daydream if it'll never come true?"

She snaps to me with wide eyes.

A still moment fleets by.

Eddy lets my sentiment linger in the air before speaking, his gaze becoming more intense by the second. "Have you ever tried talking to Kiara?" he asks out of the blue.

Taken aback, I fold my arms. "What?"

"Have you ever tried touching Kiara, outside of scaring her?"

I let silence respond for me.

"Maybe instead of humans being painful scars and reminders of our tragedy, they're precious mementos of what we used to be—*how* we used to be. *Alive.*"

Just then, an elderly ghost-less man with deep wrinkles walks out into the crematory's lobby from the hall, his hands behind him, and Rina, Eddy, and I turn to see Kiara's entire family stand—their ghosts don't move though. They close in on the gray-haired man like fierce lions hunting prey, but their nervous expressions tell a morbid tale.

I veer my attention back to Rina and Eddy, and they meet my gaze. None of us utter another word. Eddy's soft face looks onward at me with promise, Rina smiling my way, but I scowl at them with nothing left to say.

After another beat passes, I gesture for Tails to hide behind a pillar, and he scurries to the nearest one. His long nose peeks around it, but then he quickly ducks in hiding.

Beside me, Eddy flashes a grin, showing off his white teeth, and Rina extends her arms for a hug. They wait for me to cave, but I simply roll my eyes.

"Let's just agree to disagree," I mutter, entering the large crematory.

They pass through after me, and we all make our way to the front of the crowd, halting beside the elderly man. He wears a silver nametag that states he's the owner, and his plain brown pants and striped collared shirt match the dreary vibe within the place—not to mention his dusty toupee. Nevertheless, he drones on about praising Kiara's family for being so strong and something about thoughts and prayers and other super religious stuff and blah, blah, blah.

It isn't until he brings his arms around and reveals a sleek amber urn about the size of a small vase that I actually start paying attention.

"In here lies the remains of Kiara Vicily Antoinette Brown," the elder says, handing the urn to Kiara's mother who bursts into tears. Her daughters don't even try to comfort her now, and everyone in the room—including me—drops their heads. "May she rest in peace. And again, I will be praying for you all. God bless. Take care."

"What's the plan?" Eddy asks, but his voice cracks. He clears his throat and repeats the question.

I shrug, desperately trying to contain the heavy weight in my chest. "Shouldn't we be asking you that?"

My voice must sound husky and sad because Rina shoots Eddy a not-so-subtle wide-eyed look. They must think I'm in a grief-stricken daze, but I notice—that and Eddy dipping his chin in understanding.

"Actually"—he places a hand on my shoulder and squeezes—"take as long as you need. We can follow her families if you want."

"No," I say, ripping my eyes to them. "What's the plan?"

Eddy searches me for a moment.

"Slixx, don't you want to—" Rina starts.

"The fountain said *start at one, by human by way, death burns at daybreak*," Eddy says.

"That's gotta mean cremating Kiara. But I don't know—"

Just then, Kiara's father nearly snatches the urn from the mother. His hands shake as he holds it, and tears stream down his sunken cheeks. He slowly slides one hand up to the lid while most of the family on his side remain silent. "D-d-daughter," he croaks, lifting the lid.

That's when I see it.

My, Rina's, and Eddy's eyes go wide, and we lean forward

on the tips of our toes. My jaw drops. Eddy staggers forward. Rina gulps.

I inch over to the urn and feast my eyes on Kiara's shining ashes. They glow neon purple like the script on the fountain, and I start to reach out to touch it. Touch the answer to me, Rina, and Eddy's problems. Touch our stepping stone to *Bliss*. Touch my former human, who was *just* breathing yesterday— who *just* got drunk the night before yet is now no more.

I inhale.

I exhale.

Suddenly, the glass door and windows shatter. All the humans and their ghosts hit the deck, and Rina, Eddy, and I duck for cover. Jagged shards fly everywhere, raining down in mass. They clash against my back, and one piece cuts my arm. I wince in pain, but a dark shadow develops over me. I glance up at Eddy who uses his elbow pads for cover.

"What's happening?" Rina shouts, hiding behind me.

"We've got to move"—Eddy grunts—"before—"

"*Hwaaaa!*"

All of us look up at our worst nightmare. Five Hellons emerge from the back wall, clearly having come through the crematory's front entrance, and Kiara's painting falls at their crusty heels. They tow in heavier breaths than Tails, polluting the air around them, as their dagger-sharp toenails clink against the hardwood floor. They hold their round shields in front and their spears at their sides.

Of them, the biggest Hellon stands centerstage, and in a snap, its head suddenly twists around one hundred and eighty degrees. It sounds like a giant stepping over a graveyard full of bones. With its swirling dark eye now upside down, its mouth opens from the top, and the loudest deafening screech pierces the air.

Their vibrations launch gusts of wind at us, effecting even

the humans. Everyone flies back, but Rina, Eddy, and I strain to keep from falling. Unfortunately, Rina doesn't last long. The fierce wind sweeps her off her feet, and she goes flying backward with everyone else.

"Rina!" Both Eddy and I scream.

I start to let the wind take me after Rina until Kiara's urn flies out of her father's hands. Luckily, it soars upward, so her ashes don't spill out. However, in that same moment, the Hellons take off.

I lunge for the urn.

"Slixx!" Eddy cries out.

CHAPTER 10

COMPANY

Eddy's too late.

He shouts my name, but I'm already off the floor. Midair, I reach for the urn with all my might, and my fingertips graze the base. So close. But just then, the lid flies off. The urn begins to tip over, and a pinch of Kiara's ashes float up into the air. I gasp. Shifting my weight to the other side of my body, I raise my other hand, clamp the lid back down, and snatch the urn to my chest in the nick of time.

My landings always suck, though.

As I touch down on my left heel, a sharp pain seizes my ankle, and unfortunately for me, my other foot doesn't even get the chance to hit the floor. I trip over my own chain and begin to fall, staring down at the hardwood floor my ribcage is about hit.

And in that same moment, out of my peripheral, one of the Hellons catches my eye. It charges at me with only a shield, and before I can even question it, I turn to see a spear sailing toward me.

Midfall and unable to move, I simply gawk at it. So close— too close. If it were aimed at my face, it would've hit me already.

The spearhead slices through the thin air faster than I can blink, and several feet behind, the other Hellons charge. Their clobbering footsteps shake the whole lobby, and their nails clink against the hardwood floor. They now contaminate the air, fogging up half the lobby with their toxic breaths.

The humans begin to pass out from the poisonous gas, meanwhile I stare at the spear just a couple inches from my stomach before closing my eyes. I keep my clammy grip on Kiara's urn, ironically about to die with her—like I was *supposed* to. And just then, I think maybe I'm *not* the ticket to *Bliss*—if *Bliss* even exists. Maybe I just wasn't meant to make it. Maybe I was a fool to even try.

In my final moments, I wait.

I wait for the spear to strike.

And I wait to finally pass on.

But...I guess it's not my time to go yet.

Instead of a blow to the stomach, I bang against the floor, hanging onto Kiara's urn with everything that I've got. This sharp pain is even worse than the last, and a crack sounds from my ribs. My hip takes the brunt of the impact, though. I hear my arm skin scrape across the hardwood like nails on a chalkboard, worse than rugburn, but then a force yanks me up to my feet. My vision toggles, double and fuzzy, and in that brief moment, I think I see Eddy.

He takes the urn from me and grabs my hand before breaking out into a sprint. That's when I find out my aching body still works. We run out of the crematory, Eddy pulling me at lightspeed, and Tails darts out from behind the pillar and picks up cadence with us. The three of us race through the back of the plaza.

"Wait! What about Rina?" I shout.

"Hwaaaa!"

More glass shatters not too far behind us, the Hellons hot on our trail.

We all duck.

"There's no time to go back!" Eddy says.

I stop, snatching away my hand. "We can't just leave her!"

Eddy clenches his jaw as his face hardens.

I give him a second to think, but after a couple more precious moments, I whirl around.

"Hwaaaa!"

Just then, Eddy grabs my wrist, spins me back around, and pulls me into his chest. He cradles my head as we crouch down. And below, Tails lies down on his stomach with his paws over his head. The Hellons' screams pierces all our eardrums, closer than the last.

"We've gotta move!" Eddy calls out.

"But—!"

"Tails, find Rina and meet us back at Chesnutt Cemetery!"

"Woof!"

And just like that, we split up.

Tails jets back toward the chaos, while Eddy and I jump into the surrounding shrubs. We fly straight through; however, I'm in no condition to even walk—let alone *run*. My blurry vision does me no good as I can only see colors and shapes, and the left side of my body burns like I've been dipped in lava.

"How do you know the way there?" I shout.

"I don't!" He veers right, and we jet across an empty street. "I'm following my chain to the hospital! From there, I can get us to the cemetery!"

So, we follow his chain—or at least we try to. Eddy leads us down sketchy alleys where we pass homeless people and shady thugs. Then we cross full parking lots and run through an apartment complex. Wall after wall, we pass one too many unsightly humans. A couple arguing. An elderly woman bathing. A middle-aged man cooking in underwear. Two heads bobbing underneath covers. A man picking his nose.

When we finally burst outside, I heave, sticking out my tongue.

"You okay?" Eddy asks.

I shake my head, tracing his chain. Up ahead, it leads us through another complex, but I point in another direction. Catching on, Eddy grabs my free hand and darts left, so we end up taking a long way, his chain redirecting like a GPS.

However, half a block from the hospital, I suddenly stop.

Eddy spins to me wild as I turn around. "What's the matter?" he asks, urgently.

Although my vision has improved, it's still a bit blurry. I squint and search the many tall buildings behind us. The sun shines bright on the other side of them, casting an immense shadow this way. The shade resembles the bottom of a well, and not as many people walk the sidewalks over here. All is quiet. And that's the problem, especially when an odd vinegary smell wafts through the air.

"Slixx?"

"Where are the H—?" I gasp, pointing at Eddy. His skin suddenly begins to fade in and out like a flickering light, as if about to disappear at any moment. "Eddy!"

Passing me the urn, Eddy raises his arms and beholds his flickering-self. He then looks at me with wide eyes, and I examine his hazel irises. Neither of us speak, but the message translates between us. Next thing I know, we're bolting down the last quarter block toward the hospital.

Entering the hospital, we follow Eddy's chain up a couple flights of stairs before bursting out into the waiting room. Only a few people and their ghosts sit, scattered about, and they all have their heads down—telling. But with no time to scope, we follow Eddy's chain down the hall, past Mr. Strife's room. I catch a glimpse of the vacant space, the door open and no one inside but a single lingering nurse.

After turning left and right, we sprint down a wide hall. Sweat drenches both of our bodies, and beads of it fly off us. I pant, sucking in air, Kiara's urn weighing me down. My body now officially feels like a nuclear explosion. And to make matters worse, a twinge pangs my hip, and I fall into a limp, straggling behind. I curse at how slow ghost's healing abilities are as I hobble the last stretch.

Up ahead, Eddy passes through a set of white double doors, and within several seconds, I fly in after.

The sight before me steals the air from my lungs. Speechless and breathless, I dare not speak nor take another step forward. However, Eddy does. He staggers toward an operating table where his human lies sprawled out. Two ghost-less doctors poke at Mr. Strife's open heart with metal instruments, while two ghost-less nurses assist them. Also, a ghost-less anesthesiologist sits off to the side. The room is silent with the exception of clinking instruments, hushed orders, and the loud monitor. Mr. Strife's faint heartbeat echoes off the walls, barely alive though not yet dead—kind of like a ghost.

Still vanishing and reappearing, Eddy drops to his knees beside Mr. Strife's table. His chain begins to fade as the purple link grows dim, now flickering like his skin. He sobs, quiet tears dropping to the tiled floor.

Unsure what to say, I whisper, "Eddy."

"Back at the crematory, remember how you asked me and Rina why we love humans?"

"Yeah."

He sniffles, rubbing his nose. "I never gave you an actual answer." He slowly gets to his feet, his long arms swaying as if lifeless, and then he takes a moment. Standing beside the doctors, he looks down at Mr. Strife and places a hand on his.

"Everything I said back at the crematory still stands, but do you wanna know the real reason?"

"Eddy," I start, my voice low. "You don't have to—"

"I've been Mr. Strife's ghost for fifty-five years," he says. "I don't know what my life was like as a human—if it was good or bad—but after living amongst humans as a mere hollow existence, I don't think I'd trade this experience for the world. Not even another chance at life."

I furrow my brows at him, tightening my grip on the urn.

"Call me crazy, but I was happy with Mr. Strife." He shrugs. "Ever since he was a kid, he thought I was his mom who passed away during childbirth. We'd talk every night. He'd tell me about his day, update me on his father who'd become stricken with grief, and ask to pray together—at least until he lost the will to. I always wished I could talk to him...or give him a hug."

He sniffles, shaking his head. "But instead, I would flicker the lights, blow out a candle, drop a pen, or do something like that to let him know I was listening."

My "I'm sorry" comes out so soft that I doubt he hears me.

"No kid should go through what he went through. Watching his father crumble with grief and become buried in debt. Bullied for not having a mom. Paying bills at fourteen years old. Wearing the same outgrown clothes for years. It...it was nice being his solace—his imaginary friend." He forces a laugh. "An escape from the pain."

The distance between me and Eddy grows by the second like the room's expanding, but in reality, our true colors are colliding. I start to take a step forward but stop myself.

Turning around, Eddy faces me. He peers at me with a flimsy smile and cavernous lenses, which bear a painful tale like his human's. He looks just as confused as his expression— either ready to break out into tears or laughter. "I don't know if me and Mr. Strife were ever considered 'friends,' but we did help each other live. And I think whether ghost or human, all anyone needs is some company. Ghosts probably more so than humans."

I remain mute, letting Eddy's last sentiment linger around the room. It strikes a chord in my gut, and the beckoning for *Bliss* churns inside me. However, my lips curl, unable to accept his words as truth.

"I know you don't agree," Eddy says, catching me off guard. His smile evolves into a grin, and I can't tell whether or not it's forced. "Like you said, let's agree to disagree. I just wish you had a chance to talk to Kiara."

Me too, I want to say.

Turning back to Mr. Strife, Eddy leans over the table and kisses his pale human's head. His skin continues to fade in out, and I wonder how much time he has left. He then whispers into Mr. Strife's ear before backing away. "Take it easy, old man. Let's meet again in *Bliss*."

Once his hand falls off his human's, he spins around and trudges my away. "We should get going."

"Are...you sure?" is all I manage, staring at his permanently flickering state. "Can you make it?"

He looks up at me with the intense gaze of a lion. "I'm sure as hell gonna try. Now let's get to Chesnutt Cemetery."

CHAPTER 11
DIVE IN

The hospital fades behind us as Eddy and I sprint down the block. Neither of us have spoken since we left Mr. Strife in the operating room, and an uneasy silence stirs between us. Every time I glance at him, he doesn't look like his normal self, frowning and forlorn. I don't know what to say to comfort him without lying, so I keep my mouth shut.

Above, the midafternoon sun radiates, while only a couple clouds drift along the pretty blue sky. Eddy leads us to the cemetery following the main street. The race from earlier must've ended because now bumper-to-bumper traffic backs up all the roads, especially near the highway. A lot more people crowd the sidewalks, too.

Jogging, I fall behind—unable to keep up with Eddy's long strides. A cramp knots in my stomach, so I dig a thumb in it, pushing on as we cross another busy street. He then guides us over to a huge supermarket, and we cut across its packed parking lot.

I hug Kiara's urn to my chest, panting. "How much farther?"

"Just the next block over!"

"Thank goodness," I mutter.

Halfway through the parking lot, I finally catch up to Eddy, but then I recognize a duo near a gray minivan. My eyes light up. "Tails! Rina!" I call out.

Before Eddy finds them, I grab his hand and drag him to the van.

"Guys!" Rina exclaims at the sight of me and Eddy, hugging us. Her disheveled hair appears frizzier than usual with rocks and debris wrapped up in it like a jungle. "Where have you guys been?"

I look up at Eddy, but he looks away. "Uh, just running for our lives. The usual."

Rina eyes Eddy for a long beat, observing his constant flickering skin. However, she simply smiles and changes the subject. "Tails found me unconscious outside, so I must've hit the ground pretty hard. Got a few minor cuts from the glass—"she shows off her unscathed skin, though a dark bruise on her lower-back—"but they've all healed up. Now only my back hurts, but it's slowly going away. I'm healing—how cool is that!"

Smirking, I roll my eyes at her odd fascination with being a ghost.

"Woof!" Tails' bark nearly startles me—so hoarse and dry. I look down at him, and even though his tails wags in delight, his eyes are half-closed and his flailing tongue dry.

"You okay, boy?" I whisper, stooping down.

"Woof!" he says louder, and out of nowhere, a baby starts crying.

A blond man rushes around the minivan and shoos Tails away, and Tails staggers back from the car. He whines.

"Hey!" I start, charging for the human, but Rina catches my arm.

"No, that's my human's parents."

A woman with almond skin quiets the baby before shutting

the van door. Then, she and her husband quickly hop in their car, cranking it on. Meanwhile, Rina, Eddy, and I glue our faces to the back window, peering at a tiny baby in a sailor's outfit. He stares back at us, quietly sucking a pacifier, but then the corners of his mouth pinch into a small grin.

"Hiya," Eddy says, waving, and the baby giggles.

I stare at all the snot and saliva smeared across his face and his half-soaked shirt, and my stomach churns in disgust.

"His name's Pirin," Rina says, passing through the door. She makes a silly face, and the baby laughs, sweet and innocent like her. She then kisses him on the forehead before stepping back. And just like that, the baby's eyes close for a peaceful slumber as the van pulls off. "I can't wait to see him, again."

I side-eye her. "What if we don't make it back?"

She drops her head, a wave of grief rippling across her dim eyes.

"That's the point," Eddy says, his tone icy. "Rina, if you want to stay with your human, you should. Once we make it to *Bliss*, there is no coming back."

Rina pauses, her gaze wanders off into space. She starts to say something but zips her lips while Tails trots back over to us. He collapses by my side, whining.

"I'm going in the store to get Tails some water," I say.

"But the cemetery—" Eddy starts.

"And I think we all need a break." Everything inside me hurts like I'm made of glass. "Ghosts may not need sleep, but we do need *rest*." I poke his chest, which caves up and down—him exhausted like the rest of us. "That includes you."

"But, Slixx—"

I haul in air, straightening up, and gesture around us. "The Hellons are gone. It's just us, and you said the cemetery's only a block away. It'll be quick."

Eddy takes a moment to consider my proposal, but after a

minute passes, I head off with Tails. The two of us limp toward the supermarket, completely and utterly *exhausted*.

"Slixx, wait!" Eddy shouts, following us. "Rina, you coming?"

"I'll wait for you guys out here," she calls back. Her voice cracks, and from the sound of it, she's about to cry. A part of me aches to go back for her, but I shake it off, knowing she's got a lot to think about.

"She might not come with us," Eddy says in a low voice.

"I know."

"She might not be there when we get back either."

I push down a lump in my throat. "I know."

When we all enter the store, I take the lead, reading the signs above each aisle. There are so many people and ghosts inside that nobody notices Tails, a stray dog ambling without an owner.

"Bingo," I say, heading down the last aisle.

"Slixx, I think we should—" Eddy says.

"Found it." I clap, cheering with Tails, as I look both ways down the aisle like a secret agent. Tails then barks, and everyone whips their heads to him. His tail wags, smiling up at me, but I try to *shh* him. "What are you looking at?" I yap at a ghost-less scowling blond, but of course, she can't hear me.

"Whose dog is this?" she asks aloud.

Thankfully, no one pays attention to her—too many people moving through, in, and out of the store. She sucks her teeth and turns around, and after she does, I unscrew a gallon of water as discreetly as a ghost can. Meanwhile, Eddy drones on about something like an annoying worrywart.

"You want some water, boy?" I ask Tails.

He wags his tail even faster.

"Alright, lick it up quick because we're going to have to bolt before they call animal control or something."

I knock the gallon over, and it hits the floor with a hard *thud*. Everyone whirls around, again. All the humans' and ghosts' eyes point to the irritating blond lady, but she shakes her head, backing away with her red cart.

"No, I-I didn't," she stammers.

Chuckling, I sit down on the floor beside Tails who licks up the water. He slurps it up like he's been trudging through an arid desert for months. His tongue moves as fast as his tail now, and life filters back into his cute little eyes. I pet his back, basking in this moment of peace.

That is until the lights flicker.

I snap to Eddy, and he stares down at me, wide-eyed. He extends a hand before pulling me up. "Best to go out the back."

"If we can find it," I reply.

Tails splashes through the puddle of water, jumping in front like he knows the way. He scampers right out of the aisle, and Eddy and I trail him. But like a dumb human in a scary movie, I look back just as I turn the corner. *Stupid. Stupid.* My jaw drops at the Hellon standing at the opposite end, and when it screeches, the few glass water bottles in the aisle shatter. The vibrations launch a gust of wind my way, but luckily, I evade it by just a hair.

We jet into the busy clothing department of the store and fly through bright colored apparel. We zoom past everyone and everything so fast that my surroundings reduce to colors, but the approaching Hellons nab my attention. Five pop out of the aisles, barreling our way, while four more chase after us from the cashiers. Their large bodies and heavy footsteps shake the ground. With so many Hellons in one place—more than any time before—the floor rumbles beneath me, Eddy, and Tails, and we get tossed up into the air like it's a magnitude ten earthquake.

Bypassing the electronics department, Tails rounds another

corner and takes us through a sea of bikes. His small, nimble body leaps over the display bikes haphazardly left on the floor, and then he leaps over a scooter before bolting down a short hallway toward the closed auto center. He makes another turn, and we all freeze, coming face to face with a dastardly Hellon.

It stands in front of two double doors, blocking the exit. It cracks its neck, and the *cracks* sound one after another as its neck breaks in every direction. The lights flicker once before the Hellon screams, and the power cuts out. The double doors' glass windows also shatter, and a gust of wind blasts at the three of us—too close to withstand—knocking us back.

Hugging Kiara's urn, I fall on my back with a loud grunt, not sure how much more damage I can take. Now my back throbs in pain, and the rest of my body begins to turn numb. All I can hear are humans screaming in the distance. Beside me, Tails whimpers as he hits the floor. His moan is enough for me to jump to my feet, adrenaline jolting me over to him. Meanwhile, Eddy manages to land upright.

I hug Tails, burying my head in his fur. "Are you okay?"

Tails whimpers, and my heart tears in half. He pants a bit before hopping to his feet with energy. He peers into my eyes as if to reassure me, but I know we all have our limits.

"Uh, Slixx?" Eddy says.

"Are you sure you're okay, boy?" I whisper to Tails, combing a hand through his fur.

"Slixx," Eddy says a bit louder.

"What?" I snap, whirling to him.

Instantly, my limbs freeze over into ice. I exhale in one long expire, and my stomach churns in knots. My head ticks from the Hellon blocking the exit to the eight surrounding us. Mouth agape, I stare wide-eyed at the massive demons, their shields and spears behind them on their backs. They circle us, no escape in sight, and a yellow-greenish puss oozes out of their mouths. They salivate what looks like thick vomit. A strong vinegary odor circulates into the air, too, and nausea sets into my stomach.

All at once, the Hellons snap their necks. *CRACK.* Upside down. *CRACK.* Three hundred and sixty degrees. *CRACK.* Left. *CRACK.* Right. *CRACK.* Right side up. Their sharp teeth start to chatter as they creep closer, step-by-step, closing in on us. Their putrid saliva leaks to the floor, and a trail tracks behind them.

"S-Slixx, d-do you gotta plan?" Eddy asks in a hushed voice.

Paralyzed with fear, I squeeze Kiara's urn so tight I think it might break. "Shouldn't I be asking you that?"

Eddy gulps, backing up, and Tails and I back up, too. Our backs touch as we all stand side by side, watching the Hellons near us in horror. Their vile necks crack as if counting down the seconds to attack.

Sighing, I look down. Anxiety wells under my skin as I dig one of my hands into my curls. I scan the tiled floor, wracking the cracks and crevices of my mind, until an ant catches my eye. And just like that, a light bulb goes off in my head. I blink into the idea, my eyelashes fluttering, before I run the plan down to Eddy and Tails.

Once I'm done, Eddy flashes me a look. "Are you crazy?"

"Got any better ideas?" I hiss, carefully setting Kiara's urn on the cold floor.

Only a few feet away, the Hellons lean forward. Their teeth chatter quicker, and they snap their fingers and toes, readying their claws. So close to their prey, they don't even reach for their weapons. They take one final step before lunging at us.

Springing into phase one of the plan, I melt into Tails' body. Then, I (as Tails) jump up into Eddy's arms.

"I hope this works!" Eddy says.

Just a couple feet away, the Hellons charge, clawing our way.

Enacting phase two of the plan, Eddy launches me (as Tails) into the air, and we go flying over the Hellons' head. In midair, I detach from Tails and hug his body as we tumble through the floppy double doors.

I smack into a car, taking all the damage. *"Agh!"*

Now inside the supercenter's auto garage, Tails scampers from my arms and brushes his nose under my chin. He hurries for me to get up, but I can barely see.

"Hwaaaa!" all the Hellons scream, busting into the garage.

I snatch Tails under me as all the car windows and windshields break. The shards batter my back, and I curse at my slow ghost healing abilities, only healing me enough to keep moving. I scurry to my feet, and then Tails and I dart out of the garage and into the parking lot. I only glance back to count the Hellons—all nine on our trail, leaving a saliva spoor behind.

With no sign of Eddy, worry wells inside me as I lead us to the front of the supermarket. Dozens of humans and their ghosts run out of the store in a frenzy, screaming, and more windows continue to shatter. They all duck and run. Some humans cover or carry their kids, while others fend for themselves. And as for their ghosts, they just follow with the melancholiest faces. They only stop and gawk when they see the Hellons racing after me and Tails, but even then, they just do what ghosts do best: play dead.

Maneuvering through the crowd, Tails weaves between humans, and I run through them, my chain rattling behind me. We make our way to the entrance, but Eddy still doesn't show. I fix on the sliding double doors in hopes he'll pop out.

"Woof!" Tails barks as if to say *he's coming*.

But I'm not so sure.

I gulp, keeping my eyes peeled on the entrance. When we pass it, a pressure boils in my throat. We near the end of the parking lot, and I begin to hyperventilate—running over countless scenarios where my plan failed: Kiara's urn gone, never make it to *Bliss*, or even worse, Eddy devoured. I had figured that if the Hellons were just after me, then they'd chase me and leave Eddy alone, but what if I was wrong? What if something bad happened to him—because of me?

I stare back at the entrance, anticipation sweltering inside my chest. Kiara's bloody corpse flashes through my mind, and my lips begin to quiver as I fight back the onset of tears. *No, not again.*

"Woof!"

I look down at Tails who gestures his nose ahead.

Some yards away, Eddy stands on the sidewalk, waving one arm like a flag and holding Kiara's urn in the other. "It worked!" he shouts with the biggest grin.

Even though my body is on fire, a smile etches onto my face in relief. I push on running, and my heels drive into the ground with gusto. That is until I remember Rina. I scan the parking lot, whipping my head in every direction, but she's nowhere to be found. I spy the spot where we left her, but alas, she's gone. And now, even though I only knew her a short while, deep down, a piece of me hurts inside. I push her to the back of my mind, though, re-focusing on running for my *life*.

Once Tails and I reach Eddy, the three of us round the corner. We run down the last block, and the cemetery opens up on the right across a busy street. Cars zoom down the four lanes, and there aren't even any stoplights.

"I can throw Tails again," Eddy says, aware of the problem, too.

"No," I say. "He can't take another landing like that."

"Like last time, you can—"

"Neither can I!" I say louder than intended, and a part of me feels bad.

Eddy falls quiet as we near the end of the block, the Hellons screeching behind us. I dare not look back, especially not after last time. I may not wind up so lucky. Eddy, however, suddenly pushes me, and I stumble over to the side but keep running.

"What the hell?" I yell until a spear and shield fly past my neck.

Looking over my shoulder, I stare in awe at all the Hellons who have their spears cocked back and ready to throw. The empty handed one disintegrates to dust, but the others truck on. They screech in unison, and the back of the supermarket's windows shatter.

A gust blows our way, nearly sweeping me, Eddy, and Tails off the ground. Three more spears and shields sail at Eddy, but he dodges them. Another set almost catches him by surprise, but he jumps over it. Meanwhile, I suck at dodgeball—or dodge-death. One spear flies under my arms, luck on my side. But then a sharp shield nearly slices through my head, so I guess not. I throw myself from side to side like a drunk dancer until the weapons stop.

I turn around and see only one Hellon left. Smoke fumes out of its mouth as it charges at us harder than ever before.

Just a few feet away, Tails whimpers as we near the end of the sidewalk. He waves his nose as if to signal me and Eddy go on without him, and any icy frost devours my chest. I whisper his name, shaking my head, but he begins to slow down.

"Like hell!" I cry out, scooping Tails up. I kick it into high gear and lift him over my head with wobbly arms. I speed through traffic, sprinting across the street, and a bunch of cars slow down and honk. I can't blame the humans, though. I would've stopped, too, if I saw a dog *flying* through the air.

Holding my breath the entire time, I finally exhale once we make it across the street. I set Tails down beside the entrance gates, panting, before looking back at Eddy. But just as I turn my head, a hunk of hard metal knocks me out. It rams into my stomach, and in midair, I choke up spit and blood.

"Slixx!" Eddy shouts, so faintly I can barely hear.

Tails barks, too.

I slam to the ground, and my back and ribs crack. I hack up more blood. I strain to get up, but my body refuses to work, unable to move a single muscle. My lungs burn with the intensity of a million flames, and fireworks go off in my head. I inhale, but the air doesn't even make it to my lungs.

Looking down from the hazy sky, everything appears a blur. My vision toggles in and out as the world spins around me. But lying on my midsection, I spy the hunk of metal that knocked into me. A shield. The *Hellon's* shield. (Luckily the base of it knocked into me and not the sharp rim.)

A golden blur comes into view and licks my cheek. Tails. He whines, pacing about until he scoots the heavy metal off me by nudging the base. It takes him a couple tries before the shield clamors over onto the grass, but then Eddy appears in a panic. He kneels at my side with bulging eyes and sets Kiara's urn down.

"Slixx," he calls out, shaking me. "Are you okay? Are you—?"

In that moment, a large shadow casts over us, and we both know what it is. We look up to see the last Hellon towering over us. I see double, which makes it even scarier. The Hellon screeches down at us, digging us farther into the ground. The land falters beneath me, and I plummet into bedrock, wincing from the pain.

Beside me, Eddy scrambles for the Hellon's shield, and then both he and Tails scoot back. We all stare up at the mighty demon, puss dripping from its mouth. However, it stands weaponless on the sidewalk—*outside* the cemetery's entrance—and a reliving sigh escapes me. It shuts me up with another scream, though.

After a second, it disintegrates to dust, blowing away with the wind.

Eddy waits for the Hellon's wide round shield to disappear, too, but it doesn't. He inspects it, sizing up the plain hunk of metal. "That was close."

"K-Kiara's...urn?" I whisper, fighting for every breath.

Tails scoots the urn beside me, and I become at ease.

"We've gotta get to the fountain," Eddy says, standing with his new shield. He holds it from a metal knob inside and places a hand on his hip like he's some superhero.

"Woof!" Tails hops to his side like a trusty sidekick.

"Guys," I say, and they turn to me. "Can't...move."

"Right, sorry!"

"Woof!"

Carefully picking me up, Eddy pushes me up out of the pit we're in. Then, he pushes up Tails and jumps up next with Kiara's urn. "Are you able to hold this?" he asks me.

Wiggling my fingers, I will them to my stomach where Eddy sets the urn, and he suddenly lifts me up. I slide into his arms like a fitting puzzle piece. Mere inches separate our faces, so I drop my head. His cool breaths blow on my skin, enticingly smelling of mint and death. I try not to breathe them in, but my body needs all the air it can get.

Eddy carries me through the cemetery while I look down the entire time. Out of my peripheral, multiple humans and their ghosts walk along the cobblestone paths. The ghosts pay me and Eddy no mind, and the humans appear zombified—in a grieving daze. Even more humans litter the burial ground, most of them praying or sobbing at the foot of their loved ones.

Once we climb the hill and reach the fountain, Eddy sets me down. No one's on this side of the cemetery.

"How do you feel?" Eddy asks.

Grunting in pain, I sit up on the ledge of the fountain. I half-hear his question but have more important things on my mind. "Can you believe Rina left us?"

"Yeah," he chuckles.

I furrow my brows at him.

"C'mon, think back to when you first got here—all those years ago when we first met. Everything felt real—surreal—*alive*. Like we were given another chance at life with cool ghost abilities. Remember that?"

Averting his gaze, I think back to the first day I arrived here, the day that I desperately try to forget. The day I became chained to a baby and spent weeks exploring town. My eyes were starlit like Rina's, and the will to live burned bright inside me. I lost track of how many human's I kissed in the hospital, reliving their pain if only by a decimeter.

"She just got here," Eddy says. "And as I remember, the day we met, you said, 'This place is unbelievable! I want to stay here forever!'"

"What a dumb wish," I grumble.

"You also said—"

"I get it! It doesn't matter to me, anyway. She abandoned us. It's whatever."

"Woof!"

Eddy and I snap to Tails, following his gaze yonder to the shadows.

"No, I didn't," a soft voice says.

I narrow my eyes at an approaching figure.

"Rina?" Eddy asks.

Stepping into the light, she appears with her usual pure smile. She gracefully reclines beside me on the ledge, but I look away. "Don't be like that, Slixx," she says.

But I fold my arms over Kiara's urn.

"What changed your mind?" Eddy asks Rina.

She takes a deep breath. "Nothing. I'm staying."

"Then why are you here?" I snap.

She pouts. "So, that you guys wouldn't think I abandoned you."

"You did! What happened to the Rina who was so set on going, the Rina who believed we could make it to *Bliss*, the Rina who saved me back in the forest, the Rina who traveled across town with us on a slim chance that we could pass on *together*. What happened to her?"

She sighs, shifting to Eddy.

"Slixx, let's just hear her out," he says.

"No! If she was just going to walk out of our lives after everything, then I wish we'd never met."

Eddy shakes his head. "You don't mean that."

Even Tails whines.

But I turn up my nose.

"Slixx…"

"No, Eddy, it's alright," Rina says. "She's got every right to be mad at me—you do, too. I shouldn't've left you guys back at the store, but I-I was confused. I had to think about everything—going, what it would mean to give this all up."

I suck my teeth. "You're stuck between the living and the dead. Choosing that over a possible paradise? Oh, what a hard choice."

"But I just got here." She places a hand on mine, and I look at her. Her light brown eyes shimmer with warmth. "Try to understand where I'm coming from. All this is new to me. Since I've met you guys, this is the *most* I've explored outside of the hospital, and I've been here for like a *month*. I can only imagine what road trips, plane rides, and vacations to different places would be like."

She stares off into space in wonder. "I want to explore, Slixx."

Reluctantly, I open my nonexistent heart to her words.

"I want to live without the stress of being alive, for just a little longer. No worries about dying, sickness, school, relationships, or whatever else. I'm *free*."

I study her and all her radiating beauty. She oozes with passion, so I know her mind's made up—nothing left for me to say.

"Remember you said to me, 'But what good is a daydream if it'll never come true.' To me, daydreams are my own personal paradise. I want to keep it that way, at least for now."

Eddy clears his throat. "Do you really think you'll love it in this realm until the end of your human's life? On average, human's live until about eighty years old."

My eyes widen at that cold hard fact, unable to imagine even ten more years of that lonesome misery. "That's long enough to make the deadest ghost go mad," I mutter. "You might turn into a zombie like everyone else."

She shrugs. "Maybe. Or maybe I'll never lose the will to live —or maybe another ticket to *Bliss* will come along..." She elbows me. "And I'll finally go. But until then, this is my home, and I'm gonna make the most of it."

Wheeling around me, Eddy pulls Rina into an embrace. "Take care," he whispers into her ear, and she gives him a peck on the cheek. "Hopefully, we'll meet in *Bliss*."

She nods as he sits back down. Then, her attention shifts to Tails, and she pets him, sweetly murmuring into his ears. He nuzzles against her, his tail wagging fast. She giggles before retracting her hand. Tails whines for more affection, but she pans to me. "Slixx?"

I keep quiet, marinating in my mixed emotions.

"Well, I guess that's it then." She rises to her feet with a sigh before walking off.

"Wait!" I call out.

She turns around, and I stand up. We stare into each other's eyes, mine hard with contempt yet hers pleading and sincere. I start to say something, but the words don't come out. So, I try again.

"Look, I'm not very good at goodbyes, so—"

All at once, Rina hugs me, squeezing tight. "I'm sorry, Slixx."

"Don't apologize."

As we hold each other, something inside my head clicks, and finally, I get it. Because although ghosts may be able to pass on to *Bliss*, not everyone is ready to go.

"Pull a few pranks for me," I say. "And try not to go insane."

She giggles as we let go, and then waving two hands, she begins to back away. "I'm going to miss you guys! Stay safe and beware of the Hellons!"

Chuckling, both Eddy and I wave.

"Make it to *Bliss* for me!"

Eddy beams. "Better yet, meet us there!"

"Woof!"

"See ya!" I call out.

Within a matter of moments, Rina disappears into the shadows, leaving just me, Eddy, and Tails. The corners of my mouth pinch as I smile with fond memories, but without another word, I take the lid off Kiara's urn and behold her shiny purple ashes. Eddy leans over my shoulders, gawking, too, while Tails jumps onto the ledge for a closer look.

"What do you think we're supposed to do with it?" Eddy asks.

"Maybe dump it in?" I shrug. "It's worth a shot."

Pouring Kiara's ashes into the fountain, we watch the dark powdery residue submerge into the water and float atop the surface. It drifts with the currents like dead scum, and the fountain's harsh pressure butts it to the edge. But after the last bit comes out, nothing happens.

I fix on the purple ashes.

Eddy and Tails watch just as intently.

Seconds of stillness pass by before turning into fleeting minutes.

I turn to Eddy who doesn't meet my gaze. He stares at the fountain with keen focus and undivided attention—but mostly *hope*. His skin continues to flicker in and out. Any moment could be his last, and he knows it.

"Eddy…" I start.

But then the unthinkable happens.

In the fountain, the current begins to pick up. The sloshing water turns into an instant whirlpool right before our eyes, and we all watch in awe. Water splashes on us as it spins faster and faster. The purple ashes then consume the water, turning the whole thing neon. Even the script on the bottom of the fountain lights up at our feet.

Eddy creeps closer, feasting his starlit eyes on his way to *Bliss*. He steps onto the fountain's ledge and stands up, gaping down at the water. "I'm guessing we get in."

"If it's another ghost realm, Tails might not be able to enter," I say.

"Probably not."

Tails whines, looking up at Eddy.

"But it's worth a shot if you don't mind dying," he says to Tails. "Maybe you'll become a ghost, or maybe you'll get spit out of the whirlpool. Whatever the case, jump if you're not afraid to die."

As I veer my attention to Tails, he jumps in right before my eyes. His golden fur blinds me, and all I see are his small paws. "Tails!" I reach out for him, but I'm too late. The whirlpool swallows him whole.

Eddy smirks at me before saying, "Do you believe now?"

I search his hazel eyes, purple reflecting off them. I

rummage through his cavernous gaze for answers but only find hope—an unsurmountable amount of *hope*.

Without another word, Eddy plunges into the fountain, and he, too, gets swallowed whole.

Shifting to Kiara's empty urn, I run a finger along the sleek edges. For the first time, I wonder what it would've been like to talk to her—to touch her. All those years of hatred and disgust... I try to imagine what it would've been like if we had become as close as Eddy and Mr. Strife.

Abruptly, the whirlpool begins to slow down.

I step outside of my many thoughts and blink back to reality. Spinning around, I dip my legs into the water before taking one last look at Kiara's urn. A sudden tear trickles down my cheek.

"Words can't express how sorry I am," I whisper, thinking back to the alley. I wonder what would've happened if she had just gone home, if Josh would've only gotten banged up, everyone still be alive, and everything stayed normal. But I shake my head as my mind plunges into infinite what-ifs.

Unfortunately, the only thing I can do now is say goodbye.

"Rest in peace, Kiara. And if we make it, I hope to see you in *Bliss*."

Then, I dive into the fountain—no turning back now—and everything goes black.

CHAPTER 12
SLIXX

O n a hot summer's day, all the orphans run around the house in a frenzy. The littlest kids jog up and down the stairs, while the older kids branch off into groups, playing their own games. Their rosy-cheeked mama prepares sandwiches for them in the kitchen, humming a sweet melody. She stacks the fourteenth sandwich atop an old silver platter before reaching for the next slices of bread.

Three teenagers watch her from a narrow hall, peeking around the entryway. They all wear tattered clothes, and with skinny frames, one can tell they only eat three square meals a day. Two of them stand on both sides of a tall, young, curly haired girl.

"She's gonna catch you, Slim," the blond boy on the left whispers. He picks at the frays of his overalls.

Ignoring him, Slim spies on their mama in the kitchen, and a wide smirk pools on her face—determination and zest in her eyes.

"Don't doubt her," the other soft-spoken girl says.

Slim sucks her teeth. "Yeah, don't doubt me."

The blond boy glares at her.

But Slim flicks him a wink before making her move. She sneaks into the small kitchen on her tiptoes and ducks behind a long table covered by a crimson tablecloth. Without a sound, she rolls under like a spy, but her form falters to a tumble.

Her wrist hits one of the many chairs' legs, and the minute sound echoes throughout the kitchen. She tenses, stiller than a deer in headlights, while sucking in quiet breaths to calm herself.

However, after a quiet minute, she crawls to the end of the table. Lifting the tablecloth just enough to see, she looks under and spots their mama at the counter continuing to prepare the last couple sandwiches.

Slim exhales in relief.

Then, she creeps from underneath the table and rolls behind an adjacent counter, careful not to make any sudden movements. Her skinny fingers grip the edge of the counter as she peeks around the corner, watching their mama amble to the doorway. It is then that she looks back over and licks her lips at the delectable stack.

"Kids, lunch is ready!" their mama shouts, leaving the kitchen. "Kids!

Slim rubs her hands together like a mastermind while her two siblings duck from their mama, hiding in a nearby room. They wait until the coast is clear before sneaking back into the kitchen.

Out of the corner of Slim's eye, she spots them waving by the entryway.

"Hurry," they mouth. "She's coming back."

Slim nods at them with starlit eyes before sneaking to the platter of sandwiches. She takes extra precaution and looks both ways, glancing back at the door, and then swipes three sandwiches. She holds up the ends of her dress and drops them into her manmade pouch.

"What's for lunch, mama?" a little boy's voice asks from down the hall.

"Turkey sandwiches," she replies in her angelic voice, nearing the kitchen.

Slim's heart picks up speed, and she dashes for the exit. She scampers past her siblings, who follow her, but then she realizes the only way out is down the hall. Their mama's voice grows louder with each closing footstep. Her siblings shake her arm, panicked—one saying he knew Slim was going to get caught while the other prompting Slim to hide.

Thinking quick, Slim hurries back into the kitchen and slips into the closet by the entryway. She tries to push her siblings out, but they follow her inside. Their hushed voices go back and forth in alarm until Slim shoves sandwiches in their mouths.

As their mama and many other loud siblings trickle into the kitchen, the three of them are as quiet as church mice. They hear everyone nab one sandwich each and plop down at the table to eat. Most scarf the sandwiches down, while others savor it with slow bites. Crunching and chatter fill the room.

Afterward, Slim and her other two siblings slip out of the closet with the horde of quick eaters, and as they hurry down the hallway, tearing into their sandwiches, they hear their mama's voice.

"Did Slim, Jerry, and Amber come in?"

"Don't know," a loud kid says. "But ain't no more sandwiches left."

Their mama laughs, pure and in good fun. "At it again—even on her birthday. Slim, that slickster!"

"Let's play truth or dare," Slim proposes.

She, Jerry, and Amber sit on their beds in their small bedroom. All the orphans' beds are lined along both walls like a prison, but the decorations make it feel homey. The kids' home-made art hangs over their beds, and their few toys and broken crayons litter the floor. Nevertheless, a slight breeze blows in through the cracked window, rippling the holey drapes.

"Ugh, no way," Jerry says, combing through his blond hair. "That's for girls."

"How is truth or dare for girls?" Slim asks with a scowl.

"Let's just go outside," Amber says, but they don't hear her soft voice.

Jerry shrugs. "It just is."

"It's my birthday, so whatever I say goes." She drops to the floor and pulls out a beat-up shoebox from underneath her bed. After she opens it, she rummages through the various random materials inside: colored shoelaces, gum, one scratched CD, a polaroid picture, a couple dollars, dice, candy, etc.

Amber peeks over her shoulder, pointing. "Isn't that the picture that weird boy down the street gave you?"

Jerry marches over and snatches it out of Slim's shoebox. "Hey, it is!"

"Give it back, Jerry!" Slim shouts, reaching for it, but Jerry's as tall as she is and wards her off.

"Why do you still have this?"

"Yeah, how come you haven't thrown it out like all the other weird stuff he's given you?" Amber asks.

Slim finally plucks the polaroid picture from Jerry's grasp and sticks her tongue out at him.

"What are we, five?" he mocks, lying down on his bed. "How come you haven't tossed that thing. It's weird. He took it while spying on us."

Flipping the picture over, Slim beholds its contents: her. She runs a finger along their shabby orphanage in the background before sliding over to the foreground image of her face. She side-eyes someone to the right, giving them her signature smirk. Her hands are in her hair like a model, but she'd never think so.

Amber leans against the windowsill, the warm breeze whisking past her bare arms. "He's obviously got a thing for you. You should toss it."

"Guys actually *like* Slim?" Jerry gasps, feigning shock.

Slim throws a pillow at him. "You're one to talk, Mister I've Never Had A Girlfriend. We're in high school. It's pathetic."

"*Tch*. Whatever."

Slim throws the picture back into her shoebox before pulling out a skinny bottle of eyeliner and blush. She flashes them in Amber's face, and Amber's pupils shrink.

"How'd you get those?" Amber asks.

"I found them on the floor on the last day of school." Slim pretends to put the makeup on. "We should put it on and then all three of us go down to the mall."

"I'll pass," Jerry says, yawning.

Amber eyes Slim's makeup. "You know mama would kill you if she found out you had makeup, and *especially* if she found out we were *wearing* it?"

Slim shrugs before pulling lip-gloss out of her shoebox next. "That's why she's not going to find out."

Amber groans. "I've got a bad feeling about this."

"It'll be fun," Slim says, smirking. "We'll apply everything once we get to the mall."

She lifts her dress, revealing her black spandex shorts, and Jerry covers his eyes in disgust. Ignoring him, she carefully places the makeup inside her waistband before doing away with her shoebox.

Afterward, she grabs Amber's wrist and motions for Jerry to get up. They all rush out the room, run downstairs, ask their mama if they can go to the mall, and then finally head outside.

"You three, remember to be back before six, so we can all sing happy birthday," their mama says, closing the front door. "A special someone's got sixteen candles to blow out."

"Sure thing, I'll prepare my wish in advance!" Slim calls back. She dances as she, Jerry, and Amber walk down the long curvy driveway, kicking dirt with her beat-up Converse. "This is going to be so much fun," she sings. "We should play a game, too. Whoever gets hit on the most wins."

"No fair!" Jerry snaps. "Girls just don't hit on guys. And that's too ambiguous. It should be whoever gives or gets the most *numbers* wins."

Slim sighs. "It's *my* birthday but fine. The losers have to be the winner's slave for a month."

"Hell no!" Jerry folds his arms. "That's too drastic."

"Yeah, how about the losers have to do the winner's dish days for a month?" Amber suggests.

"Guys, it's *my* birthday." Slim rolls her eyes but falters—too happy to be annoyed. "But fine, whatever. We'll probably just bump into a ton of people from school."

They reach the end of the driveway and begin trekking on the grass where the sidewalk's supposed to be. Numerous trees and shrubs inhabit the street neighborhood, houses built right in the middle of a former forest. The passing homes don't look as bad or big as their orphanage, but surely, they didn't house over fourteen people. Nevertheless, a road separates the street neighborhood. No cars zoom by, though, as the area's been a ghost town ever since a highway was built on the opposite side of town.

Above, the sun shines bright, and the clear sky shows promise. The light, however, peeks through the many trees and reaches the land below scattered. Slim, Jerry, and Amber continue walking, now blocks away, and the freckled rays show across their faces.

"Not to be a Debbie downer, but I doubt anyone will want to talk to us wearing clothes like these," Amber mutters. "And it's not like me or Slim have anything to offer." She crosses her arms over her flat chest.

"Don't be like that," Slim says in a low voice.

"Yeah, that's dark," Jerry chimes in. "And you guys are... somewhat...correctly facially structured."

Stopping, Slim and Amber give him a deathly glare.

Jerry raises his arms in truce. "What? It was a compliment!"

An idea suddenly comes to Slim, and she puts her hands on Amber's shoulders. "I've got just the thing! You're wearing a bra, right?"

Bewildered, Amber slowly dips her chin.

Slim smack her shoulders, Amber wincing from the pain. Then, she starts to backtrack. "I've got just the thing," she repeats with the widest grin.

"Where are you going?" Jerry asks.

Turning around, Slim breaks out into a run. "Wait right there for a minute! I'll be back!"

"Wait!" Amber and Jerry call out in unison.

But Slim is already on her way. She runs along the "sidewalk" before veering off to a shortcut she knows within the forest—a straight shot. Her heart beats fast, and she can't tell if it's all from running or if joy's oozing from her heart. She jumps up and clicks her heels, singing about her birthday. Just a block away, she races toward the orphanage for her secret silicone pads, so she and Amber can stuff their bras later.

Suddenly, a faint bright light flashes out of her peripheral, and she slows down. She waits a moment before jogging ahead, but when the bushes ruffle behind her, she stops. She watches the spot like a hawk, putting a hand on her hip—fearless.

"Maybe it's an animal," she says to herself.

But out pops a short stout boy with buckteeth and glasses. He wears belted baggy jeans and a fancy blue collared shirt, and his overly gelled hair spikes up in every direction. A big new brown backpack hangs off his weak shoulders, the color matching his clean shoes. He nods at her as a greeting, his hands behind his back.

Slim instantly recognizes him and furrows her brows. "Are you stalking me, Elliot?" she sighs, half joking yet mildly irritated.

"No," Elliot says, looking down at the ground.

"Then why are you hanging out in the bushes—for fun?"

"I was out for a walk."

The dots connect in Slim's mind, and she narrows her gaze at him. "Were you...taking pictures of me, again?"

He glances up at her once and then twice, and then he caves. He brings his hands around and holds up a polaroid camera. "You got me."

"I thought I told you to stop, Elliot. It's creepy."

"I'm sorry," he says in a low voice. "It's just that...when my mom died..."

"I know, I know," Slim says. "She gave you this camera on her deathbed and said to use it often. But she didn't say to use it on *me*. Look, I'm sorry for your loss and everything, but it's getting creepy. My brother and sister said—"

"You showed your siblings?"

Slim rolls her eyes. "Not exactly. They actually found—"

"You weren't supposed to show anyone that." He takes a step forward, bass in his voice. "That picture was supposed to just stay between us."

"Relax." Slim scans his wide eyes, unease rising in her chest. "Just stop taking the pictures, okay?"

"But..." Elliot's tone falters. "I like you."

An awkward air taints the warm wind, and Slim rubs her arms. "I know, but I've told you a thousand times. I don't—"

He staggers forward, pushing his glasses up his nose. "Why not?"

Slim sighs. "You're not my type."

"I can be."

"You sound crazy, Elliot." Slim exhales. "Listen, my brother and sister are waiting for me. I have to go."

As she turns to leave, Elliot calls her name. "Wait—I made you something." He turns around and drops his brand-new backpack to the ground, money clearly no object. He fishes through the many notebooks, drawings, and knickknacks inside.

A silent minute passes by, and Slim taps her foot, growing antsy. "I have to—"

"Found it!" Elliot pulls out a small jewelry box, blowing off nonexistent dust. He's careful to zip up his backpack before turning around. He then hurries to Slim and stops a couple feet away from her, so she takes a step back herself. "Here. For you!"

Slim looks from Elliot to the jewelry box before finally seizing it from his chubby fingers. She unlocks the golden lock and pops the top open. Inside the box, her pretty reflection greets her, but then her eyes grow wide. She shakily opens the first drawer and sees a bunch of pictures of her stacked atop one another. Private photos. One from at school in the girl's bathroom. One inside the orphanage. Many outside. One of her posing while on a date. One of her eating. One of her drunk at a party. The edges of more photos catch her eye in the last two drawers.

"What the hell is this?" she spits.

Elliot's smile falls. "Do you like it?

"Like it?" She swipes a handful of pictures and throws them in his face. "You're fucking insane!"

Elliot's eyebrows droop down as he takes a moment to process. Then in the next second, he drops to the ground, desperately picking up every picture.

Throwing the jewelry box, Slim chucks it at a tree, and the mirror shatters. It bangs against the dirt and leaves, all the photos spilling out. "You stay the hell away from me, you freak!"

Elliot slowly rises to his feet. He reaches up to touch Slim's face, but she smacks his hand down and pushes him back. "But...I...like you."

Anger boils Slim's blood, and her heart races a thousand miles per minute. "Newsflash, dummy, the other person has to like you back for it to mean something. If I ever catch you pulling some shit like this again, I'll end you." And with that, she marches off.

She doesn't get far, though.

Elliot crumbles to tears on his way back to his backpack. He then rummages inside until he pulls out a small BB gun. He aims it Slim's back, calling her name, and she whirls around—speechless.

"I'm not crazy, Slim." He holds the gun, shaky. "I just have a big heart and really care a lot about the people I love, and I refuse to lose anyone else right now."

"Love?" Slim breathes. "Put that shit down, Elliot."

He doesn't.

"Put it down!"

"*Shh!*"

"Damnit, I said put it down!"

"*Shh!* Someone will hear you."

"If you don't—" Slim charges for him, hauling in heavy breaths. Smoke fumes out of her nostrils as she balls her fists.

"Stay back, Slim."

"Bet you don't even know how to use it."

Just a couple feet away, Elliot closes one eye. "I said get back!"

"And I said put that shit d—!"

BANG!

CHAPTER 13

REALITY

I gasp awake and jerk up as if being resurrected. I take in deep breaths, grabbing my head. My mind doubles over the dream before fixing on Slim—me, my former human self. I blink in disbelief, the BB gun plaguing my thoughts, until my white surroundings dazzle me.

Looking up, seemingly endless snow stretches for miles in every direction, and dense fog shrouds the area. I search for any other signs of nature or life, but not even trees inhabit the flat land—just mounds of snow.

"Eddy?" I whisper, my cold breath visible in the air. "Tails? Ri—"

I catch myself as a tide of realization washes over me, knowing she's gone. A merry image of her flashes through my mind as I begin to reminisce, but then my eerie surroundings jar me out of my thoughts. So much snow and fog.

Panic strikes my chest, and I try to scramble to my feet. *Try to.* As I bring my legs around, my eyes widen at my new *form.* Instead of legs, I now have a single ghost tail. My head, my arms, my waist, my chain—everything else—is normal. But my hips curve down into a squiggly tail that slithers in the snow as I walk, leaving a snake-like trail.

"What the...?"

Shivering, I grab my arms. Human weather never affected me, but now my teeth chatter while my body trembles. I inch forward, squinting through the fog, but it's too thick. Alone and in the middle of nowhere, I spin around in a frenzy. Still, no sign of Eddy or Tails. My stomach begins to churn.

"Eddy! Tails!"

All of a sudden, a low clicking sound pierces the air. I freeze in fright as the noise dies out, but then it fades in and out again. Whirling around, my chain rattles as my chest quickly rises and falls. I look left and right but don't see anything. Just snow and fog. So when the clicking sound starts again, I break out into a run.

"Eddy?" I shout, my voice cracking. "Tails! E—"

I stop at the sight of a hazy figure in the distance. It looks like a person's outline, possibly Eddy, so I creep closer. The fog clouds the shadowy figure until I'm just a couple feet away, but then the back of Eddy's head slowly comes into view. I slither around before kneeling in front of him.

"Eddy?" I whisper.

But he doesn't move. He sits stiller than a statue and stares ahead as if in a scary daze. His skin continues to flicker, fading in and out, so he must still be linked to his dying human.

I wave a hand in front of his face, but he remains unfazed. It isn't until I touch him that he shakes into consciousness. His horrified lenses peer at me, familiarity washing over them, and he exhales.

"Are you okay?" I ask.

He averts his gaze.

"Did you see...how you...?"

"Yeah," he croaks. "You?"

I dip my chin. "Homicide."

"Illness."

My voice reduces to a mouse. "I'm sorry."

He flashes me a look before standing up and noticing his tail. He then slithers in circles, studying his new form, while his chain sounds behind him. It connects from his back into the ground, and every time he moves, his chain simply extends from that same spot underground.

"Weird," he mumbles before returning to me. "But shouldn't I be the one apologizing? Murder isn't anything to take lightly."

"Neither is sickness." I stand up, too, and put on my best nonchalant face. "It was just some creepy stalker with a gun."

"Damn, that's awful. Are *you* okay?"

Forcing a laugh, I shrug. "Of course."

"Slixx," he says in a low voice, and I look up at his grave frown. His narrowed eyes must see right through me. "Stop."

"Stop what?"

"Always trying to pretend you're okay. Do you need any more proof that you *were* human with *real* emotions?"

I search his tinted hazel irises for a long beat, mute. A part of me dares to brush him off in irritation, while another part of me wishes to crumble into open arms. But the latter isn't me. Slim was brave and fearless, and so is Slixx.

"Woof!"

Spinning around, a spark of joy ignites in my chest. I scan the thick fog, only able to see a few feet in front of me, but I know that lively bark anywhere. I smile in the direction of Tails' voice. However, when a tall dark shadow approaches, I furrow my brows.

I barely have time to flee before a mighty beast pops out of the mist and attacks me. A scream gets caught in my throat, but upon opening my eyes, my jaw drops. Tails stands over me in *his* new form. He looks exactly the same except he's now over fifty feet tall like a brontosaurus!

He licks me with his giant moist tongue, and it wipes across my whole body. I can't help but laugh as Eddy creeps closer to us. He reaches out to touch Tails, and this time in his ghost form, he can. He pets Tails' soft fur, caressing one of his long legs. His fingers then slide down to his big cute paws before tapping his razor-sharp nails.

"Good boy," I say, scrambling to my tail. When he lowers his head all the way down to me, I give him the biggest hug. "You made it!"

"Woof!"

"Now we can all go to *Bliss*," I whisper.

Eddy snaps his head to me with raised brows, and I already know what that look means. He ambles over, leans forward, and puts a sarcastic hand to his ear. "What was that? Something about *Bliss*? Who believes in what now?"

Suppressing a laugh, I push him away. "Whatever. You should be asking more important questions like 'where the hell are we'?"

"Isn't it obvious?" Eddy asks, dodging Tails' attempts to lick him. But after a moment, Tails pins him to the ground, coating him in saliva, and he desperately tries to ward Tails off. "*Ghosts one – Limbo in murder and sickness, ghosts two – The Dump in natural quickness.* We made it to The Dump!"

"How do you even remember—?"

He finally manages to jump up from Tails' loving affection. "Found out I had a photographic memory as a human. Pretty cool."

I cross my arms, muttering to myself. "*Tch.* You found out you had a photographic memory, while I found out I was an orphan. How's that fair?"

"What?" Eddy asks.

I flash him a fake smile. "Nothing. Now that we're in this 'Dump,' where are we even supposed to go?"

Click. Click. Click. Click. Click. Click. Click.

My eyes widen.

Click. Click. Click. Click. Click. Click. Click.

Eddy's eyebrows tower down as he examines the mist, the noise coming from every direction.

Click. Click. Click. Click. Click. Click. Click.

A spider crawls down my spine, and I shiver. The clicks sound one after another—quick and succinct—followed by a millisecond pause. Goosebumps quiver onto my arms as the unknown sound echoes in my ears.

"What's that?" Eddy asks.

Tails steps in front of me, a low growl escaping him.

"That sound's been following me," I say.

"Following you?"

Appearing behind the fog, a large black shadow about the size of Tails nears us—fast. The clicks crescendo to an all-time high, and the nearing shadow grows larger. I hug myself, squeezing my elbows, and even Tails whimpers beside me, lowering his head. Eddy stands his ground, but judging by his clenched jaw, he's frightened, too.

I start to back away. "Maybe we should run."

"But what if it's someone who's come to welcome us?" Eddy asks, eyes peeled.

"Who would welcome us to The Dump, Eddy?"

"Friendly townspeople."

"Do you see any town around here?" I shout.

"Well—"

Click. Click. Click. Click. Click! CLICK. CLICK!

The shadow bursts out of the fog, and it's as if my guts turn inside out. Puke bubbles inside my stomach, beckoning for release. The hair on my arms shoots up, and sweat boils atop my forehead. I fall short of breath while a sharp pain engulfs my chest. And then, I scream.

"What the hell!" Eddy yells.

Tails bolts off first.

Paralyzed with fear, I stare horrified at the gigantic roach. It stands on six long, skinny legs, and its antennae flail in the air. A dark reddish-brown color plagues its nasty, flat, oval-shaped body. *CLICK. CLICK. CLICK. CLICK. CLICK. CLICK. CLICK.* Its wings twitch, fluttering with the most repulsive audio.

When the roach scurries toward us at the speed of light, that's enough to snap me out of my stupor and send me dashing after Tails. I run at the speed of light, my tail sloshing through and chucking back snow. I suck in air and spit it out in that same beat. And maybe it's my new form keeping up, or maybe I'm just running fast because Tails, up ahead, stays in my line of vision. His heavy footsteps tremble the ground, and he leaves big pawprints in the snow.

"*Ahhhhh!*" Eddy screams, hot on my trail.

The roach's shadow looms over us both, hot on *our* trail.

CLICK. CLICK. CLICK. CLICK. CLICK. CLICK. CLICK.

With no time to talk, I keep moving, propelling myself forward. Because in this new form, moving seems easier than before, though I'm definitely unaware of the logistics. All I know is that my tail powers harder than ever while the roach's incessant clicking drives me forward.

"Woof!"

Tails motions his head onward, and I squint through the fog but don't see anything. I dare not waste any breath to speak, unable to fall behind—*unable* to become roach *food*. I just keep on trucking ahead for what feels like kilometers until a bold horizontal line drawn in the snow comes into view. It runs from east to west, endless in this opaque fog.

Eddy soon catches up to me and Tails, and the three of us

race over the bold line. Even after we cross it, we keep running. I don't look back. My tail slithers through the snow, and my arms blow behind me. I lean at an angle, fixing on an unknown destination of safety.

"Slixx," Eddy calls from behind, and Tails barks as if to call my name, too.

I keep running, though.

"We're safe!"

Upon hearing those holy words, only then do I slow to a stop and spin around.

Eddy points at the humongous roach on the other side of the horizontal line. The vile insect rams its head against an invisible wall, but no matter what, it can't pass over the line. Its wings flutter as if irritated, and its antennae go haywire.

Although creeped out, I inch back over to Eddy and Tails.

"It can't get in," Eddy says, cupping his chin. "I wonder why that is."

I stop several feet behind them. "Who cares? All that matters is we're over here, and that monster can't get to us."

Eddy chuckles, eyeing me. "Monster?"

"I said what I said. Don't get me started on how you were hollering, scared out of your mind."

He throws up his hands as a peace offering.

I avert my gaze to the fog around us. Here across the line, it's much clearer, yet endless snow still stretches in every direction. The land remains flat. No sign of ghostkind or any type of civilization.

"Maybe coming here wasn't such a good idea," I say in a low voice.

"Nonsense!" Eddy slithers past me with the biggest grin. He puts a flat hand to his forehead and begins to scope out the land, pacing in every direction. "*Never rising from infliction. Move forward not back.* We just have to figure out where to go next."

I sigh as Tails joins him in playing detective. They snoop the snow like Sherlock Holmes and Dr. Watson. Meanwhile, I plop down on the snow and cover my ears, trying to rid myself of the roach's foul sound. I fix on the fog ahead and fall victim to my wandering mind. My human self resurges inside my thoughts, and my orphan siblings trickle in, too. I wonder what fun we would've had if we had gone to the mall that day—what I would've wished for before blowing out my candles.

"Slixx, Tails, over here!" Eddy calls out.

Tails gallops from the other end of the snow toward Eddy, and I rise to my tail. I uncover my ears only upon confirming no sound or sight of the roach. Then, I trudge over to Eddy who leans forward as if looking over a cliff.

Stopping beside him, the three of us look down at a set of stairs leading to a black front door. At first glance, the door doesn't appear connected to anything, but after a double take, the door is attached to an inconspicuous shack covered in snow. It nearly blends in completely, but some of the wooden planks stick out.

I look over and see many other hidden underground shacks lined parallel to this one. They extend for as far as the eye can see, and all the doors look exactly the same—black *without* a doorknob.

"Maybe we should knock," Eddy says.

"Are you crazy?" I whisper like someone can hear us. "There could be a whole gang of roaches in there—just waiting to eat us!"

Eddy skips down the stairs before halting at the doorstep. "I highly doubt that."

"Eddy, no!"

Too late. He knocks on the door three times, following some cringy tune.

Unknowingly, I hold my breath for a minute until nothing happens.

The door doesn't open, and silence settles in the air. Eddy looks at me. I look at Tails. And Tails stares at the door. None of us make any sudden movements as another silent moment ticks by.

Still, nothing happens.

I sigh before opening my mouth to say something smart.

But suddenly, a peephole on the door slides open, and a pair of green eyes on ashen olive skin studies us. They flick from me to Eddy before briefly widening, likely taken aback by Eddy's flickering skin. "Whad'ya want?" a whiny man's voice calls out —his drawl cavalier like his attitude.

Caught off guard, I zip my lips.

Eddy keeps most of his composure, though. "Uh, may we come in?"

"Mirror, mirror, on the wall, fate n' nature made us fall, daffodils bleed an' roses bloom, never cuddle a bitch, what'll we do?" the man asks as cold as ice.

Thinking quick on his feet, Eddy stammers over *uhs* and *ums* to buy time, but the green-eyed man groans, impatient. He narrows his gaze at Eddy for a response.

"Gimme an ansuh, pal."

"Um...uh...die?"

The man slams the peephole shut in Eddy's face.

Tails whimpers as Eddy turns around, puzzled.

But just then, the door bangs open. And in a flash, a large, heavyset, bull-necked man storms out and tackles Eddy to the ground. They both plummet into the snow, and layers chuck up around them.

I gasp.

"Get off me!" Eddy yelps on his stomach. He still flickers in and out but not so much that his body isn't tangible anymore.

The bull-necked man pins Eddy to the ground, pressing his forearm against the back of Eddy's neck. He clasps his hands as his other arm wraps under Eddy's arm. His thick tail—visible even in faded jeans—restrains Eddy's lower body. "Where y'all from?" he calls out, his voice rougher than bark.

He looks up at me as Eddy spits out snow, and I freeze at the sight of his one eye, the other behind an eyepatch. A brown scar runs across his face, and a severed white chain clatters behind him, sticking out of his back like our purple ones.

"We're not from around here," I blurt out.

"Ain't that obvious," the bull-necked man barks, gesturing at Tails who starts to growl.

Tails takes a step forward, but I hold out a hand for him to stay back.

At that moment, the same green-eyed man from the peephole ambles outside and leans against the doorframe. He's actually short—no taller than four foot ten—and his severed white chain ropes beneath his tail. He wears a shabby oversized hat, big clobbering shoes, and old baggy trousers—from what looks like centuries ago. A toothpick bobs in his mouth as he talks. "We know dat. Yuh pal got the ansuh wrong."

Eddy grunts in pain under the bull-necked man.

"Ain't gonna ask y'all again! Y'all from the city?"

"What? No," Eddy croaks.

"Where then?" the bull-necked man asks.

The green-eyed man takes the toothpick out of his mouth, narrowing his eyes at us like before. "Yeah, where?" he parrots.

Eddy begins to cough, too much pressure on his neck.

"*Ghosts one – Limbo*," I quickly recite from the fountain. "We're, we're from Limbo, the human realm. W-we just got here. We don't mean any trouble—we can just leave if you—"

"Limbo, eh?" the bull-necked man repeats, and he and the green-eyed man exchange some sort of mysterious look.

"Can't breathe," Eddy croaks. "Losing consciousness..."

"Please," I say, the word sounding odd out of my mouth.

Tails takes another step forward, but I keep my arm up, holding him at bay.

The bull-necked man looks from his friend to me, then Tails, then back down to Eddy. He presses against his neck a bit more. "Your skin. Why's it flickin'?"

"My human's...alive in Limbo," Eddy chokes out between coughs. His face begins to turn purple, and his eyes start to roll to the back of his head. He musters the last of his strength and shakes his long chain, rattling the bull-necked man's attention. "This is my link...to him."

"He's telling the truth!" I shout. "Just get off him!"

The bull-necked man doesn't budge, though. Instead, he glares down at Eddy for a long, quiet beat as if making sure his story checks out. I patiently wait for him to get up with high hopes, but seconds feel like hours in the face of pain, especially bearing witness to it. I watch as Eddy's face flushes firm purple, but when I lose sight of his pupils, my mouth flies open to plea.

Just as I suck in a breath, the bull-necked man finally slithers off Eddy, who gasps for air. "Rare," he says, peering yonder at Eddy's seemingly infinite chain which disappears into the fog. He backs away toward the door beside his friend. Their mysterious gazes shift from me to Eddy, but surprisingly, they both wave hands for us to enter their shack.

When it's safe to move, I scurry down the stairs and kneel beside Eddy. He clutches his throat, wheezing. "Are you okay?" I ask.

He frantically nods, mid-cough.

I reach up to rub his back but reconsider an inch away. Instead, I stand up and help him to his tail, and together, we creep toward the shack's entrance.

"Wait here, boy," I say to Tails, but he whimpers as if begging us to stay. "We'll be back before you know it."

Once inside, the bull-necked man shepherds us down a short, narrow hallway—one person in front of the other—and a creepy stillness fills the empty corridor.

When we finally reach another door, the bull-necked man opens it to a loud, whirring rush of noises and voices. The short hallway leads into some sort of speakeasy, and countless ghosts all with severed white chains sit at various tables with bubbly drinks in their hands. They all laugh, joke, and chug as the bull-necked man charges into the room, high-fiving a slew of them. He weaves through the maze-like tables until he reaches the bar and begins whipping up rounds of drinks.

Eddy and I stand in awe at the door.

"Dat's Buck Eye Gryner," the green-eyed man says. "He's the roughest, toughest ghost in alla Snowdevlin Village. He used t'be a wrestlin' champ when he was a human. But then he died inna car accident drunk drivin' after his fiancé..." He motions a thumb across his neck and clicks his tongue. "Yuh know?"

I purse my lips in alarm.

Eddy gulps. "What about you?" he asks. "What's your story?"

The green-eyed man smirks. "Name's Kaplone. Kah-Plone. An' my story? It's the same as now. Once a street thug, always a street thug." And with that, he hobbles into the bar before stopping amid the maze to chat with a table of ghosts.

I search the crowd, regret building in my chest. "Maybe we shouldn't've—"

Headstrong, Eddy strides into the bar next. He grins from ear to ear, walking down the aisles, and determination glimmers in his bright eyes. Only a few ghosts glance at him before doing a double take at his flickering skin, while everyone else must be too drunk to care.

"Eddy," I hiss after him.

He waves at a drove of ghosts who actually wave back, and he slaps hands with a couple, too. He works the room as if he's been here his whole life, but that's just the Eddy Effect.

Following him to the bar, I plop down on a stool beside him. My butt instantly sinks into the soft red cushion while I rest my elbows on the wooden counter.

Behind the counter, Gryner turns around and raises a cold brow at us. "If it ain't the travelers. What y'all drinkin'?"

"What do you got?" Eddy asks.

"What you in the mood for, Flicky?"

"Flicky?" Eddy's gaze trails down to his body, which fades in and out like a dying candlelight. "Something light, I guess."

"You look like a lightweight. How 'bout you, toots?"

I fumble for words, his one deathly eye mugging me. "Oh, uh, same."

Gryner grabs two glasses from the full counter behind him and nabs two bottles off one of the many shelves. The tinted bottles look like alcohol, but when Gryner pops off the tops, a strong citrus and copper smell permeates the air. He pours it into our glasses, and a bit splashes onto the counter. I recoil my arms just as Gryner slides us the drinks.

I inspect the thick green liquid inside, sniffing what can only be described as *bleeding fruit*. "What is this?" I ask.

Gryner's good eye peels to me, but he doesn't say a word.

I take the hint and just sip the drink. Immediately, a metallic flavor hits the back of my tongue, and I gag. But then a sweet pomegranate aftertaste kicks in. I smack my lips, feeling for the flavor, and then take another awful sip. The aftertaste punches stronger than before, and I wind up coughing. The metallic and pomegranate flavors mesh together, overpowering my senses.

"What...is this?" I choke out.

Eddy holds up his drink with sour lips. "Yeah, it's good but—"

"*Plasgood*," Kaplone says, hopping onto a stool beside me.

"Plas-good?" I repeat. "What's that?"

"Only the best rum in the realm."

"Naw, the best stuff's in the city," Gryner butts in. "Think this is good, they've got that good *good*."

I take another swig, and the powerful flavor stuns my throat. Although I wind up coughing again, the sweetness grows with each sip like fruity maple syrup—weird combination, I know. I gulp down a bit more before chugging the whole thing like juice. This results in a lot more coughing, but the sweet, lingering taste settles on the back of my tongue like ecstasy.

"What's this made of?" I ask as a rejuvenating wave washes over my body, melting away all my aches and woes.

"Yuh sure ask a lotta questions, Sheets," Kaplone says.

"Sheets?" I ask, following his gaze down to my tattered dress.

He shifts his attention to my empty glass. "Anotha onea these an' the afta effects'll kick in." Before I can counter, he knocks on the bar and tips his chin to Gryner. "Stony House on the rocks."

"Comin' up," Gryner says. He wipes his hands on his apron before turning around and grabbing a glass. He pours multiple bottles into the glass, and the liquid sloshes about, again. His hands move as if in automatic, adding foam and a fire glaze. "Flicky, Sheets, so y'all say y'all from Limbo, eh?"

I groan at our new insulting nicknames, biting my tongue.

"We haven't had visitas from there inna while, right Gryn-er?" Kaplone says.

Eddy and I glance at each other.

"Wait—what do you mean 'in a while'?" I ask.

"Have others come here from Limbo?" Eddy adds.

Gryner slides Kaplone his drink, and Kaplone swipes it up with his tiny hands, his toothpick now between his fingers. As he chugs down the foul-smelling drink, his eyelids grow heavy. He downs half of it before banging the glass down.

"Last ones who came through here was 'boutta hundred an' somethin' years ago," Kaplone says.

"A hundred and what?" I blurt out. "How are you guys still around?"

Both Gryner and Kaplone knit their brows at me in confusion.

"Don't you guys...die?" Eddy asks.

Gryner's cold eyebrows slowly rise to his forehead, and his mouth curves up into a smile. He and Kaplone then burst out into laughter. Gryner's bass bellows shake the floorboards, while Kaplone's high-pitched chuckles bounce off the walls. Kaplone slaps his small knees, rocking back and forth in the stool, as if just told the funniest joke ever.

"Y'all get a load of this one!" Gryner shouts to the full shack of ghosts, and they all fall mute, leaning forward in their seats. "These two travelers here just asked me and Kaplone if we can die?"

Instantly, all the ghosts begin to cackle, and laughter fills the room.

Meanwhile, Eddy and I scan the room, awaiting an answer. Minutes pass by, and everyone's still hooting and hollering. Some ghosts fall back in their chairs, while others bang their fists on their tables.

Growing impatient, I clear my throat out loud. "Answer the question. Can you or not?"

Kaplone flicks away a tear, licking his toothpick back in his mouth. "Sorry, Sheets. Yuh an' yuh pal's funny."

"We wish," Gryner finally says, regaining his natural scowl. The many ghosts quiet down at the sound of his voice. "This is The Dump. *The* Dump. Us ghosts here *can't* die. If anythin', we'll just be reborn on the opposite end of the realm."

"Reborn?" Eddy questions.

"Yeah, reborn," Kaplone repeats. "We got crime jus' like the humans. So say a ghost 'kills' anotha. That killed ghost then 'dies' temporarily an' goes into holdin' where it'll be reborn afta."

"Temporarily...holding...reborn," I mutter, all this flying over my head. "How long is holding?"

"Ain't nobody know," Gryner says. He grabs a rag and starts to clean the counters while Kaplone downs the rest of his drink.

"Who determines the holding time then?" I ask.

Kaplone bangs his empty glass down and exhales a refreshing sigh. His eyelids droop low like his eyebrows, and he slumps over in his chair, slurping his toothpick back in. "Yuh sure ask a lotta questions, Sheets."

I clench my jaw. "My name is not Sheets."

"What brings y'all here anyway?" Gryner asks. "Travelers don't travel for no reason."

"Uh..." I hesitate.

"We're headed to *Bliss*," Eddy blurts out, cheesing.

All at once, Gryner looks up from the bar, and Kaplone swivels in his chair with squinty eyes. The entire shack falls mute. No one utters another peep. All the ghosts stare at Eddy with such sharp eyes I don't know what they're thinking. My palms grow sweaty as an uneasy tension saturates the air.

After a long minute, Gryner finally says, "*Bliss?*"

"Did he jus' say"—Kaplone takes his toothpick out his mouth—"what I think he said?"

A mix of surprise and shock tear through the shack until Gryner chuckles. His laughs come out hardy and succinct with brief pauses between, and then all together, the entire bar cackles aloud. All the ghosts guffaw at their tables. The walls and floor shake once again, vibrations booming the place.

Eddy's eager smile curtails flat. "What?" he asks, defensively.

But everyone keeps laughing at him—at *us*.

"What's so funny?" Eddy bangs a fist against the bar. "We're going!"

"Yeah right, Flicky," Gryner says, holding onto the counters for support. "And I'm a human again." His joke sends the crowd into even louder uproar.

I stare at Eddy who glares at the bull-necked man.

"Wait, wait, an' I'ma pretty lil young thang on the beach," Kaplone chimes in. He bends his wrist like a dainty princess and imitates one strolling along a shore.

"What's so damn funny?" Eddy shouts so loud that I nearly jump in my seat.

Waving, Gryner motions for the crowd to simmer down. "Hey, hey now, let's let Flicky dream. He ain't nothin' but a kid wet behind the ears."

Just as Eddy opens his mouth to speak, outrage finds my voice. "A kid?" I cry out. "To hell with you!"

Gryner spits out a laugh while holding up his hands, feigning offense. "Oooo, Sheets gettin' ballsy, eh?" He pats his belly as if to calm himself down. "Listen y'all, we don't mean to laugh—"

"Doubt that," I snap. Out of my peripheral, a silver glimmer catches my eye from the door, and a hunched over young man in all black ambles into the bar with his head down.

"No, no, really," Kaplone says, clamping down on his tooth-pick. "It's jus' dat every time some travelers come here, they mention *Bliss*. But *Bliss* don't exist, yuh get me?"

I turn to Eddy, searching his hardened eyes.

"Yeah it does," he says. He sits straight and tall, confidence reigning in his posture. "We're gonna find it and pass on."

"*Pffft*," Gryner drivels. "Good luck with the impossible."

Eddy jumps to his tail, and his chair's legs scoot back, loudly scraping the floorboards. "We don't have to take this. If you're not gonna help us, then we're leaving."

"Relax, Flicky," Kaplone says. "It's the truth. We'd help yuh if we could. Jus' tryna save yuh some time, so yuh don't wind up like the other travelers who came through."

"What happened to them?" I gulp.

"They probably made it," Eddy mutters.

"Nope," a raspy voice says beside us.

Both Eddy and I look up at that same hunched over guy that just came in. He stands between us with his hands in his pockets, and he wears black leather from head to tail—with the exception of a white shirt: skintight pants, a long, bulky vest, and gloves. A bunch of silver necklaces also hang from around his neck. His ashen skin appears like every other ghost, but a red undertone pops out from his honey tan.

He tips his chin at Gryner, says "Usual," and Gryner goes to work.

"And who are you?" Eddy asks, sizing him up and down.

Gryner slides the leather man a clear shot glass, and he swigs it down in one gulp. He sucks his tongue after, the strong smell seeping out of his mouth. Then, he leans on the bar and turns his head to Eddy. "I'm one of those travelers."

Eddy's eyes widen at the man.

"What happened?" I breathe.

The leather man ticks his head to me—mere inches away.

Even though he looks just a few years older than us, deep, weary lines run across his forehead, and a handsome dent grazes his chin. His catlike eyes pick me apart. "Exactly what Kaplone said—wasted time. I traveled to the ends of this realm for a way to pass on, to get to my beloved Deanna who's surely in *Bliss*, but I wound up back here. And that's the end of that story."

Before I can think, the words spill out of my mouth. "So, you just gave up?"

"Givin' up is different from acceptin' reality," Gryner says.

"No, he gave up," Eddy affirms, balling his fists, and everyone looks at him. "Whatever your name is—"

"Leon."

"You must not have loved Deanna that much if you stopped looking." Eddy sucks his teeth before stalking off. He curses under his breath on his way out, weaving down the aisles.

I start after him—

"The fountain, Hellons, and rush may make it seem believable," Leon says to me in a low voice, his short lively ponytail bouncing about. "But not everyone makes it to paradise."

I stand there a moment, considering his words.

Then, I follow Eddy out with a million thoughts running through my mind. I double over all the events that led us here, and a humongous weight drops onto my chest. I wonder...

Not everyone makes it to paradise.

CHAPTER 14
FALL OUT

"What do we do now?" I ask, snuggled up against Tails' warm fur in the middle of the snow. Right back where we started, Tails and I lie together while Eddy paces around, muttering to himself.

"It's been hours, and still none of this makes any sense," he says. "For one, animals and bugs are somehow freakishly huge here? Two, they can't get past the border to eat us, but how did Tails pass through? And three, ghosts here can't die? But what about ghosts from our realm that die—where do they go?"

"Holding," a raspy voice says.

Eddy stops pacing, and he, Tails, and I shoot to Leon. He ascends the stairs before slithering through the snow with his hands in his pockets, and his severed white chain swishes behind him.

"What do you want?" Eddy sasses.

Ignoring him, I fix on Leon who stops a few feet away from us. "What do you mean they're in holding?"

"When ghosts pass on from the Limbo realm, they go into holding here. Then after however long, they're reborn."

"How do you know?" I ask.

"I was reborn."

"Then how do you know about *Bliss*?"

"Simple." Leon shrugs. "I found the fountain. The Hellons showed up and did away with me. I died—passed on into holding. Was reborn. And I've been here ever since."

I stare into his dull gray eyes. "How long were you searching?"

For the first time, Leon cracks a smile, thin and tight. "Long enough to lose track of time."

"Who cares," Eddy says. "We're gonna head out just as soon as I figure out where to go next.... Maybe there's another fountain somewhere?"

Leon smirks. "No, that was the first thing I went looking for when I arrived here. It's best if you two just give up on this wild goose chase. It leads nowhere."

"Says you!" Eddy snaps.

"Woof!" Tails barks, and his powerful vibrations send a shiver down my spine.

"Let's all calm down," I say.

Leon cocks his head to the side. "I am curious, though. How did you tame one of the wild beasts so fast if you just arrived here? Only tame animals can pass over the border."

I glance up at Tails. "Beasts? Tails is a dog."

"All dead animals are *beasts* in The Dump."

The roach from earlier flashes through my mind, and goosebumps invade my cold arms.

"We didn't tame Tails. He came with us from Limbo," Eddy says, folding his arms.

Leon raises a brow. "You...killed him?"

"No, we didn't kill him!" I shout in outrage.

"Woof!"

Leon motions for an answer, but I hesitate, searching for the right words to sound—less crazy and—more sensible. "He, uh, jumped into the fountain with us."

"Into the fountain?" Leon repeats, incredulously.

"Oh, that's right, you never made it that far," Eddy jeers, striding toward Leon. "Unlike you, we're actually gonna make it." He stops just a couple feet away. "Unlike you, we have the ticket to *Bliss*."

I sigh as confusion overcomes Leon's face, and then I raise a hand. "That would be me, allegedly."

"Allegedly?" Eddy whirls around to me, his expression softening to that of a sad puppy. "You still don't believe in *Bliss*?"

I rise to my tail, slinking over to him and Leon. But now away from Tails' fur, I hug myself—freezing. The intense winter weather numbs my limbs, and I fasten my jaw to keep my teeth from chattering. "Honestly, I keep going back and forth. But after what happened in there"—I gesture at the bar—"I'm not so sure it does."

"Don't listen to them," Eddy pleads. "Slixx…"

Suddenly, the shack's front door bangs open, and a gang of ghosts climb the stairs. I recognize Kaplone and a few others from the crowd, but they pay us no mind, simply laughing on their way through the snow. Their baggy clothes, mean mugs, tattoos (yes, those follow you as a ghost), and criminal smiles tell me they're up to no good.

Backing away, Leon starts after them.

"Where are you going?" I ask.

"To work," Leon calls out over his shoulder. "Similar to humans, ghosts have to make a living, too. Maybe you three could get jobs in the city. They're always hiring there, though the work may be a bit taxing."

"Work?" Eddy scoffs.

"What do you do?" I ask aloud.

Leon fades into the distant fog, waving a hand. "Nice meeting you three. Take heed of what I said!"

Eddy groans as Leon disappears. "Screw you!"

"Relax." I exhale an icy breath, heading back over to Tails. I bundle up in his warm fur, and he places a paw around me. "What ever happened to calm, cool, collected Eddy?"

Eddy stares at the ground. He doesn't say anything for a minute, but afterward, he lifts one of his arms and gazes down at his flickering skin. "I just wanna make it."

"But once Mr. Strife dies, you're just going to wind up here anyway," I say. "We can get jobs and find peace here—"

Eddy turns to me, deadpan. "For eternity?"

"Well, unless something happens and we go into holding."

I crack a smile, but Eddy's lips remain flat. He shakes his head. "Do you think this is funny?"

I want to say *kind of*, but I bite my tongue.

"I'm tired of living, Slixx. Maybe it's all the death I've seen in Mr. Strife's life. Maybe it's remembering that in my past life I died in a hospital bed. Maybe it's living but not yet being alive. Whatever the case, I'm finding *Bliss* and passing on—with or without you."

Just as he starts to walk off, I shout, "Let's say you find *Bliss*, what exactly is supposed to happen to you? Rebirth as a human? Heaven? The humans have so many religions, which one do you believe in, Eddy?"

He looks at me with cold eyes, and I search them, unable to ever understand him. Snow continues to fall from the infinite gray sky, white droplets piling atop both me and Eddy's shoulders. We stare at each other so long that Tails begins to whimper.

Then finally, Eddy starts off through the snow.

"Where are you going?" I ask aloud.

But he doesn't answer.

Tails whimpers, nudging me to go after him.

I look away, though. "He doesn't even know where he's going. Let's just go to the city, boy. We can start our new lives there."

CHAPTER 15

THE CITY

After asking Gryner for directions, Tails and I set off on a journey to the city. We follow along the horizontal border from when we first arrived, and the dense fog shrouds the speakeasy behind us like a fading memory. Above, the gray sky remains hopeless while the snow persists. Still, Tails and I keep moving.

When your tail feels like it's about to fall off, keep walkin' 'cus you ain't even close. But when it feels like a match lights up a gallon of gasoline in your lungs, you're halfway there. That's what Gryner had said, but judging by my bodily pain, we should already be there.

My tail burns, and a fiery sensation fills my lungs. I've been wheezing for—what feels like—hours. Not to mention, my whole body has gone numb from the icy weather. Even Tails slows down, his paws dragging in the snow. I assume either the cold has finally gotten through his thick fur, or he's just as exhausted as I am.

The next few kilometers, I begin to trip over mounds of snow. I keep my eyes on the ground—on the countless tracks and tail-prints—though. Many ghosts must've slithered through here, and I wonder how far this realm dates back, if it does.

Tails whimpers before suddenly stopping. He bends down and gestures his nose for me to get on his back.

The corners of my mouth pinch, but I shake my head, peering into his weary eyes. "I'm fine. I can walk."

However, he whines, insisting.

I consider our unknown trek and look ahead at the endless snow. It goes on and on for miles, and the fog shows no sign of letting up either. Reluctantly, I climb aboard his back, scrambling up his fur. Then, we continue onward.

It's not long before roaches clash against the borderline. Their large heads and antennae ram against the invisible wall, which deflects them back, but they crawl fast and hard. And more roaches join them, too.

Out of nowhere, a shadow casts over me and Tails. I gasp. Tails flinches, staggering back, and I grip his fur for dear life as a big black eye blinds my vision. And just then, a giant blue and white bird swoops down. It snatches up a mouthful of roaches in a snap before flying away.

Spooked, Tails gallops back from the remaining insects. He tucks his head down with a whine. We both watch the persistent roaches who continue to ram against the invisible wall, and then a spider crawls out of the fog and clashes against it, too.

I shiver, averting my gaze from the bugs. "Don't look, boy," I tell Tails. His body rises and falls, and his heartbeat races beneath me. I slink up to his neck and motion for him to look away. "Gryner said they can't get through, remember?"

He whimpers.

"It's okay," I whisper as he inches onward. "We're almost there. We've got to be."

Following along the border, spiders, roaches, ants, beetles, flies, centipedes, and other abhorrent critters bash their heads and legs against the invisible wall to get to me and Tails. Most fall behind, while a couple insects trail us—mostly hideous roaches. Freakishly huge birds swoop down from time to time and gobble up mouthfuls.

Meanwhile, Tails and I take breaks every so often. Tails collapses in the snow, and I sprawl out on his wide back. We rest for a short while before continuing our journey ahead.

Later, shock hits me as "nighttime" befalls the realm. The gray sky grows darker and darker until it's nearly pitch-black outside. A mass of swirling darkness substitutes for clouds, and the fog thickens to nearly unbreathable. Tails and I take more breaks than before, but after one too many, we decide to wait until "morning."

We rest in the middle of nowhere, and I watch the tinted sky above. The darkness drifts without purpose while an unfounded hint of light keeps the realm lit. Despair and dread taint the air as I fight to breathe. I lug in heavy breaths—winded—all night.

In the morning, the fog thins enough to breathe easier, but by then, I fade in and out of consciousness. My vision toggles, doubling everything in sight. I crumple on Tails' back as my chest heaves up and down. Despite being bundled in his fur, I shiver. More droplets of snow fall on my bare skin, and at times like this, I wish I would've died in a big ski suit.

Tails trudges on, though. I hear his paws slosh through the snow, and he pants, his tongue hanging out of his mouth. But not once does he whine. He carries our new duo like a leader and guardian, and if I could speak coherently, I'd pet his soft spot and whisper sweet words into his big ears.

FADING BACK INTO CONSCIOUSNESS, I squint at our new surroundings. We pass through a slum of tall decrepit buildings that tower over us, and chipped paint peels off at their sides. With busted windows, they appear dark inside like ancient ruins—creepy even for a ghost.

I muster what little strength I have to sit up, and even stranger, I don't see a single ghost in sight. I shiver as if someone's watching us, looking over my shoulder every five seconds.

Meanwhile, Tails leads us through a narrow main alley, several other smaller alleyways running between the buildings. It's big enough for Tails to walk through, but his shoulders graze the sides of the buildings, tearing off the chipped paint. While on the ground, debris litters the pavement—high mounds of snow on both sides.

More shivers overcome me as I search our shady surroundings. I crane my neck around in every direction, half-expecting an ambush or attack.

Tails must also sense something's off because he lowers his head.

"It's okay, boy," I croak—my throat drier than a desert. I click my tongue for an ounce of saliva, but there is none. My mind instantly shoots to the Plasgood drink I had back at the bar, craving that bittersweet flavor once more.

When we reach a dead-end, we follow an alternate path left, and as soon as we turn the corner, we see *it* in the distance. The pavement turns into a mighty steep hill, Tails and I standing at the top, and at the bottom lies a big glittery city.

Tails' head perks up at the large shiny entrance gates below, and I gawk at the thousands of ghosts swarming the plaza. I strain to hear the city's noise, consisting of faint voices and construction.

Even taller towers loom below, but these look brand new, freshly painted, and unscathed. Glitter shimmers everywhere, reflecting off the buildings' windows, like sunrays over an ocean. The tainted atmosphere of the realm seems to shift to a vibrant one down there. Countless ghosts hurry through the crowded plaza—busy, busy, *busy*—as flashing buildings' signs light up, beckoning them in.

In the middle of the plaza, I spot a small pond, and beside it, a statue of a cliché sheeted ghost, likely built to poke fun. I chuckle at the funny monument. "I think we're going to like it here," I say to Tails. "You thirsty, boy?"

"Woof!" His tail wags back and forth in excitement, and his eager tongue hangs out of his mouth, giddy. He stomps his paws against the ground as if readying himself for launch, so when I point for full speed ahead, he takes off like a bullet train.

Clutching his fur, I hang on for dear life. The wind whips my hair back, and my curls fly across my face. I spit strands out of my mouth as the gust makes my eyes water. The commotion of the city grows—remote banging and clanging of construction work and loudening voices.

Tails sprints the whole way, likely running on adrenaline. The city looked close from the top of the hill, but after countless yards, we finally reach the shiny silver entrance gates. Tails comes to a complete stop before letting me off his back, and then we both look up at a dazzling sign overhead that reads, **Nosscapé**.

Up-close, I peer inside the gates in awe of all the ghosts. The plaza looks even more crowded, but everyone slithers along with a smile. Some ghosts may bump shoulders in a hurry, but they just continue on their way, grinning. No other pets or giant animals roam about, though.

I look up at Tails. "Let's just get to the pond and go from there. Try not to make yourself look so big."

Tails raises one of his floppy ears before crouching down at an odd angle, low to the ground yet still huge. He tucks his head down like an overgrown mouse, and then he raises his other ear as if to ask *how's this?*

"Perfect," I giggle.

Then, we both enter the city and get swept into the crowd. Tails and I both move slow, trying not to stick out, but surprisingly, no one stops to eye Tails or looks at us funny. He carefully maneuvers through the crowd by wedging each of his paws between the many ghosts. Meanwhile, I keep a hand on one of his front legs, caressing it as we move along—mostly to calm my nerves. However, the many smiles around me do that with ease, infecting me, and I smile, too.

Tails guides us straight through the crowd to the pond.

Now in the center of the plaza, even more ghosts rush to-and-fro in haste, and I wonder where to. They don't carry briefcases or work bags like humans, just themselves. After Tails lies down and begins to drink the clear water, the crowd maneuvers around him, still not paying him any mind. They happily mind their business as we rest up.

"Welcome to our new home, boy," I say to Tails, but I doubt he hears me over his loud slurps. I wave at a passing ghost, remembering Leon's mentioning of finding work here. "Excuse me?"

But the ghost slithers right past me.

"Maybe he didn't hear me," I mutter before waving at another. "Excuse me!"

The next one rushes past me, too.

I furrow my brows. "What the...?" I call out to another ghost who does the same thing, and then another and then another. But they all ignore me like I'm invisible. So, I decide to take matters into my own hands and jump in front of the next ghost I see. He's a short one with a rather large belly. "Excuse me!"

Smiling, he tries to veer around me, but I sidestep him.

"Hello?" I call out in his face.

He tries the other way, but I cut him off.

"I know you hear me!"

Abruptly, the short man spins around to turn back, but I run around to stop him. I wave a hand in front of his face before gripping his shoulders.

"What's wrong with you?" I shout in unison with a construction bang.

The man suddenly leans in close to my ear and whispers, "Get out while you still can."

I freeze at the sound of his icy voice.

Pulling back, he widens his tight smile and tips his hat to me. Then, he scurries along like a ghost in the night never to be seen again, and by the time I snap out of my scary daze, a familiar bark pierces the air.

I whirl around in horror.

"*Aroooo!*"

Tails howls out in pain as a gang of ghosts in black masks injects him with several needles. He whimpers another howling cry, sluggishly swiping his paws at them, but they dodge his attacks. He puts up a weak fight as whatever serum spreads throughout his body. And in a matter of seconds, his eyes shut, and he collapses to the ground.

"Tails!" I yell, dashing back over to him. I only manage to take a couple steps though before a sharp pain nabs at my neck. I whirl around but already feel the ground slipping from under me.

A couple feet away, a ghost with baby blue eyes scowls at

me. He wears all black—a robe and a mask—like the rest, and he watches closely as I stagger about.

Struggling, I will my hand to my neck and yank a needle from my skin. "What is this?" I shout, but even my own voice sounds distant. "What..." I fall to my knees as my eyelids grow heavy. "Is..."

Everything goes black.

CHAPTER 16
ZOMBITIZED

My head hurts, heavier than a boulder. It weighs me down like the rest of my body, and my limbs are as if unattached noodles. I flutter my eyelashes—even that feeling disconnected from my body. The tiled floor is the first thing I see. Then I notice I'm sitting on a wooden chair with shackles around my wrists. I will my hands to move, but they resist.

"What is your name, girl?"

Lifting my heavy head ever so slightly, I look up at a woman standing in the center of the large room. The walls appear narrow in width—solid drapes covering the many windows—but the end of the room stretches so far it makes my eyes hurt. So, I fix on a middle-aged woman. She wears a long, unflattering, scarlet jumpsuit and looks old enough to be a mother with wrinkles—maybe an early grandmother. With her hands behind her back, she leans over with a slight hunch, while two ghosts in black masks stand guard beside her. I sense a third one behind me, though.

"What is your name, girl?" the woman repeats with a hint of annoyance, enunciating each word. "I will not ask again."

It's not that I didn't want to answer or was too scared, but rather my tongue flipped inside my mouth, unable to form words. The aftereffects of whatever they stuck me with must linger inside me.

"No matter," the woman says. She strides toward me with powerful, commanding steps before stopping a few feet away. "We don't care about your name, where you came from, how you got here, how you died, how long you've been dwelling this realm, or even if you want to be here. All we care about is the decision that you're about to make."

I try to say, "Decision?" but it just comes out as a muffled groan.

"Number Ten," she commands.

The guarding ghost from behind me walks around. He carries two glasses on a silver platter: one purple with foam on the top, the other flat blue. He kneels on one knee before me, and I furrow my brows at him, peering into those familiar baby blue eyes.

"There are but two choices in this city—both falling under the umbrella of work," the woman says aloud. "We have our trusty builders and our diligent harvesters. Which one will you be, girl?"

I want to ask, 'what the hell are you talking about?' But instead, another long groan escapes me.

"Choose your poison."

I stare at the woman a long beat, searching her bitter eyes. She keeps a straight face and doesn't move a muscle. Lines curve around her flat mouth, and deeper ones run at the sides of her eyes. She scowls down at me like a supreme force.

"Now."

I curse at her, but it just comes out as a groan. So, I shake my head.

She lifts a single brow, but the rest of her face remains a

statue like she used to get tons of Botox when she was alive. "Tip your chin and pick one, girl," she grits through her teeth. "I have very little patience."

I mutter until somewhat clear. "Yhagl...yanle...ghalez...ails... Tails. My dog?"

"Your dog?" She inspects her polished nails, nonchalant. "You mean that tamed beast? We do owe you gratitude for bringing him along as we will be putting him to work soon. It's so hard taming those animals without sacrificing hundreds of ghosts to do so."

"Wherever he goes, I go. Put us together—we'll work wherever."

"Pick your poison, and it just might happen."

She meets my gaze, and now we both glare at each other. I clench my jaw, scanning the guarding ghosts. I contemplate an escape plan for a second, but every scenario seems futile, especially without Tails.

Reluctantly, I gesture my head at the flat drink.

"Excellent choice, harvester," the woman says, smirking. "Good luck with your new job. And always remember, smile when you walk through my city of Nosscapé...or work overtime."

"Whatever. Will I be with Tails?"

The ghost holding the platter rises to his tail and holds up the drink I chose. He looks to the woman for a signal, and when she flicks her wrist, he suddenly pours the drink on me. I gasp. The warm blue liquid runs down my curly hair and my entire body, a sticky residue instantly setting in.

Two guards then undo my chains by flicking a switch on them near the floor. The cuffs pop open, freeing my wrists, and I jump up to charge at the lady. However, my tail sweeps from beneath me, and I fall flat on my face. Next thing I know, two guards lift me up by my arms, dragging me out of the room. My vision toggles over the evil lady as the guards lead me into a pitch-black hallway.

Closing the door behind them, the guards zigzag me through this maze of a building. They keep a firm grip on my shoulders and arms, but based off my recent faceplant, I can't wield my sticky body to move even if I want to—liquid still dripping from my hair. Not to mention, I'm completely blind, engulfed in total darkness. Nerves begin to claw at my skin.

Minutes later, one of the guards turns a knob, and a door creaks open. They lead me down a set of stairs, which go on forever. Even though they're dragging me, impatience gets the best of me. I groan and sigh, and my voice echoes off the finite walls, tunneling throughout the stairwell. However, the guards pay me no mind.

After what feels like a million stairs later, we finally land on solid ground, and they open another door. My head and body don't feel so heavy anymore, the remains of whatever serum they injected me with almost completely gone. I even wiggle my tail a bit and now slither on my own. The guards keep their holds on me, though.

One of the guards then turns another knob, and a wave of light hits me. I reach up to shield my eyes, but the guards grip me tight. I turn my head instead, recoiling, as the guards usher me outside.

Once my eyes adjust to the dull gray sky above, I take in my surroundings. We walk along a spacious pavement, countless buildings and numerous alleys on either side. I look up at the towering buildings as familiarity washes over me.

"Where's Tails—where's my dog?" I ask, remembering me and Tails following this path to the city.

The guards keep their mouths sealed. As we approach the end of the main alley, they veer right down a narrow alley. The three of us can barely fit, so they turn me sideways.

"Where are we going?" I ask a bit louder, catching whiff of a tough citrusy smell mixed with a rusted pennies odor. "Answer me!"

Behind all these buildings, we reach the end of the short alley where the pavement ends, and it opens up to a large light-green lake. Hundreds of ghosts populate the clearing, which is enclosed by a forest. They all float in the water, freezing with frowns. Cold breaths seep out of their mouths, and their chattering teeth permeate the quiet air. They hold themselves, shivering.

Meanwhile, more ghosts in black masks and robes stand watch on land. More than twenty of them surround the lake, staring down at the many ghosts with mean-mugs as if *daring* them to try something.

"Get in," one of my guards says, both of them pushing me forward.

Of course, I stumble but catch myself. I shiver from the cold air, solidifying the sticky liquid onto my skin, and droplets continue to drip from my damp hair. Whirling around, I march back over to the guards that led me here. "Where is my dog? That lady said we'd be together."

"Negative," one of the guards says without looking at me. "The drink you chose was for harvesting not building. You may see your beast after work today."

"*Harvesting?*" I breathe.

"Break is in a couple minutes, so hurry and get in. We need to produce as much Plasgood as possible."

I narrow my eyes at him. "Plasgood?"

But before I can ask another question, both guards shove me with such brute force that I trip and go diving into the green lake. The water hits me like daggering icicles. I swallow a mouthful before figuring to hold my breath. It's as if a million tiny needles stab my skin, and a bitter coldness eats through my flesh. Willing my limbs to swim, I bump into other ghosts and their chains on my way up.

I pop up to the surface with an immense gasp and choke out water, my throat burning like a furnace. My teeth instantly begin to chatter while my body goes numb, and I barely keep myself afloat.

Out of my peripheral, I slowly look down at my arms and see green particles peeling off my skin. They float to the top of the water before turning clear, and then I notice the same thing happening with every ghost around me. Green layers peel off their bodies and dissolve in the water, too.

"What is—?" I start to ask.

"No talking!" a nearby guard shouts.

I flinch.

"Plasgood is to be produced in peace and quiet!"

I squint at the guard for a long moment. "You call this peace? This is torture."

"Quiet!"

I suck my teeth, shaking my head. "I'm getting out of h—"

The guard kneels in one swift movement, and two others do the same. In the blink of an eye, they snatch my hair and dunk me under the water. I squirm and scream, letting out a barrage of bubbles, but they hold me under. After a minute, the water starts to scald my eyes, and green particles peel off my skin by the boatload. The little energy that I have quickly dwindles with each punch and kick.

More time fleets by as I grow weaker. Water forces its way down my throat, and I close my fiery eyes. Breathless, I lose the strength to resist and give in—to *death* (how ironic). I let the water into my lungs and allow my limbs to fall to my side. My mind flashes back to Tails, and as for my last thought, *I wonder where Eddy is?*

Suddenly, the hands from above yank me out of the water. I grip the land, hacking up water and fighting for my life.

"Five-minute break!" a guard calls out.

I lug the rest of my body out the water just as the hundreds of other ghosts get out, too. They slither around me or even over me, and I cough as they step on my back. Scrambling to my tail, I glare at the masked guard before scurrying to the edge of the forest. I take post at a tree like the others. No one speaks aloud nor to each other—not even the utterance of a peep.

That's when I try to connect the dots in my head. *Plasgood.... Harvesting.... The green lake.... The particles.... The bar back in Snowdevlin Village.... Get jobs in the city. They're always hiring.... The best stuff's in the city.... Harvesting.* Just then, the dots connect, and I slurp in a frosty breath.

Plasgood is blood.

"Last minute," one of the guards shouts. "Harvesters, start making your way back to the lake for the last harvest of the day!"

Wide eyed, I stare at the green lake in horror. All the ghosts amble past me, and they do so with exhaustion written all over their faces. They reek of despair, emptiness oozing from their aura. They walk like zombies toward a subzero doom, and not a single soul protests.

I tap a blond ghost that trudges past me, but he simply glances at me and continues on his way. I inch over to another ghost who does the same. In my final attempt, I jump in front of the next ghost, cutting her off. When we lock eyes, I stifle a gasp at the Kiara look-alike. She has long black hair and light brown skin, and a certain sense of loss plagues her eyes.

"Why do you do this?" I whisper.

She flicks her eyes from me before bumping past my shoulder. I expect her to ignore me, but instead, she responds so low I barely hear her. "Believe it or not, it makes eternity mean something." Then, she's gone.

"Time for the next harvest!"

Taken aback, I stand there in awe, replaying the girl's words, until two masked ghosts push me toward the lake. Their strength sends me flying forward, and unable to regain my footing (or tailing), I skid into the water.

"Payment will be given upon completion of this harvest!" Underwater, I barely make out the shouting guard's words. "Then you may return to your quarters for the night. Now, let the last session begin!"

As I swim to the surface, my mind wanders. Multifarious questions fuel my thoughts as I marinate on what that girl said. The lifelessness in her eyes and the hopelessness of her soul ingrain into my head, and no matter how hard I try, I can't shake it—nor this place. Nor this *life*. Maybe for the same reason humans pray in their time of need, I begin to ponder the possibility of something more—something better. A life worth living. A joy worth fighting for. And then I wonder, *did Eddy ever make it to Bliss?*

CHAPTER 17
UNEXPECTED DROP IN

Turns out, payment for today's work is just two glasses of Plasgood. However, now that I know what—or *whom*—I'm drinking, I dare not take a sip—no matter how good it is. And I know it's good because the hundreds of other harvesters gulp theirs down as they all slither into the alley. After their first drinks, their eyelids droop down, and their mouths curve up into tipsy smiles. Then after the second drink, they all begin to stumble like drunks, mindlessly babbling to each other.

I give away my glasses to a random ghost and stay behind, though. My tail sloshes snow to-and-fro as I stomp to the nearest guard.

"Where's my dog?" I demand.

"The harvesters get off earlier than the builders," the tall guard says, straight-faced. "The builders should be here any minute to complete their last task of the day. You may wait in the alleyways for your beast. And as for rest, since you're clearly new"—he side-eyes me—"choose any tower outside of the city to live in. That will be your permanent quarters."

I search his vacant eyes which stare off into the distance. His soulless gaze resembles that of the Kiara lookalike and every other ghost around here, as if living but not yet being alive. I ball my fists, rage welling in my chest, and a brief moment passes before I find my words. I want to push him—for a reaction—or throw a fit, but I flash back to the guards drowning me underwater.

Swallowing my pride, I scan the many masked guards. "Can I leave?"

The guard narrows his eyes and flicks his attention to me. "Pardon?"

"Can I leave?" I repeat. "What'll happen if I try to leave this city?"

"Nothing."

"Nothing?"

"Nothing." He returns to staring off into space.

"So, what's the point?"

He looks down at me. "Of?"

"Living?" I breathe in disbelief. "If you're not holding all these ghosts hostage, then why do they stay here?"

"Provided quarters. Nice pay of Plasgood. Work. This is similar to how humans live. They work. They die. Here, we work. We remain dead—but we have *purpose*. Suffering is just a part of the universal cycle."

I shake my head. "It doesn't have to be."

Suddenly, the ground trembles, and I whirl toward the northside of the forest. The trees quake while the leaves rustle about. Snow spatters off the branches, and bits of it tremor upon landing. Nature stirs as tremendous footsteps approach. I hear the pests before I see them, but when a roach's antennae pop out of the trees, I jump back. It slowly crawls out, followed by a thick black spider with tiny white hairs, three centipedes, a black cat, two rattlesnakes, and a golden retriever—Tails—and they all hold rusty pails.

Just as I start to run forward, the tall guard slams me back, and I fall to the ground. *"Aghhhh!"*

Snow flies up around me, pain seizing my backside. I moan as I roll over to my knees, and a sudden howl cuts through the air. I know that cry—that whimper, that plea.

Scrambling to my tail, the ground trembles, and when I look up, Tails breaks line and runs toward me, a giant pail jangling in his mouth. He only takes a few steps though before a long whip lashes his side. I trace the weapon down to a masked ghost holding it, and my body moves as if a mind of its own. I try to run to Tails again at the sight of another lashing, but the tall guard and two more shove me back.

"Tails!" I cry out, managing to keep my balance this time.

"Aroooo!"

Crack! Crack!

Tails collapses to the ground.

Tears well in my eyes, a barrier of hands separating me from him. We stare at each other from a distance that feels like countries away, and the misery in his dark eyes breaks me. A lump forms in my throat. "Tails," I croak.

"Aroooo."

Crack!

"Get up!" the lashing guard commands Tails.

Tails struggles to his feet, the rusty pail squeaking in his mouth. His paws dig into the snow for footing, but his head stays low. When he rises to a stand, that's when I see the fresh whippings on his side. They cut into his skin, red blood on the surface.

If I had a heart, it would shatter into a million pieces.

The guards push me back, farther and farther until I'm back on the pavement in the alley. They stand in front of me like a ghost gate, ready and willing to restrain me if need be. I don't try anything though. Instead, I lean against the buildings for support. Riverbeds singe my cheeks while snot scoops into my mouth.

"You may see your beast once it's done with its work," one of the guards says, stone-cold. "The first day is always the hardest, but you two have infinite chances to get it right."

"*Infinite chances?*" I mutter, sinking down to the ground.

Peering through the cracks between the guards, I watch Tails and the other animals fill their pails with the fresh lake's Plasgood and head back into the forest. After a while, they return with empty pails and do it all again. Fill. Sulk. Dump off somewhere. Come back. Fill. Sulk. Dump off. Come back. Fill. Sulk...

IN THE MIDDLE of the clearing, I hug Tails as the rest of the animals retreat into the forest. They head on home like the guards who disperse as well. Only Tails and I remain near the lake, nighttime fast approaching. I stroke his snout but dare not look at the lashes on his body up-close, refusing to shed any more tears.

He whines aloud.

"I know," I say in a low voice. "Let's leave this place and never come back."

Tails falls silent.

I look down at his drained eye, and without even uttering a sound, it's as if he whispers, "*And go where?*" He doesn't move a muscle, stiller than ice. It's as if he's lost his spirit and given up, and a piece of me dies inside.

He barks, and even without translation, I know exactly what he says. He cries out to me for better—for us to *find* better. For us to find *Bliss*.

In that moment, Eddy pops into my head. I trace him from

his thick eyebrows to his elbow pads to his ankle bracelet, and his infamous smile haunts me. The memory quickly downturns, though, upon remembering our parting from each other. Determination shone in his hazel irises, and fervor saturated his mind. More than anyone, he was dead set on going to *Bliss*. Again, I wonder if he made it.

Craning his neck, Tails looks up to the sky and shuts his eyes. *"Arooooooooooooo!"* he howls, agony and despair embedded in his voice.

I fix on him as he howls over and over again under the leaden sky. Each cry strikes me like a punch to the gut or a jab to the face, smashing me into pieces. I clench fistfuls of snow at the onset of a loose tear, and my breathing becomes unsteady. I suck in air. Then, I spit it out. The anguish in Tails' final cry cuts me to the core, and I dry my face, standing up.

Tails rises with me and rolls onto his stomach, intently gazing at me with questioning eyes.

I crack a smile. "Okay, let's—"

Out of nowhere, a horn sounds in the distance, coming from beyond the forest. Then another sounds from the city, and the two horns blow in unison.

Tails jumps up to his paws, and I whirl around the forest in terror like we're about to be ambushed. The horns keep blaring in alert. I start to run toward the forest but think better of it and dart toward the alley. But then I stop myself again, searching the clearing in panic.

Choosing the alley, Tails and I make a run for it across the clearing. I sprint past the lake before slipping into the narrow alley, but then Tails' whimper stops me. I whirl around, dumbfounded. Tails stampers in front of the alley—too big to pass through—and I mentally kick myself. I double back to the edge of the pavement, cursing myself out.

"Sorry, boy," I say, petting his big rubbly nose. "I'm going to go check the main alley real quick to see if I can ask someone what's going on. Stay here. I'll be right back."

He dips his chin.

Then, I take off down the short narrow alley before bursting onto the main alley. I whirl around in search of someone—anyone—but there's not a soul in sight. The loud horn coming from the city blares even louder, so I plug my ears. I jog down a bit and check the other various alleys but still don't see anyone. A literal ghost town.

With time of the essence, I scan the area one last time before hurrying back to Tails. But just as I veer back down the short narrow alley, a distant voice calls out, "Tails!"

I furrow my brows, thinking I'm delusional. I must be hearing things. I run faster toward the voice coming from the clearing, but once I reach the end of the pavement, a gang of ghosts bursts into the alley. They quickly scurry past me with rattling white chains, so most of their faces blur before my eyes. I catch sight of the last lanky one, though. He wears plaid with elbow pads, and I instantly know—

"Eddy?" I gasp.

He stops a couple feet away. "Slixx?"

"Sheets?"

I lean over, looking past Eddy, and my jaw drops. "Kaplone? What are you guys doing here?" I ask, but then I notice they're both wearing straps, kegs attached to their backs. Fresh wet stains on the ground catch my eye. I scrunch my face and look up at Eddy. "Are you stealing Plasgood from the city?"

"Not, not exactly," he says, waving his hands.

"Yes, exactly," Kaplone chimes in. "How else yuh think we get our drinks back at the bar?"

"What happened to *Bliss*?" I ask Eddy. "Because that's where me and Tails are going."

Eddy jerks his head back in shock. Before he can say

anything, one of the other gang members calls out from the main alley.

"Enough with that fantasy. We have to go!"

Standing on my tiptoes for a better view, I squint at the ghost in all leather. "Leon?"

Bang! Bang!

We all duck as gunshots sound off nearby. Another round fires off, approaching from the clearing, and we all hit the deck. Leon flinches. Kaplone hunches over like a snail in its shell. Eddy lunges over to cover my head.

"How do guns exist here?" I cry out.

"Yuh be surprised—anythin' can be made wit' Plasgood!" Kaplone says.

Just then, a thought overcomes me. "Tails!" I shout, weaseling from under Eddy.

I run toward the clearing, but just as I step onto the snow, a bullet hits the left building, inches from my head. Eddy grabs my wrist and pulls me back into the alley. Tripping over my tail, my body follows his force, and we both hit the building. I bump into him, our chests touching and our noses mere inches apart. My cheeks go ablaze, and my mind swirls about. We gaze into each other's eyes for just a moment.

Bang!

"Tails," I whisper, yanking away from Eddy. My tail moves without command, and I stumble out onto the clearing with my arms over my head. I do a quick scan of the area. Tails nowhere to be found. About ten masked ghosts charge my way with shotguns. The one at the forefront puts his gun to his eye and aims at me.

I suck in air.

Eddy pulls me back into the alley in the nick of time.

"Tails...gone..." I pant.

"Sheets, Flicky, we gotta go!" Kaplone cries out over the

gunshots. He dashes off in short strides, and Leon disappears down the main alley, too.

Eddy grips my shoulders. "Where'd Tails go?"

"I-I don't know. He was there before..."

BANG! The gunshots now fire off so close as if they're right next to us. *BANG!*

"The gunshots probably scared him off," Eddy says. "He's got our scent. He'll meet us."

He nods, so I nod—fright and alarm in my chest. And we both keep nodding at each other until he grabs my wrist and races toward the main alley. Once we turn onto it, Kaplone, Leon, and the other few gang members come into view up ahead. They all run with full kegs like Eddy's, Plasgood splashing around inside.

It's not long before the masked ghosts turn onto the main alley, too. They shoot at us from behind, firing off dozens of rounds one after another. They shout "thieves" and "bandits" among other insults, demanding us to stop.

"I'm not even a part of this burglary!" I cry out.

Eddy flashes me a smile. "You are now!"

We and the others duck at the overhead gunshots, but when the bullets shoot at our tails, we all hop up like in a game of double-dutch. Stray bullets ricochet off their kegs, and over-flowing Plasgood spills out the lidded tops. The other gang members call out to us, but their voices get lost in translation, stifled by the shootings. However, Eddy and I get the message when they all split up. Each of them swerves off the main alley and darts into separate ones.

A blaze of bullets fires at me, but Eddy flings me down the nearest alley, and they miss by just a hair. I run in front of him since the narrow path can only fit one person at a time. My curly hair blows back, and my dress tassels in the wind. Tails consumes my thoughts as a thousand questions shoot through my mind.

"Aye, get yuh own alley!" Kaplone complains up ahead, glancing back at us.

"What's the plan?" Eddy shouts.

"Stay up and don't get caught, Flicky!"

I start to wiggle out of Eddy's hold. "I'm just going to go back and explain to them I'm not with you guys! Me and Tails were just leaving and—!"

"Like Ms. Scarlet would eva believe dat!" Kaplone calls out.

Without any description, that name alone rings a bell. I flash back to the middle-aged woman in a scarlet jumpsuit from when I woke up inside one of the towers. My lips twist at the thought of her deep scowling wrinkles, and I have to reluctantly agree with Kaplone. She'd probably interrogate me in a chamber for eternity, accidentally kill me, find me after holding, and then do it all again!

Gunshots fire behind us.

Flinching, all of us duck. Bullets ricochet off Eddy's keg as Kaplone makes a sharp right turn up ahead, disappearing. I run with all my might, but a bullseye was bound to happen.

"*Aghhhh!*" Eddy shouts, stumbling.

Just as we turn the corner, I look back over my shoulder and gasp at the blood gushing from his tail. I look up into his pained eyes and squeeze his hand. Facing forward, the alley cuts off, and I lead us into the forest. The trees are sparse yet dense—big enough for animals to pass through—and countless pawprints, insect tracks, and ghost tracks litter the snow.

"Hang on, Eddy!" I say.

We zigzag into the forest, running like blind mice. I search and search to no avail for Kaplone. No sign of him. I don't even hear anymore gunshots—only the sounds of our restless chains. Either the masked men ceased fire and gave up, or they're lurking on the prowl for us. Indecisive, I go back and forth between the two as Eddy moans in pain.

"Which way...that way...?" I mutter to myself, scanning the ashen green trees.

Eddy drops my hand.

I spin around as he falls to his knees. His straps slide off his shoulders, and his keg rolls to the ground, Plasgood leaking out onto the snow. He falls back against a tree, slumped over, and clutches his wound at the butt of his tail.

Rushing over, I reach out to touch him but stop myself—terrified and unsure. "Eddy," I breathe. "Are you okay?"

"Yeah," he grunts, braving a harsh smile. "Just...give me a minute."

With trembling fingers, I gaze down at him. Tears burn the back of my eyelids, but I do my best to keep them at bay.

"I'm fine, Slixx—really.... I just...need a minute. That's all." He gives me a thumbs-up, but in a snap, I smack his gory hand down. His eyes widen in shock.

"Stop," I croak. A loose tear breaks through the barrier and cascades down my face. "Remember what you told me back in Limbo when I tried to save face about Kiara? Stop it."

His gaze wanders down to the snow.

I rip a piece of my dress off before grabbing the end of his tail. The bullet slowly oozes out already, so I wiggle out the rest. I then wrap the cloth around his wound, tying it tight. "A deep wound like this is definitely going to heal super slow."

"Thanks."

I fix on him, but he simply stares at the ground. "No problem."

"What made you change your mind?"

"Huh?"

He peers up at me as if bearing into my soul. "About *Bliss*?"

I take a moment to consider, choosing my words carefully.

The entire day shoots through my mind in fragments, and the humiliation, desperation, and despair make my stomach churn. "I think...I'd rather spend eternity searching for paradise than find purpose in misery."

Eddy watches me like a hawk, unmoving. His straight face and cavernous eyes block me out of his head, and I have no clue what he's thinking. We stare at each other for a long moment. But truth be told, I wouldn't mind gazing into his shimmering hazel eyes for hours—days, weeks, maybe even an eternity.

Out of my peripheral, a black shadow catches my eye, and I snap up. I squint at a short hatted man who weaves into view several yards ahead. He runs like a hobbling penguin, rocking from side to side, and his keg rocks with him.

Cupping my hands around my mouth, I jump to my tail. "Kaplone!"

Abrupt gunshots fire behind us—nearby enough to flinch— and chains clank into action.

Kaplone ducks but keeps running.

I start to call out again since maybe he didn't hear me, but the gunshots grow closer. "Can you walk?" I ask.

Eddy nods, but he uses the tree for support upon scrambling to his tail. I put one of his arms around my neck and clench my jaw as he shifts his weight on me. We then pick up cadence and run, our chains rattling behind us. His injured tail barely slithers, though.

"You weigh a lot for a skinny tall guy," I mutter.

He cracks a smile. "Did I complain all the times I saved *your* life?"

"*Tch.*" We duck as multiple rounds fire off. "Whatever."

Keeping an eye on Kaplone, we follow him through the forest. The trees work in our favor by taking the many missed bullets shot at us from behind, but Eddy and I move too slowly on account of his injury. The gunshots fire as if right on our tails. Even though I want to look back at how far the masked ghosts are, I dare not turn around, fear quaking my bones. We continue limping along.

Up ahead, Kaplone jogs to a stop, and his body turns hazy. I blink to clear my vision, but it's not me. I squint through the snow, but he remains a blurry shadow.

Eddy and I exchange uneasy looks.

Pushing onward, we sprint the last stretch, bobbing, ducking, and weaving between trees. Barrages of bullets fly over our heads and skid past us, but thankfully we make it to the end of the forest unscathed.

After a few more steps, Eddy and I burst out of the forest and into a thick foggy abyss. Kaplone's white chain and body solidify as we approach him, and then the rest of his gang comes into view. They all stare up with wide eyes, heads tilted back.

"Sorry, I lost my keg," Eddy says. "What are you guys looking...?"

We both trace the gang's gaze up into space, and I gasp. All the working animals from before surround us. The deadly rattlesnakes hiss while the roaches' antennae clash together. The three centipedes lurch back and forth, ready to charge, and the black cat winds back on its hind legs. With eight eyes, the spider's ugly little face scowls at us, too.

"Unbelievable," Eddy gulps.

Just then, all the masked ghosts run out of the forest, and dozens more emerge through the fog. They spread out around us, standing in between the animals with their guns game, while their severed white chains act as camouflage. They hold their guns to their eyes, and their fingers rest on their triggers.

"Eddy, plan?" I ask in a low voice.

"This wasn't even my plan to begin with."

"Kaplone?" I ask.

"Sheets, this might be the enduh the line for a while, but let's meet back up at the bar afta holdin'."

Whirling to him, I furrow my brows, wondering how he can so easily accept *death*.

"DROP THE PLASGOOD AND TURN YOURSELVES IN," a voice cries out from the enemy line. It echoes up to the sky from the valley of snow.

"L-let's just do what he says," I stammer. "Maybe then they'll let us go."

"Speakin' from experience, Sheets. Don't matta what yuh do now. We all goin' to holdin'."

I shake my head in disbelief, throwing up my hands. "No. I'm innocent! I—"

A low growl suddenly creeps into the sticky moist air. I wheel around, scanning every direction. Eddy, Kaplone, and the rest of the gang search, too, and even the line of gunmen looks around. As the growl grows, the animals act first. The insects begin to scatter, but the snake and cat hold their ground.

Leaping over the enemy, a big dark animal soars through the air.

I slurp in air as my mouth pulls into a grin. "Tails!"

CHAPTER 18

PROOF

Tails plows down to the ground, and snow whips back all around. Eddy, the gang, and I shield our faces, but our hair and chains belt in the wind. The snow thrashes against me, knocking me back. I trip over my own tail, but just as I'm about to fall, Eddy pulls me back and into his chest.

His back takes the brunt of the white whipping. I peer up into his closed eyes as he grunts, and then I notice the blood seeping from his wound. Without thinking, I wrap my arms around his waist, clasp my hands, and spin us around. The snow beats against my back now.

I grit my teeth.

"Slixx," he whispers under me.

"Can't say I never saved you!"

"Woof!"

I barely lift my head before a bulldozer rams into me and Eddy. We both fly up into the air, but soft fur breaks our fall. Sitting atop Tails, I look down at his golden coat, unable to stop smiling. I bend over to hug him, but he jumps back as a lash of snow hurls our way. I topple over like a ragdoll.

"Sheets!" Leon lunges over and grabs my arm. He holds onto Tails' fur with one hand and yanks me up with the other. "Must I save everyone around here?"

Another lashing of snow hurls up from the east, but before it rains down on us, I catch sight of the perpetrator's thin green eyes—the black feline. Using its paws, it chucks up snow from a distance. More lashes blast at us as white blinds my vision. I hang onto Tails' fur along with Eddy and Leon, and upon looking over a bit more, I see the rest of the gang hanging on near Tails' tail, relentless with their kegs still on their backs.

"How do we get outta here?" Eddy cries out.

"Good question, Flicky!" Kaplone shouts, hanging on to his hat.

Tails stampers back as the snow finally starts to settle.

"But like I told yuh before, ain't no way out!"

Sliding off his straps, Leon unexpectantly kicks his keg overboard. The other gang members gasp his name, but he points straight ahead. His raspy voice comes out deeper than an alto. "Either drop your kegs or plan on taking a trip to holding because those are your only two options!"

The gang members stare at him in awe for a moment, but then they reluctantly take off their kegs and push them to the ground—even Kaplone who watches his plunge to the snow.

Tracing Leon's raised hand, I fight the urge to recoil at the sight.

Not only do all the animals and gunmen surround us like before, but now a giant spiderweb entraps us. Thick silk weaves from the ground up to the foggy sky, and multiple layers overlay one another. The dark black spider with a broad back peers at us at the forefront of the enemy's round line. It begins to creep closer along with the hissing snakes, yellow venom dripping from their fangs.

At the center of the chaos, Tails takes a step back but has nowhere to go.

Kaplone takes off his hat and slides to the edge of Tails' back, and the rest of the gang follows him. "Jigs up," he says. "C'mon, guys."

Leon stays put, though. "Kaplone—"

Kaplone glances around at the enemy closing in on us. "Meet back at the bar. See yuh, pal." He then waves two fingers and slides down Tails' back, and the rest of the gang trail him. They all hang onto Tails' fur before landing on the ground with a tuck and roll.

Leon curses under his breath.

"For someone who gave up on reuniting with the love of his life, you sure don't like to quit," I say.

"I didn't give up!"

Just a couple yards away, the enemy creeps toward us, confining us to a tight oval. Below, they shout commands at Kaplone and the gang who do as they're told. The gang walks with their hands up, slowly passing between the cat and insects, but then without warning, the gunmen knock them upside their heads. They fall to the snow like corpses.

"Kaplone!" Leon shouts.

Tails stampers in place, whimpering, so I pet him with shaky hands. Fear quakes my bones and chain as the spider nears us with its eight beady eyes. My stomach also churns at the sight of the two centipedes—whose legs clack into motion —and prowling black cat.

Both Tails and I recoil—me more so in disgust. A shiver tingles my spine, but I fight the urge to shake, balling my fists. "Somebody do something! Me and Tails have somewhere to go."

"Sorry, Slixx."

I spin around before locking on Eddy.

With his head propped on his chain, he lies in fetal position, clutching the end of his bloody tail. "I'm not really...of much use right now."

"Eddy," I breathe, scrambling over to his side. "Are you okay?"

"Healing," he grunts. "Slowly but surely. But by the looks of it, we'll be in holding soon."

"Don't say that!"

Below, a few gunmen break line and retrieve the gang's fallen Plasgood kegs. The rest advance in multiple rows, like roman soldiers, until just a few yards away from us, and then they all take their marks. "LAST CHANCE. TURN YOURSELVES IN NOW."

Ice spreads through my chest as Tails whimpers. Yet, my fingernails dig into my palms, and a beckoning will proliferates from my gut. I clench my jaw, analyzing Eddy's pale face. "Are you coming to *Bliss* with me and Tails or not?"

His vexed eyes flick up to me.

"Would you quit babbling about your dumb fantasy," Leon mutters. "We better get down before they shoot us up here. If you die in long-range pain, you get reborn that tenfold."

"I'd rather die on my dog than die at the feet of the enemy."

He turns around to me, and we both glare at each other. Neither of us blink. Neither of us say a word. Grotesque noises —clicking and hissing—sound from the nearby animals, but we just stare at each other for a long, silent moment.

That is until the gunmen shout out one final command, and Leon averts his gaze. He turns away from me and scoots to the edge of Tails' back, raising his hands to the enemy. "Suit your-selves," he says in a low voice before sliding down. But just as he does, a blinding white light bursts out of nowhere.

Both Eddy and I shield our eyes.

"What is that?" I shout.

"I don't know!" Eddy says.

High above, the light radiates like an eclipsing sun, and the gunmen behind me cower from it, too. It dazzles the entire area, dipping our sight in stinging shimmer. The rays twinkle and beam with zest, but then after a moment, I notice the gunmen put their arms down. I wonder if it's safe to look. *Maybe the light has dimmed; maybe my eyes have adjusted; or maybe I'll go blind.* I contemplate for another split second until Tails pokes his head up, and I decide to look, too.

Big mistake.

I gasp as if the air's been vacuumed out of my lungs.

Ruby eyes bear into mine. Verquen. He stares at me—or rather *through* me—aloof yet focused.

My lips quiver to speak, but nothing comes out.

"My Ticket to *Bliss*," Verquen says, and his glassy voice makes my skin crawl. He caresses my cheek. "The time has come for you to show me the way."

I reach up to smack his hand, but it's as if I'm trapped in a daze. His sinister yet beguiling face paralyzes me, erasing all thought from my mind. The longer I stare at him, the more a snaky lust slithers into my body.

Although when gunshots erupt, I snap out of it. Fear overcomes me, and I gasp back into myself. Tails jerks his head down, knocking me off balance. I try to latch onto his fur but can't get a grip. I squeeze my eyes shut as an immense pressure builds behind me. Elliot flashes through my mind. Face to face with *the* gun from my past. A crippling dread eats away at me as I spiral to my demise.

"Frost Fix!" Verquen cries out.

I wait to crash land in the snow, but after a moment, the still air beckons me to open my eyes. When I do, Tails' fur shades my vision. I then look up, and my jaw drops at the frozen barrage of bullets overhead. I glance around at the many shells mere feet away. Behind, even all the gunmen and animals appear motionless. They don't move a muscle.

However, what startles me the most is *myself—floating* in midair. I bring my tail down as if I'm about to swim, but I can't move from this spot. I squirm to no avail until a hand extends down to me.

I trace the palm to its source before swatting it away. "What'd you do?"

"Slixx!"

"Eddy?" I shout.

"Who are you?" Leon asks.

"I have come to retrieve my Ticket to *Bliss*," Verquen says.

He then flicks his index finger, and I float up into the air, lighter than a feather. I kick and flail my arms but just keep rising. I round over Tails, and Verquen guides me through the air until hovering before him. He holds me for a moment, inspecting me from head to tail, and it's then that I notice *his* new tail. It's long, like his former human legs and curves from under his cloak, but I now realize the black chain around his neck must be his actual link. I wonder why his is *black*, though.

Questions start to swirl in my head, but then he drops me in midair. I land rough on my back, and Tails whimpers from the impact. *"Agh,"* I grunt. "Sorry, boy!"

"Look," Leon says, "I don't know who you are or what they've told you, but *Bliss* doesn't exist."

Verquen flips his platinum hair to Leon, expressionless. "You do not believe that."

"Excuse me?"

"What's going on?" Eddy calls out in the background.

"You are a loss believer," Verquen continues.

"How do you know that?" I chime in.

"Because I can read his soul. Leon Craftsmith. Human Profession: Medical student. Cause of death: Blood loss. Age of death: Twenty-two. Died with much regret. Years in The Dump: One-fifty. Current occupation: Thief. Am I missing anything?"

Leon seals his lips, gulping. "You can freeze time, read souls, and appear from some heaven like a God? Exactly who are you?"

For the first time ever, Verquen cracks a smile. A corner of his mouth pinches, and a single wrinkle curves around it. "I am no God. And I am from someplace opposite of 'heaven.' I have come for my Ticket to *Bliss* as she will lead me there to finally pass on."

Leon shakes his head. "It-it doesn't exist," he mutters.

"Because *you* have never found it—because *you* cannot. Only Tickets can, and they are but rare jewels that die with regret." Verquen rips his gaze to me. "I am afraid we must be going now, Ticket."

"Like hell," I spit, scrambling to my tail. "I'm not going anywhere with you. Me, Eddy, and Tails are going to find *Bliss* ourselves."

Verquen cocks his head to the side, inquisitively. "You ticketed fool. What look of discovery and horror will mask your face when you realize that they cannot get in."

My voice comes out so low and weak that I barely hear myself speak. "What?

"He's lying!" Eddy yells.

Gunshots erupt again. They sound loud, long, and drawn out as if in slow motion, and gradual gunfire smokes in the distance. The once-frozen bullets begin to move through the air, too. They near us atop Tails' back while new ones fire simultaneously.

Verquen whirls to me, extending a hand. "Will you come without a fight, my Ticket?"

I flinch. "You'll have to kill me first."

"No matter."

He heads for me, lifting his cloak. And just then, smoke

begins to seep out of his mouth, and his body starts to fade with it like before. Eddy hurriedly limps to me, but Verquen's faster. His long, able tail propels him forward as he speaks with each stride. "My ability is wearing off, and those deathly bullets are quickly approaching. I will spare you this time, Ticket. But when we meet again..."

I try to take a step back but teeter on the edge of Tails' nape —about to fall off. Verquen slithers inches from me, and I turn my head. His smoke cocoons us. I try to push him away, but he flicks his index finger, forcing my hands down. He then cups my chin and whispers into my ear.

"You will lead me to Bliss. Thirty seconds."

When his hold crumbles from my skin, I break away. "Thirty seconds?" I whisper, searching his dissolving icy eye. But then it hits me as the last of him fades away in smoke. I suck in air. *Thirty seconds to escape.*

Tails moans aloud, quivering.

"Slixx, are you okay?" Eddy asks a couple feet away.

I shift from him to Leon, who still stands in shock. Thirty seconds. Without a word, I do a quick scan of all the bullets closing in on us at different angles, and although they speed up with each passing second, they're still relatively slow. Thirty seconds. I stroke Tails' fur as an idea strikes me.

"Full speed ahead!" I shout. "You guys better hang on because we're charging through!"

"Are you mad?" Leon snaps. "Those are bullets, shooting at *us.*"

"Yeah, Slixx, we can't—" Eddy starts.

"If a bullet train hits someone at two hundred miles per hour, would it hit the same at half speed?"

"What?" both Eddy and Leon ask in unison.

I roll my eyes before clutching Tails' fur. "I believe in you, boy. Let's go!"

Charging ahead on command, Tails keeps his head tucked down. He burrows through the giant spiderweb full force and tears through the thick silk barrier with his canines. With every bite, he growls in his throat, mustering every ounce of strength to barrel through.

Atop his back, I bury myself in his fur while swatting down bullets with my tail. I use as much force as I can, and the bullets go flying in the opposite direction. They're picking up speed, though. At first, they only hit with a sting, but as they grow faster, they hit like heating fire.

I look up ahead just as Tails leaps into the air, ripping through the web with all his might. The many overhead bullets hit him, but he doesn't waver. He soars over the rows of gunmen.

"Aroooooooooooooo!"

Now at regular speed, the fiery bullets zip through the air.

I grit my teeth as a stray shell grazes my shoulder. "*Agh.* Almost there!"

Finally bursting out of the spiderweb, Tails lands with a stumble, but he doesn't stop. He continues running—far away from the enemy behind us—into thick fog. Fresh gunshots fire at us, though. Two more scrape past my arms. A yelp sounds from either Eddy or Leon. Tails' fur belts back like my curly hair, and his gashes bleed like mine. We all suck it up, though.

That is until Tails collapses miles away.

IN THE MIDDLE OF NOWHERE, Eddy, Leon, and I fall off Tails' back. Piles of snow mound around Tails, and more plops up as I hit the ground, my chain coiling around me. I instantly seize my shoulder, but my arms hurt almost as bad. I feel for a hole or bullet, but thankfully, they're only flesh wounds.

Eddy, however, groans aloud.

I scurry over to his side, and my eyes widen at a deep bullet lodged in his neck. Blood oozes out as if from a leaky pipe. Eddy points to his throat, emitting muffled choking noises. I stare in horror, frozen. He gestures for me to help, but I *can't*. For a brief moment, I wonder if I should dig it out, but all the gore makes my stomach churn. Vomit wells inside me. Making its way up my throat. I—

Green gook spews out of my mouth and stains the pure white snow.

"Move!" Leon shouts, scampering past me with a hand inside his long vest. His rattling white chain clinks loud in haste.

I wretch once more before turning around. But then my mouth falls agape as I stare at Leon's fingers in Eddy's throat. "What are you doing to him?" I shout, but he's already pulling out a small silver bullet with forceps.

Eddy gasps in a breath like he's just been saved from drowning, but then his eyes roll to the back of his head. Blood now squirts out of his open wound, and I can't help but gag. Meanwhile, Leon rummages through his vest, revealing the many Velcro pockets inside, before snatching out what looks like a thick towel and gauze.

I throw up, again.

When I look back up, Leon firmly presses the bloody towel to Eddy's neck with both hands. He snaps to me and jerks his head for help. Beneath him, Eddy flickers in and out faster than ever before.

"Sheets, I need you to dig in my pocket for a syringe!"

I watch his lips move but don't hear a word. He repeats himself twice more before I snap out of it, and without thinking, I do as he says. He yells for me to look inside the left side of his vest and retrieve a syringe from the bottom corner pocket.

And I do everything he says until he orders me to draw my blood.

"I'm not sticking myself with that thing?" I shout.

"A plasma transfer could save your friend!"

I clench my jaw in fright, staring down at the dastardly syringe. My fingers tremble.

"In case you haven't noticed, he's dying!"

"I know that!"

"Then save him!"

I hesitate.

"Now!"

Squeezing my eyes shut, I look away and stab myself with the syringe. The pinch hurts worse than the bullets, and it takes all my willpower to pull the lever to draw blood.

"Slow and steady," Leon says, but his voice drowns to the back of my head.

"Is it full?"

"Keep going."

"Is it full?" I repeat louder.

"Almost there." Just as I open my mouth to ask again, Leon calls out, "It's full!"

Yanking it out, I try to hand it to Leon, but with his hands tied, he looks from the syringe to Eddy to me. We exchange uneasy eye contact, and then what he's trying to say washes over me. "I'm not sticking him!"

"You *have* to."

"Why can't you do it? We can switch positions."

"If I move from this spot, he'll die, Sheets. You've got to do it."

My gaze trails down to Leon's bloody hands and Eddy's ghastly neck, only the whites of his eyes visible. I shake my head.

"Stick him on the left side of his chest—where his heart's supposed to be."

"I-I can't..." Eddy's choking noises morph into gargles, and I recoil. I want to crawl into a hole. I want to escape from this crime scene. I want to go back to Limbo. I want to be anywhere but here.

However, Tails' whimpering rips me back to reality.

I puff out a breath before ramming down the syringe. I refuse to look, but I feel the scary needle jam into Eddy's chest. Reluctantly, I follow Leon's instructions and slowly inject my plasma into Eddy.

It takes a second, but Eddy finally stops gargling.

I slowly glance at him over my shoulder—damn near traumatized.

He now lies with his eyes closed, and his face appears relaxed. Although he continues to fade in and out, the rate returns to normal speed, flickering intermittently. He now rests easy beside his seemingly infinite purple chain—bound to his human, Mr. Strife, somewhere in Limbo.

Sliding one hand into his pocket, Leon pulls out a bandage. He removes the towel, wraps the bandage around Eddy's neck, and collapses in the snow. His black leather outfit sticks out like a sore thumb.

"Is he okay?" I ask.

Leon sighs. "He'll be fine."

I exhale in relief. After a still moment, my adrenaline dies down, and the wintery weather begins to chill me. I cross my arms and shiver. "Aren't you cold?" I ask Leon.

"After a while, you get used to it."

I think back to what Verquen had said about him. I contemplate whether or not Leon even knew he'd been here a hundred and fifty years and how time works here. But just as I engross myself in thought, I look back at Tails and become breathless.

He lies on his side with his long tongue hanging out. He chest quickly rises and falls, and he inhales rapid breaths. Red blood stains his fur coat. Bullets ooze out of his skin before falling to the ground.

A yell gets caught in my throat as I run to him, and then suddenly, my knees buckle. I tumble into the freezing snow. My eyelids droop down as my body fades from me. I try to call out to Tails, but my limbs beckon for rest.

Leon ambles past me to Tails. "I forgot to mention a side effect of the plasma transfer. The donor becomes extremely fatigued. Nevertheless, don't worry about your beast—pet. He'll be in pain for a little bit, but he'll heal quickly." He walks around Tails, inspecting him. "There doesn't appear to be any fatal wounds like Flicky's."

I turn my head to Eddy, who remains unconsciousness.

"He'll be alright," Leon says, petting his nose, and Tails snuggles under his touch.

"How'd you even...?" I ask, unsure what I'm trying to say, but he gets it.

"I used to work part-time at an animal hospital in my past life." Leon slides down beside Tails, and a hint of jealousy consumes me. "Back in the city, I ran into this guy when me and the gang were on the run, and we just hit it off."

"On the run," I mumble, slowly. Words flow out without me even thinking. "Why'd you want to become a doctor?"

He pauses for a second. But then he cracks a smile and gazes up at the hollow sky. "A deadly plague killed my city. My dad and I were one of the few lucky survivors. Ever since that day— watching all those bodies in the street, piled on top of each other in the dumpsters and overflowing the graveyards, so many corpses that the officials started burning bodies—I vowed to cure the ill-stricken. Years later, my dad came down while I was in medical school. I was going to save him...but then...a tsunami hit. I don't know what became of him."

With each blink, my eyelids grow heavier, and my consciousness slips further away from me. "I'm sorry."

He faces me, but when he speaks, his voice goes in and out as I hear every other word. "A year later...another plague swept through the country.... I kept bleeding.... Red everywhere... everything faded to darkness.... But no matter...I'm dead now.... Wanted to ask you...Verquen...*Bliss*...ticket...?"

I blink once. Then twice. And then, I'm out like a light.

CHAPTER 19

WINDSTORM

"So now *you're* a believer?" Eddy mocks.

He, Leon, and I all sit atop Tails as Tails walks onward into the unknown foggy abyss. I sit at the forefront on his neck and grip his fur, Eddy and Leon doing the same behind me. Initially, Eddy tried to hold my waist, but I swatted him off.

Around us, all is quiet except the sounds of paw crunching snow and rustling chains.

"Where did that Verquen character come from?" Leon asks. Oddly enough, he's been asking me and Eddy a bunch of questions about our journey through the realms thus far.

I side-eye him, though, and Eddy turns up his nose. Leon's searching gaze shifts between us for answers, but we both give him the cold shoulder.

"Well?" he presses.

I sigh. "For the last time, we don't know. He's a serial killer who followed us here from Limbo. He believes I'm the ticket to *Bliss* and am going to lead him there. A bunch of nonsense."

"But it's true," Eddy chimes in, his tone now soft.

"No offense," Leon says, "but why is *she* the ticket to *Bliss*?"

I feign hurt. "Ouch."

"Well, for starters, this Verquen guy showed up at our dead-end town and killed humans and ghosts—" Eddy says.

"Technically, he didn't *kill* the ghosts in Limbo," Leon interrupts. "They passed on here to holding—"

Eddy talks over him. "Then, Slixx's human died, but she didn't."

"That still doesn't explain how—?"

Eddy speaks even louder, so I lean away. "Out of everybody, *her* chain snapped, and *she* didn't pass on. *She* led us to the fountain—"

"Technically you did," I mumble.

"And this almighty Verquen guy's been stalking us ever since! Slixx's the ticket to *Bliss*—she's gonna lead us there!"

Leon folds his arms. "Still sounds like fantasy to me."

"Nobody asked you to come," Eddy says. "Shouldn't you be heading back to the bar anyway?"

"Shouldn't you be heading back, too?" Leon snaps. "You did join the crew, remember?"

I chuckle. "He's got a point there."

"Heyyyyy!" Eddy whines.

"Woof!"

Giggling, I pet Tails' head. "You feeling better, boy?" He barks in response, and I smile. Then, he barks again as if to ask *where are we headed?* "Uh, we should probably figure that out. Guys, where are we going?"

"So much for a ticket," Leon says, coldly.

Unable to speak with conviction, I bite my tongue.

Eddy leans forward at eye level with me. "Where do you think we should go?"

Unease and uncertainty sinks into my skin, and I tense. "Umm..."

"Let's try The Myriad Desert of Dreams," Leon blurts out.

Both Eddy and I whirl around to him. A moment of silence passes by before either of us speaks.

"Why are you here again?" Eddy mocks.

"The Myriad Desert of Dreams?" I repeat.

Leon averts his gaze. "There are no fountains in this realm, but that place has the closest thing to it."

I scrunch my face in confusion. "What's there?" I ask.

"A waterfall."

"A waterfall?" Eddy asks.

Leon nods.

"In the middle of a desert?" I ask.

Leon dips his chin.

"Will it..." I gulp. "Lead us to *Bliss*?"

Leon peers at me with those small catlike eyes of his, analyzing every inch of me. His last sentiment comes out with a hint of hope yet cold and renouncing. His tone holds true to the story he's told us—about Deanna and searching—and now without a doubt, I know that he once believed in *Bliss*. That is until time told him to give up. "It's the closest I ever came. Worth a shot."

He, Eddy, and I exchange glances: Leon's longing; Eddy's eager; and mine anxious but ready. Tails breaks our mute dialogue, though, with an animated bark, and his tongue-hanging smile warms my soul.

When Leon points west, Eddy immediately questions him, but Tails sets off. Eddy and Leon bicker back and forth for miles. Even though I try to tune them out, Eddy's yapping pierces my ears. I sigh countless times, occasionally chiming in with "shut up!" They don't listen, though.

When the sky begins to darken, we set up camp and rest in the middle of nowhere. Only snow surrounds us. Leon strays away from us for fresh air, while I pet Tails. He closes his eyes at the touch, letting my hand gently glide down his golden fur.

Beside me, Eddy plops down in the snow for small talk. His teeth chatter the entire time, but as for me—I don't know when my bones or skin adjusted to this icy weather—I shiver just once.

At nighttime, we take off again under the nearly pitch-black sky. Leon swears he knows where he's going by following the murky clouds, so Tails follows his directions, leading us through the thick fog. However, when I look up at the sky for directions like Leon, I only see swirling darkness above.

Tails' walk eventually turns into a run sometime during Eddy and Leon's arguing match. I sigh the whole way, preoccupied with the dull, snowy landscape. Later, we rest awhile before setting out again. Run. Argue. Sigh. Rest. Run. Argue. Sigh. Rest. Run...

The cycle tires itself out well before we arrive at our destination.

Under the dim daylit sky, Tails trudges through the snow—now perfectly healed. The couple bullets that penetrated his skin have oozed out, and his ghostly healing ability has patched his wounds and scratches up. Meanwhile, Eddy still clutches his tail. He's no longer bleeding from there or his neck, so I can't tell if he's just being overdramatic or is still in pain. As for myself, only scars remain. And as for Leon, I don't notice any injuries other than his leather snagged in a couple spots.

"The Myriad Desert of Dreams is just up ahead," Leon says from behind. Both Eddy and I look back at him. He points straight ahead, and we follow his finger. "You all might want to brace yourselves."

"For what?" Eddy and I ask in unison, both of us obliviously peering through the fog.

Even Tails utters a confused moan.

"The windstorm," Leon says. "It's upon us."

I furrow my brows at him. "What windstorm?"

But instead of answering, Leon bends over and grips handfuls of Tails' fur. He buries his head down, too—appearing ridiculous in the calm air.

"Start talking," Eddy says, folding his arms. "What wind—?"

All of a sudden, a humongous gust erupts. It rams at us full force and even blows Tails back. A blast nearly sweeps me away, too, but Eddy catches me by my waist. My hair whooshes back as curls cover my face, and my chain whips overhead in the current. I swallow my screams, shutting my eyes tight.

"Keep going!" Leon shouts from behind, his voice muffled yet audible.

Beneath me, it feels like Tails is moving, but I can't quite tell. I keep losing my balance, unable to get a grip on his fur. I jerk around like I'm on a raging horse or wild bull. My skin stings from the thrashing snowstorm, and my mouth dries to a desert. I yelp, but the sound doesn't come out.

Opening one watery eye, I squint down at Eddy's thick brown hair. His head is buried into my side, and one of his elbow pads wraps around me. I only catch a glimpse of Leon's same rigid form in the back until another gust hits me. I yank myself down just in time or else I might've really been swept away.

I heave bushels of Tails' fur in my rough hands. And even though I don't hear it, I know he whimpers in pain, and a pit forms in my stomach.

"This is it!" I shout over all our clattering chains.

"We have to make it to *Bliss*!" Eddy says.

"Keep going!" Leon yells at Tails.

Another gust lashes from ahead, and a heap of snow knocks me upright. I strain to keep my balance, but then another wave hits me. Not even Eddy's grip can save me from this one. The wind hurls me into the air, and my screams get lost in the gale. My entire body tenses, either frozen numb from the weather or discombobulated from the chaos. I squeeze my eyes tight in horror as my chain belts in the wind. Ironically, thoughts of death race through my mind, and I can't shake the thought of holding and rebirth.

All I hear is the wind as it batters my ears.

Mustering the courage, I flick open my eyes. Bad idea. The spanking white snow blinds my vision, and the harsh wind brings tears to my eyes. With no sign of Eddy, Leon, or Tails, I glue my chin to my chest and seal my eyelids again. My chest pounds hard as if I have a heart. A massive pressure clamps around my throat, choking and sucking the life out of me. Death awaits me.

Or so I thought.

I continue to aimlessly flail in the wind until it abruptly lets up. Oddly enough, a heatwave now burns beneath my skin, and the chokehold around my throat vanishes. Too scared to open my eyes, I plummet to the ground in terror—hoping the snow will break my fall.

My body, however, blisters from the sudden heat. Maybe it's coming from inside my horrified bones, or maybe I'm hallucinating the temperature change. Either way, just before I hit the ground, I open my eyes to a lush golden caramel color. Then...

BAM!

My landings always suck. I alight flat on my face with a thud, and a brisk pain travels throughout my body. That becomes the least of my worries, though, because I start to *sink* into the ground.

Startled, I jerk my head up and look down. I narrow my hazy eyes at the tiny grains of sand beneath me. The land swallows my hands before stopping at my wrists—thankfully this is regular sand and not quicksand. The foreign terrain extends out in front of me, and I trace it several yards away to three blurry figures.

After a moment, my vision toggles from fuzzy to clear, and I see Eddy, Tails, and Leon who all run toward me. Eddy and Leon's tails and chains slither in the sand, leaving an imprinted trail behind them, while Tails leaves pawprints. The tiny particles of sand around me jumble into the air as they near.

I slowly scramble to my tail, the pain reducing to a minute sting.

"Slixx!" Eddy cries out in the distance.

I wiggle my tail to make sure I can walk, but it falls flat. So, I limp toward everyone. (Meaning, my tail slithers but falters, and I nearly trip each step. It doesn't really hurt, though.)

Hurrying over, Tails ambushes me first. He licks me, and his long, thick tongue knocks me over. I fall back onto the ground, and sand plops up around us. The warm air brings out his scent of sugary almonds, enticing my nostrils. Any ounce of pain temporarily fades to the back of my head as a buttery sensation soothes inside me. I try to ward Tails off, laughing, but he licks and licks until he's satisfied with his barrage of love. He pants so hard that his whole body heaves up and down. He even scampers around me—restless.

His barks sound like music to my ears, a sweet angelic verse. I spin around to catch him, and when he stops, I kiss him on the snout.

His mood, however, flips like a switch, and his tongue rolls back into his mouth. He peers at me with a knowing intensity before dropping on his hind legs and reclining on his front ones. Although he's physically huge, he somehow shrinks down to comfort me—as if sensing my pain. He whines.

"I'm okay, boy." I caress his paw. "Really. It was just a minor fall. I'll heal in no time."

Just then, Eddy and Leon run into view.

Eddy's eyes light up. "Slixx!"

"Are you injured?" Leon asks straight away, scanning me from head to tail. He fixes on the minor scrapes and cuts on my upper body before staring down at my tail. He analyzes the purple bruise on it and reaches out to touch it, but I swat him away.

"For a stone-cold leather brute, you sure are a softie," I say.

"Doctor instincts," he replies.

"Correction"—Eddy sidesteps in front of Leon—"*medical student* instincts. You probably failed the test."

Leon folds his arms, stalking off. "*Tch.* You don't know what you're talking about."

Eddy then turns to me, and once again, his expression softens to that of a sad puppy. "Slixx, are you okay? What happened?"

I gaze into his promising hazel eyes for a moment before brushing past him—before I can get trapped in his charming spell. "I'm fine." Limping back to Tails, I find Leon. "Hey, Christopher Columbus, is this The Myriad Desert of Dreams place?"

He nods.

I slowly dip my chin, the previous chaos rattling about my head. "So, what the hell was that windstorm back there?"

Eddy's eyes widen, and he storms to Leon, snatching him by the collar. "Yeah, we could've gotten killed!"

Unfazed, Leon simply stares at him. "Even so, only temporarily." He slaps Eddy's hands off him. "But if you two must know, each terrain in this perilous realm is different, and windstorms are the gateway in."

"Like a deadly border," I joke under my breath. "You people must not travel too often then."

"Well since you know everything, where's the waterfall, genius?" Eddy asks Leon.

Leon jerks his chin, gesturing behind us.

I lean back over Tails' paw and put a hand to my forehead to block out the bright light above. I glance up in search of a sun but only see blinding rays of various hues streaming about the sky: crimson, canary, amber, and a hint of periwinkle. Averting my attention back down, I spot huts in the distance. They just look like square dots, so I squint to get a better picture and discover miniature villagers roaming about.

"Where's the waterfall?" I ask.

Leon mounts Tails' back and takes a seat near his tail. "In the village, of course," he says.

I narrow my eyes at his smart mouth.

"How long is it going to take us to get there?" Eddy asks.

"Not long if we run," Leon says.

I follow Eddy aboard Tails, and I take a seat at the front. Eddy tries to sit close, but I shoot him a death stare. "What's so special about this waterfall, again?"

"And how's it gonna lead us to *Bliss*?" Eddy adds.

"I never said it *would*." Leon's quick reply casts thick doubt into the air. "I said it was the *closest* I ever came to it."

"Pray tell," I say, leaning over to one of Tails' ears. My voice falters to a whisper. "Are you okay, boy? Do you need to rest a bit?"

He doesn't bark or utter a sound, and I get the feeling he wants to ask *me* those questions instead. But truthfully, most of the minuscule pain has subsided. I kiss him on his thin-haired dome as reassurance, so he sets off with an enthusiastic bark.

"There's a cave under the waterfall, and inside of it, there are hieroglyphics. Seemingly, they appear as just a bunch of pictures with surface tales, but I'm sure there's something more to them."

"Like a code waiting to be cracked?" Eddy mutters, twiddling his thumbs.

I ponder the idea myself. The fountain from Limbo was clearly a riddle, so maybe this next one will be the same. But then again, the riddle from Limbo flowed with ambiguity yet sense. Maybe each riddle is harder than the next. Maybe this time, we might not be so lucky.

But then I look over at Eddy, and I can already tell his gears are turning. I exhale in relief.

"So, all we have to do is crack the code and go to *Bliss*," Eddy says, looking back at Leon, but Leon doesn't meet his gaze.

"If it were that simple, I would have figured it out long ago," Leon says. He crosses his arms as a still moment of silence passes by. "And this '*Bliss*' place still might be just a fantasy."

Before Eddy can say anything, a wretched anger surges from my gut, and I whirl around to Leon. "Then why are you following us?" I snap. "Why didn't you just stay back in Snowdevlin with the rest of your thug-bar friends? No one asked you to come."

Slowly turning his head, Leon's calculating catlike eyes fix on me, his thin pupils keen and still. He pauses for a long moment.

"Or is it because you believe...?" A bead of sweat trickles down my nape—the blasted heat taking effect. "That maybe, just maybe, there's a chance you might be reunited with your beloved Deanna?"

He lowers his head, casting a grave shadow on his face. His detached eyebrows knit together, and his mouth curves into a frown. He reminds me of the prowling black cat from earlier, tamed and clever yet still an outsider.

After another minute, I render his silence an answer and face forward. Eddy mutters my name but dares not push for a response, and then at the height of tension, he even whispers Leon's name.

Locking my mind on just me, Tails, and *Bliss*, I let both of them and the past wash off my back like water down a sewer. Because after living for so long—even as a ghost—you get tired. *I'm* tired.

Immortality isn't all it's cracked up to be.... Eternity is a long time to idle.

CHAPTER 20

AFTER DEATH

"Uh...guys!"

Eddy's voice rattles me out of my nap.

Halfway to the huts, my eyes had become heavy, and I dozed off. The warm weather practically put me to sleep, too, but now as I awake, sweat drenches my face. Beads of it stream down from my puffy hair to my neck. My dress also sticks to my body, wet stains under my armpits. I click my dry mouth for moisture but come up short. (At least the pain from my fall has completely subsided.)

"What is it?" Leon calls from the back, his voice hoarser than usual—dry like he just woke up, too. "Don't fret. Myronians practically worship travelers."

Sitting up, my vision wanders from the bright, blistering sky down to the small village before us. There are dozens of beige huts made of clay with carved-out squares for windows, and at the top of their flat roofs, long wooden bridges connect each hut to another. Large gray stones surround each home, too, while hammocks composed of cheap fabric hang from supporting wooden pillars. Meanwhile, all the white-chained villagers with dark skin—about a hundred or so—kneel before

199

Tails. They all wear long, white, thin tunics that drape around their ashen tails.

I furrow my brows in confusion at the sight. "What the...?"

"This place—" Eddy cuts himself off.

Sliding down Tails, Leon strides ahead to an elderly couple at the forefront of the villagers. Beads of sweat trickle down the sides of his face.

Unlike all the villagers, the couple wears zealous sapphire tunics with golden embroidery stitched around the necks, and instead of kneeling, they bow their heads. Their flawless chocolate skin shimmers under the radiant sky, glowing with much melanin. A few pleasant wrinkles decorate their faces, but their age only projects from their gray hair.

When Leon stops before them, he bows his entire body at a ninety-degree angle, and they look up at him with wide smiles. Although Leon's much taller than them (and everyone else), the dominant energy in the air stems from the elderly couple.

"Lovely to see you again, Mrs. Gryah," Leon greets before lowering his tone. "Old man."

"Watch it, buck," the elderly man snaps. His flat lips curve down into a natural frown, and his tight, slanted eyes hide his pupils. Not only does his sapphire tunic assert authority but also his presence—similar to that of a commanding military veteran. "Remember, we are the Gryah's—the Chiefs of Myro."

Out of the blue, a blond child shouts "It's Leon!" from the crowd. She even points at him in excitement, but her mother hushes her.

"Leon!" another kid on the opposite side cries out, and in the next second, his name spreads through the crowd like wildfire.

"Alright, alright, settle down now," Mrs. Gryah says, her voice soft yet husky. She giggles in cute chuckles as the crowd dies down, and her healthy afro appears as lively as she. "*Eri Eri*

Spah. Lovely to see you too, Leon. It's always a pleasure having you."

Eddy leans over to my sweaty ear. "Can you believe people actually *like* this guy?" he whispers.

I crack a smile before sliding down Tails' fur, and Eddy follows after me. The heat now boils my skin. It's as if I've been placed in a scorching inferno, and my flesh is being burned alive. While Eddy appears moist and glistening like the villagers, I look like I've just stepped out of a sauna, digesting deep breaths.

As we both inch over to Leon, all the Myronians fix on us with wide eyes. Their jaws drop, gawking in marvel, and it's then that I realize they're not staring at *me*—they're staring at *Eddy*. They watch his skin flicker as he fades in and out of existence. Even the kids point at his chain behind us, which extends off into the distance, and hushed whispers spread through the crowd. The voices die down when we approach the Chiefs of Myro, though.

Unsure how or if we're supposed to, Eddy and I awkwardly dip our heads to the Chiefs of Myro, but they prove to be unresponsive. Mr. Gyrah keeps a straight face while Mrs. Gyrah simply giggles. Meanwhile, the villagers continue staring in awe at Eddy's phenomenal yet dying skin.

Uneasy, Eddy starts to raise a hand to say hello, and I fight the urge to roll my eyes because surely our embarrassing bows just did that. However, just as he raises his hand, the sound of clinking metal fills the whole area. Eddy's hands shoot up. I gasp as all the villagers jump to their tails and switch to attack mode. They pull pocket-sized daggers out of thin air, pointing them outright at Eddy. Even the kids possess small knives!

The villagers at the front of the crowd hold their daggers inches from Eddy's neck, including the Chiefs of Myro. Sweat trickles down his flustered face, and he stares up at the sky as if praying.

"Maybe we shouldn't have come here," he squeals.

Behind us, Tails lets out a low growl.

I glance from the silent but deadly villagers to Eddy, shocked.

Leon, however, steps over to Eddy's side in haste. He shakes his head and dries his hands as if they're wet, and before I can raise a brow at the strange gesture, all the villagers' eyes shoot to him. "He didn't mean to offend!" he says aloud. "He just transcended from Limbo—he's new here—and unfortunately, does *not* know the rules!"

"Y-yeah, yeah, I-I'm new," Eddy squeaks, still scared out of his wits. "D-don't know the rules."

"I can vouch for him. He's harmless."

Eddy clears his throat. "Y-yeah, h-he can v-vouch for me."

"*Gulikwa*," Mrs. Gyrah spits, scowling. Her once smooth and playful face now appears hard and rigid. She keeps a firm grip on her sharp dagger and presses it closer to Eddy's neck, and Eddy gulps. "What's wrong with his skin?"

"I..." Eddy's voice falters.

"He hasn't fully passed onto The Dump yet," Leon cuts in. "His human is dying in Limbo. Nothing more."

The Chiefs of Myro snap to Eddy, and Eddy jumps. They size him up from head to tail before looking him dead in the eyes. "*Perigwa Banti*," Mr. Gyrah grits through his teeth, his tone reigning with bass and power like his sapphire robe. "Keep your hands down unless you want to fight. For we've been burned by travelers before—our kindness taken for weakness—but never again."

Eddy frantically nods in agreeance and jolts his hands down to his side. "Never again!"

The Chiefs of Myro begin to put away their daggers, and the

villagers follow suit. They conceal the weapons up their long sleeves.

"He can be a bit dense, but he's good people," Leon says.

"Don't push it," Eddy slights.

Once all the daggers are away, I finally exhale the breath that I've been holding. I inhale for fresh sandy air, but then the Chiefs of Myro turn to me.

"How about the girl?" Mr. Gyrah asks, beady-eyed.

Tails barks, sticking up for me.

"She's—" Leon starts, but I interject.

"I can speak for myself." My stomach twists into knots, regretting my pride. Even though the villagers' daggers are put away, I gulp. "I just came from Limbo, too. We're on our way to *Bliss*."

Mrs. Gyrah's scowl vanishes, and she flutters her long eyelashes in awe. "*Bliss*?" she repeats.

Searching the rest of the crowd, I notice their similar blank expressions. "*Bliss*" spreads through the crowd like Leon's name had, and the chatter grows in volume as if hopeful. I scan various children's grins and the adults' starlit eyes. The tension in my stomach wanes while a fire burns deep inside me.

"Can you guys help us?" I blurt out.

"Slixx—" Leon warns in a low voice.

Suddenly, Mr. and Mrs. Gyrah exchange looks before extending their hands to us. "Come now, my child," Mrs. Gyrah offers me with a smile.

I look down at her hand—hesitant—but she beckons for me to take it. So, I do, slipping my clammy hand inside her dry, adapted one. And Leon takes her other hand, while Eddy gets stuck with Mr. Gyrah. They both look less than pleased, especially considering Eddy's horrified quivering lips.

Mrs. Gyrah takes the lead and ushers us through the crowd of smiley villagers, and Mr. Gyrah follows closely behind. At close range, I scrutinize the many people, examining their glassy dark skin and frizzy blond hair. I only spot a few with long dark hair and one albino. Many have blue irises, while a slim woman with red lenses catches my eye. I blink in disbelief before doing a doubletake, but the woman disappears. One second, I see her, and then the next is as if she gets lost in the crowd.

Mrs. Gyrah pulls me forward, weaving us through the wide-eyed villagers. "Let us have a proper sit down."

"What about my dog?" I ask, carefully trying not to step on her chain.

"Don't worry," she says. "He's in good hands. Since he can't fit in the village, our people will take him around back to join the other animals." She then snaps her fingers, and I glance back to see Tails being herded around the perimeter.

Once we break through the crowd, the villagers disperse. Mrs. Gyrah leads us down one of the many shady narrow alleys between the huts, skylight peaking in through the bridges' cracks overhead. We walk one in front of the other, so Leon temporarily takes the lead until we reach the end of the alley. The next one is a bit bigger. Then, we bypass an open clearing guarded by four wooden pillars, and three hammocks gate the space. Huts dominate the village, though, seemingly clumped together at random yet methodically placed in order.

After passing through another narrow alley, I spot small wooden stands and various supplies behind them—like lumber, gallons of Plasgood, and metal daggers. I assume this to be the market, wondering if we've reached the center of the small village yet.

Mrs. Gyrah guides us through one more alley before leading us to the largest hut. It sits between two smaller ones—the size of those two combined—and has a red carpet at the doorstep.

Although other than that, the square carved-out windows, flimsy wooden door, and everything else looks the same.

Mr. and Mrs. Gyrah only let go of our hands as we step inside their hut. They push the door open, and a loud high-pitched bell jangles at the top.

Immediately upon entering the place, the smell of lavender and cedar hit my nostrils. They enchant my nose, over-whelming my senses, and smoke from burning sage fills the air. It fumes from the back corners of the room, near a primitive clay fireplace.

Gazing in mystic wonder, I follow the traveling smoke to the ceiling before noticing the red painted walls and tiny golden cursive above each window. Red rugs like the one outside litter the floor, and in the center of the room, mats line around a coffee table. On the right side of the room, counters lie under-neath a narrow staircase which leads upstairs.

Mrs. Gyrah counts the four mats with her finger before gasping. "Oh dear, baby, we don't have enough seats! I'll go get another mat." She starts for the staircase like a cute, old, worried lady, but Mr. Gyrah stops her.

"Baby, it's fine, it's fine."

"Since this isn't my first time here, I know what breaking out the mats means," Leon says, lingering by the door. "And I have a feeling you're going to have the same conversation as the one the three of us had before—me, you, and the old man."

"Watch it, boy," Mr. Gyrah snaps.

"I can just make a round through the village and come back later."

Mrs. Gyrah's frowns, but she reluctantly nods. "Fine. One round."

And with that, Leon bows on his way out.

The door slams closed in unison with the bell, and I flash an uneasy glance at Eddy. His nerves appear worse than mine, so I do my best to keep a straight face. Nevertheless, Mrs. Gyrah summons for us all to sit down around the table.

All our chains rattle as we take our seats. I choose the cot nearest the door and recline on my knees. My chain wraps around my tail, while Eddy's chain trails out the door, attached to that same spot back in Snowdevlin miles away.

Mrs. Gyrah beams, while Mr. Gyrah watches us with cold hawk-like eyes. "What are your names, dears?" she asks.

"Slixx."

"Eddy."

She dips her chin. "And what are your stories?"

The gun flashes through my mind followed by Elliot's menacing face, and I gulp, staring down at the table. I think back to the orphanage with my mama, brothers, and sisters. I wonder what became of their merry smiles and childish games after I passed away, leaving them with only bittersweet memories.

"Uh..." I choke.

"Cancer," Eddy blurts out.

I jerk my attention to him. Even sitting down, he towers over all of us in the room like Leon. His clenched fists lie atop his knees as he stares straight ahead, aloof. A drop of sweat drips off the tip of his sharp nose, and I watch it fall. His elbow pads draw my attention next. This tall, lanky scaredy-cat was once a brave fighter, likely saving face for his loved ones amid pain—like all the times he had for me. Thinking about it, we're not so different.

"I was diagnosed on my seventeenth birthday. Didn't make it to my eighteenth." Eddy clears his throat, his eyelashes fluttering back to reality. He shrugs the tension off, though, like it's that easy. "I passed away the day before."

"I'm so sorry," Mrs. Gyrah whispers.

Eddy's mouth pulls up into a thin smile. "It's fine."

"Death is never fine."

"If only it were that easy," Mr. Gyrah chimes in. He then pans to me. "How about you, er uh, Slixx?"

I blink, and the gun plagues me behind closed lids. I fight the urge to jump, stiffening my entire body. "I...was murdered."

Neither Mr. or Mrs. Gyrah say anything, waiting for me to continue.

However, a lump gets caught in my throat. "Um, I..." Words escape me as my stream of consciousness blanks in fear. My tongue twists in my mouth while my palms grow even clammier. I suck in breaths. The room seems to shrink. A gunshot goes off in my head, and I gasp.

They all look at me, startled.

I pause.

"Did you just see it—your last human moments?" Mr. Gyrah croaks.

I dip my chin, coming back into my body. When Eddy places a hand atop mine, I peer up at him, and his twinkling eyes brighten up the already well-lit room. The lines in his irises dance, extending a hand for a comforting waltz. I yearn to stare longer as my stomach grows light, but my head says otherwise. I avert my gaze and snatch my hand away, too.

"Um, I had a stalker," I finally say. "A kid about my age. He liked me...a lot."

Mr. Gyrah strokes his braided gray goatee. "Weapon of choice?"

"A gun."

"That coward," he curses under his breath.

"I'm so sorry, Slixx," Mrs. Gyrah chimes in. She lays an arm on the coffee table and motions for my hand.

Instinctively, I slip a clammy one into hers, and she lightly squeezes it. In that moment, I remember my mama and how much fun it was pranking her. I allow myself to reminisce the only fragment of my human life, and a wet stream singes my cheeks. I quickly flick away the tear. "I'm fine."

"Hmm, I see you're like your lover," Mrs. Gyrah says.

I jerk my head back, flicking a flustered glance to Eddy, and he meets my stare with tinted red cheeks. My body temperature shoots up one hundred degrees as my face burns hot. I shake my head at the Chiefs of Myro who side-eye us.

"We're not—" both Eddy and I say in unison.

Mrs. Gyrah giggles like a young school-girl. "No need to explain."

"No really—" I say louder than expected. My voice bounces off the walls, and a moment of silence fleets by. My face feels like it's being baked in a furnace. I look to Eddy for help, but he only stares at me like a blushing deer in headlights. His mouth moves without sound, neither of us sure what to say.

"Nevertheless, death is always hard for newcomers." Thankfully, Mrs. Gyrah steers the conversation back on track. "Because—unlike Limbo—The Dump reveals ghosts' causes of death, everyone becomes haunted by their human deaths. It usually stirs in sudden flashes like PTSD, or it may just haunt one's every waking moment. Just depends. But whatever the case, Slixx, Eddy, you two are not *fine*—you're *feeling*. It's all part of the process."

"What process?" Eddy whispers loud enough to hear, sheepish and shy.

"Toward acceptance of your new state in this realm."

"But we don't plan on staying," I interject. "We're headed to *Bliss* to pass on."

As if on command, the corners of Mrs. Gyrah's mouth pinch. "Slixx, what is *Bliss*?"

Taken aback, my lips sink apart. I study her cavernous and wise eyes for a second, and then, Eddy and I exchange an uneasy glance.

"What do you mean?" Eddy asks. "*Bliss*. Paradise."

"Heaven?" Mr. Gyrah offers.

I fold my arms while Eddy cocks his head to the side. "Sure?" I mutter.

"Do either of you know exactly what *Bliss* is?"

"Paradise," I say.

"And?"

I try to exchange another puzzled look with Eddy, but this time, he doesn't meet my gaze. Instead, his attention rests on the wooden table between us.

Meanwhile, Mrs. Gyrah giggles at my answer. "Are you sure *Bliss* isn't reincarnation or rebirth? Akhirah even? Heaven *is* the most common answer we get, though."

I take a second to digest her sentiments, and my mind whirls at the remembrance of human beliefs. They all hit me, but only the bits and pieces of information I know. I connect heaven to Christianity and rebirth to Hinduism and Buddhism, but that's all I naturally remember.

Eddy finally looks up, a grave line under his flat mouth. "What's the answer then?" he asks. "What is *Bliss*?"

Mrs. Gyrah giggles again—cute and high-pitched—and for the first time, Mr. Gyrah cracks a smile. "What do you think?" she counters. "Humans war over this subject, and millions die. Shouldn't you two know where you're going before you get there?"

Mr. Gyrah then takes over. "Rebirth means to be born again after death where your soul transfers into another physical being. You may shift from human to butterfly"—he snaps his fingers—"like that. A new chance at life. Or you may ascend to the purest paradise, Heaven. Or maybe wind up at Akhirah, awaiting judgment." His deep stare shifts to me, bearing into my soul. "No one knows, but if anyone has ever made it, of course there's no evidence of such."

Mrs. Gyrah squeezes my hand, reclaiming my attention. "So now tell me, my dears, where are you going?"

Even though I take a moment to collect my thoughts, Eddy fires off at the mouth. I turn to him, staring at his strong convictive face just as intently as the Chiefs of Myro. His hardened eyes fix straight ahead at Mr. Gyrah while sweat drizzles off his chin. He speaks sonorous and with certainty, his dire tone taking me aback.

"Heaven."

"Eddy," I breathe.

"Oh, and how are you so sure?" Mrs. Gyrah asks.

Eddy rips his gaze to one of the many windows. "In my past life, I remember my mom and dad used to read scriptures over my hospital bed. They were both pastors. We'd all pray together every night before my medication set in. I used to know bible verses by heart, but now it seems they're just a hazy memory.... I'm sure my parents are in Heaven now, so I just gotta meet them."

"You do know there are far more religions than the ones I've mentioned, dear?" Mrs. Gyrah asks. "Are you sure, you're sure?"

He nods, and then the Chiefs of Myro turn to me. Their probing stares rattle my already frazzled thoughts. I look between them, searching for an answer but come up short. My mind doubles over all the faiths we've discussed and the many others that I don't even know. They all flow separate—too far apart for me to even compare.

Thinking quick on my tail, I force myself to speak before being spoken to. "What are your stories?" I ask them.

Out of the corner of Eddy's eye, he glances at me as if catching on to me and my deflection.

"Old age," Mrs. Gyrah says.

"Really?" I say. "You look so young."

She giggles low and sweet, lighting up the mood. "'Black don't crack', I suppose."

Both Eddy and I chuckle.

"What about you, Mr. Gyrah?" I ask.

However, he keeps his head down, twiddling the ends of his goatee. He clears his throat aloud as his face flushes like a tomato. His vision wanders around the room, looking anywhere but at us, and Mrs. Gyrah laughs at her suddenly sheepish husband.

"I...femina umina grr..." he says, starting loud before reducing to grumbles.

I furrow my brows, and Eddy and I exchange confused looks.

"What was that?" Eddy asks with a hand to his ear.

Mr. Gyrah's cold eyes shoot up to Eddy, and Eddy jumps in fright. The old Chief keeps his head tucked down which appears even scarier, a shadow overcasting his long face. This time when he speaks, his voice comes out loud and forceful as he grits each word through his teeth. "I. Fell. Down. The. Stairs."

I stare at him for a long moment, Eddy too. We pause for just a second to digest one of the *Chiefs* of Myro's cause of death, and then an uncontrollable guffaw surges up my throat. Eddy and I roll in stitches until Mr. Gyrah lurches his head up to us. His scowl sucks out our laughter, and we seal our lips.

"By a clumsy accident," Mrs. Gyrah adds. Even she holds a gentle hand to her mouth to contain her laughter. Her husband sucks his teeth before stalking from the table, while she shrugs off his embarrassed attitude. "Everyone here in The Dump has died by natural disasters. Nothing to be ashamed of, baby!"

Mr. Gyrah crosses his arms on his way upstairs, and his noisy chain rattles behind him. He stomps up a few steps—the end of his tail lashing the wood—but stops halfway up and plops down. He sits hunched over with tight, angry eyes, yet his red cheeks tell the tale of his untimely demise.

"Shouldn't Leon be back by now?" Eddy asks Mrs. Gyrah.

She pouts her lips. "*Should* be. With him, there's no telling what he's strayed off into."

"Will you take us to the waterfall?" I blurt out.

Mrs. Gyrah grins, rising to her tail. "We actually have a surprise for you all waiting there."

Eddy's eyes light up. "I love surprises!"

My lips curl at his over-enthusiasm.

Heading for the entrance, Mrs. Gyrah gestures for us to follow her, so we do. She waves for Mr. Gyrah to come too, and surprisingly, he's the first one out—probably to escape his humiliation. He hurries past me and Eddy, slamming the door open, while the doorbell jingles in alarm. Mrs. Gyrah catches the door and holds it open for me and Eddy.

I follow him out, but just as I'm the last to leave, Mrs. Gyrah whispers something in my ear.

"*Know where you're going before you get there, or you may end up somewhere wretched. Think on it, Slixx.*"

CHAPTER 21
LITTLE HUMMER GIRL

We barely take a few steps from the Chiefs' hut before a random blond villager jogs our way. He pulls Mr. and Mrs. Gyrah to the side, and they converse amongst each other in hushed voices. That lasts for a short minute, and then Mrs. Gyrah instructs us to stay outside their hut until they come back. Something about preparations for our surprise.

Eddy and I nod, and the three of them slip into an alleyway, heading in the opposite direction that we initially came. Their jangling chains carry them on their way.

Meanwhile, I lean against the wall, minding my own business. I survey the land full of huts, bridges, and alleyways, and the desert sand beneath my tail beckons my attention, too. Although the peaceful fresh air feels good with every inhale, the hotness and humidity swelter me in an inferno. My entire dress is now completely soaked and glued to my body, and sweat cascades off my sticky skin. The intense temperature forces me to sit down before I pass out, my chain clattering into a pile beside me.

Eddy awkwardly kicks rocks—the weather clearly not

affecting him as much. A serene moment of silence fleets by, but he always has to open his mouth. "So..."

I sigh, mustering the energy to look up at him. He stands over me, blocking out the radiant sky, and his silhouette shades me. I think to ignore him, but a sudden thought pops into my mind that I've been dying to ask. "How'd you and Leon become so close?"

"Close?" Eddy scoffs. "That guy's the worst."

"You two seem pretty chummy to me. Did you bond before or after I left Snowdevlin?"

"*Tch*." He kicks a large rock down the road. "After you left for the city, I went searching for *Bliss*. With no direction or inclination. I trudged through the snow for however long it took for me to pass out from hypothermia."

"Next thing I know, I'm waking up in a warm wooden room. Leon, Kaplone, Gryner, and all the rest of the gang were hovering over me asking if I'm dead. I jump up determined to go to *Bliss*, but they laugh.... They tell me it doesn't exist, but of course, I don't believe them. At least not until Leon tells me his story.... I hate to say it, but that guy deserves to go to *Bliss*. He's been through a lot. But anyway, they offered me a job and purpose and..."

In that moment, I wonder what Leon told Eddy. I imagine that he went into detail about what he told me back in the snow. About the plague that ravaged his home, the tsunami that took his father's life, and the following plague that took his —how horrific and scary those must've been. And surely, he divulged word about his beloved.

I try to fathom the amount of pain between he and Eddy's causes of death. The natural yet incurable maladies that took their lives. They *deserve* to go to *Bliss*. I, however, reflect on my unfortunate passing from the human realm and ponder: *If someone drives another to their breaking point, do either deserve to find peace?* Elliot's face pops into my head, startling me. I then remember my siblings and I gossiping about him. *Maybe if I had been a bit nicer?*

Jolting me back to reality, low humming sounds just a couple yards away.

"What's that?" I ask, but Eddy's already creeping toward the noise, careful not to make too much commotion with his chain.

I scramble to my tail as buckets of sweat fall from my face. I jog to catch up to him, but after I do, it's as if he's being pulled ahead by a string. His focused eyes fix on a nearby alley where the loudening hum comes from. The high-pitched melody grows sweet like from that of a woman.

Just a few steps away, Eddy rattles out of his daze as we stop before the singing alley. I glance at him eerily and nervous, and he looks at me the same. We both take deep breaths before slowly poking our heads around the corner.

I gasp.

Eddy's eyes widen in disbelief.

"Leon?" I call out.

He turns around amid zipping up his pants, and the humming woman steps out of his shadow. Her red eyes catch me off guard. She nonchalantly slips on her short silk dress straps, the gown hanging off her wide hips, while a tunic rests on the ground around her tail. She's tall like Leon, and their tails and chains briefly intertwine, resting atop each other. They pull apart at the sight of us, though. Leon starts toward us as the humming woman shimmies into her tunic.

"How'd the talk go with the Chiefs?" he asks us, cool like nothing's happened.

Stunned, neither Eddy nor I speak.

"They bring up faith and afterlife and all that fantastical garbage?" He stops feet away from us, and we stumble out into the open. A bright red mark now plaques his neck. "Don't tell me you two bought into—"

Before I can say anything, Eddy jumps the gun. "What happened to your beloved? I thought you were so in love and dying to join Deanna in *Bliss*?"

One of Leon's brows twitch in confusion, but then realization settles in. He looks over his shoulder at the approaching woman, her long black hair swaying along her butt. "Oh, her? That's Leira." He rolls the R in her name. "She's an old friend."

Eddy shoves Leon's shoulder. "I don't give a damn who she is!"

"Watch it, Flicky."

"What about Deanna? You said you were going to reunite with her in *Bliss*—that she was your one true love."

"She is."

"Then what's this?"

"You're cheating on her," I whisper, taking a step forward. "What about your vows?"

"Well, we never quite made it to the alter," Leon yawns. "Hence, fiancé. And you can't expect a dead person—ghost—to be faithful. I'm trapped in this eternal hellhole, and I still have needs."

Eddy opens his mouth to speak, but Leira then joins in on the conversation, her and her white chain slinking out of the shadows. "It's true," she says with a heavy accent, locking her sights on Eddy. She leers at him with sensual red irises, and Eddy's face relaxes a bit. She steps over to him—her big chest brushing up against his arm—and his face reddens. He doesn't move, likely too flustered, but for some reason, my blood boils. "This is the damned. They don't call it The Dump for no reason."

My body moves as if a mind of its own, and I cut between

Eddy and Leira. I peer up into her crimson eyes and snap, "We're going to *Bliss!*"

She shifts her gaze down to me, looking me up and down. "It doesn't exist."

"Yes, it—" I start.

But she turns around to Leon. "I'm surprised you're actually back pursuing this dream."

"You and me both," Leon sighs.

"He couldn't get in alone before," Eddy interjects, "but now we've got the ticket to *Bliss.*"

"Oh?" Leira smirks. "And what's this ticket you speak of?"

Eddy places a hand on my shoulder. "Slixx."

Leira averts her gaze back down to me, and all of a sudden, I feel exposed. She studies me like I'm a naked specimen. I can't help but look away, folding my arms. "This flat chested girl is the ticket?" she asks.

I whirl to her. "What'd you say?"

This time, Leon cuts between us. He grabs Leira's shoulders and backs her up, and she reluctantly follows. "Sorry, Leira's known for her mouth."

"And the things that go in it?" I scorn.

The corners of Leira's mouth pinch. "Spicy, like me—I like her."

"That makes one of us." While I'm riled up, I finally blurt out what's been on my mind. "So Leon let me get this straight, you want to reunite with your beloved in *Bliss*, but until then, you sleep with whores to satisfy yourself?"

Leon rakes a hand through his hair. "You don't get it, Sheets. Nor you, Flicky."

"All ears!" Eddy calls out.

"You two just got to The Dump, and ever since, you've been on the move. You don't know what's it like to actually *dwell* and marinate in this wasteland, drifting for an eternity with nothing and no one. Even ghosts need companions. Look at you two."

I look up at Eddy, and he looks down at me. My cheeks grow hot while his are still tinted bright red. I jerk away, clearing my throat. "This is just a circumstantial arrangement," I say, but Eddy refuses to back me up.

Leon and Leira side-eye us like they know something we don't, and the next moment of silence builds a weird lovestruck tension in the air.

"Eddy, Slixx!"

We all turn back to the road where Mrs. Gyrah's voice comes from. The four of us exchange unfinished looks before leaving the alley. We wave our hands to get Mr. and Mrs. Gyrah's attention, and they meet us halfway from their hut.

"Nice seeing you again, Leon," Mrs. Gyrah says. Then, she winks at Leira, and Leira bows at her and her husband. "I see that's where you strayed."

"It's always nice to get reacquainted with old friends," Leon replies.

"Mhmm." Mrs. Gyrah gestures down the nearest alley on the righthand side, and we follow her and Mr. Gyrah. "If you must go now, we have prepared somewhat of a going away party. We welcome and celebrate any and all guests with music and drinks."

"You may leave after the farewell speech," Mr. Gyrah says.

"I didn't know we needed permission," I mutter.

While walking, he shoots a deadly glare back at Eddy, and Eddy knits his brows in fright. He frantically shakes his head, but Mr. Gyrah must think my snide came from him. Although instead of rightfully blaming me, Eddy just seals his lips until Mr. Gyrah faces forward.

"Sorry," I mouth to him as we weave through the next alley. Eddy flashes me a brave smile, though.

The Village of Myro is actually bigger than it looks. We weave down another alley before I even hear the faint sound of trickling water. The Chiefs of Myro zigzag and lead us down a few more alleys, and the trickling sound grows into cascading water. Then, after one more alley, the land changes from sand to rock, expanding into a mountainous clearing.

Although the village ends behind us, all the villagers stand on the many layers of salmon rock which rounds around to a waterfall. Straight ahead, the clearest blue water gushes down from the highest peak, falling into a pure pool of sublime wonder in the middle of the clearing.

The villagers hoot and cheer for us as scattered musicians begin to play music in harmony with their stirring chains and the waterfall. Drums boom from the far left of the precipice while rainsticks echo falling showers. Even zithers sound a sweet melody of remembrance. Leira begins to sing amid an onset of hummers, and as much as I hate to say it, her soulful angelic voice graces us all. Her mouth opens long and wide to produce operatic sounds, enunciating consonants and vowels of a different language, and the villagers all sway to the slow music as they drink from their wooden cups of Plasgood.

Mr. and Mrs. Gyrah lead me, Eddy, Leon, and Leira through the peaceful crowd and up the mountain. Under the hot sky, my face boils with sweat, and the warm ground singes my bare feet. We climb layers of rock before pacing to the peak.

Tails pops into my head as we near the top, and I think back to the whippings he received in the city. I shiver, suddenly doubting this place, but then I spot yellow fur just beyond the peak. My tail kicks into gear, and I jog past everyone to get to Tails, towing in heavy breaths.

Upon reaching the top first, I stop beside the waterfall and behold the breathtaking view—almost as pretty as the clear pool below. Rocky mountains stretch for miles beyond, and the radiant sky shines down on flat valleys between. A river origi-nates from as far as the eye can see, flowing downstream to the waterfall.

I pan across the high summits before looking down at the yellow fur coat. Turns out, it isn't Tails but rather a much smaller blond dog with a tiny pug face. It rests a couple yards away, and next to it lies a bigger black dog. It salivates almost as much as two skinny dogs on the opposite side. Although they don't look nearly as cute as Tails, I gaze at the canines in wonder, warmth spreading through my chest. I scan the new land of rocky mountains and spot more dogs yonder, and one in particular catches my eye, straying from the rest at the sight of me.

"Tails!" I shout.

He bounds over to me, majestic and starlit. He jumps at me for joy, and his tongue knocks me over, relentless licks of love following. The Myronians' music speeds up amid our lively reunion. Although I uncomfortably land on my chain, the pain drifts to the back of my head. I simply laugh—overwhelmed with affection—and after Tails' last lick, I hug him tight.

Suddenly, the music stops.

I whirl around and see Mr. And Mrs. Gyrah now at the top of the peak with their hands raised for silence. They face the villagers below, while Eddy, Leon, and Leira stand behind them. Eddy gawks down at the waterfall, mere feet away, before looking back in amazement at the rocky mountains and dogs.

Mrs. Gyrah waves for me to come hither, so Tails and I head over to join the group.

"*Spicily!*" Mr. Gyrah cries out over the loud waterfall.

"*SPICILY,*" the Myronians repeat with bass and pride, and I jump in surprise.

"We have visitors today," Mr. Gyrah continues. "They have traveled here from great lengths and come in peace. They are passing through on their journey, so we must celebrate them. For we live by a set of codes and..."

With Tails behind me, I stop between Eddy and Leon as the view sucks the air from my lungs. I gawk at the display before me—like Eddy. The vertical angle of the grand waterfall, the tentative calm Myronians crowded around it, and the beautiful view of the architecturally patterned huts grace my eyes. The land entraps me in a mesmerizing trance until Leon elbows me.

Blinking back to reality, I look around at everyone staring at me.

"Your name," Leon mutters.

"Oh, Slixx!" I say much louder than intended.

Since Eddy isn't paying attention either, I do the same as Leon did to me, and he blurts out his name, too.

Mr. Gyrah grumbles under his breath, shaking his head in disapproval, but then he clears his throat to save face. Mrs. Gyrah steps in, though.

"We welcome thee four travelers," she says. "And we wish them luck on their journey, so in turn we may bear good fortune. Because the first code reads as such..." All the villagers recite the code with her—almost like a chant. "The Dump sends travelers to Myro, we welcome, we greet, we bestow in honor, hail the Realm who sent, good fortune amen, we settle for peace, one day godsend, to dwell, to remain, to lay rest..."

Nerves begin to claw at my skin as the speech comes to an end. I look over at Leon, who stares down at Leira's butt, and nudge him. "You're disgusting," I mumble.

"What do you want?" he asks, casually.

I glance over at Eddy to make sure he's not listening—good thing he's absorbed in the ambiance and music. "How do we get to *Bliss*?" I whisper to Leon.

"Should I be worried that the 'ticket' is asking me this?"

"Just answer the question."

He sighs. "Look, I'm not promising anything. All I know is that there's hieroglyphics and script in the cave similar to the script on the fountain in Limbo, and Leira will translate. Whatever 'ticket' magic you do, will be done in there."

I ignore his sarcasm. "How exactly do we get *there*?"

"Leon, Slixx, Eddy, and Tails," Mrs. Gyrah continues. "We send you off with love, care, and kindness. And may you return the savor ever in our favor."

"*Spicily!*" Mr. Gyrah chants.

"SPICILY."

The music starts again as all the Myronians begin to play and sway to the beat. Leon leers down at Leira—who hums a sweet melody in chorus with the other harmonious voices—but Eddy and I shake our heads in disapproval.

Just then, Mr. Gyrah waves for us to descend the peak, and Leon takes the lead. Leira follows him along with Eddy, and Tails and I trail last. The Myronians make way for him, parting a wide path for us all. But out of nowhere, a familiar voice whispers in my ear. I don't even have to turn around to know who, but I think back to the discussion of faith from the hut.

"*Remember what I told you.*"

I gulp, an answer still out of reach.

"Isn't this cool?" Eddy says to me over his shoulder. "Although everyone here almost tried to *kill* me, they're good people."

I wipe a heap of sweat off my forehead, transferring it to my forearm. I try to shake away my uncertainty and fake a smile. "Yeah, they did almost slice your head off."

"For no reason!"

"Trust me, based off the travelers they've encountered in the past, they have good reason," Leon says.

"Were they really that bad?" I ask. "What'd they do?"

Leon nods. "Yes, but unfortunately, that's not my story to tell, so I can't say. You and Flicky just keep your hands down."

"You too," Eddy snaps. "And to *yourself.*"

Leon cracks a smile.

"He's got a point there," I tease. "When we make it to *Bliss,* I'm telling Deanna!"

Leon rolls his eyes yet adds, "Maybe you should find a new sheet to wear before interfering with my love life."

"Very funny," I say, stifling a laugh.

At the foot of the pool, the five of us face the dazzling waterfall. It crashes down at the center while ripples carry out to the edges. The clear blue water reveals the many rocks and pebbles far below, starting off shallow but showing depth ahead.

Without warning, Leon dives into the water, and Leira follows. Water splashes on me and Eddy, who both stand on land in shock.

"C'mon!" Leon calls out over the music. He and Leira swim through the water like slick fish, cutting through the surface with their flat palms.

Taken aback, I blink in awe. "A warning would've been nice!"

"*Tch.* That guy," Eddy grumbles, taking off his elbow pads.

He removes the first one just as I look down at my dress, and a gruesome scar about his elbow steals my attention. I gasp.

He must hear me because he looks up in confusion. He traces my gaze down to his scarred arm and instinctively hides it behind his back. "It's nothing. I'm fine."

I shoot him a narrow look.

His face drops as he takes off his other elbow pad—same scar. "It...it was the cancer."

I slowly dip my chin. "In your cause of death, did you see it?"

"No. Kinda glad I didn't."

"Me too." I point to Leon and Leira who duck and swim through the cascading waterfall. "Last one there smells like rotten Plasgood."

Eddy scrunches his nose. "*Phew*. I smelled the old stuff back at the bar and *pee-yew*."

I giggle before plunging into the pool, sinking underwater. Although Eddy cries out at me for being a cheater, I take advantage of my head start and swim onward. "C'mon, boy!" I shout to Tails, and he plops in after me. The resulting current carries me farther ahead, so I ride the wave until it lets out, the warm water rejuvenating my sticky, sweaty skin.

Tails' loud paw-nipping swimming technique splashes water in every direction. The backlash weighs my limbs down, and since I'm already a pretty bad swimmer, it's like I'm barely moving.

Back in Limbo, I learned that I lacked aquatic skills when Kiara and her mother vacationed at various lakes and beaches for spring break. One time, Kiara ventured out for a midnight swim, dragging me along. Both of us nearly drowned. Ever since then, we took to lounging on land with the tanners while the other humans and ghosts swam.

Both Eddy and Tails catch up to me in no time.

"Cheaters never win!" Eddy says.

I laugh, slicing water out of my way. "That's what the losers say!"

That must light a fire under his butt because he kicks it into high gear and swims faster. I continue laughing, though, and the guffaw in my gut refuses to let me speed up. After a minute, I attempt to catch up, but then I give up upon seeing him a yard ahead, nearing the waterfall.

Unfortunately for me, he passes under first, and I lose. However, Tails gestures for me to get on his back, so I hitch a free ride. His cute big paws wildly nip at the water, and his long tongue hangs out, brushing along the surface.

When we approach the cascade, Tails dives under. I hold my breath and hold onto his fur tight, hunching over. The torrential water batters my back and stings, but it only takes a few strokes to pass through.

Once on the other side, I look up and digest my surroundings: we're now inside a large ill-lit cave with rocky icicles hanging from the ceiling. Only a hazy glimmer of light from outside casts through the waterfall. Jagged stones stick out from the sharp walls, and the sudden drop in temperature contrasts with the arid weather above ground. Although the cool air graces my once sweltering skin, I shiver—soaked from the swim.

Eddy, Leon, and Leira stand on shore, so Tails swims us over to meet them.

"It's about time," Eddy jokes.

"Ha-ha, very funny," I say.

He straps the Velcro straps on his elbow pads, tightening them back on his arms. "What can I say? It's the athlete in me."

Tails pushes himself up out of the water, and I slide down off his back to my tail. "Whatever. I let you win." Before Eddy can respond, I turn to Leon who stands with Leira several feet away—too close for comfort. She holds a thick stick as he rubs two pebbles together, lighting a spark over it. "Hey, cheater, where's the hieroglyphics?"

"The irony," Eddy mumbles.

I shoot him a cold look, though, and he zips his lips.

A moment later, Leon finally creates a spark big enough to light up the stick, and Leira hands him his new torch. He then moseys over to the only tunnel inside the cave. He holds up his torch to the dark passageway, lighting up only a couple yards ahead. "This way, Sheets."

"W-we're g-going in there?" Eddy asks.

"Don't tell me you're scared, Flicky?" Leon says. "A big fellow like you?"

I laugh, patting Eddy's back. "You've got to do better." He shoots me a scowl, but I shrug. "C'mon, boy," I say to Tails, patting him along, and Eddy stumbles after us.

We all follow Leon through the long one-track tunnel which curves at every corner. Our shadows trail us on the walls, and the faint sound of crunching gravel accompany each of our footsteps (or tailsteps). Leon's torch guides us forward along with the eminent darkness behind us. Up above, hundreds of more rocky icicles point down at us.

Leira hums a saccharine tune, and her angelic voice echoes throughout the cave. Her song calms me at first, but after a while, with the end nowhere in sight, my tail begins to hurt. I fix on the ground, frowning the rest of the way. Tails tries to cheer me up with nudges, but I shake my head, declining his invitations to hop on his back. I figure he deserves rest after that exhausting swim.

"How much farther?" I ask.

"Yeah, feels like we've been walking for hours," Eddy says.

Leon sighs. "Relax, we're here."

Looking up, I scan the wide clearing before us. The narrow passageway opens up to this circular barren dead-end, and it's completely empty. Leon's torch lights up the area while our shadows dance on the walls. He and Leira slither into the clearing, but Eddy, Tails, and I take baby steps—Eddy more so in fright.

"Where's the hieroglyphics?" I ask aloud, and my voice echoes back at me. *"Where's the hieroglyphics...glyphics...glyphics... glyphics?"*

"Over here, Sheets," Leon says.

"It's Slixx," I grumble, stalking over to him with Tails at my side.

We both stop beside Leon and Leira, and I widen my eyes at the glowing walls. Leon's torch reveals many golden lines running in every direction. They stream along the walls in loops —curvy and round—forming hieroglyphics of some sort. Stick figures connect to each other along the horizon, while foreign script runs vertical above and below.

I touch the engravings and run my finger along two stick figures. Even though one reaches for the sky and the other runs in the opposite direction, they both hold hands. I trace the running figure to the next which jumps up into the air. The running figure holds down the jumper by its chain, and the stick figure on the opposite side grips the jumpers' foot.

"Alright. Work your magic," Leon says to me.

I roll my eyes. "It's not magic."

"You sure? Because that's what your boyfriend keeps making it out to be with this 'ticket' nonsense."

"He's not my—" I stop myself, seething heat through my teeth. "It's not magic."

"Hmm. That's interesting because I recall you saying that you, your beast—"

"Dog."

"And Flicky all jumped into the fountain and wound up here." He looks down at me with a blank expression. "Is that not magic? Maybe even black magic. I didn't know ghosts could practice."

I curl me lips at him. "You look like black magic."

His eyebrows shoot up.

"Can you read it?" Leira asks, turning to me.

I narrow my eyes in confusion, glancing from her to the foreign script on the walls. Starstruck, I point. "That?"

She nods.

"Uh, no. Can you?"

She returns her attention to the mighty walls. "I'm afraid not. My people are only able to decipher the hieroglyphics, not the script." She begins walking, so Tails, Leon, and I follow her to the middle of the cave walls. "It is said that a traveler will come one day and translate all of Myro's secrets which will unlock the Realm."

"What does that mean?" I ask, gazing up at the many columns of cursive script. It looks like a combination between Japanese and Arabic but more complex. At first glance, the script can be mistaken for small pictograms as lines strike through each loop. A pressure builds in my chest at the thought of this translation standing in all our ways to *Bliss*, and I gulp.

"I cannot say more than I've already said," Leira answers. "Because that's all I know. That prophecy has been passed down for eons by The Great Silent Elders."

"Well, where are they?" I ask. "Maybe they can—"

"In holding. They voluntarily serve as sacrifices in our solstice rituals as soon as they are reborn." Leira touches one of the stick figures and traces it down as it falls out of line from the rest. Her slender index finger goes from its head to toe before rounding up to its hand and flying chain. Strangely enough, it doesn't connect to another, but rather the chain of figures starts over, continuing like normal. "The Great Silent Elders choose to die the minute they come back. Since we cannot pass on further than this realm, they feel holding is the closest to peace."

"Fake peace..." I muter, fixed on the ground.

Leira must hear me because she dips her chin. "Yes, kind of like fake peace."

"Like Limbo..."

"Exactly like Limbo," Leon says. "Those from Limbo may pass on here to The Dump, but it ends here. Death is holding, and holding is to be reborn. I used to believe—but how does *Bliss* exist if there's no way out?"

Tails moans, dropping to his paws. He hopelessly lies down, and his whimpers melt my nonexistent heart.

I stare back up at the stick figures. An immense weight drops on me, and I nearly collapse from the burdensome pressure. I wonder if our journey to *Bliss* ends here. *I'm the ticket*, I repeat in my head. The thought of letting everyone down churns my stomach, eating away at me from the inside out. The somber look on Tails and everyone else's faces stabs me in the back, but the scribble on the walls is just that. Scribble. Nothing magically clicks. Nothing appears the least bit familiar. In fact, the more I look at it, the more confusing it gets. I pose a jarring question to myself: *Am I really the ticket to Bliss?*

"Hey, guys!" Eddy shouts.

Whirling around, I find Eddy at the end of the clearing near the tunnel. I stare at him in confusion as he stomps the ground. He does that a few times before dropping to his knees and putting his ear to the floor.

"What are you doing?" I ask.

"Come look!"

Tails, Leon, Leira, and I exchange muddled looks before meeting him. He's now stomping the ground, again, and needless sweat trickles behind his ear.

"Eddy—" I start.

"Listen," he says. To his left, he pats the ground with the tip of his tail, and it sounds like regular gravel until he taps the spot before him.

We all look at each other.

"Sounds shallow," Leon says.

Eddy stomps the hollow ground, again. "Whatever it is, something's down there."

"Like what?" Leira asks in unison with Tails' bark. "This cave has been here since the beginning of this Realm."

Eddy smirks. "Someone must've built it—or rather *created* it."

In that moment, Mrs. Gyrah's words ring in my ears. *Know where you're going before you get there, or you may end up somewhere wretched.* I know where Eddy stands on *Bliss*, so I have an idea of Who he's referring to. Me, on the other hand, all the beliefs are fragmented puzzle pieces—impossible to connect.

"Shine the light over it," Eddy instructs Leon.

"Woof!"

Leon wields the torch over the ground, but it looks no different than the rest of the gravel. Eddy stomps down on the hollow spot, though.

"Maybe it's nothing," I say.

"Then how come the rest of the ground sounds normal?" Eddy asks. "This could be the way out of this realm?"

"I highly doubt it."

"Why do you have to be so negative?"

Taken aback, my eyes widen. I stare into Eddy's offended ones but hold my tongue. Because, truth be told, neither one of us knows what the hell we're doing, or if this is actually the end of our adventure—if we'll never truly pass on.

I take a deep breath. "Tails, could you dig for us?"

Without hesitation, Tails licks me—all too eager—before shoveling away at the ground with his paws. He chucks away at the surface dirt and rocks, while Eddy, Leon, and Leira wait on the edge of their seats.

Crossing my arms, I refuse to hold out hope over some hollow sound in the ground. Unless they dig a reverse tunnel to a swirling vortex, I'm not buying it.

Annoyed, I amble away from the debris Tails lashes into the air and somehow find myself along the middle of the wall. In the dim light, I run a hand over the fallen stick figure and script below it, but still, nothing clicks. More doubt begins to cast in my head, but I remind myself that I never believed in this "ticket" nonsense in the first place.

The fallen stick figure captivates my attention, though. I analyze its misplacement and odd pose, wondering why the rest of the figures appear normal before and after it. That one earlier stick figure who was jumping up had another holding it down, but this one reaches out its hand for help. And no one takes it.

"Leira," I call out over the noisy digging. "Can you come here?"

Of course, Leon comes with her.

"What does this hieroglyphic say?" I ask.

"You can't read one without the others." She takes us all the way back to the entrance of the cave. "Which way do you want me to read?"

"Uh, does it matter?" I ask.

She dips her chin. "Each way tells a different story. One of light. And one of darkness. Which way would you like?"

I scan the cave in confusion, befuddled at how pictures—*stick figures*—can tell two different stories. It looks so plain and empty inside, but deep down in my gut, something tells me that there's more to this place than what it seems.

I gulp. "Darkness."

Turning to the right, she traces a finger over the first stick figure before brushing along the wall. She walks and reads, pouring the story and language of her people into me and Leon. Maybe it's her words or maybe it's Leon's torchlight, but the stick figures almost seem to come alive.

"This is a story about a woman and her son. Her name was Martha, and his name was Markus." The first stick figure simply stands holding hands with the next shorter one—

mother and son. Markus then connects to Martha who appears in a series of images climbing various terrains. "Martha roamed The Dump for centuries, before ghosts and time even existed. After looping around the entire Realm once, she discovered the land to be barren, so she circled back around and planted valleys, sprouted deserts, built mountains, cried rivers, and sprung snow."

The hieroglyphics then shift to Markus falling. Five following stick figures of Martha grip his chain though, pulling him back to land, and Markus appears, standing beside her and holding her hand, again.

"One day, a windstorm came. And something that can only be described as 'darkness' infiltrated Markus' head. He fell ill with *Nilli*—consumed by dark thoughts. He attempted to take his own life countless times, but Martha would always save him with herbs and rescue him from drowning. That is until she sparked bright light in the sky. She hoped that would cure him, and it did...for a short while."

A stick figure even bigger than Martha shows holding Markus' hand. Markus appears on the other side of it yet smaller, and this sequence repeats until he's nothing more than a dot.

"The *Nilli* took over him. His mind. His soul. And in turn, his body. He became nothing more than a hollow shell of a person, so Martha knew what she must do. She let him go."

At the center of the cave's walls, we stop before the fallen stick figure.

"Let him go, how?" I ask.

"Exactly how it sounds." She looks at me with the gravest expression. "*Vedidae*. Martha sacrificed her son by burning his ashes, and then she sent his remains beyond this Realm and created *Osolá*. Holding."

I clutch my head, desperately trying to understand. "But

why would she kill her son? Just because he was depressed with *Nilli* or whatever doesn't mean—"

"I believe you've already answered your own question."

I scrunch my face in confusion before realization sinks in.

"Fake peace," Leon and I both say in unison. We exchange uncanny quick glances.

"Since Martha's son became a ghost of himself, she put an end to his suffering and laid him to rest," Leon says, putting the pieces together.

Leira nods, pointing to the next stick figure. "Thus, the cycle begins again."

"You said there were two stories: one of light and one of dark. What's the light?"

"We found something!" Eddy cries out.

Snapping our attention to him, Leon's fiery torchlight whooshes through the air as he turns. He starts for Eddy as Eddy calls for light. Leira and I remain where we are, though, our conversation left unfinished.

"Unlike the story of darkness which detailed the demise of Martha's son, the story of light shows all the love and kindness Markus had in his heart. He was troubled and ill, but there is not darkness without light."

I look back at Markus' fallen depiction. Although he's normal size at the end of his life, he fell without anyone to catch him—not even his own mother. I wonder if he wanted to live in misery or if he thought things would get better, but I guess I'll never know. His mother must've done it because she loved him, though. If he could never reach *Bliss*, she gave him the next best thing.

"What do you believe?" I ask Leira.

She cocks her head to the side ever so slightly. "What do I believe?"

"Uh...faith or something like that?"

"Oh, the Realm, of course. Martha created The Dump from her son's ashes, so that we could all live here in her paradise."

"I see," I whisper so low I can barely hear. Her words ring bells in my head as if I've heard this story somewhere before. My scattered brain tries to connect the dots but ends up blanking, so I shake away the thoughts.

"Slixx, Leira, come take a look at this!" Leon says.

Just then, a glimmer off to the left catches my eye. Leira fades from my peripheral as she runs to her affair, but I trail along the wall, passing the story of light. I pay no mind to the hieroglyphics, but rather an imaginary string pulls me forward. I near the end of the cave. And although there's no sign of the glimmer I saw, I continue ahead.

My gut takes me to the foot of the tunnel—Eddy and the others just a couple yards away. Leon's torchlight only lights up several feet beyond the cave, so I stare straight ahead into the black abyss. The dark tunnel bears no light, no hope, and not a soul. However, if I concentrate really hard, I can hear the faint waterfall in the distance.

Suddenly, another glimmer twinkles out of my peripheral. I turn around to the story of light, expecting it to be gone, but there it is—bright yet tiny. I pass the first hieroglyphic before stopping a few feet away.

On a depiction of Markus sleeping, a minuscule sparkle twinkles inside his blank face. He sleeps soundly while his mother holds onto his chain and foot beside him, and upon noticing, that strikes me as odd. I slowly reach up and touch the light. Nothing magical happens or spontaneously combusts. At first, I scratch away at the light, and lit particles fall from the twinkle.

As soon as they hit the floor, they burn out.

"What the...?" I mutter to myself.

"It's just a cheap plate of metal," Leon says aloud, his voice bouncing off the walls.

"No, there's words on it!" Eddy defends.

"No, they're hieroglyphics," Leira says. "It'll take me a moment, but I can translate."

For some reason, I dare not turn around as if trapped in a vortex. The captivating light lures my undivided attention, but I listen to the others just fine. Leira begins to lowly mutter in her language, stumbling and doubling over words, while Eddy and Leon argue about what it could mean. Tails barks when he agrees with either of them.

Meanwhile, I stand here in awe.

Leaning closer, my finger hovers over the light. I narrow my eyes to inspect the twinkling spec, and it shines bright like a radiant star in the vast human galaxy. I try to remember what beyond the human realm's sky looked like but fall short of just illuminations amid darkness. The twinkling spec before me draws me in close— mere inches away—and I begin to ponder the different stories.

One of light. One of darkness.

I scrutinize Markus' sleeping stick figure before me—and the many other relaxed depictions of him along the wall. In this story of light, he doesn't move too much—just sleeps, stands, and sits. His poses strike me as odd and just that—*poses*. It's as if he's staging himself for his mother while she builds the realm. And then it hits me. Maybe this isn't the story of Markus before he fell ill, but maybe it's the story of him *hiding it*.

A longing sensation arouses in my gut, and I trace a finger around his sleeping face. It's as if the twinkle inside channels something within me. My mouth opens without me even thinking, and a single word slips out.

"*Nilli.*"

Suddenly, the cave begins to quake.

Tails barks in an uproar.

"What's going on?" Leon shouts.

"Slixx!" Eddy cries out.

I whirl around to him. We lock eyes as rocks fall around us, but then the shaking ground throws me off my tail. I stagger back before slamming into the wall. My body takes the brunt of the crash until my head bangs back. My vision dips in black for a second. I flutter my lashes to regain my sight, and even though it comes back, I only see blurry colors.

The ground rocks me to the side next. My tail slips from beneath me, and I fall to the ground. My entire body trembles as if amid a seizure, while Eddy, Leon, and Leira's loud voices further tremor the cave—Tails, too, with his panicked barks.

"Tails, Eddy, Leon, Leira!" I shout.

During a series of blinks, I see two dark figures nearing me. They're mysterious until they speak, and I recognize Tails and Eddy's voices. Eddy kneels beside me and cups my face while Tails ducks his head to us.

"Are you okay?" Eddy asks.

"Woof!"

"Fine," I blurt out, smacking Eddy's hands down. Annoyance pricks my skin, tired of holding his hand during times of distress, and I think about how Leira's always been behind Leon —ever since we got here. Then, I flash back to the many occasions between me and Eddy where *I* was like *Leira*. After the stabbing. The Hellons in Limbo. The City. Now. Shaking my head, I know that's not how I want to get to *Bliss*.

Just then, the earthquake ceases.

I rub my eyes hard, desperately trying to clear my vision. I rub and rub and rub. My sighs flow out in exhausted breaths as I regain my balance. Still rubbing my eyes, I stand up.

"Unbelievable," Eddy says in a low voice beside me.

"What is that thing?" Leira yells.

Tails lets out a low, vicious growl.

My eyes flutter now with semi-normal vision, so I exhale in relief…until I look up. When I do, the air gets vacuumed out of my lungs, and I stiffen. Fear and déjà vu overcome my limbs. My eyelids widen in horror at my worst nightmare—the Hellons. *They're back.*

Two big ones as tall as the ceiling. Their cone heads creak from side to side, and their sharp teeth click, the eerie sounds sending a shiver down my spine. They scowl at us below, irate smoke fuming out of their tiny noses, and their broad shoulders expand with each huff and puff.

Unlike the many ones before, these two do not have weapons.

I count my blessings—thankful since we're trapped in this confined clearing.

However, the Hellons abruptly bend to the side toward each other. Their horns bang against each other before interlocking, and they exhale dark toxic breaths. We all watch in terror as burning flames erupt around them—darker than the black and violet swirling in their one eyes. The loud ring of fire crackles, bouncing off the cave walls, while the Hellons *merge* into each other.

Their big, scaly, dragon-like bodies mesh together like water and alcohol, and their incessant clicking teeth hammer together fast and hard. Their single eyes become one giant cycloptic one; their teeth fuse together, doubling to that of a mutated shark; their scales even double, protruding from their skin like old hard boogers on a wall; and their harsh breaths now permeate the air with an overwhelming vinegary odor.

The newly merged Hellon stands hunched over—*twice* their normal size. Its back inflates with each inhale, and its thick arms dangle at its side. It glares down at us with the meanest mug.

Tails barks.

Eddy gulps.

My clammy hands blister with sweat, but I do my best to keep a brave face. That is until the Hellon screeches with the screaming power of a bionic banshee. Its piercing cry quakes the cave even harder than before, and if there were glass around, it'd surely disintegrate.

We all cover our ears, but the vibrations overpower us. Tails hides his head between his front legs while his fur belts in the wind. Meanwhile, I stumble backward but catch myself, my hair and dress whipping behind me. Eddy loses his footing, too, but I push him back on his tail. He looks back at me with jittery eyes, and I meet his gaze. I see the hazel spark in his irises desperate to save face, but deep down, my chest warms at the sight of his raw emotion.

"It's going to be okay!" I lie. He probably doesn't hear me anyway.

Though before he can respond, rocky icicles drop from the ceiling near the entrance. The Hellon steps forward just in time to dodge them, but they land snug in the ground behind it, blocking the way out. They're at least ten feet long and way too sharp and thick to climb.

I look at Eddy and Tails before looking over at Leon and Leira. Leon shields Leira, but underneath him, she screams at the top of her lungs, hugging the metal plate.

Just as I turn away, Leon and I make eye contact, and he mouths something. Although I don't hear it, his lips read pretty clear.

"What did you do, Sheets?"

But in that moment, all I can do is shake my head.

"HWAAAAAAH."

CHAPTER 22

FIGHT OR FLIGHT

The Hellon lunges at Leon and Leira first.

Tails bulldozes into me and Eddy, and I yelp until we land on his back. I clutch his fur, Eddy gripping my waist from behind. We both hang on for dear life as Tails rounds the wall toward the Hellon.

Looking over at Leon and Leira, I crinkle my brows. Leon scampers off like a frantic rat—torch still in hand; however, Leira doesn't move. She stands paralyzed by fear, hugging the metal plate and whispering foreign tongues. He must think she's following him.

"Leon, get Leira!" I shout.

He whirls around, puzzlement written all over his face. He blinks at the empty space behind him before finding Leira several feet away at the Hellon's mercy. It bounds on all fours, sprinting at her, and green saliva drools from its open mouth.

"Leira, run!" Leon cries out.

But she doesn't. And he doesn't either.

With the Hellon mere steps away from Leira, contemplation masks Leon's face, and my lips twist in disgust. I shout one final time for him to save her, but he flashes me a quick look before glancing at the clicking Hellon and running the other way. His short ponytail breezes back, and his jewelry jangles around his neck. The tips of his torchlight waft in the wind, too. Though most noticeably, his shameful tail slithers fast *in the wrong direction.*

"Leon! Ugh—" Turning my back on him, I lean forward like a horseback rider and tighten my grip on Tails' fur for him to go faster. "C'mon, boy!"

The Hellon cracks its neck with each step toward Leira. It grates its teeth in between clicks, and even more polluted breaths emit from its mouth. The air becomes thick and dark, the little light from Leon's torch appearing dim over here.

Just then, the Hellon lunges for attack.

Leira drops the metal plate.

I gasp as Tails soars her way.

Eddy squeezes my waist.

Leon's fiery torch whirls around somewhere far-off.

In that moment, the Hellon screeches, and a gasp gets caught in my throat. I nearly freeze in fright, but a burning passion spurs me into action. Maybe it's adrenaline or fight or flight. I don't know, but in that moment, I plant a fond kiss on Tails' back—telepathy translating between us—and unclamp Eddy's hands from around me. With no time to explain, I stand up, squeeze his startled hand, and jump off Tails' back, pulling Eddy with me.

He yelps. I yell. We fall. The sound of teeth sinking into flesh blares.

Midfall, I command myself not to look, but I do. I glance over my shoulder, and it's as if a hammer bangs against my chest. My eyes widen in awe. Tails bites the Hellon's neck, tackling it away from Leira. Red blood squirts out while the Hellon screeches a cataclysmic cry of a thousand pains.

The loud sound knocks me off my tail. What was supposed

to be a tuck-and-roll quickly turns into a faceplant-and-roll. I land badly on half my face before rolling on the ground, and a stinging pain overcomes my body. Somewhere during the mix, I lose Eddy's hand, but as soon as Leira crosses my vision—still standing in distress—I scramble to my tail and scurry for her.

Growling like a mongrel, Tails tackles the Hellon to the wall and clamps down his teeth even harder. The Hellon screeches again, but my ears reduce to ringing. I grit my teeth through the pain upon reaching Leira. My hands fly up to her shoulders as if instinctive, and I shake her. I shake her so hard that her hair jolts around her banging head. However, she remains unresponsive, simply muttering in tongue and blinking in a daze.

"*Esseo lux damne gididi. Esseo lux damne gididi. Esseo lux damne gididi....*"

With no time to waste, I grab hold of her hand and jerk her forward. At first, it's like moving an iceberg, but eventually, her tail begins to work. We run away from the warzone behind us.

I spot Leon off along the edge of the wall, while Eddy waits for us straight ahead. Eddy's wide eyes stare at us for a beat, but then he runs to meet us.

"Are you guys okay?" he asks, sizing me up. He reaches out to touch my likely purple-bruised face, but I hand him Leira instead. "Where are you going?"

"Tails—" I start.

Suddenly, a piercing whimper erupts. I whirl around and gasp at the sight. Tails chokes out blood as the Hellon sinks its claws into his side, and now with the roles reversed, the Hellon bites Tails with its sharp daggers. Tails cries out again, choking out more blood. A pool of red gore surrounds them—most of it coming from my *best friend.*

My tail jolts out to race for him. "Tails!"

But just as I start to run, the Hellon throws him across the cave at lightspeed. A gust of wind knocks us all back as Tails hurls past us, but it's as if I watch him fly in slow motion. I study his tight eyes, scrunched nose, and the claw marks on his body. The back of my eyelids burn.

"Tails," I whisper.

He slams into the wall harder than two colliding meteors. Debris breaks out, and a vicious wind belts back. The cave dims in wake of the catastrophe, Leon likely trying to save his diminishing flame from going out.

"Tails!" I scream.

Eddy pivots around me and pulls me down, shielding me from the blast, and Leira ducks under him, too. I struggle out of his grasp, but he holds me back. I jump up to see Tails, but a cloud of smoke shrouds him. Flying rocks scrape up my face and shoulders, but I barely feel a thing in the heat of the moment. The wind lashes my hair and tears backs.

I just want my dog.

Once the gust dies down, I break free from Eddy and dart to Tails. I run into the swirling yet settling smoke with my mouth covered, but debris still manages to get in my throat. My coughing and hacking are the least of my worries, though. I barely see a thing in this dusty vortex as Leon's torch must be on its last leg.

However, I continue aimlessly stumbling until I spot a big dark shadow. I run toward it, and I don't know if it's the hope in my chest or not, but the little light inside this cave seems to grow brighter. I run faster, slithering quicker than ever before.

When Tails finally comes into view, I shout his name, but a dastardly face cuts me off. Leon. He kneels beside Tails, stroking his snout, with a long green test tube in hand. Although his lit torch is propped up against the wall behind him, its fire has reduced to a weak flame.

Anger seizes control of me, and I rush over and smack the

tube out of his hand. "Get away from my dog," I grit through my teeth.

"Dammit, Sheets!" Leon shouts, scrambling to pick up his spilled tube. Light green Plasgood leaks out of it and onto the newly stained ground. "This could save him."

"Like you could've saved Leira?"

He averts his gaze, shifty-eyed. "You...you all were closer—"

"That's *bullshit*. And you know it."

"Listen, Sheets..."

I take a step closer to him, towering over his pathetic existence. "No, *you* listen. You're nothing but a phony! All that crap about wanting to be a doctor to save lives and cure your dad was *bullshit*. You don't care about anyone but yourself. Sure, you save lives but only when it's convenient for you—only when *your* life isn't on the line." I back away toward Tails. "You're nothing more than a coward."

Leon's eyes widen. "I..."

Averting my attention to Tails, I fling my arms around him and hug him tight. "I'm so sorry, boy."

One of his eyes flutters open, but a deep gash cuts through it. When he looks down at me with a moan, that's all it takes for me to breakdown. Riverbeds stream down my cheeks instantaneously, and a heavy pressure weighs down my body. The pain in his eyes crushes my dead soul.

"T-Tails," I choke out, but he just whines another moan. "This is all my fault. I should've protected you. I should've—"

"Sheets," Leon says, low and serious. "Let me help."

"To hell with your help!"

"Sheets, he's dying."

"He'll heal!"

"Not before he bleeds out."

I pause, clenching my jaw. My scowl softens as I look up at Tails. His many bloody wounds bring another tear to my eye, and a lump gets caught in my throat as I try to keep it together. I can't breakdown any more than this—not in front of Tails and surely not in front of that coward.

Just then, a warm wet liquid touches my tail. I slowly look down in horror before gasping. Tails' blood pools around me, and it appears bright red in the wake of death. It marinates beneath his wounded body, quickly spreading on the ground.

Tails lets out a mixture between a moan and a howl.

"In my past life, I died on the operating table as several doctors and nurses in quarantine gowns tried to pump my stomach," Leon says. "The second wave of the plague was even worse than the first. Made us all vomit. Wretched our guts out —blood and mucus—until we passed. I don't want your dog to go out the same way I did."

I ball my hands, pride reigning in each of my fists. My mind dances around the idea of his help, but I dare not utter a word.

Leon sighs. "Look, Sheets, I may be a coward—a coward who wants to save lives but fears death himself—but everyone's scared of something. And from the little time that I've known you, I know that you are, too. Scared that you'll never find *Bliss*, but even more scared of what'll happen when you do. You pretend to be brave, but I know you're just as afraid as the rest of us."

I fold my arms, digesting his sad but true sentiment.

"Please, *Slixx*," Leon pleads. "Let me help...before he's gone to holding."

I glance up at Tails who moans, again, but this time it's as if he's reasoning with me. Blood stains his fur and drips down his body, and the pool at my tail continues to spread. I dig my fingernails into my palms, pride surging through my bones.

"You don't get to be a team player or hero when you want to," I finally say. "Either you're with us, or you're not." I meet his gaze. "So, what's it going to be?"

He stares at me for a long moment with those invasive catlike eyes of his, but instead of picking me apart, he bears into my soul as if to gain an understanding. Then, he dips his chin. "I'm in."

Tails barks with what little energy he has.

"Then save my dog," I say.

Springing into action, Leon slides closer to Tails and asks him to open his mouth. Tails does as instructed, and Leon begins to slowly pour the elixir into Tails' mouth underneath his tongue. Though a quarter way through the elixir, the Hellon suddenly screeches, and we all jump.

Leon strokes Tails' snout, trying to calm him down, while I whirl around. The smoke has almost completely settled, so I see through it, staring directly at the dark Hellon across the cave.

Rounding Leon, I pick up his dim torch from off the ground. "Borrowing this," I say as I stride off into the warzone.

"Be careful, Sheets."

I stop on my heels (or the tip of my tail) before glancing back at Leon, who starts pouring the rest of the elixir into Tails' mouth. The sound of my nickname out of his mouth again makes me crack a smile. "You had it right the last time."

The corners of his mouth pinch.

"You too," I follow up.

Then, I jog off through the debris, and in less than a minute, I burst out onto the battlefield. I spot Eddy and Leira in the same spot where I left them—the Hellon, too. I knit my brows in confusion as I run over to them.

"What's going on?" I ask Eddy.

"Slixx!" Eddy shouts, overly excited. The fear in his eyes transforms into relief, and he hurls me into a big embrace. I barely have time to react before he pulls me away, gripping my shoulders. "Is Tails okay?"

I nod. "Leon's giving him an antidote to heal faster. What's happening over here?"

"Nothing." Eddy points at the Hellon who stands hunched over near the wall. "He hasn't moved from that spot. But when I started to creep over for a better look, it screamed out of nowhere."

"But it didn't move?" I ask.

Eddy shakes his head.

I pan over to the Hellon, sizing it up from head to toe, but nothing appears unusual. Blood drips from the fang marks in its neck, and a pool of it wells around its feet. I squint at the demon.

"Maybe it's healing itself," I suggest.

Eddy shakes his head, again. "The Hellons didn't heal back in Limbo."

"Maybe they're evolved here."

"I highly doubt that."

I raise a brow at his sassy remark. "I'm Slixx, remember? Not Leon."

"Sorry."

Rolling my eyes, I return my attention to the Hellon. Its broad shoulders expand and contract with each pant, and its toxic breaths further taint the atmosphere. Although I hold up Leon's torch for more light, the darkened air makes it hard to see.

Not to mention, the Hellon's strong vinegary odor has increased tenfold, engulfing the cave in acidity. Either my nostrils adjusted during all the commotion or I just didn't notice until now, but my nose burns like a fiery sun. My throat starts to itch, too. However, given the trapped circumstances, covering my face seems futile.

A hacking cough sounds behind me, and I turn around to the culprit. Leira coughs into her arm while holding her throat.

And it is then that she finally speaks. "The—*kaff! kaff!*—metal plate."

Eddy and I exchange confused glances.

"Look yonder," she says. "*Kaff!* When you neared the Hellon, it screeched—*kaff!*—but didn't move. I have a feeling it's guarding that plate."

"But why?" Eddy asks.

"What did the hieroglyphics say on it?" I ask.

She shakes her head. "I didn't get a chance to finish translating."

"Well, just tell us what you could make out," Eddy says.

"That's not how my people's language works. Nothing can be made out unless fully read—especially an artifact like that without context."

"Then we have to get the plate," I say, turning toward the Hellon.

However, Eddy catches my free hand. "Whoa there, Slixx. If you get any closer than I did, that Hellon is gonna do more than scream."

I exhale in annoyance but reluctantly stay, knowing he's got a point. "Leira, how much longer would you need to translate?"

"*Kaff! Kaff!* Probably a few moments. Why?"

Eddy looks to me. "You gotta plan?"

My lips curve up into a sly grin. "Maybe."

"But...but...but I'm the plan man."

A chuckle escapes me, and I playfully roll my eyes as I gather him and Leira into a huddle. I hold Leon's torch in the middle to light up each of our faces.

Just as I open my mouth to speak, Leira chimes in. Her tiny pupils highlight the fear in her glassy eyes while her gaze remains aloof yet present. "Before I do anything for you travelers, you tell me what kind of situation we're in. What the hell is that demon over there?"

"Technically, it's a Hellon," Eddy says.

"Meaning?"

"It basically appears in our way every time we get a step closer to *Bliss*," I say.

Falling silent, she takes a minute to process everything. Only the crackling flames from Leon's torch sound while our shadows dance around us. After another second, she finally mutters under her breath, "Hail the Realm. Hail the Realm. *Massio Dix Yoku.* Hail the Realm." She must place great trust in those words because she then nods for me to go on.

I take a deep breath. "Okay, here's the plan..."

CHAPTER 23

HELL FIRE

After I finish explaining the plan, Leira doubles back toward Tails and Leon. Although she's not a fast runner, she runs as fast as she can, and her long jet-black hair whips behind her. She soon disappears into the debris, leaving Eddy and I to do our part.

"You know this plan is suicide, right?" Eddy says, telling more than asking.

"You got any better ideas?" I ask.

"Not at the moment."

"Then try not to die."

Eddy flashes me a nervous yet confident smile, my words lighting up his competitive streak. "You too."

"Ready?"

"Ready."

And with that, we both take off. Eddy rounds the left side toward the Hellon while I round the right. We both sprint a yard before the Hellon screeches, and its vibrations hit us. We keep running, though, pushing through the fierce winds. It screeches again as we draw near. Then, again. Then, it attacks.

The Hellon veers left for Eddy as planned. Although I ran

fast, I made sure Eddy was just a few steps ahead of me—closer to the metal plate.

Lunging for Eddy, the Hellon screams, and the gusting vibrations nearly knock him off his tail. He closes in on the metal plate, but the Hellon's just inches behind him.

I stop and shout, "Eddy!"

Bang!

Eddy kicks the metal plate diagonally, and it goes skidding my way. I stifle a gasp, tightening my grip on Leon's torch. Eddy tucks and rolls as the Hellon's teeth chomp down, but then the Hellon cracks its neck to me. My limbs freeze like blocks of ice. It takes everything in me to move. The Hellon crawls for me at lightspeed, and in a matter of seconds, it dives at me with a swinging claw.

Out of my peripheral, I spot Eddy now on the opposite side. When the metal plate reaches me, I swat it to Eddy with my tail, and it goes skidding, again. The Hellon's dark eye recalibrates to the right; however, its claw still comes down over me. Its immense shadow is enough to make me shiver.

"HWAAAAAAH!"

With my body too heavy to move, I miss my brief window of opportunity to jump out of the way. The Hellon's claw rams down overhead. My panic-stricken mind scrambles, but not a single thought formulates. The Hellon's feet jolt to the left as its claw hammers down on me.

My mind blanks to gray.

"HWAAAAAAH!"

Without thinking, I raise Leon's torch and shut my eyes. A gust of wind whooshes down on me, and my eyes burst open. I watch in horror as the Hellon's claw just barely misses my head. Those sharp daggers pass right before my eyes, and its long shiny nails appear even pointier up-close. I wheeze.

The Hellon charges for Eddy.

Although I want to stand there in terror and wish every-thing away, I pull myself together. *Bliss* seizes my mind, and I picture me, Eddy, Tails, and Leon there. I imagine it to be a white background surrounding a lush green garden. We all rest in the grass while Tails circles around us, wagging his tail. A fire burns bright in my gut, calling me home to this paradise.

Suddenly, a whipping wave erupts from Tails and Leon's side of the cave. Leira must've successfully translated the message to them, and Tails used his tail to lash up another smokestack of debris. Gravel and soil explode in the air as the thick smokestack shrouds the other side.

Snapping into action, I bolt left.

Eddy kicks the metal plate to me and tucks and rolls like before. The plate then skids to me, but this time, I kick it and dive out of the way. The Hellon screeches, impatient and irate. It chases after the plate, but Eddy passes it back to me.

Waiting to kick it one last time, I stop at the foot of the smokestack for our final part of the plan.

The Hellon storms my way—angrier than ever—and in a matter of seconds, it towers over me and screeches. I try to withstand the gusting vibrations, but they're too powerful. My hair belts back before I fall on my butt. Leon's torch rolls out of my hand. The metal plate even blows from under me. My eyes widen in shock as the plan slips through my fingertips.

"Slixx!" Eddy shouts.

His voice nabs my attention, and I come to, realizing the Hellon's claw is raining down on me. I push off my tail in haste. The Hellon's shadow collapses over me. Both it and I lunge for the metal plate. It screeches again, and my hearing flatlines to ringing.

I propel myself forward with one hand and reach for the plate with the other. Fully extended, I stretch my arm as far as I can, and my fingertips brush against the metal plate. Meanwhile, the Hellon's claw continues to drop on me. It reaches for the metal plate with its other claw, too.

"Almost there!" I shout, my tail scrambling in the gravel.

I thrust myself up an inch and snatch it. The Hellon's claw rams down just a few feet away. I think to toss the plate but doubt my weak, stringy arms, so instead, I throw it back over my head and kick it with my tail. I aim for the debris, and the metal plate goes skidding into the thick smokestack.

I start to exhale in relief, our part of the plan completed, but then I yelp at the Hellon's claw that's about to rip me into oblivion. I think to roll out of the way, but there's no time. I contemplate the chance of survival after those sharp nails sink into my skin, wondering if Leon has some type of antidote to bring *me* back to life.

Even though the metal plate skids away, I can tell by the dark, livid look in the Hellon's eye that it's not sparing me like last time. Its legs break out for the plate but not before it finishes the job—to send me to holding. Its claws head straight for me.

Adrenaline surges through my veins.

Eddy calls my name in the distance.

I picture all of us lying in the grass with Tails frolicking about.

I can't let that go.

Snatching Leon's torch, I fling myself up and push off on my hand and tail. I hurl through the air like a frog. Hope reigns over me, but the Hellon's reach is far greater than I imagined. Its main claw clamps down before stealing the soil. I hit the ground rolling but not out of range. The Hellon's claw slices at my thigh, and I cry out, Leon's torch falling out of my hand. I go tumbling, chucking up dirt, until I hit the wall with a bang.

When I open my eyes, I catch a glimpse of the Hellon disappearing into the debris. A small smile etches onto my face as everything goes according to plan; however, a grand stinging pain like that of a million papercuts seizes my body.

"Slixx!" Eddy shouts, sliding to his knees. "Are you okay?"

Fighting through the pain, I try to sit up, but he presses me back down. "I'm fine," I grunt, but he shoots me a glare. "Okay, I'll heal."

His frantic eyes probe over me, while his trembling hands make me uneasy. He doesn't move for a second, but then he tears a sleeve off his plaid shirt. He moves quickly, scurrying down to my tail with the cloth.

I hold in groans as his touch incites more pain. "How...bad is it?"

"Uh, bad," he gulps aloud, wrapping the cloth around my thighs. He awkwardly chuckles to relieve some tension, but I continue to moan. "You'll heal, though."

"Ouch!"

"Too tight? Sorry."

I sigh, palming my face.

Just then, on the opposite end of the cave, Tails and the Hellon burst out of the debris. Adrenaline takes over, and my upper body shoots up. Out of my peripheral, I spot a puddle of my own blood, but an even grander sight catches my attention. I watch in awe as Tails tackles the Hellon, biting into its neck again. Both of them soar through the air, and the Hellon's blood squirts out.

My plan worked—surely the Hellon was caught off guard in the smokestack. I worry about Tails' condition, though. I hope Leon's elixir worked, but I question whether or not it healed Tails completely in such little time.

The Hellon bellows in pain, its scream shaking the entire cave. Rocks slide down the walls, and the rocky icicles quake above. Tails tackles the Hellon to the ground before slamming it against the wall, not making the mistake of holding onto it this time.

Screeching, the Hellon's collision quakes the cave even more. It falls to the ground and doesn't move for a second as its neck bleeds profusely. However, Tails doesn't give it time to rest. He bounds over to it and jumps atop its limbs, and that's when I notice Leon riding atop him. I barely see him in the wake of his dying torchlight somewhere on the ground.

The Hellon screeches like music to my ears. It cracks its neck in every direction, but Tails pins him down tight, snarling like a rabid mongrel. He rips into its neck. The next screech sounds even louder than the last, but Tails doesn't waver, the Hellon's squirming and screaming proving to be futile.

"It worked," I pant. My mouth curves up into an unbelievable grin, and the pain at my side melts to the back of my head. I rise to my limp tail. "It really worked."

Eddy watches in wonder, too, before snapping out of his daze. He gestures toward Leira who stands on the edge of the settling smokestack, so we run over to her.

"What does it say?" I blurt out upon reaching her.

She clutches the metal plate with trembling hands, but her lips remain sealed.

Eddy snaps in her face, but she still doesn't respond. He even waves a hand in front of her but nothing.

"We don't have time for this," I say. I take a deep breath and raise my hand. "I apologize in advance."

Eddy looks at me in confusion until I slap Leira across the face.

Her cheek turns tomato red from my hand, but a scowl overcomes her face. She charges at me in an instant, snarling. "*Gidi negit hoctu crackri—*" she curses.

"Whoa, whoa," Eddy says, stepping between us. He holds her back, but I shoo him away.

"We don't have time for this!" I shout in unison with the screaming Hellon, and we all jump. "What does the plate say?"

Leira's gaze trails down to the small hunk of metal. "Uh...I-I'm not exactly sure what it means, but—"

"Just spit it out!" I say, impatient.

"Okay! It literally says, *darkness begets darkness with a fiery blade, so may light shine only after the eye to the nape is slayed.* I-I don't know what that means."

I look to Eddy, but he's already twiddling his thumbs in deep thought. Even though I suck at these riddles, I try to piece it together or at least make some sense of it. However, the whole thing translates as mush.

"Look, this whole thing is crazy!" Leira cries out, her disheveled hair strung about her frame. Her face is coated with debris, and her small pupils hint at her frightfully lost sanity. She steps to me in rage. "Your whole plan is insane—all of us are going to *die*. You've got Leon up there like a knight who's—according to your plan—supposed to give your beast back up against an otherworldly demon. But the catch is, your beast is also going to die."

"Watch it!" I snap.

"No, you watch it! I trust the Realm and all, but I cannot trust a foolish girl like you. Take me back to Myro." She points at the rocky icicles. "'Have your beast break the barrier.'"

"Even if he did, do you really want a demon rampaging through your village? Myro would be no more."

She clenches her jaw.

"This 'foolish girl' is trying to save your life, so let me."

"I got it!" Eddy says, coming to. He whirls to Leira. "Hand me your dagger."

Leira knits her brows.

"The ones that you all pulled out on me when we arrived. Hand me your dagger."

She opens her mouth to speak but shakes her head, reaching up her sleeve. A strap clicks, and she pulls out a sleek dagger. "Now tell me what—"

Eddy swipes the dagger from her. "Darkness begets darkness with a fiery blade," he recites. "I'm thinking we use what's left of the torch fire to light this baby up and take down the Hellon."

"That little dagger is hardly a blade—let alone one big enough to take down that demon," Leira says.

I roll my eyes from her to Eddy. The Hellon continues to screech in the background while Tails growls back at it. "I hate to say it, but she's right. There's no way we can kill a Hellon with that."

Eddy shakes his head. "No, listen. *May light shine only after the eye to the nape is slayed.* All we have to do is cut it from the eye to the nape, and that shining light will lead us to *Bliss!*"

"You sound mad—" Leira starts.

"Let's do it," I say with sweaty palms.

Eddy's eyes light up. "Seriously?"

Suddenly, the Hellon screeches—a screech like no other—as if gaining strength from the depths of *Nilli*. I whirl around before sucking in a breath. The Hellon's neck lurches up, and it clamps down on one of Tails' front legs. Tails whimpers a high-pitched howl. His cry echoes around the cave, likely even down the tunnel, as blood squirts into the Hellon's vicious mouth.

It digs its teeth into Tails' leg even harder, and Tails cries out for help, crushing my soul. Tails doesn't let up, though. He pushes through the pain and bites the Hellon's open neck wound, and it screeches in turmoil. He keeps the Hellon pinned down, but with blood gushing down his leg like that, I'm not sure how much longer he can hold on.

"We've got to hurry," Eddy says. "We—"

Before he can finish, I snatch Leira's dagger from his hands and take off. I break left for Leon's torch, Eddy calling my name from behind. He runs after me, but I don't look back. I dash along the cave wall before retrieving Leon's torch, only a weak flame crackling above it, providing the dimmest of light.

I dip Leira's dagger into the fire and hope its scorching by the time I reach the Hellon.

Catching my eye, a glimmer twinkles from above. I whip my head to it and spot Leon's silhouette jumping in the air. His jewelry shines as he arcs over Tails, heading straight for the Hellon. I furrow my brows at the small shiny instruments in his hand, but as I near the scene, I recognize them as scissors and a needle.

Freefalling, Leon cocks the arm with the needle back, and in the next instant, he lands, stabbing the Hellon in the eye. It roars with more piercing screeches, and its body squirms like a roach with its head cut off. Its claws scrape Tails in the commotion, but Tails simply growls through the pain.

Leon tries to hang onto the Hellon's poked eye during all its writhing, but that and the spouting blood must make it an impossible feat. He rams his other hand down in the nick of time, and his scissors ram the Hellon square in the eye, too. The Hellon squirms even more like holy water on a burning sinner, throwing Leon off.

"Leon!" I shout.

I start to run for him, but the heating blade in my hands keeps me on track. I round the Hellon and Tails just as it bites both of Tails' front legs. He cries out again—sorrow and despair cracking my heartless body. I slither as fast as my injured tail can go.

Tails nearly topples over, but when he sees me, he reextends his front legs, restraining the Hellon's limbs. Up-close, thick streams of blood run down his head, and a deep gash cuts through his closed right eye. I want to crumble at the sight of him. However, this won't all be for naught when we get to *Bliss*.

"Slixx, wait!" Eddy shouts from behind.

I continue ahead, though, and don't stop running until I'm several feet from the Hellon's eye. It persists scratching and biting Tails, but Tails bites it back every so often with the last of his strength.

I pull Leira's dagger from the weak torch and hold it up, steam emitting from the red-hot iron. "*May light shine only after the eye to the nape is slayed*," I mutter to myself. Although I don't exactly have a plan for slaying the nape—especially since its pinned down—I charge for the Hellon's eye. Half of me hopes that if I stab hard enough, it'll strike a core with the nape, but the other half of me knows this to be a pipe dream. I don't have a plan. I don't have a backup plan. I just want this Hellon to get the hell off my dog.

I dodge the Hellon's stray claws.

Tails does his best to keep it still, but it spirals out of control. I jump over another claw before noticing white foam bubbling out of its mouth. I squint to inspect it, but the Hellon's mouth lurches out at me. I gasp. Its sharp rows of teeth head straight for me—its range too wide for me to jump out of the way. I clutch Leon's torch in one hand and the dagger in the other.

Letting out a war cry, I stand my ground. Even though I'm up against a giant, I swing my dagger at it—not going down without a fight. But luckily, Tails stomps on its head, so I run straight for the detained Hellon's bleeding eye, white puss also oozing out.

It swings at me with its newly freed arm, though.

I tuck and roll once. Then twice.

The Hellon screeches on a rampage. It begins to slice Tails' side up, and he howls in agony. I snarl my lips in ire before sprinting for the Hellon's eye again. Tails' cries fuel me, firing me up with rage, and smoke fumes out of my nostrils. I push off the tip of my tail and lunge for the Hellon's eye.

My war cry hollers over the pandemonium as I impale its eye, digging deeper in the same fresh cut that Leon created. Its mouth opens wider than Tails' head, and it lets out a bass-booming ear-splitting scream. I jam the dagger in as far as it can go. Blood and puss submerge my hand, but I stab over and over again.

Tails keeps its head in place while I cut deeper into its eye.

"HWAAAAAAAAAAAAAAAAAAAAAAAAH!"

I stab relentlessly, and gore squirts onto my face. "May light shine only," I pant, "after the eye…to the nape…is slayed!" Tears begin to sing my cheeks as Tails yelps. Out of my peripheral, the Hellon continues to slice up his side, and all Tails can do is fend him off with his teeth. "Dammit! Why won't this work?"

After the hundredth stab, tears drench my face. The Hellon's eye is completely covered in blood and puss, blinding its vision, and its free claw slices everywhere. I roll out of the way before impaling its eye again. I cut as deep as I can—through flesh and veins—but the nape seems impossible. My hand grows tired and numb while my other is sore from my tight grip on the torch. My breaths come out heavy and uneven, too.

"Die already!" I cry out.

But my tears are futile.

I give it all I've got, but it's not enough. The Hellon squirms and screams, and there's not a damn thing that I can do about it. I stab once more before holding the dagger in the air. The weapon shakes in my trembling hands as I contemplate giving up. I picture me, Eddy, Tails, and Leon lying in the grass, again, and a heavenly peace drifting between us all. Such serenity. Such tranquility. Such…*Bliss*.

"Slixx!" a distant voice calls out, snatching me to the present.

I jerk my head up and find Eddy and Leon on the opposite side of the Hellon.

"Toss the torch!" Leon says.

He and Eddy raise their hands, ready to catch it.

I glance at the weak torchlight, and without thinking, I throw it to them. It arcs through the air before falling, and Eddy jumps up and catches it. Leon then grips the handle, too, and they cock it back.

"On three!" Eddy shouts.

I blink in awe as realization comes over me. And then I nod. "On three!"

"One..."

The blind Hellon screeches and squirms, but Tails keeps one firm paw on its head. I dodge its stray claw before jumping back into place.

"Two..."

I wield Leira's cold dagger, channeling all my strength into this last stroke.

"Three!"

In unison, I ram the dagger into the Hellon's eye, and Eddy and Leon swing the torch at the Hellon's nape. The light vanishes, burning out in an instant, as the Hellon roars in agony and fury. Darkness consumes us all. Leira screams, Tails howls in distress, and both deafening cries quake the cave. Then the sound of rocks crashing down thunders, and perhaps a rocky icicle falls on the opposite side because a large bang goes off, debris blasting at us all.

I dare not move.

But after moment, all is quiet.

I hear only Eddy and Leon's heavy breathing mixed with my own. "What's happening?" I whisper.

"Is everybody alright?" Leon asks. "Leira?"

Leira cries aloud, terror in her shaky voice. "Leon!"

"Slixx, you okay?" Eddy asks.

My lips tremble. "E-Eddy?" I gulp. "Tails?"

Silence reigns over the cave.

Like Leira, I begin to breakdown, too. I fall to my knees in the darkness and land in a puddle—probably the Hellon's blood and puss. It's as if the weight of this afterlife plummets on my shoulders, and I begin to sob. My sniffles quickly turn into wailing. I cry outright and unapologetically because darkness feels even more depressing when you're alone.

Eddy's pleas and Leon's condolences fade to the back of my head. I only hear myself crying and on replay. My mind becomes engulfed in blackness as dark as my surroundings, and nothing seems to matter anymore.

That is until a weak whimper chimes.

I gasp. "Tails?"

Suddenly, rocks begin to crack aloud. It's as if someone takes a giant hammer to the walls, or the cave begins to crumble. I whip my head around in search of the source, but the cracking bounces off the walls—as if coming from every direction. Rocks fall from the ceiling and trickle down the walls, and the splitting cracks grow louder.

"What's going on?" Leira screams.

"The cave is falling apart!" Leon shouts.

"Slixx, I'm coming to find you," Eddy says. "Say something —anything!"

My words come out without thought as I rise to my tail. "Stay where you are. It's too dangerous."

"Slixx—"

The cracks finally cease. The cave quiets itself, while the rest of us inside panic. I haul in a deep breath, scanning the still darkness.

"Is everyone alright?" Leon asks. "Did anyone get hurt?"

On the back wall, a blinding white light beams through a crack. The single beam of light lights up the middle of the cave, but then more light streaks through the many cracks on the back wall. The light breaks through as if fighting to pry its way into the darkness, and it does, lighting up the whole cave. I stare in awe at the thousands of beams streaking through the countless cracks.

Like finding the light at the end of the tunnel, a tall, narrow portion of the cave's back wall shatters. The pure bright lights burst through, and I shield my eyes from the blinding radiance. Leira shrieks, caught off guard, while Eddy and Leon groan.

With my back turned, I slowly open my eyes. My lashes flutter until my eyes adjust to the luminosity, but when they do, the Hellon's lifeless corpse is the first thing I see. It lies in a puddle of its own filth, and dark blood drips from its claws.

I pan over some more and spot Tails collapsed on the ground on the other side of the Hellon. I slurp in air at the sight of his red and dark stained coat. My legs move without command, and I leap onto the Hellon, running over him. I then jump to the ground and behold my dog.

A tear cups my chin as I walk around to his field of vision. I mindlessly pass Eddy and Leon who stand between Tails and the Hellon, and a couple yards away, Leira fleets by the corner of my eye. My gaze remains on Tails, though.

When I stop before him, he looks at me straightaway, and I stare into his good eye. "Hey boy..." My voice cracks like the countless fissures that were in the wall. I creep closer and place a hand on his snout, and he whines. "I know I keep saying this, but I'm so sorry."

He whines again as if to reject my apology. Like it's not my fault, but I know it is.

"Leon, is there anything you can do?" I ask.

He quickly circles around Tails before stopping beside me. "Some wounds look surface, while others look deep—like the ones on the left side of his body and the gash on his eye. I don't have much antidote left and just a wee bit of Plasgood, but I'll do what I can."

"Thank you. Is there anything I can do?"

He pats my shoulder. "I'll take it from here." Then, he opens his vest and rounds the left side of Tails, pulling out large gauzes and a clear white bottle.

Looking away, I crawl closer to Tails and collapse beside him. I lie down against his dry matted fur, and he whines as I hug him.

Without a word, Eddy kneels in front of me. He lies down against Tails, too, and places a gentle hand on mine. I glance up at him for a brief moment, his glossy hazel eyes channeling every ounce of comfort possible. He doesn't speak. Although silence prevails, an unspoken consolation airs between us.

I close my eyes at the sound of Tails' high-pitched whimpers. I try not to think about what medical aid Leon is rendering to him or how painful it must be. I squeeze my eyes tight and hug Tails even tighter, and I force my mind back to *Bliss*. I imagine all of us in the grass—no more humans, no more demons, no more pain, and no more living. Just peace.

Without a sound, Leira tiptoes over. I peek through one eye as she plops down and buries her head in her lap. She weeps while Tails moans. Eddy and I remain silent. This keeps up for what feels like hours until Leon walks back around and sits down beside us.

I open my mouth, but a lump gets caught in my throat. Tears well behind my lids at the question swirling around in my head. I yearn to know the answer but cannot ask.

Thankfully, Eddy does. "Is he gonna make it?"

Leon drops his head, and a tear trickles down my face. He

rubs his neck, avoiding eye contact. "I don't want to make any promises," he says. "It's a waiting game now. We just have to wait and see if the little antidote and Plasgood that I had worked. I gave it to him orally in his mouth and physically applied some on his wounds. It wasn't nearly enough, though.... But I also gave him a shot to put him to sleep. Bodies heal most when they're not actively working, and he needs as much rest as he can get right now. Only time will tell if he wakes up or..."

I sniffle, wanting to keep it together so bad, but I can't. Not right now—not like this. I stroke Tails' hard fur before giving him a soft kiss. I dare not face the blinding white light because paradise means nothing if your loved ones will never make it. My gut tells me to go, but my soul beckons to stay. So, I stay.

And I wait.

I *hope* and wait for my best friend to wake up.

CHAPTER 24
CALLING

I doze off. I awake. I doze off. I awake. I doze off. I... This cycle repeats until Leira's snoring wakes me up. She finally cried herself to sleep, resting on Leon's lap. She breathes like a grizzly bear, and her snores resemble a barracuda.

My gaze instantly flicks to Tails. Although his eyes remain closed, his body expands and contracts, and I exhale in relief. Just his breathing is all the hope that I need. I peck his fur before finding Eddy staring at me. Neither of us speak, but his eyes shine as bright as the blinding light behind us, supporting and hopeful, too. To my surprise, I look down and see his hand still atop mine.

"Slixx, Eddy," Leon says.

We both turn to him.

"This might not be the right time, but I've got to know. That Verquen character, was all that stuff you told me about him back in the snow true?"

Eddy and I exchange uneasy looks before he answers, "Yep."

"Do you believe now?" I ask. My voice comes out froggy and

weak like my current state, but I don't care enough to clear my throat. "In *Bliss*?"

Leon looks straight ahead toward the barrier of rocky icicles. He takes a moment to gather his thoughts, contemplation written all over his silhouetted face. "Not sure."

"After all this, what do you mean n—" Eddy says, furrowing his brows.

But I cut him off. "Let him speak."

Eddy's expressions softens as he recoils with a pout.

"Perhaps it exists," Leon continues, "or perhaps it doesn't. Regardless of what's happened, none of us can say with certainty that *Bliss* is one hundred percent real. None of us have ever been—not even that Verquen character."

Eddy sighs. "I hate to say it, but he's gotta point."

"Fair enough. But what if that's the entrance?" I ask, gesturing to the blinding light. "What if that's the way to *Bliss*? Would you go?"

Leon hesitates.

"Eddy, what about you?"

Nearly jumping up, Eddy widens his eyes in enthusiasm. "Hell yeah!"

I crack a smile.

"Would you?" Leon asks me.

I pause. His query elicits a natural response from me, but I stifle the three letters. Gulping, I avert my attention to Tails. "I would, but not without my dog."

Eddy drops his head, while Leon dips his chin in understanding.

"You never answered, though," I say to Leon. "Knowing what you know now, would you go?"

Mumbling, Leon repeats my question to himself. He rakes a hand over his sleek ponytail, and his jewelry jangles around his neck. His thin catlike eyes appear calm and calculating. He looks down at Leira without an ounce of warmth present. He combs the hair from her face, but he moves robotically more so than affectionately. "To tell the truth, even if I wanted to, I'm not sure I could get in."

"What do you mean?" Eddy blurts out just as mystified as me.

"Why wouldn't you be able to get in?" I ask.

He looks up at me and Eddy, keen and meticulous. "I've done things in my past life—things that I'm ashamed of. I swore I'd take it to the grave, and I did. My memory of it all rushed back when I came to The Dump, though."

Staring off in a trance, he caresses Leira's cheek. "You've already faulted me for my *fickle* ways. But there are so many more unmentionable and despicable things about me. I am a sinner. And sinners never find peace."

I narrow my eyes at him, digesting his confessions like a hard pill to swallow. I search his hollow irises for certainty, and they tell a tale even graver than his expression. My mind scrambles for a response, but nothing seems quite right to say.

Eddy, however, finds the words as per usual. (Hence, the Eddy Effect.) "You can always repent—or pray for forgiveness."

"Pray to who?" Leon asks with a hint of sarcasm. "A mighty ruler in the sky? Or a slew of worshipped animals? Or maybe a holy man walking among us in ghost world? Perhaps even hail the Realm like the Myro's? It all sounds ridiculous."

I take a moment to consider as Mrs. Gyrah's advice rings in my ears. *Know where you're going before you get there, or you may end up somewhere wretched.*

"Everyone believes in something." Eddy removes his hand from mine before sitting up and blocking out the blinding light. "When a person is at their lowest, they turn to someone or something. Who do you turn to?"

"Myself," Leon says.

"And how far has that gotten you?"

He falls silent.

"Look how far that's gotten *you*," I snap to Eddy. "You're a hypocrite. Faith or no faith, we're all in the same boat right now." I turn to Leon. "If your faith is yourself and you believe you can do anything, then keep believing that. I think some people need a set of rules or beliefs to be a good person, but if you trust your judgment, then that's on you. Nothing wrong with that."

Leon dips his chin. "Thanks, Sheets."

"Who do you turn to then, Slixx?" Eddy asks, leveling his voice.

I shrug. "Even in my past life, I'd never thought about it. I guess I'm still figuring it out. But when I do, try not to judge me too hard."

His gaze trails down to the ground. An apologetic twinkle shines in his eyes, but his face remains taut. "Sorry."

"As much as I hate to say this," Leon says, "you're a good guy, Flicky."

Eddy whips to him, starry-eyed. He stares at him in wonder before returning a grin. "Right back atcha, Leon."

He reaches out and touches the left side of Eddy's chest. "Don't lose that heart."

"And don't you lose those medical skills," Eddy says, and we all chuckle. "You'll become that doctor. I'm sure of it."

"And you'll become that renown athlete."

I smack Leon's hand down. "Alright already. Enough with the sappy antics."

"Is it because you're not a part of it?" Eddy mocks.

I suck my teeth. "Yeah right."

"I always suspected you were the jealous type," Leon says.

"Jealous?" I roll my eyes. "You two are delusional."

Eddy and Leon lean toward each other, cupping their hands

around their mouths as if I can't hear them. "She gets like this all the time," Eddy whispers. "Very possessive."

Leon raises his brows. "Really?"

"I'm right here, ya know!"

They zip their lips.

Meanwhile, Leira's snores break off into wheezes. She sucks in air, regaining consciousness, and rubs her eyes awake. Her long hair brushes along her waist as she sits up. "Can I go home now?" she mumbles.

Eddy, Leon, and I each exchange looks. We glance at each other in deliberation of who's going to spill the unfortunate news of no news. However, as we open our mouths to speak, something large moves behind us.

Startled, I jump around to my knees. "Tails?" I shout.

Although weak and faint, he barks. He *actually* barks.

I bury my face in his fur, embracing him in a great big hug. The matted parts chaff against my skin, but I caress the hard and soft spots all the same. His one good eye opens, and his mouth curls back into a feeble smile. He slowly rolls out his tongue and licks me.

Tears of joy escape me. "Thank you," I murmur to no one in particular.

"He's alive!" Eddy exclaims.

Both he and Leon stride to Tails' ear, but when they both go to rub his soft spot, they scowl at each other. Leon shoots Eddy a frown; Eddy glares at him. They snoot their noses at each other before petting different parts of Tails.

My mind swirls as an array of emotions overcomes me. I squeeze Tails harder just to feel his body cave in and out with each breath, and the thought of losing him vanishes from existence. I no longer have to imagine a comatose world without him, but instead, he and I will be going to *Bliss* after all.

I hug Tails one last time before standing up. Then, I wipe

my tears and snot with my forearm and face the blinding light. "Who's ready to go to *Bliss*?"

Eddy comes up beside me. "Wooh! I'm in!"

"Let's find out if it this fantastical place exists," Leon says, crossing his arms on my other side.

"Take me home." Leira steps in front of us, and her entire body becomes a living shadow. "Now that your beast is undead, have it part the barrier, so I can leave."

"He might be too weak—" I start.

Tails slowly ascends to his paws. He barks, offering me reassurance, but still sounds hoarse and weak. Although he walks with a limp, I dare not stand in his way. We all follow him to the tunnel, and once there, he headbutts one of the rocky icicles. He rams his dome against it several times until the rest of us join forces and push the rock from the bottom.

Even with everyone's help, it takes a few minutes before the sharp rock topples over.

Leira then shuffles past the barrier in a hurry. She backs away into the dark tunnel and blows Leon a kiss before flashing the rest of us a thin smile. After, she turns around to head out. Her long hair sways along her back, and her hips rock from side to side. She begins to disappear into the darkness.

"Wait!" I call out.

She wheels around, her hair flipping over her shoulder.

I break formation and jog over to her. She studies me as I come to a standstill, but I avoid awkward eye contact. "Hey."

"Hey?" she says as a question more so than a statement.

"You know we're going to *Bliss* to finally pass on. You don't have to go." My gauche words come out forcefully, so I take a moment to compose myself. "Despite everything that's happened, you can come with us. If Leon's tagging along with us now, anyone can."

She chuckles. "Thank you for the offer. Although tempting, I must return to my people."

My eyebrows droop down in bewilderment. "But why? Don't you want to go to—?"

"Of course. As much as I love my village, *of course* I want to leave this wasteland. The Dump is PTSD for ghosts, and it's hell reliving your demise. You never forget about it. You never forget what was, what could've been, and all the what ifs that could've happened after you left the land of the living. Every day, it's like I'm burning—just without the fire."

She takes my hand. "But like my people, I believe in the Realm, and I trust whatever it has in store for me. That being said, something tells me you four are the travelers that we've been waiting for. So go. And may we reap what good fortune you may sow. Good luck, Slixx."

A lump gets caught in my throat. I swallow her rejection like hard alcohol, but I squeeze her hand in return. Then, we part, both backing our separate ways.

"May we meet again in the next life."

She turns her back, and I turn mine, heading back to Eddy, Tails, and Leon. They talk amongst themselves until I return.

"What was that all about?" Eddy asks, his hands clasped behind his head.

"Uh...girl talk." I flash a smile.

"I take it you were talking about me," Leon says.

"So vain." I roll my eyes. "You were the last topic of conversation."

"So, I was a topic?"

"Woof!"

Shaking my head, I walk off. They all follow me, and we trek across the cave before stopping at the foot of the blinding white entrance. It's as wide as all four of us standing in a line. We shade our eyes from the intense rays, but the brightness never wavers.

"Ready?" Eddy asks aloud.

Tails barks, and Leon and I nod.

Leaving the rest unspoken, we all take off running.

We sprint as fast as we can to our heart's content, and our chains rattle like sweet music behind us. Eddy hops into the air with zest, while Tails keeps up with us even with limp paws. Leon even jumps for joy. Excitement bursts out of me, too, and I shout at the top of my lungs.

"To *Bliss*!"

The light grows brighter the farther we run. I see nothing but white all around me, and I'm blinded by the intensity. Happiness overfills me. I exude sweet euphoria and wonder if this is *Bliss*. I smile from ear to ear, and my tail slithers so fast that it feels like I'm flying. I run toward the light with all my might to the jolly sound of rustling chains and cheerful voices.

Tails gallops at my side, and Eddy and Leon chase paradise full of spirit. The light intensifies tenfold. My arms blow back in perfect ghostly running form, and my curly hair belts behind me. The light vanquishes my vision, Eddy, Tails, and Leon vanishing from my peripheral.

I keep running, though, because I know their spirits run alongside me, and that's all that matters. I run. *We* run. We all chase the unattainable.

The light amplifies beyond anything I've ever seen.

And dazzling wonder overtakes my consciousness.

CHAPTER 25
DEAD BOY, AGAIN

I stare up at a burning red sky and immediately know this can't be *Bliss*.

Sitting up, my back aches, and my limbs throb. I guess it's from running so hard, but then I notice the uncomfortable barren terrain under me. Bedrock extends for miles ahead, and big cracks separate the dry stones. The land looks like it hasn't touched water in eons.

A bubbling noise sounds behind me, but just as I turn around, Eddy pops into view. I gasp, grabbing where my human heart attack would've been. I curse under my breath before hitting him.

"Sorry," he grumbles.

A hand then extends down to me, and I trace it up to its origin. Leon. He stands beside Tails who sits like a good dog. A scar runs through Tails' closed left eye, and dry blood still stains his fur coat. However, the wounds now appear fully healed, lingering only as permanent reminders of battle. He breathes hard and eager with his tongue hanging out of his mouth.

My eyes light up at the sight of him, and he barks as if to greet me.

"I take it we're not in *Bliss*," Leon says.

Shifting my gaze to him, I sigh. "Doesn't look like it."

I grab Leon's hand to pull me up, but when he does, I don't land on my tail. Matter of fact, my tail doesn't even hit the ground. I glance down at my lower body and do a double take. I'm floating. *Floating?* Yes, floating!

"What the—!" I gasp, backing away.

I know my feet turned into a tail before, but this is beyond preposterous. I float in midair like a stereotypical ghost, and my lower body now takes an indefinite shape. Beneath my tattered dress, my skin swirls like a mixture of contained gases. And even more ludicrous, my tail rounds beneath me, so I look over my shoulder only to discover my *new* tail. It appears indefinite like the rest of my lower body, but the tip is solid, sharp, and *lethal*. It shines under the deadly skylight, resembling my same metal chain.

"Apparently this is our new form," Leon says.

Eddy wags his pointy tail in excitement, and his extended chain rattles behind him. Unlike in The Dump, it now extends from his back up to the perilous sky for as far as the eye can see. His skin, however, continues to flicker at the same rate—thankfully. "It's pretty cool."

"Cool?" I slowly touch the tip of my tail. "Ouch!"

Tails whimpers, stooping down to inspect my prick. He whines as I suck my bleeding finger, but after a second, the bleeding stops. The sting lingers for a minute, though.

"Yeah, don't touch it," Eddy says, holding his hand. "Been there, done that."

Leon shoots him a dark look. "You actually grabbed yours, you fool."

"Who you calling a fool, nincompoop?"

"Nincompoop?" Leon asks.

Tails raises an ear.

I even raise a brow. "Eddy, that's your best comeback?"

Eddy's gaze trails down to the ground, and he lowers his voice to a mumble. "I ran out of them."

Both Leon and I shake our heads.

"Where exactly are we?" I ask, scanning the dry land. I finally behold the bubbling behind me, and my eyes widen at a fiery river. Bubbling lava flows down a narrow stream no wider than my thumb, but the red-hot bubbles blister and bust aloud all the same while dark cooled lava plagues the edges. I float toward it, the front of my dress dragging on the ground.

"Your guess is as good as mine," Leon says, staring up at the pained sky.

Above, the various red hues range from bright blood to crimson, and they intertwine with rotten pumpkin orange and blazing yellow. There are no clouds. No sun. No light source. The sky just burns bright like an eternal inferno, and melancholy looms over the land.

"Well, according to the fountain from Limbo, we're in the third realm," Eddy says.

"How do you know?" Leon asks.

He shrugs, nonchalant. "Photographic memory."

Jealousy creeps up my spine, but I try to swallow it down. Although I can't help but roll my eyes, I clamp my lips shut at the onset of a snide remark.

Eddy recites the original riddle. *"Ghosts one – Limbo in murder and sickness, ghosts two – The Dump in natural quickness, ghosts three – Almost in self-witness.* My guess is we're in Almost."

"What an odd name for a realm," Leon says.

I stare down at the sweltering lava before tracing it yonder in both directions, wondering its source and where it streams to. "But if this is Almost, then this is the last realm. All we have to do is find another fountain, and it'll lead us to *Bliss*."

Leon crosses his arms. "I highly doubt that."

"You got any better ideas?" I ask with narrowed eyes.

"No, but I know your little plan is too simple to work. For starters, we're in the middle of nowhere. Secondly, The Dump brought us here by cave not fountain. And lastly, we don't even know where to begin."

I bite my tongue at his valid points, especially the second one. With no clues or new riddles, it's like starting all over, again.

"How about following the lava stream," Eddy suggests.

Leon shrugs.

"It's worth a shot," I say. Tails creeps up behind me, and I pet him with a smile. "Which way?"

"Left."

"Right."

They both respond in unison, and I sigh. They start to bicker back and forth, insults sailing through the air. My temples pulsate at the onset of a headache, so I massage them. Even though my ears don't ring anymore, I wish they did to tune out these idiots.

The barren terrain stretches for miles in every direction, and the stream runs the same. It's a gamble either way.

"You joined my team back in Snowdevlin, remember?" Leon says. "Without me, we never would've gotten this far. I say left."

"*Psh*. Me and Slixx were doing just fine without you."

"Traveling aimlessly?"

"No! I'm the one who found the fountain in Limbo!"

"Give me a break."

"No, you—"

Out of nowhere, we all jump at the sound of heavy panting. Tails hops in front of me in attack mode, growling, while I whirl around to find the source. But no one else is out here. The panting grows heavier and louder as the rugged breaths draw near, and clanging metal also sounds in the distance.

"W-what's that?" Eddy asks, his voice shaky.

Despite the situation, sarcasm escapes me. "Clearly not the wind."

"It sounds like it's coming from—" Leon starts, but midsentence, he gasps.

Both Eddy, Tails, and I wheel around to him before gasping, too.

A short kid with shaggy blond hair and bony shoulders passes *through* Leon. His body appears translucent blue, and a severed black chain stems from his back. It drags on the ground as he runs straight ahead in fear. His droopy eyebrows are scrunched together, his sunken mouth curved down. His running arms propel him forward, but he holds onto something in his right hand. I try to lock on it but can't get a good view.

"Leave me alone!" the boy shouts, passing through Leon.

Leon barely has any time to react before the boy runs through him and disappears. He pats his body down, while the now invisible boy continues shouting at the unknown. The boy's chain rattles ahead as his breaths grow farther away.

"Leave me alone!"

"Wait," I call out.

"S-stop!" Eddy says.

All goes quiet except the bubbling stream of lava.

"I said stay back!" the boy cries out.

My hands shoot up, and I gesture for Eddy and Leon to raise theirs. Eddy puts up his, and Leon reluctantly does, too. Even Tails puts up his front paws.

The boy lugs in heavy breaths like he's been running for hours.

I blurt out the first thing that comes to mind. "We come in peace."

Leon shoots me a look. "Really?"

I shrug, ushering him to say something.

"Look, kid, we just arrived here," Leon says. "We don't have any weapons or cruel intent. Maybe you can help u—"

"Stop trying to turn me into something I'm not!" the boy shouts.

We all look at each other in confusion, and Tails raises an inquisitive ear. Our puzzled expressions quickly turn into panic, though.

"H-hey p-pal, you okay?" Eddy asks.

"I didn't ask to be here!"

Tails and I exchange uneasy glances.

"Maybe it's a ghost mid-lifetime crisis," Leon whispers to us.

We flash him glares.

"What? It happens."

"Maybe we can help you!" I shout to the invisible kid. He respires deeply, so I know he's still here. "Just come back—"

"You never listen!" The kid chokes up as he begins to sob. "It's always my fault, but I can't help it, Dad!"

I find myself subconsciously floating forward—toward the boy's voice. His intonation and tone resonate with me, and Elliot's face pops into my head. Although instead of shaking it away, I let it marinate in my mind this time. That sick face. My *killer's* face. I creep toward the invisible boy's tears, replacing Elliot with his shaggy blond hair and terrified frown.

His sob quickly evolves into a wail.

"Slixx, wait," Eddy says behind me.

But an unseen magnet attracts me to the boy, his pain evoking my past trauma. The boy cries out for help. The backs of my eyelids sting. His voice rises along with his bawling. A lump gets caught in my throat, but I gulp it down. Then suddenly, a metal slide clicks.

"If you don't want me here, then I'll just go!"

I freeze as my eyes widen in awe, and the boy and I speak in unison.

"Stop," I whisper.

"Stop!" he shouts.

BANG.

My jaw drops in horror as the boy's lifeless body becomes fully visible. He collapses on the ground, landing on his ivory face, and bright red blood gushes from a blasted hole in the back of his head. The gore puddles under him before spreading out to his chain. More and more blood—more than a body possesses—rushes out of his wound with no sign of stopping. Meanwhile, his tail shrivels up while his eyes flush red.

I cup my mouth.

"What the...?" Leon asks in a low voice.

Tails barks, galloping to me. He curves around to shield me from the wretched view, but I catch a glimpse of the boy's left hand shaped like a finger gun—his thumb and index finger pointed. Splattered blood plagues his hand as if a real weapon. I begin to question it, but at this point, anything's possible.

"I think I'm gonna be sick," Eddy says.

Burying my head in Tails' fur, he snuggles against me. I squeeze him tight, desperately trying to shake away Elliot's intermittent appearances in my mind—him and the real gun that took my human life.

"Where the hell are we?" I choke out.

Eddy walks up from behind me and places a hand on my shoulder. I cave at the touch and fall into his arms, and he caresses my wild hair. I can tell that he's as much in need of this hug as me. "Almost," he says.

"Almost to peace but not quite," Leon says. "Makes sense."

I don't cry. Maybe after a million tears, I can *no longer* cry. Maybe I've become so numb to the pain that nothing feels real anymore. Like I'm going through the motions of life without even being alive.

Pulling away from Eddy, I take a deep breath to collect myself. Then, I walk back to Leon, and Tails and Eddy follow. We all huddle together, staring at the bloody blond boy from a distance.

"I'm assuming this realm is for those who took their own lives then," I say.

Eddy drops his head.

Tails whimpers.

"Instead of simply knowing their deaths like in The Dump, they relive them," Leon suggests.

Just then, our suspicions come true. The blond boy begins to absorb the gallons of blood on the ground, and it quickly soaks back into his wound. It leaves no stains or traces of gore. And once it's all gone, the boy's eyes burst open. He blinks twice before rising to his tail, floating in the air.

He robotically places the finger gun inside his mouth as if rapidly rewinding his past actions, and just as fast, he puts his hands to his side. His mouth opens wide, yelling like earlier, but nothing comes out. His veins pop out, though. All the despairing emotion in his previous shouts now show while his tears suck back into his whole red eyes.

I suck in air at those *familiar* red eyes—from that fateful day. Back in the dark alley. "Verquen..."

"Where?" Eddy snaps, whipping his sharp tail around like a weapon.

Leon instinctively whips his lethal one around, too, and he holds up his hands as if to catch the threat. Tails also bites out a vicious growl, revealing his canines. Their heads whip to-and-fro in search of the enemy.

"Those eyes..."

Settling down, they all follow my gaze back to the boy. A

mental image of Verquen catches me off guard, and I nearly forget to breathe. The boy's unchanging eyes remain engulfed in red as he moves backward through time. His skin remains solid, too.

He shouts a final time before running backward—past the spot he passes through Leon—going back the way he came.

"Should we follow him?" Leon asks.

But I'm already ahead of him. I slink after the boy before breaking out into a run to chase after him. He moves faster than he came, flying backward through time, and Tails, Eddy, Leon, and I pursue him.

When the gap between us and the boy grows too far, we hop on Tails' back. His healthy paws hit the ground running, but I remind him to be careful of the lava stream which we follow along. It grows wider the farther we run, and the hot bursting bubbles louden. The warm temperature also rises just enough to produce beads of sweat above my upper lip. However, this little heat pales in comparison to Myro.

Eddy, Leon, and I cling onto Tails' fur as we race after the boy risen from the dead. A hopeful part of me thinks that maybe he'll lead us to *Bliss*, but my churning gut says otherwise. I clench my jaw, wondering what wicked ways lie ahead.

CHAPTER 26
NOISY HOT NOISY HOT

The stream gradually widens the farther along we run, but after a few kilometers, it flows into a large ocean—a piping, hot, *lava ocean*. Tails slows to a stop at the edge of the land as the blond boy runs backward across the large body of lava, floating over it. Meanwhile, the rest of us stare in shock at the sight before us, a massive heatwave hitting us straight on.

Instead of sea ice, chunks of barren land—like the one we're on—float on the ocean's surface. They somehow withstand the smoldering lava and slowly drift with the current. These sea lands stretch for as far as the eye can see, but even more shocking, thousands of red-eyed ghosts like the blond boy run backward toward a distant burning forest several miles away.

They mindlessly rewind through time in silence while pants and screams fill the air from other invisible ghosts. I assume they're running *to* their deaths but can't figure why the solid ones backtrack toward the remote forest. Smoke fumes up to the sky from the burning trees yonder.

"He's getting away," Eddy says, snapping me back to reality.

Tails stammers in place with a whimper.

Wiping the sweat off my upper lip, I peek over his head and down at the boiling bubbles of lava below. "Tails can't go through that!"

"We can float across," Leon suggests.

I suck my teeth. "And leave Tails behind?"

Eddy points ahead. "Uh, he's getting away!"

We all trace his index finger to the blond boy who gets swept up in the mass of dead ghosts. Because although the population is sparse on the outskirts where we stand, sporadic breaths and few bodies bypassing us every so often, it becomes denser closer to the burning forest.

"Why are we following this particular ghost again?" Leon asks.

"Because we don't know where to go, and he's our only lead," I say.

"I'd hardly call this a lead."

"Do you have any better—?"

Just then, Eddy blurts out, "Over!"

"Over?" Leon and I repeat in unison.

I glance back at him over my shoulder, and his hazel eyes light up with the idea. He gestures with two fingers on his palm. "Tails can just jump over the lava and onto the next rock."

I knit my brows, shifting my gaze between him and the yards of lava between us and the nearest sea land. "What if he falls in?"

"Canines are very agile."

"Let's hurry this up then," Leon says.

My jaw drops. "What? No way—!"

Without warning, Tails leaps into the air, and I nearly fly off his back. I manage to grip his fur, but a shriek escapes me. My head whiplashes back; then it jerks forward when Tails lands hard. My stomach churns in knots at this abrupt roller coaster.

"Hey, boy, you know you don't have to—"

But he jumps again. He leaps over the lava and lands quickly on his feet. The gaps between lands widen, but he just takes a running start. I cling onto his fur for dear life, desperately wanting to get off this bumpy ride.

The screams and heavy breaths louden as we near the smoky forest, whereas the solid mute ghosts run through and all-around Tails. They float through the air like a hook reels them in. I lose sight of the blond boy, but Tails continues hopping in driven pursuit.

"Are we almost there?" I shout.

Instead of a response, Tails breaks out into a growl, and I yank my head up in surprise.

My eyes widen just as fast at a Hellon a couple yards away. It looks exactly like the one from the cave, standing weaponless and hunched over, but smaller—now the same size as Tails. Out of my peripheral, I catch sight of another one before panning over to another. About ten of them stand on various pieces of land surrounding the burning forest island.

"You've got to be kidding me." I sigh. "Eddy, I don't suppose you have a plan for this, do you?"

"Uh...not at the moment."

"Well, we can't take on all of them," I say, thinking back to the aftermath in the cave. "And who knows how many more are guarding the other sides of the forest."

"But look closely," Leon says, his tone low and keen.

Looking ahead at the many Hellons, I try to no avail to pick up on Leon's clue. Even Eddy doesn't get it because he asks, "What are we supposed to be looking at?"

Leon groans. "They're not moving. We see them, so surely, they see us. Why aren't they attacking?"

"The last one didn't attack until we stole that plate of metal," Eddy says. "Or maybe we're not close enough. Could be either or both."

"There's only one way to find out."

I whirl around to them. "Have you two lost it, *again*? We can't just jump into another fight."

"Why not?" Leon motions to Tails. "Your dog seems to be healed up, and now we know how to kill them."

Eddy grabs the back of his neck. "Fire to the nape and dagger to the eye, remember?"

"Do either of you have fire?"

"Lava," Eddy quickly answers.

Frustrated, I blow smoke out my nostrils. "Do either of you have daggers?

Leon turns to the side. "We have our tails."

"Not the same thing. Who knows if they'll work."

"And who knows if they won't?" he counters.

"I hate to say it, but he's gotta point," Eddy chimes in.

I narrow my eyes at him, but he averts my deadly gaze. "Fine. But if we die, it's on you two. And I doubt there's a holding in this realm. Who knows what'll happen to us here."

Leon studies me with those calculating catlike eyes of his, picking apart my existence even from a distance. "Lucky for you, I'm not in the business of dying."

I grit my teeth, matching his straight face, yet an odd sense of relief washes over my doubt. Sweat trickles down the sides of my face from the heatwave, and a bead of it drips from my chin. The corners of my mouth pinch as I turn around.

"To *Bliss!*" Eddy cries out.

Both Leon and I chuckle, and Tails barks.

"Let's go, boy," I say, patting Tails.

Taking off, he leaps onto the next piece of land. He moves quick and nimble like a wild animal, and for the first time, it dawns on me that Tails has a past, too. I wonder what he's been through—who used to own him. Was he owned when we found him in the cemetery? Since he was collarless, was he abandoned?

Orphans like me get street smart, so I assume the same for abandoned pets, tapping more into their innate instincts.

Eddy, Leon, and I all hang onto Tails' fur as he soars across the lava. He backs up before jumping to the next piece of land. He scans the area for the quickest and shortest route but is also careful not to come too close to the Hellons. I stare in awe at his high-speed mind as he jumps from side to side, pushing off the lands with tremendous strength. His fur coat breezes back along with my wild hair and chain, and in the blink of an eye, we pass between two Hellons.

Although they remain motionless, they both screech. Their cries trigger a domino effect, and one by one, the other Hellons let out piercing cries. They echo around the sides of the island, the screams growing more and more distant yet still thunderous.

I glance back at Eddy and Leon, and the three of us exchange uneasy looks. I then shift my attention to the Hellons behind us, and they fall silent after their initial screeches. Thankfully, they don't chase after us—they don't even turn around.

A relieved smile etches onto my face; Eddy returns the expression; and Leon nods. Facing forward, I behold the burning forest before me. Fire ravages the treetops, and the lush green leaves burn brightly. Up-close, they strangely retain their color. Never do they shrivel to brown ash, but they just...burn. And above, a smokestack pipes up into the air from somewhere within the forest.

Tails makes one final leap and stops on the forested island. A massive influx of ghosts runs backward into the forest, and they all enter from the center. Even louder screams and pants echo from the depths of the fiery jungle—the hub of death.

Tails barks out of nowhere, but then I catch a glimpse of the blond boy. He hurls between the two center trees like the rest of the ghosts before flying out of sight.

Reclining on his paws, we quickly dismount our ride. Meanwhile, Tails rolls out his exhausted tongue, panting. I do a quick scan, and luckily, there's not a scratch on him. He barks for us to hurry.

Leon takes the lead, running for the forest.

"Wait," I cry out, and he whirls around. "Tails can't fit!"

Tails whimpers but shakes his head all the same as if to say *go without me.* He's as tall as the treetops, and the forest appears too narrow for him to squeeze through.

"We can't leave you," I say.

But he barks in protest.

"We can meet him on the other side," Eddy blurts out. "We'll go into the forest and see if we can find anything. Do or don't, either way we'll meet him on the other side."

Leon starts for the forest, again, and Eddy breaks into a sprint with him.

"What if we get lost?" I call out.

Eddy glances back over his shoulder. "Then we follow the ghosts out and round the outskirts of the island!"

Tails pushes me forward with his nose, but I still hesitate. He pushes me again and whines, begging me to go, and it's only then that I cave at those puppy-dog eyes. I kiss him on the nose before running after the boys.

They're not too far ahead, so I chase them down as they near the gateway to the forest. Invisible voices and breaths whisk past me, and I swat the sides of my ears. The subtle whispers send a chill down my spine while the cries produce goosebumps on my arms. These pained ghosts cry out in despair for eternity. I wonder *what if I had ended up here?*

Gaining on the boys, Leon suddenly stops at the foot of the

forest's tall, wild, evergreen grass. Eddy bumps into him, but I halt a safe couple feet away, slowly approaching them with curious brows.

"He's getting away!" Eddy says, peering into the dark ghost-sucking abyss.

"What's wrong?" I ask.

Both Eddy and I slowly tick our heads in Leon's direction to the left and gasp. I grab my chest, caught off guard, and Eddy jumps into the air. He rockets off the ground and up miles into the sky before drifting back down.

Just centimeters from Leon lies a tall skinny girl with cinnamon skin. She nearly blends in with the tree bark, but her butterscotch shirt, tight black spandex, and black chain give her away. She stands as straight as a board, her arms by her side, and her long straight hair drapes behind her back. She appears as a pretty statue—unmoving and still—staring dead ahead.

Leon waves a hand in front of her unblinking face. "Hello?"

"Think she's dangerous?" Eddy whispers.

I roll my eyes at him. "Yeah, especially with all those weapons she's carrying."

Leon raises his tail, angling yet concealing it high behind his shoulder—ready for attack. He snaps his fingers in front of her, but she still doesn't blink. "Hello there." *Snap. Snap.* "Hey."

The girl's full lips remain sealed like a doll.

Tails creeps up behind us, curious too.

I swat at the sides of my ears again—at the many voices—while the influx of retreating ghosts breezes past me. The eerie wind makes my skin crawl. "Should we just go in?"

"I don't know," Eddy whispers like it's a secret.

Leon flashes us an unsure look. "Will she stop us?"

Eddy whisks in air to speak, but then the girl's head snaps left toward Leon. They stare into each other's eyes mere inches apart.

"No," she says in a cold, flat voice.

"AHH!" we all cry out, simultaneously.

Taken aback, Leon and I freeze while Eddy jumps back into the air. Tails begins to growl only after our reactions; however, after a moment, I melt back into my body and pet him calm.

"You're real?" Eddy gulps, floating down.

The girl's icy glare glosses over each of us. "Yes."

"Well maybe you can help us," I say. "We're looking for—"

"A way into the forest," Leon interjects, forcing out a laugh. He glances back at me with a phony smile, but I give him a black look.

Gesturing, the girl tips her chin at the centered trees. "You were on the right track." She then faces forward without another word.

I look to Eddy for an explanation of what's going on, but he shrugs just as clueless as I am. So, I elbow Leon's back. "What are you doing?" I murmur, but he shakes me off. And at that point, I've had enough. I sidestep to the front, bumping his shoulder. "My name's Slixx. This is Leon, and that's Eddy. Who are you exactly? And what is this place?"

She turns to me on command, expressionless. "I am the temporary keeper for the time being, and this is Almost." She answers curt like she's cutting herself off, but she remains looking at me—or rather *through* me.

"Okaaaaay..."

Eddy steps on the other side of me. "What do you mean by 'temporary keeper'?"

She shifts her remote regard to him. "Every blue moon, one ghost is chosen from the pool to become cognizant and observe the realm."

"As a punishment?" I ask.

"As a *blessing*," she corrects.

Leon dips his chin as if in understanding. "To temporarily relieve eternal pain?"

"Yes," the girl says.

"Oh…" I twist my mouth, realizing the circumstances. "Well, how often are these 'cognizant ghosts' chosen? Is 'every blue moon' like a day or a month?"

The girl cocks her head to the side ever so slightly. "Time doesn't exist here."

Both Eddy and Leon flash me shrewd looks like I should've known that.

"What's inside this forest?" Eddy asks, studying the raining embers.

The girl shifts to him. "The Hub. Or the pool's source."

"Well, do you know anything about Bl—" I start.

But Leon talks over me, *again*. "Bless your soul! It was a pleasure meeting you."

I scrunch my face at him but bite my tongue. Eddy even raises a defensive eye, and we glower at Leon together.

"We'll just be going then," he continues, slinking into the forest.

I flash the girl a fake smile before ripping my attention to Tails. I peck him on the snout one last time and grin. "Meet you on the other side, boy."

He barks, licking me after.

As I turn to the forest, a scowl re-masks my face. I march in after Leon, and Eddy follows at my side. We all enter the dark green abyss, but the fire far overhead lights up the dim grassland enough to see. Embers fall from above and prick our skin, yet they burn out before contact, serving as mere mosquito bites.

Since the trees part to form a path, we follow it straight ahead. Countless ghosts run backward through and all around us, while various invisible voices cry out for help. They talk over each other, sounding in unison with our clanging chains. Whispers and screams fill the air with despair.

Meanwhile, I swat at my ears like the voices are in my head, triggering déjà vu with me and Kiara. I remember scaring her in her sleep, and a corner of my mouth pinches at the fond memory. I let if fade, though.

"What the hell was that back there?" I ask, shoving Leon from behind.

"Yeah, why'd you keep cutting Slixx off?" Eddy asks.

Leon sighs but doesn't turn around. "Safety precautions."

"Meaning?" I say.

He sighs, again, as we walk deeper into the forest. "Meaning we don't know her, anyone here, or anything about this realm. Had you told her what we were here for, she might've tried to stop us. She kept her mouth closed, so, so should we."

Eddy shakes his head, lowering his voice. "He's gotta point."

"But what if she knew something and could help us?" I ask, twitching as the voices grow louder.

Leon shrugs. "What if she didn't?"

"I'm not doing this with you again."

"Let's just take it one step at a time," Eddy says with a shiver. "Find the Hub and go from there."

"Fine."

"Fine," Leon says.

The three of us fall quiet for the next few minutes. The voices eventually get to Leon, and he plugs his ears with his fingers. He leads us through the forest with his macho shoulders and squeaky leather, while Eddy walks beside me with his head down. He stares at the ground with such intensity, and the tension in his face reigns over his stiff posture. He shivers every so often but keeps his hands in his pants. As for me, I flinch and tick like a mad woman. The voices erupt in various volumes, so some pierce my eardrums while others fire off in my head. It only gets worse the farther we travel into the burning forest.

After another moment, Eddy breaks the silence. "I've been thinking about this Hub," he shouts over the voices. "From what that girl said, it's where all these ghosts come from. They wind up here from the human realm after taking their own lives, but what becomes of them?"

Leon glances back out of his peripheral. "They can't die, remember?"

"I know that. Their bodies can't. They're trapped in this infinite loop here. But...what becomes of their souls?"

I gaze at Eddy's remote yet twinkling eyes for a beat before pondering his query. "I'd never thought about that," I whisper.

"That girl back there said one ghost becomes cognizant at a time in this realm," Eddy continues. "But cognizance doesn't equal consciousness."

I think back to the cinnamon-skinned girl. She looked like us and breathed like us, but she wasn't *all* there. "Come to think of it, something was a little off about her."

"What happened to her soul?"

Leon lowers his head as if he's thinking.

"And from what I gather, Verquen's from here."

I gasp, a sudden dastardly image of him emerging in my head.

Leon jerks his head up. "How do you figure?"

"Slixx, I think you figured it out, too—earlier when we saw that boy rise from the dead. Back in the human realm, Verquen's eyes were red before they turned white." Eddy pauses. "This is all just a hunch, but something tells me it's true."

When I try to speak, my voice cracks, so I clear my throat. "Yeah, I had a suspicion."

"So, he's here?" Leon asks, raising his lethal tail.

"Most likely," Eddy says.

"Then everyone stay alert and close together. We'll notify Tails once we make it to the other side."

I nod.

"Copy," Eddy says but dry and out of character.

I hate that I never know what he's thinking. A part of me wants to give him a hug, but he's probably not in the mood right now. "Are you okay?" I whisper to him.

He looks up at me with the blankest expression and says one word: "No."

Recoiling into a recluse, I return my attention to up ahead. My focus shifts to tuning out the chorus of voices as the tense atmosphere carries us the rest of the way. The three of us float onward in silence while cries for help echo all around us.

Thankfully, after another yard, we stumble upon an open clearing. A well lies in the center, composed of old jagged stones stacked atop each other, and a small wooden pail rests beside it. Countless red-eyed ghosts hurl themselves into the well, while new voices erupt from it every millisecond. In a never-ending cycle, the solid ghosts get sucked away only to return as invisible beings to relive their deaths.

All of us clamp our ears shut with flat palms.

I cringe at the agonizing screams and cries, and spiders shoot down my spine with each passing breath. "This must be the Hub!"

With scrunched faces and clenched jaws, Eddy and Leon frantically nod their heads. Eddy creeps forward first, and Leon and I follow. Gusts of wind whip past us in every direction as ghosts zoom in front of us, behind us, on both sides of us, and *through* us. The deafening voices increase the closer we get to the well.

After a couple more steps, the vibrations seize my body, and my knees buckle. I drop to the ground. Lush grass meets my knees, but I can now feel the embers sting my skin.

"Slixx!"

I glance up at Leon. He stares down at me with inquisitively concerned lenses, while behind him, Eddy surveys the well.

I nod my head for him to go on without me.

"You sure?" he shouts.

I nod harder, and he goes on to investigate with Eddy. Meanwhile, I crawl to the nearest tree and prop myself up against it. More embers fall on me, but the volume's a decimal lower over here. (Which is not much. But I'll take it.)

Eddy and Leon round the aged well thrice before looking at each other in confusion. They shake their heads at each other, unable to find anything, but Leon motions for them to try again. So, they round one more time, digging their palms against their ears. Eddy lowers himself to the ground and crawls alongside the well for a closer look, and Leon leans over it.

He slowly sticks his head over the ledge for a look inside, but when he does, a giant gust knocks him back. He hits the ground with a thud and yelps.

Scrambling to my floating tail, I muster enough strength and run over to him. Eddy, however, obliviously continues crawling around the well for clues.

"Are you okay?" I yell.

"*Agh!*" Leon's hands fly back up to his ears. "Dammit!"

I wish I could help him, but with my hands to my ears, all I can do is curve my tail under him to prop him upright. He rocks to and fro, cursing under his breath, until another piercing scream fires between us. In an instant, his curses evolve into shouts as he begins to tremble uncontrollably.

"Eddy!" I shout for help.

With his back turned, Eddy doesn't hear me.

I start to call again, but Leon yelps in pain. He hunches over, burying his head in his chest, and it takes everything in me not to drop to my knees in panic. Thinking quick on my feet, I float around to his back and hook my tail around his. He's so tense that his tail remains bent and rigid like his body, making it a perfect fit.

At first, I drag him out of the clearing easily, but then I lose strength partway through. My tail drops to the ground, so I slither the rest of the way—like back in The Dump. And I don't stop until Leon's tail unhooks from mine.

He collapses in the grass—the volume a few decibels lower out here.

"Are you okay?" I ask, dropping my hands.

He pants like the few hushed voices that whisk past us. "Yeah.... Fine.... Thanks, Sheets."

"It's Slixx."

"Mhmm.... Right."

"Slixx! Leon! I got it! I got it!" Eddy's voice breaks through the sea of invisible whispers, and he repeats our names until he bursts into view. With his hands behind his back, he looks from our trail in the dirt up to us before raising a brow. "What happened?"

Shaking our heads, Leon and I find our footing (or tailing) and float to our tails.

"What'd you find?" Leon grunts.

Eddy's eyes light up in excitement, and he unveils what's behind his back. "Tah dah!"

I frown at the wooden pail in his hands. "Seriously?"

Even Leon washes a hand over his face, muttering curses.

"No, wait, look," Eddy says, flipping the pail upside down. He blows dust off the bottom and hands it to us with the widest grin. "Another riddle."

Glancing at each other, Leon and I hesitate.

"Go on! See for yourselves."

I reluctantly grab the pail from him; however, my frown turns upside down once I notice a tiny inscription in the middle. I become speechless. "What the...? Eddy..."

"What does it say?" Leon asks, squinting over my shoulder.

I, too, narrow my eyes at the small print, especially in this dim lighting. "*The soulless burn lost forever, the soulful yearn in heed of treasure, the soulless want what is never to be had, while the soulful search for what is never to be found, cross fire, in desire, single ticketed to sweet peas and canines, may the wretched fall or may wretched seeds plant even after, after.*"

Looking up at Eddy and Leon, they look just as perplexed as me.

"So..." Leon starts. "*Bliss* does exist?"

I whirl to him. "After all this, seriously?"

He shrugs. "I still have yet to see it."

"Keep talking like that and you might not get in."

He cracks a smile. "Alright, gatekeeper."

A smile spreads across Eddy's face from ear to ear as he snatches the pail back, frantically tapping the print. "We just have to make it to *Bliss* before Verquen does!"

"What if he's already at the entrance waiting for us?" I ask, crossing my arms.

"It's possible," Leon says.

Eddy freezes, staring at us for a moment, before wagging a finger. "Not likely." He then turns around, tucks the pail under his armpit, and starts back to the clearing, and Leon and I follow him.

"How do you figure, Flicky?" Leon asks, re-plugging his ears.

I plug mine, too. "Yeah, how do you know?"

Abruptly stopping, Eddy wheels around with the widest grin and smacks the left side of his chest. He bears into each of our eyes, and his infectious merry attitude casts a warm, fuzzy feeling in my stomach. "I've got faith."

"Eddy..." I whisper.

"I don't know how or when—in this lifetime or the next— but I know we'll make it."

I double over his words in my head. *In this lifetime or the next.* My stomach churns in trepidation and indecision. *Know where you're going before you get there, or you may end up some- where wretched.* I stare into his promising hazel irises and wonder my own fate—like what realm I'll end up in next? Hopefully, the one in my daydreams.

Leon places a hand on Eddy's shoulder. "Of course we will."

I gulp, swallowing my fear, and stroll past them. "Then we better get a move on. Last one out the forest smells like canine butt cheeks."

The three of us exchange looks before taking off. We fly as fast as we can, and I take the lead until we reach the clearing. Leon swerves in front of me, dashing along the pathway parted by the trees. The voices and red-eyed ghosts slow me down, but when Eddy passes me, I'm determined to catch up.

We race down the pathway, our laughter and jolly chains curing the tainted air.

CHAPTER 27
TAKE OFF

We stumble out of the forest, and my vision immediately locks on Tails. He lounges by the shore, facing the fiery ocean. Eddy, Leon, and I step off the grass and onto the rocky barren land, nearing him, but he doesn't turn around. He remains still with his back turned, and immediately, I know something's wrong.

Rushing over to him, I cup his face. I pat his snout down for any injuries while inspecting the rest of his body, but there's not a scratch on him. "What's wrong, boy?"

He whines before gesturing toward the boiling sea.

Eddy and Leon come up beside me, and all three of us follow Tails' gaze. He directs our attention north, and it is then that I notice a narrow bridge connected to this island. It lies several feet away from us and runs all the way to a distant volcanic island. The remote shore appears black, and a mighty volcano occupies the entire width of the isle. It stretches all the way up to the chaotic multicolored sky, lava likely brewing inside.

"*Cross fire, in desire,*" Eddy mumbles. "That's the way to *Bliss!*"

Staring in the distance, Leon puts a hand to his forehead. "Technically, the print on the pail never explicitly said *Bliss*, but I'll go with it."

Just then, a strong zealous sensation explodes in my gut. It surges throughout my body and casts a driven fervor in my chest. I wipe the sweat from my upper lip with a slick smirk, and my hands ball into radiant fists. I glance over at Tails and place a gentle hand on his cheek. The image of him, Eddy, and Leon in the garden resurfaces in my head, fueling the fire inside me.

"I don't know about you guys, but I'm ready to finally pass on."

Tails' eyes flick to me with a glimmer of hope.

Eddy cheeses my way.

And even though Leon doesn't look at me, the corners of his mouth pinch.

"I don't know if we're the first," I continue, "but we're going to be the next ghosts to paradise."

Tails perks his head up.

"Then what are we waiting for?" Eddy calls out, heading for the long narrow bridge. "It'll be just like before when we ran into the light—only this time we'll make it."

"Woof!"

Remembering our gay laughs and zest, I peck Tails on the snout, and he rises with me. I lead us all to the bridge where I stop beside Eddy, Tails behind us.

Eddy flashes me a pearly white grin, and I can't help but do the same. "That's the Eddy Effect," I say.

He raises a confused brow, but I shoo the notion away. Looking back, I find Leon in the same spot. He stares ahead at the thousands of sea lands littering the boiling ocean for as far as the eye can see, but he mostly locks on the volcano yonder.

"You coming?" I ask.

"How do you know we'll make it, Sheets?" The skylight highlights Leon's clenched jaw. "What's gotten us this far?"

"Uh…" Open and honest, I blurt out the first thing that comes to mind. "My gut."

"*Tch*. That's what we've been banking on?"

I drop my head, but Eddy grabs my wrist like old times. I look up at him. His sweet eyes capture me in a daze, and his gentle touch warms my skin. Somehow, he looks different than he did back in Limbo. My cheeks burn just looking at him— mesmerized by his sparkly clear skin and thick eyebrows.

He looks back at Leon. "Slixx is in tune with her body and the realms, and that's what got us here—so close to the finish line. She trusts nature. So, if her guts saying go, then I'm going."

I gape at Eddy in wonder. *His words…* I'd never thought about it like that.

"You coming or not?" I repeat.

Leon rips his gaze to us. "After all you two have put me through, I'd be a fool not to." We all crack smiles as he joins us at the foot of the bridge. He falls into line beside Tails. "But if this fantastical paradise doesn't exist, we're going to have a harsh exchange of words."

I roll my eyes, and Eddy makes a silly face, mocking him.

Tails barks before giddily panting with his tongue hanging out.

"Though before we go, I must ask"—Leon points down at us—"are you two officially an item now?"

I furrow my brows in confusion until I realize Eddy's still holding my wrist. In a snap, I snatch my hand away, while Eddy obliviously takes another moment to catch on. I pat down my hair, trying my best to act normal, and clear my throat. "*Ahem*… no, what, what are you talking about? That's crazy—!"

Beside me, Eddy cracks a smile before stealing a kiss on my cheek. His smooth full lips peck the side of my face, and my cheeks burn bright. I nearly gasp with wide eyes, but within seconds, he takes off running.

Leon places a hand on my shoulder. "I knew it all along. Deanna and me. You and Flicky. Maybe we can double tryst in *Bliss*."

Just as I come to, Tails barks, and he and Leon take off after Eddy. I blink in confusion, trying to digest everything that's just happened. The realm seems lighter, and the land seems bigger. An unbreakable smile etches across my face. I touch where Eddy's gentle lips grazed my cheek as butterflies flutter around in my stomach.

"Maybe," I mutter under my breath in response to Leon. "Just maybe..."

Scurrying off, I propel myself forward with flailing runner arms. I catch up to Eddy and Leon, but none of us say a word. We just smile, flashing each other knowing glances. Eddy's hazel eyes flicker to me, and I meet his warm gaze.

I giggle.

He chuckles.

Leon nods out of my peripheral.

Meanwhile, Tails simply jogs alongside us just to keep pace.

My cheeks still burn, but I begin to laugh. The dream of all of us lying in the grass soothes me. I sprint ahead fast, desperate to make it a reality.

CHAPTER 28
OFFENSE

As we near the volcanic island, it's as if a mighty fist punches me in the gut. Gasps sweep through our unit, and Tails erupts into a vicious growl. I blink as we near the isle, sprinting the last couple miles.

I rub my eyes to no avail, wishing they deceived me, but an unimaginable nightmare lies dead ahead. The black land that we saw earlier from a distance comes into view and is actually a multitude of Hellons. They litter every inch of the island. They look identical to the still ones we saw earlier, simply breathing, but these seem different. They face the bridge as if waiting for us.

"No way," I breathe.

Eddy's quivering lips keep silent.

"Holy hell," Leon whispers from behind.

Tails hacks out a rancorous bark.

"M-m-m-maybe they're harmless," Eddy says in a low voice.

I shake my head, my vision locked on our new enemies. "Not this time."

"Should we turn around?" Leon cries out, short of breath.

"And go where?" I ask.

"Somewhere safe!"

"I don't think such a thing exists in this realm."

Eddy gulps before dropping to a grave tone. "Th-then we fight."

"Are you mad?" Leon shouts.

I ball my hands into fists, succumbing to the burning fire inside me. "If they don't engage, then we just pass. If they do, then we tear our way through until we reach paradise. If anyone wants to bow out, now is the time to do so. And that goes for you too, Tails! I'm not your owner—I'm your friend!" A lump gets caught in my throat, but I swallow it down. "Do whatever you want!"

An air of silence transpires between us all. No one utters another word, but a vengeance electrifies in my bones, thundering each of my limbs. I suck in breaths and spit them out just as fast, while my floating tail soars across the bridge. Each step that I take, I get that much closer to achieving my dream—that much closer to *finally* resting in peace.

Suddenly, Tails bulldozes into me, Eddy, and Leon from behind. We fly up into the air before plopping down on his back. To my discomfort, I land sitting on my chain with a hard bang, and my hair whips across my face. Meanwhile, Eddy lands farther back in the middle, and Leon rides in the back like usual.

"*Owww,*" I moan, pulling my chain from underneath me.

Tails gallops full speed ahead, though. He speaks in a series of barks, and I lock onto each of his yaps. Although I don't understand him, a warm buttery feeling melts in my chest. I decode his sentiments in abstract and rejoice, hugging his neck, and I savor the precious scent of his sugary almond coat.

"Let's go to *Bliss* then, boy!" I say.

"Woof!"

Running even faster, Tails sprints the rest of the way with ease, and we hang on for the ride until he slows down several feet from the island. He prowls toward the Hellons who stand in strict columns and rows while Eddy, Leon, and I serve as his extra pair of eyes and ears.

"Think they'll attack?" Leon asks.

Just as Tails steps off the bridge and onto the island, an icy voice stops us in our tracks.

"No."

In a flash, Tails breaks out into a ferocious growl, and I whip my head around in search of the voice. *That voice.* It booms with cold bass and fills the area, carrying clear and with a slight echo.

"Not unless I tell them to."

"Who goes there?" Leon shouts.

Out of my peripheral, I spot Eddy jump to his tail. "Show yourself!"

"That voice," I mutter.

"Ticket," the melancholy voice calls, and I finally spot the source on the ground.

Below, Verquen sits on a rock between one of the centered Hellon columns. He looks the same as always—with those heinous flushed ruby eyes and that black chain around his neck —but something about him *feels* different. Something that I can't quite place.

I look from Verquen to the large volcano not too far behind him. A spiral pathway ascends around the mountain, surely leading to the top, but from down here, the volcano looks infinite and never-ending—like it's connected to the sky. I wonder if Verquen's as strong as the deadly magma inside.

"You have finally made it," he says.

Eddy takes the words right out of my mouth. "What the hell do you want?"

Verquen flicks a loose strand of his long platinum hair over his shoulder. "I have been waiting for you, Ticket." He points at me. "It is now time for you to lead me to *Bliss*."

"Like hell!" I yell.

"Is this your army?" Leon interjects, sizing up the many mighty Hellons.

Verquen nods before rising to his floating tail. His deadly eyes fix on me—his target—and he extends a hand my way. "I have spared and saved your life twice before, and it is now time for you to return the favor. Will you show me the way? *Bliss* awaits."

I narrow my eyes at his hand, wishing that I could smack it down.

"She's not going anywhere with you," Eddy growls in unison with Tails.

I suck my teeth, glaring down at him. "Even if I knew the way, I'd rather die before I help you. You're a murderer."

Verquen glances down at his hand and slowly retracts it. "Mur-der-er?" he repeats like it's a foreign word. "I helped those people in Limbo—both human and ghost. I believe the proper word is a *savior*. Or rather a God."

My mouth flies open to respond, but Eddy fires off before I do.

"Damn you!" And without warning, he jumps off Tails' back.

"Eddy!" I shout.

"Don't be a fool, Flicky," Leon calls out as Eddy lands soft on his tail. "Get back up here!"

I slide to the edge of Tails' back and start to jump myself, but Leon quickly grabs my arm. I look up at him, but he continues surveying our surroundings. His pupils move at light-speed as his head whips around, scanning the army of Hellons.

"I'm sick of this guy always getting in our way," Eddy says.

He stomps toward Verquen with clenched fists, but Verquen's attention remains on me. "Hey, I'm talking to you, pal!"

Nerves claw at my skin with each step that he takes, and my breathing becomes unsteady. I choke out my words with clammy palms. "Eddy, stop!"

"Mind your temper, Flicky," Leon says. "Look around. We're outnumbered."

"I don't care," Eddy spits, stopping just a yard from Verquen. He bends over with his hands out in a fighting stance, and his sharp tail springs up over his head.

"No!" I scream.

Tails' growls morph into savage barks. He tries to spring into action and prowl after Eddy, but Leon commands him to stay for our safety.

"This guy thinks he's a *God*," Eddy says, taking off. "Well, how about I knock him down to ghost size!"

My shriek booms in my own ears. "Stop!"

"Don't!" Leon shouts.

But it's too late.

Eddy flies through the air as fast as a shooting star, and a swift gust lashes back at us. Leon and I shield our faces while Tails turns his head away. Verquen, however, appears steadfast, his ghastly red eyes still laser focused on me. Not even Eddy's battle cry fazes him, his expression deadpan.

That is until Eddy's tail shoots in the air. He aims it at Verquen, and the sharp blade glimmers under the skylight— now mere inches away. He spins around, ramming his tail down on Verquen's head.

"Eddy!" both Leon and I shout.

Just as his strike lands, Verquen unleashes his own tail at lightning speed. It lurches over his head from under his cloak— much longer than any of ours. And his attention finally shifts from me as he comes face to face with Eddy.

CLANG! Their tails clash like pieces of metal.

Eddy gasps.

Although Verquen looks at him, he speaks aloud to me. "Ticket, I only have the need for you, so unfortunately your people must be disposed of."

Eddy grunts before their tails repel. He blows back but then lunges at Verquen again. "You son of a—!"

Before Leon can react, I jump off Tails' back.

"Slixx!" Leon calls out.

Landing with a stumble, I race after Eddy. Tails barks, stammering behind in uncertainty, while Leon calls me back. I keep running, though—but perhaps not fast enough.

Eddy belts out another battle cry as his tail whips around. He wields it like a blade, slicing it through the air, and his short hair breezes behind him. Instead of another hammer fist, his tail jabs with a right hook this time.

"Get outta our way!"

Unable to make it in time, I scream Eddy's name.

Verquen's tail shoots over and blocks Eddy's attack again, but this time his tail hooks around Eddy's straight one. In the blink of an eye, it takes the form of a snake and wraps around Eddy's tail in a spiral.

Eddy gasps, looking over his shoulder and trying to pull away. I near them just a few feet away. Tears burn the backs of my eyelids. I hear Tails' paws hit the ground running behind me. But within the same second, Verquen's whizzing tail lurches forward and pierces straight through Eddy's stomach.

I stop.

Tails' paws stomp one final time.

Leon yells Eddy's name.

"No..." I whisper, buckling to my knees.

I collapse to the ground with trembling fingers and quivering lips, and my hearing flatlines. I slowly shake my head in disbelief. I watch as Eddy looks down at the dagger in his gut. His eyes burst wide open, bulging out, and his dilated pupils quake in awe. His cheeks puff out like a frog before he chokes out blood. It splatters through the air while the rest floods his chin.

I reach out a hand for him as he looks up at me. "Ed-dy...?"

His pale lips shudder to speak, but he only spits out more dark blood. Some of it lands an inch from my knee, but I fix on Eddy. A purplish tinge invades his wan complexion as if he's being choked to death.

He mouths something that I cannot decipher. His lips move slow, but they barely open, slurring the words. I squint but only catch his last word, clinging onto it with my body and soul.

Bliss.

Tears singe my cheeks.

His mouth explodes with more blood before Verquen slings his body behind him. Eddy lifelessly tumbles across the barren land until his back hits the volcano. He doesn't move a muscle nor an inch. With his head facedown, he simply lies there like a corpse.

My hearing fades back in all at once to my earthshattering screams. I yell at the top of my lungs before wobbling to my tail. I start to take a step forward, but out of nowhere, Leon runs up from behind and wraps his arms around my waist, holding me back. Although I squirm to break free, he holds tight and presses his head against my back.

Earsplitting yelps tremor my vocal cords.

While, in the background, Tails howls in one long cry.

CHAPTER 29

DEFENSE

Straight-faced, Verquen turns to me. It's as if his obtuse gaze stares *through* me, but I stare past his blood-thirsty eyes at Eddy. I wail aloud for my friend, fighting to reach him. However, Leon still holds me back. I continue squirming, though—even when Tails nestles his head against mine.

My screams eventually taper off into hushed cries. "He'll heal, right?" I ask Leon, but he remains quiet. His head shudders against my back, and I assume he's crying, too.

Just then, Verquen extends another hand. "This is your last chance, Ticket. Will you come now, or will it cost you your friends' lives?"

Sniffling, I wipe away my tears with my forearm before breaking Leon's clasp around me and petting Tails away. I rise to my floating tail with tight fists full of vengeance.

"Don't do anything rash," Leon says in a low voice behind me.

"If I go with you"—I gulp—"what'll happen?"

"Your friends will live, and you will open the gateway to *Bliss* for me," Verquen says.

Leon steps in front of me with a guarding hand. "And what becomes of Slixx?"

"The Ticket will open the gateway. That is all I can say."

Leon grits his teeth, and Tails begins to growl.

"Like hell I'd lay down my life for you," I say.

Backing away, Verquen floats toward the volcano. He drifts there, nonchalant, before stopping at the foot of the spiral pathway—next to Eddy's body. "Very well. If you will not do it by choice, then you will do it by force."

I narrow my eyes at him.

"What the hell does that mean?" Leon shouts.

Verquen cocks his head to the side ever so slightly and holds his gaze on us. His hair drapes over his shoulder as he stares for another moment. Then, his tail lurches outright and stabs Eddy's back.

"Eddy!" I shout.

Tails rips into an even louder growl.

"Leave him alone!" Leon cries out.

Verquen, however, picks up Eddy's body and digs his tail through Eddy's chest.

Eddy's closed eyes pop open. He chokes out blood, and it splatters on the ground. His retch soon turns into wheezes, and then his head drops to his chest, dangling as if disconnected from his body.

Upon squinting, I see that his shoulders are moving up and down ever so slightly. "He's still breathing," I whisper.

"When you are ready, Ticket, come find me," Verquen says. And with that, he strides up the spiral pathway, carrying Eddy with him.

I start to chase after him, but all at once, the army of Hellons snaps to us. They all turn right and left, dispersing out of their neat rows and columns. A gang jumps in front of me, and as I look back, one jumps between me and Leon, separating me from him and Tails. A bunch of other Hellons surround them, too.

"Sheets!" Leon shouts.

"I'm okay! You and Tails, stay together!"

Out of the corner of my eye, I catch a glimpse of Eddy's pale face. His veiny eyelids crush my soul, and his cracked lips stir my tear ducts. What I would give to take his place or to see those infamous, hopeful hazel eyes of his. But alas, Verquen continues climbing the pathway and pulls him out of sight.

"Remember, fire to the nape and dagger to the eye," Leon calls out.

Facing forward, I study the Hellons surrounding me. I count five of them, but of course, there are many backup lines behind just waiting to attack. My gaze then darts to the bubbling ocean behind the Hellon closest to the shore.

"Stab them and dump them in the ocean," I shout.

Tails barks as if knowing his part.

"I was just thinking the same thing!" Leon says.

Screeching, the Hellons lunge at me in sync. Their claws rip through the air as they charge, and their clobbering feet shake the entire land. Their eyes swirl with darkness, too—fixed on me. *Their prey.*

I jump high into the air, though.

And below, they all crash into each other. Their horns tangle together, so I take my window of opportunity and tailspin toward the nearest one. Gravity carries me straight back down, and as the Hellon's pull apart, I stab one dead in the eye.

Blood spews out and squirts on me. The Hellon's mouth flies open with an earsplitting roar. The vibrations nearly blow me away, but I yank my tail out of its eye and push off its face in the nick of time.

Leaping left toward the next Hellon, I catch this one off guard, too. As it finally untangles its horns, I whip my tail around and puncture its big eye. More blood splatters across my face while it roars in pain. It flails its head around like a maniac, so I dig my tail deeper into its eye, bracing myself.

Behind, another Hellon claws at me. Its daggers whisk through the air from above, so I think quick on my tail. Can't jump up. Can't double back right—all the Hellons are free and untangled now. And with the boiling ocean just inches away, I can't flee left either.

Precious time escapes me.

Another Hellon claws at me from the newly freed masses—and then *another*. Then before I know it, multiple claws slice through the air to get to me, and if another second ticks by of me riding this roller coaster, I'll be done for.

Suddenly, a wholesome image of Eddy emerges in my head. He grins from ear to ear, and his skin glows bright. His plaid shirt and tattered jeans define him, contributing to his infamous Eddy Effect. But unfortunately, that image flashes to a new one of his bloody body on Verquen's tail. He hangs stiff and limp while choking out gore. But even on his deathbed, hope twinkles in his pale eyes. *Bliss*, he'd said.

Anger boils my blood, hotter than the ocean. Retribution inundates my bones, and my head submerges into savagery. I grit my teeth so tight that they might crack. My hands re-ball into fists as I snatch my tail from the crazed Hellon's eye. With time of the essence, I shut off my mind and trust my body—and the land.

Too close for comfort, a claw nabs at my neck. I jerk back, but it only misses by a hair, literally chopping off strands of my own. I close my eyes from the many attacking claws, bend over, and leap off the Hellon's face. Gusting pressure passes over me as I dive headfirst to the ground.

Midway, I open my eyes and shift my weight to my tail, landing softly above ground. I whip around and spot Leon and

Tails a couple yards away. Tails bulldozes into the Hellons like bowling pins and knocks them into the ocean, while Leon leaps from Hellon to Hellon, stabbing them in their eyes. His tail's drenched in red blood like mine.

"Leon!" I shout as he lands on the ground. The screeching Hellon's drown out my voice, so I call out his name louder.

Meanwhile, the Hellons from above start to look down and notice me.

"Sheets!" A claw rams down at him, but he does a handstand and slices across the Hellon's wrist. The claw falls to the ground, its fingers squirming like a roach with its head cut off. "Find Eddy!" He tucks and rolls from another Hellon's claw. "We'll be right behind you!"

Although Tails charges out of view, he barks in agreeance.

"Leon..." I whisper.

Above, all the Hellons begin to bend over and reach for me.

"You can't take on all these by yourselves!" I shout, backing away.

Leon slashes across one Hellon's Achilles heel—much more skilled than me—and the Hellon buckles to its knees. I think back to the other gang members back at the bar and wonder if that's where he learned to fight. "Slaying a few more!" he pants. "Then making a run for it! Go!"

I nod before taking off. The Hellons swipe at me, but I leap out of the way. My pupils shoot about my eye, scanning the many speedy claws, and I barely have time to assess them all. With the Hellons now fully bent over, their claws hack at me with the swiftest of ease. I tuck and roll out of the way—only to scoot to the foot of another. I try to run straight, but they block me in.

I stand cornered, encircled by Hellons, and curse under my breath.

All of a sudden, a piercing scream erupts from above. The

male voice belts a single shriek, and I immediately recognize it as Eddy's. His dry voice explodes into the sky as if he's being tortured, agony and despair drawing out his cry until his voice gives way.

I gasp. "Eddy!"

His scream, however, means nothing to the Hellons. They continue stealing for me, and I spring from side to side on my tail. My stomach churns from Eddy's cry, compelling me to take a page out of Leon's book. I lunge ahead and slash off a Hellon's claw. It falls to the ground with squirming fingers like the one before, and I repeat the savage act a few more times.

After a minute, I stop and wipe the sweat from my eyes. My entire face is soaked, and I pant out rugged breaths. The Hellons still come at me all the same, though, and it's then that I realize: *Fighting* them wouldn't be the problem, keeping up my stamina to slay them all *would*.

I flare my nostrils before peering up at the countless claws above. With the Hellons bent over, their long pinecone-shaped heads block the sky, and their arms, claws, and horns overlap and intertwine. Their sharp daggers swipe at me, so I keep bouncing around.

I look both ways for an opening, but they've caged me in like a bird. Although I could fight my way through, there's no way I'd be able to take on all these Hellons by myself—who knows how many stand in my way from here to the volcano. I look up instead, and a sliver of hope dawns on me. *Even if I could get past their claws, their heads—*

"That's it," I whisper at the onset of an idea. "Their heads. If *they* won't move out of the way, then I'll *make* them move."

I leap over a claw and onto the next wrist that nabs my way. I run up it, but then another claw swipes at me. I sidestep out of the way, but another rams at me from behind. I whip around, facing the Hellon just inches away from my head. I start to jump up, but a deadly shadow looms overhead. So, I jolt my body down into a crouch.

Although the Hellon misses my head, one of its claws scratches up my back as I bend down. I yelp. The agonizing pain surges through my body like a thundering rush, and it's as if a butcher knife carves down my spine. My screams ring in my ears. A metallic flavor bursts in my mouth. I hear Tails bark and Leon call my name in the distance, but it sounds as if it's coming from the bottom of a well.

A cough overcomes me, and I cup my mouth, hacking out dark blood. Tears stream down my cheeks, but more claws hurl at me from all directions. Quickly, I grab the Hellon's claw that scratched me and pull myself up onto its arm. I try to stand but fall to a limp.

Slicing an inch from my neck, a missed claw blasts cold wind at me, and I lose my balance. I plummet from the Hellon's arm but luckily land on a nearby stray claw.

"Oof!"

My arm breaks my fall, and a newfound ache seizes my body. I clench my jaw through the pain, my back wound still burning as if someone's taken a lit torch to my skin. I try to focus my mind on me, Eddy, Tails, and Leon lying somewhere tranquil in the middle of a field, and what little chance we have left of making it to *Bliss* fuels me to get up.

I jump onto another claw and then another before springing up a yard and stabbing a Hellon in the eye. It bellows, hurling its head back, but I grab onto its horns.

When it screeches up at the sky, I lean toward the volcano, muster every ounce of strength within me, and push off its face with all my might. I fling through the air at the speed of light— over all the bent Hellons.

Flying too fast, I stab my tail into the side of the volcano to stop myself from soaring into the ocean. It scrapes across the mountain, causing a rockslide, but I barely slow down. My eyes widen as I near the foot of the fiery ocean. I reach out for help, but there's nothing to grab on to.

Only a few feet away from plunging into the lava, I shut my eyes. Rocks continue to pour from under my tail, but eventually, they dwindle to pebbles. I open one eye to see the edge of the pathway and lava several yards beneath me.

"That was close," I mumble, dangling upside down.

"HWAAAAAAH!"

Whipping around, reality rushes back to me as Hellons fill my vision. They storm after me with bloodthirsty eyes, and they steal the air with their sharp claws. I push off the volcano to get away, but my tail's stuck inside.

"No. No. No."

I yank and yank to no avail.

"Dammit!"

With the next pull, I use everything I've got, and my tail finally pops out. I go tumbling to the ground though, coming down on my back, and I choke out a yelp. My eyes bulge out; my limbs stiffen to ice; and it feels like my back has been ripped open, again.

The ground rumbles from the approaching Hellons, but I can barely breathe. I scramble to my knees, placing a hand on the wall for support. Then I scurry up the spiral pathway. A trail of blood drips from my back, but I hurry as fast as I can on a limp tail, leaving the chaos behind me. Because although my body is in hell, my mind is on *Bliss*. We have to make it.

"Me." I seethe out a breath. "Eddy. Leon. And—"

I stop.

"Tails?"

We'll be right behind you, Leon had said.

I glance back but now only see the sweltering ocean. Then, I look down at the narrow pathway that neither Tails nor a

Hellon could fit on, and my tail moves without a second thought. I start to double back down to Leon and Tails.

However, I don't make it any more than a couple steps before another shrill scream erupts from above. I whip around and look ahead at the ascending pathway. "Eddy!" But then I look back down to Tails. My imaginary heart tears in half, and confliction cascades over my wounded body.

"*AGHHHHHHH—!*" Eddy screams again before abruptly cutting out.

My heavy chest drops into my gut, and I suck in air.

I'll come back after, I tell myself. *Just hang on, guys.*

I repeat these words as I continue slithering up the spiral pathway. They serve as a chant, swirling about my brain, but I can't tell if it's because I need something to cling onto or if it's because I'm trying to convince someone—*myself*.

I'll come back after. I will. I will.

Every few paces, I choke up blood. It stains the ground, and behind me, my rattling chain drags through it, splatter soiling the metal links. I keep going, though.

I dig my nails into my palms through the excruciating pain, and my teeth grind against each other. I rush up the pathway as Tails cries out in distress. His high-pitched whimper cracks my soul, but I chant the mantra in my head, hoping him and Leon hold the Hellons off for just a little while. At least until I save Eddy and find *Bliss* for us, or I save Eddy and we retreat.

Rounding the last corner, I spot the end of the pathway just up ahead, and the sound of boiling lava fades in. It grows louder with each step that I take as if warning me to turn around. Although my bones quake in fear, I limply sprint the last stretch —for my friend. My tail sloshes in haste as Eddy's screams haunt my ears, carrying me faster, and I run to him.

When the top of the volcano comes into view, it's unlike anything I've ever seen before. It's shaped like a cone, funneling up to the sky, and the walls are lit up with a vermilion hue. Layers of elevated rock stack atop each other, while the ground tapers up into jagged edges. In the center, a vivid lava ring boils bright, appearing ebony with a neon orange glow beneath.

I gaze at it in awe until I spot Verquen kneeling on the opposite side of it. He clutches Eddy's hair in one hand, but Eddy's head hangs lifeless.

"I thought that would make you come faster," Verquen says without looking at me.

"What'd you do to him?" I ask, my voice shaky.

He rises to his floating tail and drags Eddy up, too, still holding him by his hair.

It's then that I see Eddy's face and gasp. Air escapes me in one long exhale, and new tears trickle down over my dried ones. My lips quiver to speak, but I can only shake my head. Sadness devours me into a pool of despair as I barely recognize my friend.

Fresh third-degree burns scald half his face, emitting hot smoke. Big thick holes erode through his flesh and tissue, and black char covers his singed eye. His scorched skin resembles dark soot, puss and blood oozing out of his open wounds. He still flickers like a candle, too.

I stumble forward. "Eddy!"

In the blink of an eye, Verquen flings Eddy's unconscious body across the volcano. He goes rolling on the ground while his limbs flail about. I watch in horror as he skids up the layered walls and bowls to the edge of the mountain. The rocks break his fall, slowing him down, but half his body teeters on the edge.

"Come now, Ticket," Verquen commands.

Ignoring him, I limp toward Eddy. I shake my head in disbelief as riverbeds massacre my face. My chest caves in with each uneven breath, and my entire body quakes. Everything—this realm, this life, *existing*—seems unreal.

Who would've thought that my worst nightmare would be a fear that my mind couldn't even imagine?

I near Eddy, just a couple yards away. His shoulders move ever so slightly, so he must still be breathing. I pick up the pace, fighting though the pain in my back.

CRACK!

Jerking my head up, I snap to Verquen. His tail penetrates the ground, and a clean crack cuts through the jagged land. It runs past the ring of lava, in front of me, up the layered walls, and crackles around Eddy. Then, the land beneath Eddy cracks aloud. It landslides by mere inches, ripping apart from the volcano, and Eddy's body now teeters on a slanted cliff.

I run for him, but just as I take a step, Verquen's icy voice stops me in my tracks.

"Take another step, and he will die. I said come now, Ticket."

In the distance, Tails howls in unison with screeching Hellons.

Every part of me aches. Doubt and uncertainty cloud my mind, casting me into a shadow realm of turmoil. "What do you want from me?"

"To open the gateway to *Bliss*."

"I don't even know where the hell that is—or even how to do it!"

He retracts his deadly tail from the ground, and it hovers over him as if a mind of its own. "Your life."

I furrow my brows in confusion. "What?"

Striding off, he heads for me, but when he gets too close, I start the other way. We round the ring of lava—across from each other—and I make sure to keep a safe distance. Our chains clang behind us, stirring with tension befitting of the situation.

He points to the bubbling lava. "Your undying chain will open the gateway to *Bliss*."

I gulp, trying my best to save a brave face. "You expect me to believe this fiery ring is the gateway to *Bliss*?"

He nods. "*Single ticketed to sweet peas and canines.*"

"You know the riddle?" I narrow my eyes at him. "Then you should also know that the soulless can never pass on. I know you're from Almost."

"You may have figured that out, but you are not all knowing. I will leave this wasteland and pass on to peace."

"Not without a soul."

"Once the gateway is open, nothing can stand in my way. However, as for you, your sly journey was all for naught. You have done a selfish service leading your people to their deaths. All for you to betray them in the end and try to pass on without them."

I glance back at Eddy as I pass him. "What are you talking about? You're standing in *our* way. After you're out of the picture, me, Eddy, Tails, and Leon are going to *Bliss*."

He suddenly stops, so I stop, too. We stand directly across from each other, a trail of my blood at our tails. "*True peace you seek—to Bliss—despite hellish way, those might make it with a plum severed chain,*" he recites from the fountain. "*You* are the only one with a plum severed chain. Detached from your human's. Only *you* did not pass on from Limbo."

I stare at him in awe, petrified.

"*Single ticketed to sweet peas and canines.* Once the gate is open, only one person may pass on per Ticket. But I take it you knew that already."

Every word that he utters strikes me to the core. I connect the dots in my head, but I just don't believe it—I *can't* believe, especially not when Tails and Leon yell in the distance. A piece of me dies inside, and a piece of me wishes to have never existed.

"No," I whisper.

"Back in the Myronian cave, Martha sacrificed her son to finally put him to rest. Passing on means sacrifice, and sacrifice is nonnegotiable. You knew that all along, did you not?"

I shake my head in shock—on the verge of hyperventilating.

"Someone has to cut the chain off your back. Bring your people along to do it and then before you bleed out, abandon them and find *Bliss* for yourself—"

"No, I didn't know any..." I grab my head, rummaging through my hair. "You don't know what you're talking about!"

"No?" he asks, his tone flat and cold. He stares at me as Tails howls, and more chaotic clashing and clinging erupt from thousands of feet below. The Hellons screech, too, but it all fades to the back of my head like static.

"I didn't know any of those things." I sniffle, wiping away snot and tears. "And I don't believe a word you say."

His tail shoots up into attack mode. Overhead, it points at me, and the tip gleams under the burning sky. "You do not have to believe me as I will be taking *Bliss* for myself."

"You'll taint wherever you go," I bark, raising my tail, too. I let rage consume me, and my tail floats off the ground. I must be healing but not quickly enough.

He takes off his cloak, revealing a tight leather bodysuit underneath. His abs show through the material, while the turtleneck fits snug around his neck just below his black chain, which binds to his back. "I see you have made your decision then. By choice or by force. I will just have to kill you then. And since you are already wounded, this will not take long."

I spit out a clump of blood before crouching down with balled fists. I reimagine me, Eddy, Tails, and Leon lounging somewhere off in a field with clear minds and serenity. Although I've never smelled a sweet pea, I know a sweet smell will marinate over us, plunging our senses into a saccharine wonderland.

I hang onto that dream as if my life depends on it and fight through the pain reigning over my body. Then, I take off. I leap across the ring of lava for Verquen, and my lethal tail soars over my head at him. "Last one standing goes to paradise!"

CHAPTER 30

SHOWDOWN

I fly *through* him.

My tail lunges at Verquen's head, but he uses *Pellucid*, making his body transparent. I whisk in air as I land on the ground, but out of my peripheral, I catch a glimmer of his tail. I pivot to the side and strike mine against his. Our tails clash like two titanium swords. He pushes down on mine, clearly stronger, so I jump back onto higher land.

He wastes no time and hurries after me, though.

When his tail hurls down on me, I roll out of the way. It spikes the ground and cuts several feet deep, chucking up rocks, but he simply yanks it out and runs after me. I start to dodge another one of his airstrikes but decide to plant my floating tail instead. I meet his attack head on, and our tails clash again.

This time, however, I deflect and strike again. He does the same. Our tails clash and clank slowly before powering into hyperdrive. They then blitz blow after blow, moving at lightning speed, and my tail starts to move at its own will. I aim for his head and neck, but he repels me and targets my chest. Clinking metal fills the warm air, our chains causing just as much commotion as our tails.

This keeps up for what feels like hours. Sweat cascades down my face, and my matted hair sticks to my skin. I pant out rugged breaths as my lungs burn with the intensity of a thousand flames. My body begins to weigh down, and even more blood drips from my back wound, splattering on the ground by the bucketful.

Still, we continue attacking blow after blow. He cuts right. I cut left. He carves down. I carve around. He breaks right, so I slice left. But suddenly, his blade snakes around mine like it did with Eddy's. It slithers up before stabbing at my face, and my eyes widen. I try to yank back my tail to block him, but I'm stuck in his grasp.

Verquen's eyes light up as his blade touches my forehead.

I suck in air. His blade pierces my skin, and blood spatters out. I lunge back, finally retracting my tail, but my body's too slow. I grit my teeth, mustering everything I've got. More blood squirts out, but then his blade cuts straight *through* me.

His eyes narrow.

"You're not the only one who can use Pellucid, ya know!" I shout, stumbling back. I grab my forehead to stop the bleeding, which streams down my face, but thankfully, it's just a flesh wound.

He stares at me—deadpan. "Very well. But by the looks of your injuries, you will not be using it again."

Just then, a clump surges up my throat, and I grab my mouth. *"Kaff! Kaff!"* I look down to see blood in my hand. *Damnit.*

"You are depleting your strength and sustaining injuries much faster than you are healing. At this rate, you will tire out, and I will slay you and use your chain as my Ticket to *Bliss.*"

"No, I'm getting my friends, and we're getting the hell away from here!"

"Oh, and going where?"

I hesitate, all the realms shooting to the forefront of my mind.

"Ticket, you have seen the afterlife in its entirety. Limbo, The Dump, Almost. This is the finish line, and this is the end of your story."

I shake my head, tears singing my cheeks.

"I am not sure what will happen to you after I dismember your chain"—he starts floating toward me—"but passing on will be the least of your worries. Your friends will perish. You will no longer be the Ticket." He stops a few feet away. "And both your human and ghost life will be all for naught."

A gunshot—*the* gunshot—pierces my ears. Elliot's face floods my mind, and it's as if I'm right back in the forest with him. *Put that shit down, Elliot. Put it down!* Rage surges through my bones, and my hands ball into fists. I vent a vicious scream.

"I said...PUT IT DOWN!"

I float to my tail before charging at Verquen. For a second, his brows knit together in confusion—studying me—but then in an instant, he rushes for me, too. Our tails whizz through the air as they collide with a bang. He slices right. I slice left. He curves a hook, and I jab it back. Again, we hammer blow after blow.

However, when his next strike assails at my chest, instead of attacking head-on, I duck under it with a spin and ambush his thigh. He gasps. I smirk as the blow tears into his leg, but then he lunges at me. Although my tail digs deeper into his skin, he grunts through the pain and kicks me in the head.

The butt of his tail connects to my chin and sends me flying back. My face numbs with a mighty sting, and my vision blurs over the blazing sky. One second, I hurl through the air, and the next, I slam into a wall. My metal chain rams into my back, digging into my open wound.

I shriek.

Hacking up blood, I fall to the ground. My whole body scalds in pain, and my bruised knees hurt, too. I stare down in horror at the load of dark blood beneath me, but then I spot red blood drops a couple feet away. I jerk my head up in shock, Verquen towering over me. Quickly, I throw myself to the side as he slashes at me, and debris and rocks blast into the air where my head would've been.

Midfall, Verquen and I lock eyes. His red ones chill me, but I scowl at him all the same. We glare at each other for just a moment before he jumps off the wall and launches himself at me. His tail propels over his head, while bright blood drips from the gash in his thigh.

Stifling a scream, I regain my tailing and scurry backward. My back aches to give out, but I bear through it, rising to my floating tail. I sprint right just as a gust blasts at me from behind, and a massive yet precise pressure slices at the back of my head—Verquen's tail missing by just an inch.

He crashes into the wall by the pathway, and the land quakes.

I race toward Eddy, who still lies unconscious on the edge of the mountain. I yearn to save him or at least pull him to safety, but Verquen flies at me from behind. I round the ring of lava, leaping out of the way of his repeated strikes. I tuck and roll until my body screams as if in a furious firestorm.

Landing across from Verquen on my butt, I pant out heavy breaths, but my lungs only fill with rapid ones. He slowly floats toward me like a prowling lion, but I can barely move. I scoot back until my back hits the wall, flinching from my open spine injury. My tail rests over my shoulder as I can barely lift it.

One single word repeats in my head: *Escape.*

With no time to think, plan, or deliberate, I grip the wall and pull myself up to my tail. Verquen then picks up the pace, and his float turns into a swift glide. His tail shoots up at me while I slither *at* him. My mind doubles over this bad idea, but my tail moves before I can think—and now there's no turning back.

I push off the ground and lunge at him, and our tails clash. He barrels down on mine, forcing my own tail to my neck. His face remains expressionless, but his vacant eyes reek of regretful sin.

"Agh!" I cry out, turning my head away.

He presses my tail to my neck, and I scream louder.

Floating closer to me, he grabs my throat beneath my tail with one hand. He squeezes as his tail presses against mine, and I cough up blood. His other hand then glides up my waist and past my chest and neck, stopping at the side of my face. He caresses my cheek.

"My precious Ticket," he whispers.

More and more blood rushes up my throat, but I can barely breathe to choke it up. I try to push my neck back, but his free hand slides to the back of it and holds me still. He pushes me forward, and my own lethal tail penetrates my skin. I cry out in pain like Tails, Leon, and the screeching Hellons below.

Verquen's free hand drifts down to my back before stopping at my chain. He grips it while sliding his tail down to the butt of mine. He now pushes my tail into my neck from the bottom, so the tip of his can curve around my back.

Suspense builds in my chest as his blade nears my skin.

"Now to open the gate," he says.

Prying into my open wound, his tail stabs me in the back, and I scream. I scream louder than anytime ever before, blowing out my own eardrums. I scream as he butchers my back by slicing off my skin. Buckets of dark blood plummet to the ground by the gallon.

My screams echo up to the pained sky above. My entire back heats on fire, and my past life flashes before my eyes. I see my orphanage, my siblings, Elliot, *the* gun, and then the images flicker to recent times: Rina, the alley, Kiara's death, the fountain, the bar, Gryner, Kaplone, Myro, Mr. and Mrs. Gyrah, Leira, the cave, and the blinding white light. It ends with a serene grassland, but it's empty. None of us lie in peace.

Melting back into my excruciating body, I choke on my own blood.

You'll have to kill me first! I scream in my head.

Just then, my mouth flies open, and I spit a clump of blood in his face. His eyes close on reflex, and for just a fleeting millisecond, his grip eases. I smack his arm off my neck and kick him across the face with the butt of my tail. The tip of my blade slashes at his cheek before he goes flying through the air.

Then without a second thought, I race for Eddy. I slither with all my might, and hope gleams in my eyes. I focus on the plan. *Escape.* I figure if we can all make it out in one piece, then we can all come back together. And if what Verquen said was true, we'll find a way for *everyone* to go to *Bliss.*

Upon reaching Eddy on the slanted cliff, I glance back over my shoulder. A smokestack of debris clouds where Verquen landed, so I squint to see him. I waste no more than a second searching, but then a low breakage sounds at my feet.

"Slixx..."

CRACK!

Just as I turn back to Eddy, the cliff breaks off from the mountain. My eyes widen in awe. I exhale a cold cruel breath as the cliff falls to the ground below. I reach for him, but it's too late. His body spirals down into the chaos below, and I drop to my knees. Metal and lead seize my mouth. Snot curls over my lips while riverbeds cascade down my face. I extend a hand over the precipice, but all I can do now is watch his body flail through the air.

"Ed-dy," I cry.

He freefalls to his death, but when he nears the ground, his body begins to rapidly flicker like a windy candle—the quickest it's ever done. He disappears. He reappears. He disappears. He reappears. He disappears. He... I trace his chain up to the troubled sky, and it flickers the same, too.

Below, a Hellon opens its mouth to devour him whole, but just before he falls into its clutches, he flickers out one last time and disappears for good.

My mind shoots to his human back in Limbo, Mr. Strife, and a flatline rings in my ears. I cup my mouth, grieving the unimaginable. My soul shatters into pieces, and my spirit crumbles right before my eyes.

Trembling uncontrollably, I spot Tails and Leon near the pathway below. Tails plows into a swarm of Hellons near the shore, while Leon yanks his tail out of a Hellon's eye. It screeches in anguish as Leon jumps back onto Tails' slashed crimson back for rest. And it is then that I see a gory gash at Leon's side—his leather soaked in blood.

Meanwhile, the Hellons corner them.

Tails backs away toward the pathway with nowhere to run, and suddenly, Hellons begin to rise from the ocean. Their entire bodies blaze on fire, the backs of their necks bubbling and bursting in the lava; however, their eyes remain intact. Leon probably couldn't slay them as fast as they came, so Tails likely just pushed as many as he could in the lava.

Still alive, Hellons trudge out of the shallow ocean.

"Leon," I whisper, clutching my heavy chest.

In that moment, Leon looks up at the volcano. His gaze pans from the opposite edge to me, and we lock eyes. Although despite the distance between us and how I can barely see through my tears, I swear he smiles.

But all at once, the Hellons storm him and Tails. The ones on land charge at them while the fiery ones attack them from the ocean. Tails growls before lunging forward. Leon jumps off his back and stabs the nearest Hellon in the eye. Then he leaps and stabs another one, and hope ignites in my gut. The thinnest smile curves onto my face. Adrenaline amps me, so I start to jump up and run to help them.

However, in the blink of an eye, a Hellon catches Leon soaring through the air and flings him in its mouth—into those *ferocious* sets of teeth. It clamps down on his body, and blood squirts out from between its teeth. Leon—crushed. Just like that—all while the other Hellons slash up Tails' fur with their claws. He yelps and whimpers before they shove him into the ocean.

Just as he falls, I jerk my head down and cover my ears.

"*AWOOOOooooooooooooooooooo...*"

I ball my nonexistent heart out as my dream disintegrates to nothing. I think to throw myself off this cliff now, leaning over, but a hand snatches me back. I tumble on the ground before skidding to a stop near the ring of lava.

When I look up, Verquen slithers over to me. Blood gushes out the long slash across his face, and his long disheveled hair sticks to his sweaty skin. He glares at me with wide demented eyes—lustful to finish what he started. "I will now open the gate," he pants, limping my way.

I start to move but wonder the point.

He stops before me and stomps on my lower back. I yelp from the force, but it's as if I've become numb to the pain. I catch a glimpse of his wild tail just as it stabs me in the back. I simply turn and stare down at the boiling ring of lava, though. The bubbles swelter and burst like life before death. Dried tears stain my cheeks. Sadness grips my soul. Nothing hurts anymore because nothing *matters* anymore.

After Verquen carves out my chain from my back, he steps over me with it in hand. He clutches it as he rounds the other side of the ring of lava. "Finally…" He gawks at my bloody chain. "The time has come."

"Just go," I croak, bleeding out. "And I hope you wind up somewhere wretched."

A glimmer twinkles in his eye as he stares me down, and in that moment, his red eyes soften as if with the slightest of a soul. But then they harden in the next instant. He throws my chain into the ring of lava, and the entire fiery pit explodes into water. The shower cascades down into a small pond, and I behold the clearest and bluest water that I've ever seen. The gentle drops ripple across the pond, lessening the burden and guilt in my soul. My eyes widen at the gateway to paradise.

"*Bliss,*" I whisper, a smile creeping onto my face.

I reach for the pond as Verquen jumps into it. He grins with starry eyes, and for the first time, his emotion seems genuine. We both lunge for a chance—the *only* chance—to pass on. I picture my dream with me, Eddy, Tails, and Leon in the field, and joy overwhelms me. I hurry to touch it as euphoria calls out to my gut.

Gaping at the water in wonder, *it* finally occurs to me. *Know where you're going before you get there, or you may end up somewhere wretched.* I know now. *I know!* I shout inside, gay.

I hang onto my dream as my steady fingers near the gateway. Eddy, Tails, and Leon pop into my head one by one, and happiness bursts in my chest. "I'll come back," I whisper.

And I don't know who touches the pond first, but suddenly, everything goes black.

Acknowledgments

In the famous words of Drake, "I mean, where the f*** should I really even start?"

In all seriousness, my deepest gratitude goes out to all my wonderful Backers who supported *Ghost to Paradise* on Kickstarter. You guys believed in my book baby when it was just an idea and rough drafted manuscript, and for that, I truly appreciate each and every one of you. Special thank you to Ariel Brinkley, Brant Cooper, David St. John, Dylan Ohrwaschel, Terril Fields, Maria Williams, Clyde Pope, Lauren George, and Frances Hawkins-Islar.

Also, thank you so much to my mommy who's believed in me since the beginning! To my siblings, couldn't have done it without you guys, too.

And to all my precious readers, my next book is for you.

About the Author

Kris A.S. grew up in the Atlanta Metropolitan Area. (Yes, just outside of Atlanta—not Atlanta *Atlanta*. She knows to clarify for the real Atlanta folk.) With an affinity for storytelling, she has been writing novels since elementary school. Her debut novel was successfully crowdfunded online, and she has many more stories left in the tank. When not holed up inside writing, she enjoys long walks, hot weather, performing spoken word poetry, and making people laugh.